Santa,
Please Bring
Me a
Boyfriend

BOOKS BY SOPHIE RANALD

Santa, Please Bring Me a Boyfriend

SOPHIE RANALD

Bookouture

Published by Bookouture in 2022

An imprint of Storyfire Ltd.
Carmelite House
50 Victoria Embankment
London EC4Y 0DZ

www.bookouture.com

ISBN: 978-1-80314-476-4
eBook ISBN: 978-1-80314-475-7

For Christina, my guiding star at Bookouture for four years. Every author needs an editor like you in their Christmas stocking.

CHAPTER ONE

It was late November and Christmas had officially arrived in London. Or, to put it from my perspective, it had arrived drunk, vomited copiously everywhere and decided to stick around and make itself at home for another month. It was here to stay, no matter how pointedly you cleared up around it, coughed discreetly and said, 'Gosh, is that the time?' and even – peak British way of suggesting a guest had outstayed their welcome – slapped your thighs, said, 'Right!' and got to your feet in a marked manner.

Christmas had arrived, and I was marking the occasion by meeting my best friends for an alcohol-fuelled afternoon tea at Liberty, the city's most iconic department store. (If 'most iconic' was even a thing? I had no idea, but I was an estate agent and we lived and breathed exaggerated descriptions.)

Not that much exaggeration was necessary when describing the total over-the-top festiveness of Carnaby Street in the heart of London on that sparkling, frosty winter day. Festoons of lights and baubles arched across the road; elaborate displays filled every window with shiny red, green, gold and silver decorations; even the red telephone boxes, which were there all year round, looked as if they'd been dropped off by central casting to contribute seasonal vibes to the scene.

And, as if that wasn't enough, I was entering Liberty through the annually created Christmas department. In spite of myself, I paused there and looked around. There were decorations everywhere: racks and boxes of glowing glass baubles in all colours, swags of tinsel as thick and glossy as tigers' tails, wreaths made of pine cones and wreaths made of holly and wreaths made of cinnamon sticks.

There were boxes of chocolates, tubs of dried fruit and nuts and stacks of boxed cakes, mince pies and stollen. There were festive room fragrances and festive tea towels. There were stockings for children to hang up on Christmas Eve and discover the next morning bulging with expensive gifts.

And in the beauty hall next door were all the things I'd hope to find in my own stocking, if I had anyone generous enough to fill one for me. Perfumes made by famous-name houses, serums that would make me look like a twenty-five-year-old goddess who'd just slept for nine hours, blushers and bronzers and highlighters that would make me glow like a woman in love.

I lingered for as long as I could, taking in all the glorious things I couldn't afford to buy, furtively spritzing a tester of the new Le Labo fragrance on my wrist and wincing when I noticed that a bottle would cost as much as my and my daughter's monthly food budget, stroking a coral-coloured Chantecaille lipstick against the back on my hand.

And then, my head reeling from the sensory overload, I climbed the wide wooden staircase to the second floor to meet my friends.

All three of them were there already, seated on a horseshoe-shaped blue velvet banquette, getting stuck into Bellinis. I bent over to hug and kiss them, noticing the new piercing in Naomi's ear, the lighter blonde highlights in Abbie's hair, and Kate's gel manicure, which featured tiny sprigs of holly on her middle fingers.

'It's still November, Kate,' I chided. 'What's with the festive nails? It's bad enough that the bloody lights have been up on Oxford Street for a week.'

'Someone get the Grinch here a drink,' Kate said as I slid into the booth next to her. 'I for one adore Christmas, and I plan to milk it for all it's worth. I started a week ago with a trip to the Harrods food hall, just to get my vibe going.'

'The fruit for my Christmas cake has been soaking in booze for three weeks already,' Naomi said. 'I went for rum this year, changing it up a bit.'

'I've already bought Matt his Christmas present,' Abbie said. 'Dodgy pair of trainers. But they're limited edition apparently – he's been stalking them round the internet for months, waiting for a pair to come available in size twelve. I spotted them and snapped them up.'

'We're off to Patch's brother's place,' Naomi said. 'They live in Yorkshire and I know it's not exactly the North Pole but there is a decent chance it might snow. Do you think you can do snow dances? Like rain dances only… I dunno, different?'

'Put on welly boots and stomp around singing "I'm Dreaming of a White Christmas"?' Abbie suggested. 'What are you up to, Kate? I bet it's something fabulous.'

'I'm going to Paris for a few days with Andy. Us single Pringles need to have each other's backs, right? Although there have been murmurs that he's met someone, but he's refusing to divulge any info.'

'Oh my God!' I said. 'You're going to have to pump him for all the details you can get. Andy's been single for almost as long as I have.'

'You could join us in Paris,' Kate suggested, 'and pump him yourself.'

For a second, I allowed myself to dream. But this relatively affordable afternoon tea was already pushing my fun budget to its limit. I knew that if I accompanied Kate and Andy to Paris, they'd either be offering to treat me to meals and drinks all the time, or moderating the fabulousness of their trip to bring it within my financial reach – which it wouldn't be however much they curbed it.

So I shook my head regretfully.

A waitress placed a fresh round of drinks in front of us, and Kate ordered afternoon tea all round. We all clamoured for more intel about Andy's new love interest (he'd been single for the longest time and used to lead a pretty chaotic life fuelled by whatever mind-altering substances he could lay his hands on before getting clean a year or so before), but Kate either didn't know more or wasn't saying.

I hoped that that nugget of gossip would distract my friends from my own Christmas plans or lack thereof, but I'd reckoned without Kate's tenacity.

'So you see, Rowan,' she said, 'everyone's getting excited about it already, November or not. It's just you. What gives?'

I shrugged, taking a gulp of my cocktail and biting into a sandwich. Turkey. Obviously.

'It's just... It doesn't feel like there's that much to get excited about. Clara used to be totally giddy about Christmas weeks before, but now she's a teenager she's gone all cynical.'

'Can't think where she gets that from,' Abbie teased.

'Ha ha. And anyway, it's her year to spend it with her dad, and they're going to Wales to stay with Paul's parents. My mum and dad are heading off on one of their cruises next week – they reckon there's no point "making a fuss" if Clara's not going to be around. And I'm too skint to do anything fabulous, even if I had anyone to do it with.'

'Oh no.' Naomi's face fell, and she reached over to give my

hand a squeeze. 'But I thought you were going to make loads of money in your new job, like *Selling Sunset*.'

'Selling sub-zero, more like,' I said. 'I showed a massive mansion in Mayfair to an applicant the other day – it was truly epic, marble everything and an *actual* Picasso on the wall – but the heating hadn't been on for ages because the seller lives abroad, and it was freezing in there. We could legit see our breath, and there was frost on the windows like something out of *A Christmas Carol*. The buyer couldn't get out fast enough.'

When I'd accepted the job at Walkerson's Elite a few months before, I'd been elated, full of *Selling Sunset* dreams of my own. I'd get to look at all the property porn I wanted, and in the flesh, not just online. I'd get to show rich men around zillion-pound mansions and surely it would be just a matter of time before one of them fell in love with me, swept me off my feet and whisked Clara and me away to live in the lap of luxury.

Not that I'd need a rich man, of course, because I'd be rich myself. The basic salary I was offered was modest, but on top of that were commission and bonuses. I worked out that I'd only have to have two or three of 'my' buyers a year purchase a property for me to be absolutely rolling in money.

The only problem was, I didn't have a single buyer. The second the phone rang, my colleagues Brett, Marty and Kimberley pounced on it like a pack of hungry wolves, claiming the applicant for themselves and thus a share of the commission if they went on to buy a home. And all the sellers, I'd learned, 'belonged' to Julz, the branch manager, who negotiated the terms of their contracts with the agency.

And so Clara and I were skinter than we'd ever been, scratching a living on my pittance of a wage, and I was finding the atmosphere in the office more and more toxic by the day.

But this was meant to be a celebratory get-together – a treat to kick-start the Christmas season – and I didn't want to put a downer on the fun. So I helped myself to a mini mince pie off the cake stand and concentrated on glugging some more of my Bellini, determined not to ruin the vibe by offloading my woes to my friends.

'Maybe I just need to focus harder on getting into the Christmas mood,' I said. 'Fake it till I make it or something.'

'That's the spirit!'

As if by magic, Kate had summoned another round of cocktails.

'I strongly recommend a trip to Harrods. It's so gloriously tacky, you can just gaze round and imagine what it would be like to spaff nine hundred quid on a set of three Cartier baubles, and part of you thinks it would be great and the other part is just really relieved you're not that person.'

'Those are the people who buy houses from us,' I said. 'I showed a place to one guy the other day and he said it wouldn't work because it only had parking for six cars, and he had twenty. I bet he'd think nine hundred quid for Christmas decorations was small change.'

'Or you could do other stuff that's Christmassy,' Naomi suggested. 'Have your own Christmas fayre in your flat, like those ones that always get into local papers.'

'Where Santa's been on the extra-strength lager since seven in the morning, the reindeer are moulting, the elves swear at small children and there's mud everywhere,' Abbie said, giggling.

'No! I meant a nice one, with churros and Baileys hot chocolate and an ice bar,' Naomi protested.

'You could get Clara to dress up as Elsa and sit in a corner and sulk,' suggested Abbie.

'The sulking bit's easy, at any rate,' I admitted.

'Or you could shove a pillow up your top and go for a ride on a donkey,' Kate offered.

'Find three random blokes to turn up at my door with presents I don't know what to do with,' I said.

'Yeah, but you'd need to rent a stable first,' said Abbie. 'Camp out there in the cold for a couple of nights. That would get you in the mood.'

'Or I could just cook enough food to feed twenty people, get drunk and have an argument with myself,' I said. 'You know, the full family Christmas vibe.'

We were all giggling now, enjoying our own ridiculousness.

'Spend a fortune on gift wrap and ribbon and tags at Paperchase and then flagellate yourself with guilt when you realise none of it's recyclable,' Abbie said.

'Eat nothing but cold roast potatoes for a week,' I said.

'Buy a tub of glitter, chuck it on your carpet, spend several hours hoovering, then hoover again every day for six months and still find glitter,' suggested Kate.

'Make a Spotify playlist that's only got "Santa Baby" on it and listen to nothing else for a month, until eventually you rip your own ears off.' Abbie was laughing so hard she had hiccups.

'You see, Ro,' Kate said. 'We're all here to help.'

'Don't know what I'd do without you guys.'

I brushed away a tear of laughter, leaving a smear of mascara on my hand. My friends *were* here to help – they *did* help. But the one thing they couldn't do was change the fact that I was facing yet another Christmas without a man in my life.

I remembered Clara, when she was a little girl, writing her list to Father Christmas every year, and every year including 'A pony' on it, even though she knew there was no chance she could have one. If I was writing my own list, I'd put 'A boyfriend' – and the chance of my wish coming true was about as small.

We'd finished the food by this stage, and were slightly light-headed from Bellinis and giggling, and as we all had work the next day, we ordered a final round of drinks and asked for the bill. I wasn't sure whether it was the company of my friends, the food and drink, or the acceptance that Christmas would come and go as it did every year, so I might as well make the best of it, but I felt more cheerful than I had in weeks. Maybe not festive exactly, but I found I was actually looking forward to my walk back to the Tube in the frosty darkness, the lights arching above me, the shop windows glowing with promise.

* * *

Two floors above, Alex was gazing around in bewilderment at a world he never thought he'd find himself in. Normally, he was a last-minute-shopping kind of guy and would make almost all of his purchases online. But this Christmas was different, and he had someone new to buy gifts for.

Also, he was pretty certain that, after today, he wouldn't have much opportunity to visit actual, bricks-and-mortar shops and wouldn't be around to take delivery of anything he ordered online. And besides, he hadn't been in London that long, and circumstances had significantly curtailed his opportunities to sightsee, so he was killing two birds with one stone by getting his present-purchasing under way and doing a spot of exploring.

He'd been for a run along the river earlier, then treated himself to a massive steak lunch, the remains of which were wrapped in a hopefully leak-proof foil parcel in his bag for him to take home, where he knew the leftovers would be greatly appreciated. He'd called in at the Science Museum, giving way to his inner nerd and remembering how much it would have thrilled him when he was a child.

And now he was here, in the children's department at Liberty. He looked at the tiny, perfect, costly outfits with marvel and incredulity. When he was a kid, he'd worn his older brother's hand-me-downs; anything new his mum had purchased had never come his way. Not that he'd minded – everything ended up muddy from the football pitch, ripped from climbing trees, or outgrown as Alex did what his mum called 'shooting up'.

The other kind of shooting up – the kind that happened on the rougher streets of Glasgow not far from his childhood home – was a trap he'd fortunately always managed to avoid.

Apart from a three-year stint abroad at an American university, Alex had imagined he'd always call the city of his birth home. He loved its handsome, weighty Victorian architecture; its habit of battering and deep-frying absolutely anything – from a pizza to a Mars bar – and calling it a regional delicacy; even the length and coldness of its winter nights.

London, by contrast, felt positively balmy. Even on this winter day, the sun blazed from a clear sky, melting the frost on the grass almost before it had formed. Christmas here would be strange, new and unfamiliar in more ways than one.

Last year, he'd still been living with Leila. They'd both known their relationship was limping to a close but had stuck it out for one last Christmas, marking the day with sadness thinly disguised as jollity. In January, without too much acrimony, they'd gone their separate ways, relieved to finally acknowledge that their two years together had been, if not a mistake, not right enough to go any further distance.

Shortly after, Leila had got back together with an ex. Alex didn't want to think too hard about what that had meant about why he and Leila had got together in the first place, but he certainly didn't wish them ill.

He'd been ready to move on, and now he had. He was here, in London, settling into a new job and with other irons in the fire as well. He might not have moved here for a woman, but he had one in his life, for which he was grateful. He had a roof over his head and company at night.

And now, he needed to buy a Christmas present for a person he'd never met. It was a tricky ask, but Alex had always enjoyed a challenge.

Half an hour later, his task achieved, Alex emerged onto Carnaby Street, the amethyst-coloured carrier bag tucked safely in his rucksack. The sun had gone down while he was shopping, but the evening was still bright, the Christmas lights and illuminated shop windows glowing against the black sky. He could see a full moon rising and no doubt once he was on his way home, cycling along the river, he'd see stars too, guiding him on the still unfamiliar route.

He paused, taking in the atmosphere: the shops were closing early, because it was Sunday, and crowds of people were spilling out onto the street, making their way to the stations and bus stops, or stopping to peruse the menus of bars and restaurants before pushing open the doors and entering the welcoming warmth within.

He could do the same – have a pint in a pub or a quick, solitary meal before heading home. But that wouldn't be fair. He thought of the leftover steak and the eagerness with which it would be received, and turned to make his way to the rack where his bicycle would be – he hoped – still waiting for him.

His eye was caught by the door of Liberty swinging open and a group of women emerging, laughing, maybe slightly tipsy after a long lunch. There were four of them: one blonde, one red-headed and two dark. The light from within caught their smiling faces and swishing coats, and the brisk wind carried their voices to him.

There was something about them – a glamour, a togetherness – that made him stop, watching as they parted, hugging and kissing each other, still spinning out whatever running joke had made them laugh.

One of them in particular struck him. Her hair was long, glossy as a piece of coal left out at Christmas for a badly behaved child – not that anyone ever did that. Her skin was pale, almost luminous under the lights. She moved with a kind of assured grace that impressed him.

Alex watched as she turned, lithe as a dancer, and strode off in the direction of the station.

And although he knew it was impossible, in this city of millions, he found himself thinking, *I wonder if I'll see you again.*

CHAPTER TWO

'Rowena? Jesus Christ, it's like talking to a brick wall sometimes.'

I managed not to jump as Julz, my boss, appeared behind me, his cloying pine-scented aftershave announcing his presence even before his posh, booming voice. At first, I'd corrected him when he accidentally-on-purpose called me a name that wasn't mine, but I'd given up, realising that he took as much pleasure in my protestations as he did in his own deliberate mistake.

'I was just focused on the particulars for Portland Mews,' I lied. In fact, I'd been gazing at the glossy photographs on my screen, imagining myself living somewhere like that, with a four-poster bed for Clara and a swimming pool in the basement and a kitchen that probably cost more than the value of my entire flat. 'The floorplan's come in and I'm not sure they've got it quite right – the downstairs cloakroom—'

'Never mind that. I need you to do the viewing at Gloucester Gardens. Marty and Brett are both busy and Kimberley's at the dentist. I have a potential new listing, so I'm going to have to head out there sharpish. Chap that owns it is flying out to Kuwait at five. Which means you'll have to hold the fort here this afternoon.'

'But I...' The words formed on my lips, but I didn't bother saying them. I was contracted to work half-days, having insisted at my interview that I wanted to be home when my daughter finished school in the afternoons. But Julz took as much notice of that as he did of my actual name.

Resigned, I reached for my phone and texted Clara to let her know I'd be back late and she'd have to walk home from school (which, at fourteen, she was perfectly capable of doing but still bitterly resented). Then I ran a comb through my hair, kicked off my trainers and forced my feet into the four-inch heels Julz insisted projected the desired 'professional glamour' image.

With Julz's nasal breath ruffling the hair on the back of my neck, I teetered out of my chair to make my way to my little green Ford Fiesta. Pushing open the door, I was met by a blast of icy air – the morning's frost had long since melted, but the day was still midwinter cold.

'Mind you park that shit-heap around the corner when you get there,' Julz said. 'Not exactly the impression we want to give, is it?'

Although just the previous day, when the car had refused to start in the late November chill, I'd called it worse names myself, now I felt fiercely defensive of my ancient little runaround, in which I'd had to sink all my spare cash – plus two hundred quid borrowed from my ex-fiancé – in order to be able to accept Julz's job offer.

'Must have own transport,' the ad had said. Clearly turning up on a bus to show a potential tenant around a seven-million-pound Chelsea apartment would be even worse image suicide than turning up in Portia, as I'd ironically christened the car.

'It gets me from A to B,' I told Julz calmly, for about the millionth time, hoping he hadn't noticed the crumpled McDonald's wrapper Clara had left on the passenger seat, nor the family-size tin of Quality Street I'd failed to conceal in the driver's side footwell. I'd have to smuggle it into my bedroom without my daughter seeing, or risk her giving me The Face, one eyebrow raised and one side of her mouth lowered in something that was almost, but not quite, a sneer.

I'd caught her practising it in the bathroom mirror a few weeks back, and she'd had the grace to blush and pretend she was tweezing her brows, but that hadn't stopped her deploying the look on me when I did something she deemed particularly cringe, which was often.

'Well, it needs to get you to Gloucester Gardens, stat,' Julz said. 'Don't forget to show them the wine cellar. But don't let them open the middle door in the walk-in wardrobe – that's where the client keeps his fetish gear. And if they ask you about the service charge—'

But whatever gem of wisdom he might have been about to impart was drowned out by the rattle of Portia's engine stuttering to life. I pulled off in a series of jerks, firing up the satnav as I went in a manner totally forbidden by the Highway Code.

Unfortunately, I realised after a fifteen-minute drive west, Gloucester Gardens didn't appear to exist. Where my satnav told me to go was only a cobbled mews that didn't seem to have a name, leading to a dead end off Gloucester Place. Increasingly anxious as the scheduled viewing time approached and then arrived, I parked Portia and climbed out, cursing my high heels again as I staggered over the cobbles, the embossed folder of glossy brochures clutched in my increasingly sweaty armpit.

I walked through the mews, then back, consulted my phone then turned to retrace my steps.

And then I saw a powder-blue sports car, low and sleek, pull up directly in front of a tall, stucco-fronted mansion block and, as I watched, a sign I hadn't noticed before seemed to materi-

alise above its black-painted front door: 'Gloucester Gardens'.
Right. So it was a building, not a street.

I hurried towards the car, my heels skidding on the stones,
and a woman swung out of the driver's seat and directed a
blinding smile at me. She was about my age, about my height
and also had dark hair. But there the similarity between us
ended. Whereas I was sweaty and flustered, the waistband of
my pencil skirt cutting painfully into my middle, my Primark
coat both uncomfortably warm and unable to block out the
chilly wind, she was a living Instagram post.

Her trousers were white leather, the sort of thing you only
wear if you're never going to take public transport or cook a
meal and you're one hundred per cent confident you'll never,
ever sit on someone's discarded chewing gum. Her hair fell in
glossy, bouncy waves over her cream faux-fur jacket (or it might
have been real fur for all I knew), and the high neck of a white
cashmere jumper showed above its collar. Her face was a
perfect, serene mask of Botox, fillers, highlights and contours
that I knew would have taken the best part of an hour and at
least a dozen products to achieve, yet gave the appearance of an
effortless natural glow, like she'd just stepped off a ski slope or
just had the most amazing orgasm of her life.

'You must be from Walkerson's,' she said, dazzling me with
a hundred-watt array of flawless teeth. 'I'm Tatiana. So excited
to meet you.'

She extended a cool, moisturised hand for me to shake.

'I'm Rowan,' I muttered, rendered awkward and charmless
by her gorgeousness. 'I'm so excited to be showing you the
apartment. Come on in.'

I fumbled the keys off their slot on the leather folder and
inserted what I hoped was the right one into the black door,
swinging it open.

As we looked around the apartment – itself Insta perfect,
with dark polished parquet floors, tall windows overlooking a

garden square, a space-age kitchen and a marble-tiled bathroom complete with a free-standing steel bath and vast walk-in shower – I tried to remember Julz's pointers for conducting viewings.

Give them the sales patter, he'd said, but ask them about themselves too. Make them think you're interested.

He'd have been genuinely interested in Tatiana, that was for sure – anyone with a penis would, unless of course they swung the other way, in which case they'd immediately be filling out the application form to become her new gay best friend.

'Would you be moving here with your family?' I asked, hoping my question didn't cross the line from 'interested' to 'intrusive'.

She gave me her radiant smile again and said, 'Oh, no. The flat's not for me. I run a concierge service helping people who are moving to London to find homes, schools for their children – that sort of thing.'

I'd like to say her words rang a bell at the time, and they should have done – enough bells to rig out all Santa's reindeer.

But they didn't.

CHAPTER THREE

Over the next couple of days, though, I barely gave Tatiana another thought. I had the regular, humdrum parts of my job to focus on and a daughter to parent (although sometimes, parenting Clara felt like sharing the flat with a sullen ghost – the Ghost of Christmas Presents, perhaps, since her sole topic of conversation seemed to be whether she was going to get the new Fenty Beauty lipstick in her stocking) and a mountain of laundry to tackle.

Still, on Thursday evening, waiting for Clara to return home from her dad's, I indulged in a massive wallow. I'd hung the final load of washing on the rickety airer in the living room, which was the only place in the flat where it fitted, poured myself a gin and tonic that was light on the tonic, kicked off my sheepskin slippers and flopped on the sofa with my phone.

The flat was chilly, because I'd put the heating on a timer and it had only kicked in a few minutes before I arrived home, and I was wearing a towelling dressing gown over my tracksuit bottoms and a red acrylic jumper that had shrunk in the wash, meaning I could no longer wear it anywhere but at home. The sofa was still the same one Paul and I had inherited with the flat, its faded pattern of curly leaves and stylised peonies so familiar now I only occasionally noticed how ugly it was. On the mantelpiece above the gas fire were a couple of early Christmas cards and a swag of gold tinsel I'd picked up in a half-hearted attempt to make the place look festive. As I'd told my friends, the Christmas spirit was at a pretty low ebb in me, but I promised myself I'd make more of an effort in the coming days, if only for my daughter's sake.

The door to Clara's bedroom was closed, so at least I couldn't see the chaos. I'd gone nuclear at her a few weeks back and told her that I was no longer setting foot in there to tidy, if she wanted to live in a pigsty she could knock herself out, and her washing wasn't being done unless she put it in the bathroom laundry hamper, to which she'd responded with The Face, a shrug and a 'Fine'. I knew that behind the door, clothes would be scattered on every surface, make-up spilled on the carpet, plates and coffee cups mouldering on the floor.

Massive own goal there, Rowan, I told myself. I couldn't go in and sort it out, because then I'd be backing down. I couldn't make Clara do it without resorting to bribery, which would in turn lead to escalating demands, like negotiating with Nigerian pirates.

Although it wasn't as if my own room was much better. Neat and clean, certainly, but hardly a bower of bliss. At first, after Paul pushed off, I'd tried to make it a haven for me, with pretty white broderie anglaise sheets and curtains and a string of fairy lights over the bedhead. But the fairy lights were long dead, hanging limp and dim like a reproach. The buttons had come off the duvet cover and the quilt hung out of the gap like a lolling tongue – the only oral action my bed had seen in a good few years. There was a cobweb in the corner of the ceiling that had been there since the summer, which I couldn't bring myself to remove because I didn't want to make some poor spider family homeless.

Not that anyone ever saw inside my bedroom except for me – and Clara, when she sneaked in to raid my precious stash of professional-quality cosmetics, which was dwindling by the day.

Oh, and Paul.

Although I was alone in the flat, I felt my cheeks colouring as I thought about what had happened – what I'd allowed to happen, over the period of almost a dozen years since we'd separated.

The first time, I think it was brought on by an overwhelming sense of loss on both of our parts. He'd moved out a month before, and the shared parenting arrangement was just finding its feet, with poor little bewildered Clara clinging to me and crying when Paul came to take her to his place for the night, then clinging to him when he dropped her off again. He'd stayed for a cup of tea that time, and the two of us had talked to our daughter, comforting her with promises that Mummy and Daddy still both loved her very, very much and always would, but sometimes grown-ups just couldn't live together.

Her tears dried eventually. She fell asleep and I carried her to her bedroom, before returning to Paul. We looked at each other, overwhelmed by the enormity of what we felt we'd done to our little girl, even though she'd wept just as heart-rendingly the previous day when I'd cut her cucumber into sticks instead of rings. Seconds later, I started to cry and so did he, and we ended up in each other's arms, having desperate, silent sex so as not to wake our daughter.

I'd clung to him myself, afterwards, almost praying that this would be what it took for him to change his mind. The sex had reminded me of what had been right – the life we'd shared together – and made me forget all the things that had been wrong. The rows that had got worse and worse since Clara's arrival; his refusal to do his share around the house, something that had become entrenched since I'd been on maternity leave and picked up all the slack; him accusing me of being a nag and no fun any more before finally announcing that he couldn't do this any longer, and he was leaving. But he prised my arms off his shoulders as tenderly as he had Clara's an hour before and said he had to go.

There'd been more times after that. More than I could count – more than I'd admitted to anyone, even my closest friends. More than I even liked to acknowledge to myself. When Clara was asleep; when she was at her grandmother's; when we'd dropped her off at a friend's place after her gymnastics class.

Lots and lots and lots of times.

There'd been intervals, of course, when it hadn't happened for a while. When Paul had been seeing someone else; when I'd put my foot down and told myself (and, slightly less firmly, him) that for the good of all three of us, this had to stop.

But it had never truly stopped, mostly because we – at least I – didn't really want it to. It wasn't about pleasure or even desire – not for me, at least. It was about satisfying a deeper, less physical need – the need to feel wanted, to be touched by another adult, to recapture some of the closeness we'd had back in the beginning. Which is a hell of a lot to pack into five minutes, let's face it. Perhaps that was why I let the same five minutes happen again and again.

Morosely, I took out my phone and flicked back through the photographs, all the way back to when we first met.

I'd been twenty-two and, if I say so myself, quite the knockout. Knock-out enough to get me a few not-that-well-paid modelling jobs, until I'd realised I had a shelf life and standing around in freezing studios was no way to spend my days, and retrained as a make-up artist. But in those early photos, all that was still ahead of me.

There I was, with Paul on what must have been our first Valentine's Day together. He'd taken us out for steak and chips

– his favourite meal, which I soon learned to say was mine too –
and afterwards we'd gone to a club to dance. I'd dressed up for
the occasion in an appropriately rose-red satin dress, which had
been way OTT for the restaurant, but we couldn't have cared
less.

Paul had a digital camera back then, and he must have
asked our waitress to take the photo. I was smiling, my model
smile, all teeth and eyes, but the smile had been genuine, I knew
for sure. God, I'd been so self-conscious in those days, so
worried about my mouth being too wide, my ears too sticky-out,
my skin too prone to breakouts and my hips too prone to
lardiness.

But I looked amazing. Radiant, even. The way Clara was
beginning to look now, when she wasn't pouting for selfies or
hunching her shoulders because she wasn't used to having
breasts.

And there she was, a few years and many photos later. Our
surprise baby. Paul had a better-quality digital camera by then,
and the picture of him, Clara and me taken in hospital just after
she was born was crisp and clear. I looked like shit, obviously –
I'd just given birth, my hair was slick with sweat and I had no
make-up on – but triumphant, deliriously happy, with my puce-
faced baby girl cuddled against my bare shoulder. Paul was
grinning like he'd just invented the wheel.

And then, before Clara's third birthday, it had all gone
wrong: from happy to miserable to bitter, and after one particularly toxic row, Paul had decamped to his brother's place and
later moved to a flat of his own, and never come back.

After that, there weren't that many pictures of Paul and me
together. Hardly any, in fact, and none that Clara wasn't in too.
And we'd all changed. The goatee beard Paul had when I met
him had been shaved off, then replaced with the full hipster
version he'd adopted when Clara was about eight, then shaved

off again. I'd gone from slim to not-so-slim to downright gaunt and then to where I was now.

The only linear progression seemed to be in Clara. In each photo she was a little older, a little taller, a little more like herself and less like a jigsaw made of bits of her parents and grandparents.

In each she was more beautiful, in the more recent ones more contemptuous, and, still more recently, visibly mortified by the fact that she was being asked to smile for a camera held by her mother rather than her or one of her mates.

And here – with a crash of the front door against the wall that would add to the hole in the plaster and earn me a 'God, stop nagging, Mum' if I mentioned it, a blast of cold air and a clatter of keys – was Clara.

She came into the living room looking quite cheerful and dumped her half-open bag next to me on the sofa. With a sweeping glance, she took in the loaded clothes airer, me, my G&T and my phone, and her expression changed to her more usual one, the way she used to look at broccoli when she was little.

'Did you wash my cream jumper?' she asked, without preamble.

'Hello, sweetheart.' I remembered something I'd read in *How to Survive Parenting a Teenager*, about modelling behaviour. 'Did you have a good time at Dad's?'

Clara ignored me and turned towards the damp washing, rifling through it and sending several pairs of my knickers sliding to the floor.

'I've got nothing to wear,' she said in a tone as full of self-pity as someone doing a juice fast complaining they hadn't had a square meal in days. 'All this stuff is yours.'

'Anything that was in the laundry basket in the bathroom, I've washed,' I said. 'If there's stuff in your bag or in your room that needs doing, just put it in the machine and we can stick another load on now.'

'But it won't be dry. God, why can't we have a tumble dryer like normal people?'

Because there's nowhere to put one and no money to buy one if there was.

'We can make space,' I relented. 'Drape some stuff over the radiators.'

With a martyred sigh, Clara sloped off to her room and returned with an armful of dirty washing. She dumped it in a pile in front of the washing machine, then rummaged in her bag for more. Then she looked at me expectantly.

'The detergent's in the cupboard under the sink,' I told her.

She sighed again and shuffled through to the kitchen. A few seconds later I heard her muffled voice saying, 'I can't find it.'

Inevitably, I broke. I got up, taking my glass with me, found the washing powder (literally right under my daughter's beautiful ski-jump nose), loaded the machine and switched it on. Then I poured another, even larger gin.

'Have you eaten?' I asked. 'There's some leftover lasagne I was going to heat up, and we could make a salad.'

'There's at least three units of alcohol in that, you know, Mum,' Clara pointed out in an identical faux-helpful tone to the one I'd used when I'd told her where to find the Daz. 'We had a lesson about it today in PSHE. Apparently rates of problem drinking are sky-high among millennials.'

Which would have nothing whatsoever to do with their Generation Z children.

'Yes, well...' I hunted feebly for a valid reason to be getting stuck into the gin alone at six on a Thursday evening. Having no one to drink with wouldn't wash, I suspected. 'It is nearly Christmas.'

Clara rolled her eyes. 'That's what you said when you bought that tin of Quality Street.'

I remembered another phrase from the author of *How to Survive Parenting a Teenager*: 'Take a deep breath, then rise above it.' Gritting my teeth, I opened the fridge and took out the veggie lasagne. The beeswax wrap that covered it – Clara having banned cling film from the house a few months back after learning about marine microplastics in Geography – hadn't stuck to the dish and the pasta had dried out a bit round the edges. I held it out to her with what I hoped was an inviting smile.

'Shall we bung this in the microwave?'

Clara made the broccoli face again. 'Is there cheese on that? You know I don't eat dairy any more. Anyway, I'm not hungry. I'm going to my room.'

Which meant I'd be left with the task of sorting and hanging up her washing.

'Have you done your homework?'

'I'll do it in bed.'

How much, if any, would get done in between chatting to her mates on WhatsApp and scrolling through TikTok, I didn't know. 'Sometimes you have to let them make their own mistakes,' said *How to Survive...* in my head.

'Want me to bring you a cup of tea?' I asked.

Clara shook her head, her dark ponytail swishing. She'd done it in a new, fancy way, I noticed, with an extra bit of hair underneath to give it more volume. My heart twisted, as it often did, with how beautiful she was, this perfect girl Paul and I had made, and I sent up a silent prayer to whoever might be listening that she wouldn't always hate me.

Then she changed her mind and smiled, the increasingly rare smile that lit up her face and showed her slightly crooked front teeth. There'd be orthodontist's bills in my future, if she decided she wanted them fixed.

'That would be nice. Thanks, Mum.'

Phone and tablet clutched to her chest, my daughter headed

back towards her bedroom. She opened the door, kicked aside three random trainers, then turned back to me.

'Oh, Mum. Dad and Hayley are getting married. She's asked me to be a bridesmaid. How cool is that?'

Cool? Like having a bucket of icy water chucked over my head, more like. I forced a smile and tried to share in my daughter's excitement, but all I could think was that I wasn't good enough for Paul. I never had been, and now I'd never have the chance to make myself be.

An hour later, I'd finished my gin, eaten a few forkfuls of cold lasagne from the dish by the open fridge door before scraping the rest into the food-waste caddy, and retreated, like a wounded animal seeking its burrow, to bed.

The duvet cover around me was littered with Quality Street wrappers. I was forcing myself to make my way through all the toffees before starting on the good stuff, which of course would mean I'd end up eating even more of them than I would otherwise, and wake up in the morning hating myself even more deeply.

If that was even possible.

For what felt like the thousandth time, I picked up my phone and tapped through to WhatsApp. There was the Girlfriends' Club group, where my best mates, Kate, Naomi and Abbie, would be at the touch of a keyboard to give me virtual hugs.

We'd met years ago when our boyfriends used to play five-a-side football together, and what had begun as a casual meeting up of a group of girls who had only that in common had somehow endured and been forged into the closest friendships I'd ever had. Naomi was Clara's godmother; Kate had come round with doughnuts and a box of tissues when Paul left; we'd all rallied round Abbie last year when her twenty-year relationship had almost hit the skids.

I loved them fiercely. I could tell them anything.

Except maybe the truth about just how close Paul and I had remained, and the hope I'd nurtured, barely admitting it even to myself, that somehow, someday, he and Clara and I might have been a family again.

But now he was getting married. I'd known about Hayley, of course – if Clara hadn't told me that there was someone new on the scene, the abrupt cessation of intimacy between me and Paul would have. He'd never said anything specific to me – but then we'd never said anything specific to each other about what had been going on between us for so long, only come together in sudden furtive surges of longing that left us sated and guilty, a bit like the sweets I was eating by the handful would.

I swiped away from WhatsApp and through to Instagram. Clara was too young to have an account, but I'd given in to her increasingly desperate pleas ('But everyone else does, Mum! God, don't you want me to have friends or what?'), bearing in mind *How to Survive*'s advice that picking your battles was key to... well, surviving parenting a teenager.

I'd insisted that she kept her account locked down and private, and that I should vet any new followers, and as far as I could tell she had complied. She was followed by a handful of her friends from school, by Paul (not that he ever posted anything), by me and by Daily_Hayley, who, as her username implied, posted regularly every day.

Masochistically, I searched for her (like I'd follow her myself – stalker alert!) and flicked through her feed. I wasn't sure if she had aspirations to become some kind of influencer, but it sure looked that way – the images of her life were as perfectly curated as if she was a celebrity.

There was Hayley in the gym, her face perfectly made-up, her strawberry-blonde hair in a deliberately messy topknot, her skimpy sports bra colour co-ordinated with Lycra leggings that revealed not a speck of cellulite, swinging a kettlebell with a big smile on her face. There was Hayley clutching several bright yellow Selfridges carrier bags, a red double-decker bus whizzing past in the background. There was Hayley walking her cock-apoo in the woods, the autumn leaves a perfect match for the dog's curly fur and Hayley's vintage tweed coat. There was Hayley pouring a green smoothie into a glass, her skin as glossy as the fresh spinach artfully arranged on the marble kitchen counter.

There was Hayley's slender, manicured hand, a silver charm bracelet on her wrist and a diamond ring on her finger.

The worst thing was, I couldn't hate her. The captions on her posts were self-deprecating and sweet. The reels she posted showed a bubbly girl who addressed her viewers as 'you guys' in a slightly husky voice that always seemed about to break into giggles. And she was so young – so fresh and unspoiled. At least five years younger than me, which would make her almost ten years younger than Paul.

No wonder Paul had fallen for her. No wonder Clara was excited about having this fun woman as a stepmother.

As if ripping off a plaster, I closed the Instagram window and tapped through to the Girlfriends' Club, where I posted without preamble.

Rowan: So Paul's getting married.

There was a pause. Normally, my friends were quick to respond, especially to news as earth-shaking as this. But it was half past seven in the evening; Kate would probably be heading out for a cocktail in some glamorous bar, Naomi would be putting her two-and-a-half-year-old twins to bed, Abbie and Matt would be settling down on the sofa together, their black-and-white cat stretched across their laps.

But I should have known I could rely on them.

Kate: OMG! That's... er... sudden. How long have they been together again?

Naomi: Have you met her? Is she nice?

Abbie: Fuck. Are you okay?

No, I'm not okay. I'm absolutely, abjectly miserable. But, I realised, Clara's bombshell wasn't the only cause of that. It was the culmination of what felt like years of increasing dissatisfaction with my life, with myself.

Rowan: Been better. It just feels so kind of brutal.

Like he's rejected me, once and for all, I typed. Then I deleted that.

Like he's really moved on, and I'm kind of stuck, I wrote instead.

Stuck in a job I'd only taken because my career as a make-up artist, specialising in weddings, had imploded when suddenly no weddings were allowed during lockdown, and which felt too daunting to try and re-establish. Stuck in a flat that had only ever been meant to be a rung on the ladder and now felt like a prison. Stuck with a daughter I loved more than life itself, who was moving further and further away from me as she grew up.

Stuck with a bunch of stale dreams I now knew would never come true.

Rowan: I mean, she seems nice and everything. I think they've been seeing each other for six months, so it's kind of quick. But Clara likes her. And obviously I want Paul to be happy. I'm not bitter or anything.

I'm bitter.

Kate: God, that's always the bloody way, isn't it? These commitment-phobes put off marriage to a woman who's perfect for them for years and years and then it ends, and then suddenly someone else comes along and there's a ring on her finger before you can say, 'It's not you, it's me.'

Rowan: To be fair, Paul and I were engaged. And then Clara came along and it just didn't seem like the right time to get married, and then obviously everything went tits up before it could ever happen.

Which was kind of how it had gone down. Kind of. When I was pregnant, I'd suggested to Paul that we trot along to the local register office and get married, just the two of us and a couple of witnesses. But he wanted to do it properly, he said. And then there wasn't the time or the money or – later – the love left for that.

I didn't regret anything – certainly not Clara. And those stolen moments with Paul? At the time, it had felt necessary. I'd wanted so much to be wanted and needed and loved by someone who wasn't my daughter. It wasn't his fault that deep in my heart – deeper than I could ever tell anyone about – I'd hoped for more.

Abbie: Still, though. It must hurt.

Rowan: Yeah, it does, I'm not going to lie.

Although if they asked me when we last slept together (slept – as if!) I couldn't promise I wouldn't lie about that.

But my friends didn't ask. Whether because they were too tactful or because they genuinely had no idea just how long

Paul's and my... thing, whatever it was, had been going on, I wasn't sure.

We chatted a bit more about other stuff, and I ate a few more chocolates, and then the speed of my friends' replies slowed down a bit, and I imagined them getting on with their evenings, their work as my emergency support system done for the time being.

Reluctantly, I got up to clean my teeth (I knew from bitter experience that waking up at two in the morning with my mouth tasting of sour chocolate wasn't worth it), tapped on Clara's door and said goodnight, and then returned to bed.

I switched off the light, but sleep eluded me. I lay there in the darkness, imagining Paul and Hayley lying together, her honey-coloured hair spilling over the pillow, one shoulder in a baby-doll nightdress visible above the covers.

Then my phone illuminated with a WhatsApp message, and I grabbed it and glanced at the screen.

Naomi: We should do something lovely for Rowan. She's had a tough couple of years and it's Christmas after all. Let's get our Santa hats on!

She can't have meant to post in our group – she can't have meant me to see. And clearly she hadn't, because the message was deleted almost immediately.

But when I fell asleep, shortly after, it was with the beginning of a glow of comfort inside me.

CHAPTER FOUR

When he was a teenager, Alex – like most of his friends – had been obsessed with computer games. He had other hobbies – his mum made sure of that, sticking her head round his bedroom door and demanding whether he was going to fester in the dark in his own filth all afternoon or get out in the fresh air and get some exercise. To which Alex had replied that the air might be fresh, but that was because it was downright dreich out there, and she'd said she didn't care how dreich it was, he was going to rugby practice because she wasn't having him letting the team down. And, of course, Alex had gone.

But computers had been – and remained – a big part of his life. Teenage Alex, though, hadn't followed the trend and played *Grand Theft Auto* and *Half-Life*. His obsession was with the old-school games, the ones that had been right at the vanguard of the genre. He'd tracked down – and paid handsomely for – a beta version of *Prince of Persia*. He'd discovered the original *Brickout* for Mac. His rationale was to get under the hood – to discover the underpinnings of the medium. In his dreams, he was going to become a games developer and make a fortune.

Obviously, that never happened.

But he'd retained a fondness for those clunky, pixelated, buggy proto-apps, and remembered with happiness the hours he'd spent staring at the screen, his fingers cramping from gripping the mouse ('You'll wreck your eyesight for sure,' his mum had said).

And now, on this icy December morning, he was reminded of those days. Not only were his eyes dry and scratchy from staring at a screen all night, but he was basically playing *Tetris*.

Okay, not actual *Tetris*. But that was what the daily ritual of loading up his van with parcels of all shapes and sizes, in an order that approximated that in which they'd need to be delivered – last ones at the back and underneath, first at the front and on top – reminded him of.

Alex was no expert – he was a rookie at the game, as he'd be the first to admit. His colleague Damon loaded his own van in a fraction of the time it took Alex, even on occasion humiliatingly asking if he needed a hand. But he was improving, albeit slowly.

His efficiency wasn't helped by the fact that – his mum's voice again, 'You're daydreaming again! Away with the fairies!' – Alex found the repetitive nature of the task invited distraction. When he was engaged in something mentally challenging, he could focus just fine. But now, cold, sleep-deprived and frankly bored by the necessity to stock his van with the parcels that would constitute the one hundred and seventy deliveries he was due to make that day, he couldn't help allowing his mind to wander.

Nice Mrs MacAllister had another Waterstones order. Chatting on her doorstep a day or two before, Alex had asked why she didn't switch to digital books, but she'd said she preferred reading hardbacks, even though the weight of them played havoc with her arthritic wrists. She liked the smell, she'd told him, while her dog sniffed eagerly at Alex's ankles, analysing the scent of all the other dogs he'd encountered on his round.

Number 60 Thorntree Hill were having an early Christmas party, he guessed – yesterday, he'd dropped off a weighty, clinking crate of bottles; today's was much larger but feather-light, presumably filled with disposable plastic champagne flutes and paper plates. Not for the first time, Alex considered the environmental implications of transporting oversized boxes that were mostly filled with air.

And, as always, there were a number of parcels for the residents of the Falcons estate. Alex had to admit it wasn't his favourite place to stop. The four low-rise blocks and two tall towers made for a lot of hauling stuff along walkways and up stairs, not least because the lift in Curlew Court seemed to work only intermittently – on odd-numbered days or alternate weeks on a day with an 's' in it, Alex had ruefully speculated.

The pretty Asian lady with the cute toddler daughter had several parcels, he noted – she was clearly an organised Christmas shopper. Just the previous day, he'd arrived to find her wrestling a load of Tesco bags up the stairs and had given her a hand with them, and she'd confided that she was planning on making an early start on the cooking and putting everything she could fit in the freezer well ahead of twenty of her friends and family descending on Christmas Day.

And, for the first time, Alex noticed a parcel for her neighbour at number 74 – or possibly her teenage daughter. Alex had only briefly glimpsed the two of them on his rounds: the girl pretty but as sullen-faced as Alex remembered his own sister being at the same age; the mother as tired and harried-looking as Alex supposed his mum must have been, getting the two of them through high school on her own.

There had been something about the mother that had seemed familiar to Alex, but he hadn't been able to place it.

After all, he'd been in London only a few months – what were the chances of him having ever encountered her before?

But that was enough. He'd been away with the fairies for sure – but nonetheless, his van was loaded and ready to go.

With a cheery wave at Damon, who – ahead as always – was already reversing neatly out of his parking bay, Alex slid into the driver's seat and fired up the van's engine.

CHAPTER FIVE

The rain, which had more or less held off all day, started in earnest just before I left the office. I looked out through the shopfront windows, past the boards of properties sold and for sale, and watched it lashing down on the almost-dark street, sending tourists and shoppers dashing for cover, umbrellas blowing inside out and newspapers held futilely over their heads for shelter.

For a second, I considered staying at work for an extra hour or two to see if the weather would improve, but I abandoned the idea almost straight away. It was three o'clock; I liked to get home before Clara returned from school, even if I couldn't always pick her up. The traffic, which I could already see inching bumper-to-bumper towards Piccadilly Circus, was only going to get heavier. And besides, I didn't want to give Julz any ideas about my willingness to put in extra hours for no extra pay.

So I pulled my coat over my head, cursing myself for leaving my own umbrella in the car, and made a dash for the underground parking.

Soon I, too, was edging along in the seemingly endless crocodile of cars, Portia's inefficient heating leaving my feet chilly on the pedals and the windscreen misting up as fast as I could clear it with the threadbare towel I kept on hand for the purpose.

It took me almost two hours to complete the journey home, which would have taken a quarter of that on public transport. Not for the first time, I cursed the necessity of having a car for work, then reminded myself of the terse reply I'd heard a radio announcer give an irate listener once: 'You're not *in* traffic, you *are* traffic.'

Contributing to global warming and congestion was what I was doing, as Clara never tired of reminding me (except when she needed a lift somewhere).

'Don't feel bad, Portia,' I said, reversing carefully into my parking space at home. 'You're a car. This is what you do.'

Although the little Ford's environmental rating was so bad that, before my next vehicle tax payment was due, I might have to consider investing in a replacement. How I'd be able to afford that, or bear to part with my rattly little green friend, I had no idea.

I made another mad dash through the rain to the lift, only to find that it was on the blink yet again.

'Shit,' I muttered. 'That's all I need.'

It was only two weeks before that I'd sent my most recent strongly worded email (okay, if I'm honest it was more a forlorn plea for help) to the building's management company, and received an assurance that regular maintenance work on the elevators was ongoing and normal service would be resumed as soon as possible, followed by a helpful-not-helpful reminder that in the event of fire, residents should always use the stairwells.

'Like I'd have a choice.'

I turned towards the concrete stairwell, bracing myself for

the seven-storey climb up steps that always smelled strongly of some sort of industrial-strength cleaning product.

But before I could begin my weary ascent, a voice behind me said, 'Excuse me,' and a man stepped past me and set off up the stairs at a brisk clip. He was a delivery driver, I guessed, from his baseball cap and high-vis jacket, and the huge cardboard carton he was carrying, balanced awkwardly on one shoulder.

I set off behind him, thinking that my climb would be somewhat improved by the view of his tight denim-clad bottom just about at my eye level and the fresh scent of whatever man beauty products he used that trailed behind him. But I didn't get to view it for long; he was already at the first landing when I started up, and by the time I'd turned the corner, he was out of sight, only the drumming of his boots above me telling me that he hadn't already reached his destination.

Beginning to sweat in my winter coat, my high heels pinching my feet and my breath coming in puffs (God, I was so unfit. Yet another disadvantage of driving to work every day), I laboured on upwards, the pale yellow fluorescent lights dazzling me with each corner I turned.

Above me, the thumping of the delivery guy's boots had stopped. He must have been going to the floor below mine, although I could no longer be sure whether I had one more flight to go or two.

But I'd climbed faster than I realised. I emerged onto a walkway and saw, like a beacon of hope ahead of me, the number 71 on a red-painted front door. Thank God – I was on my floor already.

Gasping, my legs feeling like hot jelly under my tights, I turned the corner and trudged towards my front door. But someone had made it there first. The delivery driver was standing on the doormat, his hand impatiently raised towards the bell. As I approached, the door opened and Clara looked out, peevish as she always was when she had to answer the door without being one hundred per cent sure it was a delivery for her or one of her mates come to visit.

Her face almost immediately relaxed into a smile, however.

'I've got a package for Rowan Connell,' I heard the man's voice say. He had a hint of an accent – Scottish, maybe? – that elongated the Os of my first and last names, making them sound almost like a caress.

'That's me,' I panted, coming to a stop behind him.

He turned around, smiling, and I could see why Clara's surliness had melted away so rapidly. His grin was wide and engaging, and his eyes under the turquoise peak of his cap were the brightest blue I'd ever seen.

'Package for you then, I guess,' he said. *Definitely Scottish.* 'Careful, it's a bit awkward.'

'Didn't look it when you were legging it up the stairs,' I observed, reaching out for the box. He was right: although not particularly heavy, it was so large I had to stretch my arms out to receive it and could only just see him over its top.

Which meant he could only just see me – probably a good thing, given how red-faced and sweaty I felt after my climb.

'I get plenty of practice running up and down stairs,' he said, unclipping a device from his belt. 'I just need a photo.'

Clara leaned in towards me, automatically putting on her selfie pout while the driver tapped his camera, even though as far as I knew he only needed to photograph the door and the parcel, not our faces.

'All done?' I asked.

'All done,' the driver confirmed, meeting my eyes for a moment then breaking into a grin, like delivering my parcel was the best thing that had happened to him all day. It was certainly the best thing that had happened to me. 'Have a good evening. Don't get too wet out there!'

'Don't worry, we're not going anywhere.' Clara smiled again. 'Are we, Mum?'

'Not if we can help it,' I agreed, cheered by my daughter's sudden good mood.

The driver turned and headed for the stairwell at a jog, then paused, turned again and sketched a wave before disappearing into the stairwell. I heard the thud of his boots again as he descended at what sounded to me like reckless speed.

'So what is it?' Clara asked, gesturing at the parcel.

'Oh.' For a moment, I'd almost forgotten it was there. 'I've got no idea. Let's open it and see.'

'I'll get a knife from the kitchen.'

I carried the parcel through to the living room and laid it on the floor. My name and address were on the label, so it was definitely for me. But what was it? I couldn't remember ordering anything recently, apart from a couple of small gifts for Clara, which even packaging-happy Amazon wouldn't have put in a box this size.

I knelt on the carpet and Clara joined me, a paring knife in her hand.

'Well?' she asked impatiently. 'Are you going to open it or what?'

'Maybe later,' I said. 'Why don't we just look at it for a bit? Maybe run the hoover round first.'

'Mum!' Clara rolled her eyes, and we both laughed.

It felt like the first proper laugh we'd shared for ages.

'Go on then.' I held out my hand and Clara passed me the knife, handle first, the way I'd taught her when she was a little girl.

Carefully, I ran the blade down the thread-reinforced tape that sealed the edges of the box. I felt the snapping resistance as the knife slit through the tape and the threads, all along one side, then I moved on to the next, carefully unsealing that too. I could hear Clara breathing and smell her peach shampoo as she leaned close to watch.

'There we go.' The last of the tape cut, I eased the lid of the box open. It was so large it couldn't lie flat, and I had to prop it up against the coffee table.

But we barely noticed that. I pushed aside a layer of bubble wrap, but I could already see what lay underneath. There was a printed image of the iconic faux-Tudor facade of the Liberty department store, clad in snow, all coloured in frosty blue, grey, white and silver, drifts of glitter dusting its surface.

'Oh my God,' Clara breathed. 'It's the Liberty beauty advent calendar.'

'Looks that way.' My heart pounding with excitement, I lifted the box out of its packaging, kicked the cardboard aside, and laid it across my outstretched thighs.

'Mum, if there's a Le Labo under-eye serum in there, can I have it? Can I please?'

Only if you fight me for it, I thought.

'Only if you have my wrinkles too,' I said.

'But prevention's better than cure – everyone knows that,' Clara argued, then she changed tack and said, 'Besides, you don't have any wrinkles, Mum. You're beautiful.'

'Flattery won't get your mitts on my Liberty beauty products,' I said, and Clara glared, then giggled.

'Shall we have a look inside?'

The front of the calendar was split vertically down the middle, its two sides opening outwards like doors to a magic castle. I eased them apart and we looked down together at the array of little drawers inside, twenty-five of them, printed with the store's art deco design, each with a tiny slot in the top to pull it open with a finger, and each concealing its separate treasure. A waft of fragrance came up from the cardboard, reminding me of the beauty hall where I'd lingered, wondering what it would be like to be able to buy anything I wanted.

'Go on, Mum! Open them. God, you're so slow.'

'I'm savouring the moment.'

'Who sent you this, anyway? You never bought it for yourself? I mean, it would be amazing if you had, but...'

But I'm always telling you we can't afford stuff, and spaffing hundreds of pounds on a shameless indulgence for myself would make me the worst mother ever.

'Of course I didn't. I couldn't. I think it must be...'

Then I remembered the WhatsApp message I'd seen a few nights before, from Naomi, which had appeared and been deleted so quickly I might have thought it had been a dream, if it wasn't for the notification that had been there the next day: *This message has been deleted.*

It had said something about doing something lovely for me, because I was having a hard time.

I didn't feel like I was having a hard time now – I felt like the luckiest person alive.

'I think it might have been Auntie— I mean Naomi. And Abbie and Kate, I expect.'

When Clara was small, my friends had jokingly referred to themselves as her aunties, as she had no real ones. But recently she'd taken to rolling her eyes at the pet name, and dropping 'Auntie' altogether, except when she forgot.

'Let's have a look, shall we?' I lifted the calendar and put it on the sofa, propped upright. 'Do you want to go first?'

'But it's yours.'

'You open the first one, for today, the first of December.'

'But then you won't get to open one until tomorrow.'

'Well, we could just—'

'God, Mum. Don't you know how it works? You open one a day, every day until Christmas.'

This is what I get for teaching my daughter about the importance of following the rules, I thought.

'Fine,' I agreed reluctantly. 'You do today's and I'll do tomorrow's.'

Carefully, almost reverently, Clara hooked her finger in the top of the door with a '1' printed on it in gold. Her face was transfixed, her bottom lip caught beneath her teeth. Gently, she eased the little box out of its slot.

'Ooooh,' she breathed. 'It's a lip balm.'

'Not just any lip balm,' I corrected. 'That's Malin+Goetz. It's super fancy.'

'Wow.' Clara's hand closed over the tube. 'Mum, can I...?'

Over my dead body, I thought. Then I thought, *It's almost Christmas. How often does Clara get something really special like that?* And if I conceded on this, my bargaining power if we got the eye serum would be significantly increased.

'Oh, all right,' I said. 'Mind you don't take it to school and lose it though – you'd be gutted.'

I was wasting my breath, I knew – she mostly wanted it so she could whip it out of her bag during double Maths and impress her mates.

'Thanks, Mum. I do love you.' Clara leaned over and brushed my cheek with her lips (soon to be rendered smooth and flake-free via a unique blend of fatty acids, I thought enviously). 'Tell you what, let's cheat and check tomorrow's, just so we know what you're getting.'

'But you said—'

'Just this once. Go on, Mum.'

There was no way I was going to be able to hold out, not now I'd seen the lip balm. I located the drawer with the number '2' on it, and carefully slid it out.

Clara's face fell. 'It's empty.'

Baffled, I turned it over, my brain whirling. There should have been some sort of plastic wrapping over the whole thing, surely? But there hadn't been. And the box did feel suspiciously light, now I thought about it. Even if the products were small enough to fit into the drawers, lots of them would be full-size and some in glass packaging. Perhaps it had been tampered with. I'd have to tell my friends, and perhaps the handsome, smiling delivery driver with the sparkling blue eyes would lose his job.

Although if he was responsible for stealing my epic beauty haul, he deserved to lose more than a job, the thieving rob-dog.

I replaced the number 2 drawer in its slot.

'It's okay if we check the others now, isn't it?' I asked.

Clara nodded. She looked like she might be about to cry.

'It'll be okay,' I assured her. 'If there's been a mistake, they'll sort it out. Promise.'

I checked the number 3 drawer, but that was empty too. So was number 4.

'Stop!' Clara ordered. 'We know there's nothing in them.'

I swung the doors of the calendar closed, lifted it and gave it a gentle shake. There was no inviting rattle from within, and now it felt even lighter than before.

'I'm going to have to tell them. It feels so awful, ruining their surprise.'

Reluctantly, I took my phone out of my bag. There were already three new messages on the Girlfriends' Club WhatsApp.

Kate: It's been delivered. Have you got it, Ro?

Abbie: She must've done. Come on, Connell, get a move on and open it.

Naomi: Perhaps she's fainted from shock. Earth to Rowan??

Hastily, I typed a message.

Rowan: Guys, I'm really sorry. It's here and it's lovely and I'm so grateful, but something's wrong.

Abbie: What's the problem?

Rowan: It's empty. Apart from today's, there's nothing in any of the drawers I checked.

Kate: Oh no, how awful!

But she added a crying-with-laughter emoji.

Rowan: What? What's so funny?

Naomi: Admit it, Ro. What would you have done if there'd been something in all the drawers?

Rowan: I'd have opened one every day until Christmas, obviously.

Abbie: Pants. On. Fire.

Naomi: You might have managed that for the first three days. But then you'd have opened two, and by the end of the week you'd have gone through them all. You know you would.

Rowan: I would not!

But, deep down, I knew they were right. I might have opened them in my room, in secret, pretending to Clara that I didn't know what was there when we opened them together later. But it was true – curiosity would have got the better of me. It already had.

Rowan: Okay, maybe I would.

Kate: So you're going to have to be patient. You'll get one instalment delivered every day.

Abbie: And it's not all beauty stuff either.

Naomi: Ssssh! No spoilers.

Abbie: Sorry.

Rowan: OMG! This is immense. How am I going to handle the suspense?

Kate: You're just going to have to find a way.

I thanked them again and put my phone aside, looking at Clara's expectant face. I explained to her what was going on, and she squealed with delight like a little child.

I could have squealed too. The weeks until Christmas suddenly felt full of excitement and promise – and I knew that my friends would enjoy the journey as much as I would.

But I don't think any of us realised just how bumpy the ride would be.

CHAPTER SIX

When I drove to work the next morning, I could still feel a warm glow of happiness, tinged with pleasurable anticipation. When I arrived home later that day, there'd be another parcel waiting for me. If I was lucky and early, I might even get to see the blue-eyed delivery driver again. And if not, there'd always be the next day, and the day after that, and all the days leading up to Christmas.

London seemed to have upped its festive vibes, too. As I drove past Hyde Park, I was grateful for once for the heavy traffic, which allowed me to stare out of the window at the mist rising off the Serpentine, shrouding the trees in grey haze, the sun glowing above like a matte gold Christmas bauble.

But when I arrived at the office, Marty and Brett were already there – unusual, as neither was a morning person, except on the occasions when they hadn't made it to bed the night before – ready to harsh my mellow.

They were in the middle of what looked like a doozy of a row.

'Mate, Roddy Leibowitz is my applicant.' Marty switched on the coffee machine and put a mug down next to it with unnecessary force. As usual, he was wearing trousers that were just slightly too short, showing a few inches of bare ankle above his tasselled loafers. I wasn't old enough to be his mum, but still, every time I saw him, I wanted to tell him to put some socks on before he caught his death of cold.

'Yeah, and I showed him Rupert Court.' Brett pushed back his chair and clasped his hands behind his head, faux-casually, a wide smirk on his face. His suit was just too bright a blue, the lapels a touch too wide, the knot in his orange-and-magenta floral tie fractionally too large for the sophisticated man-about-town look he aimed for.

'So what if you did?'

'So you said, if I did, I'd get sixty per cent of your commission.'

'I never. Jesus. Do you think I'm stupid? Sixty per cent for one viewing, when I've been dragging that fucker round London for months?'

'You did,' Brett insisted, the smirk becoming more like a snarl.

'Yeah? Prove it.'

I knew, and both of them knew, that the arrangement would have been made on the fly, Marty faced with a diary clash but determined not to let down a potential buyer; Brett scenting a rare moment of weakness, like a hyena moving in on a dying antelope. Brett's share of the commission on the multimillion-pound property would be a sizeable whack, and he'd have earned it given the notorious pickiness of Roddy Leibowitz, who did something massively lucrative in the City.

I was used to the two of them having these kinds of scraps, mostly over money, but sometimes over something as stupid as Brett having nicked Marty's stapler, or Marty having put three sugars in Brett's tea when he knew full well Brett only took two. It was part of their endless, childish power play.

At first, I'd expected that Julz, in his position as the branch manager, would intervene, but he never had. I'd begun to think he even encouraged it – that he believed the adversarial nature of their relationship made them hungrier to bring in the big bucks.

Now, he was watching them idly from behind his computer screen, in between apparently polishing his fingernails on his trouser leg.

'We shook on it!' Brett protested. 'Gentleman's agreement, and all.'

'Gentlemen don't make up agreements that never existed, mate. I'll give you thirty.'

'Fifty.'

'Thirty-five, and that's my final offer.'

'Forty.'

'Deal.'

'And I'm putting it in writing and you can bleeding well sign it.'

Like a couple of cats backing off from a fight, their tails still fluffy with aggression, the two of them stared at each other across the office. Then Kimberley walked in and their animosity faded almost instantly. Kimberley had been hired a few weeks previously, and the pair of them had greeted her with hostility hidden by a thin veil of what they would probably have described as banter.

Two cats clocking another cat that they dislike even more than they do each other, I thought.

As always, Kimberley was rocking a strong look. Today she was wearing a neon-orange trouser suit, a white crop top showing off her toned midriff, the trousers split at the ankle to reveal her white stilettos.

If I'd worn shoes like that in this weather, they'd have been trashed within minutes, covered in rainwater and grit salt, but Kimberley seemed to have an almost supernatural ability to repel the elements. Her hair hung in perfect platinum waves down her back, unfrizzed by the rain; her white-and-silver French manicure was unchipped in spite of the force with which she pounded her keyboard; her matte nude lipstick unsmudged even though she was sucking furiously at her vape pen.

'Right,' she said into her phone, exhaling a caramel-flavoured cloud. 'I'll pass that on to the vendor. They were looking for offers over four million, but we'll do our best for you. I'll come back to you as soon as I hear back. Right? Right. You have a good day too.'

Brett and Marty watched as she topped up her water bottle and took a seat at her desk.

Then Brett said, 'What's the difference between an Essex girl and a shopping trolley?'

'You've got me there, mate,' Marty said.

'A shopping trolley's got a mind of its own.'

They both laughed far more uproariously than the feeble, offensive joke justified.

Kimberley, tight-lipped, was bashing away at her keyboard. As I watched, she pulled out her Airpods and slotted one into each ear, feigning indifference.

Next to me, my desk phone began to trill.

'What do you call an Essex girl with half a brain?' Brett asked.

'Dunno, mate. Gifted?'

Brett bellowed with laughter. 'Got it in one.'

The phone was still ringing. Normally, my colleagues would pounce on it before I'd even noticed its summons – whoever took the call got the applicant. But today the urge to bond over goading Kimberley was apparently even stronger than the drive to nab a new potential buyer.

If it was even a buyer. It was just as likely to be someone trying to sell us a new photocopier contract.

I reached out my hand and picked up the receiver.

'Walkerson's Elite, Rowan speaking. How may I help you?'

'Oi!' Brett and Marty knocked off the banter, united in outrage that I'd had the audacity to actually take a call. I pressed the phone to one ear and my hand to the other so I could hear the caller over their protests.

'Hi,' a woman's voice said, 'I'm calling about a property I saw online – the flat on Kildare Terrace.'

'Of course,' I said. 'I'll just take a few details from you, if I may.'

Getting her into the database was key – once that had happened, she'd be my applicant and there would be nothing anyone could do about it. Not that Brett and Marty wouldn't try, especially if it turned out she had north of five million pounds to spend.

The woman gave me her name, which I had to ask her to spell out because both first and last names were unusual, and recited her telephone number and email address, which I repeated twice for fear of getting it wrong and losing my first-ever actual applicant before I'd even begun.

'The property's still available,' I told her. 'But there have been a few viewings in the past few days and quite a bit of interest. So I'd advise getting you in to see it as soon as possible.'

The flat – I navigated to a different part of the system and checked the listing – had been on the market for a couple of months with no offers, which suggested that it wasn't exactly being fought over. But creating a sense of urgency was part of the job, I'd learned.

I'd also learned that being less than honest with people didn't sit well with me, but I'd have to live with that or have no chance of ever getting any commission added to my meagre salary.

I arranged to meet the woman at Kildare Terrace early that afternoon, thanked her and ended the call.

'You may as well give her the particulars for Mortimer

Gardens as well,' Kimberley said. She seemed to have a data-base inside her head with the details of every single property on our books, which made Marty and Brett's jibes about the stupidity of women from Essex even more unfair. 'And the penthouse on Talbot Road, and the other one a few doors down. I'll get the details over to you.'

'Great, I appreciate that.'

I texted Clara to let her know I'd be late, hastily ate the cheese and pickle sandwich I'd brought from home, and then hurried to Portia's parking spot, hopped in and headed off to do my viewing.

I found the property easily enough – it was a modern block, ugly as anything from the outside but, thanks to its location, highly sought-after, as the marketing literature said. A lift had been installed (which I was willing to bet was more reliable than the one leading to my own flat), and parts of the original estate had been converted to a leisure centre complete with swimming pool and gym.

It wasn't anything to write home about, going by the kind of places Walkerson's Elite normally marketed, but by my standards it was the lap of luxury.

I swung Portia into a free parking spot and looked around for my buyer. Normally, as I knew from conducting viewings on behalf of my colleagues, Walkerson's Elite clients would arrive in a sports car, as Tatiana had, or in a black cab, as many did if they were visiting from abroad and didn't know their way around London. Occasionally, one had even shown up in a chauffeur-driven limo.

But the car that pulled up next to mine was a normal white sedan, a Toyota, only a couple of notches above Portia in the car hierarchy. An Uber, I guessed. I knew from the price of the flat that my applicant wasn't in the same league as many of our super-wealthy buyers. That was okay. She only needed to buy one relatively humble property for me to make a wedge of commission that would make all the difference to Clara and me.

I watched as the door of the cab swung open and a woman's legs emerged. Then the rest of her followed – slowly and cumbersomely, because she was clearly in the very late stages of pregnancy.

I hurried over. 'Mrs Choudhury? Here, do you need a hand? I'm Rowan from Walkerson's.'

'Thank you. God, the state of me! No one tells you it'll be like this, do they?' Her voice was pleasant, with an accent that reminded me – briefly and pleasurably – of the handsome delivery driver who'd brought my parcel.

'If they did, that would be the population explosion sorted in one easy step, right?'

We exchanged smiles. She was a pretty woman, about my own age or a couple of years younger, although it was hard to tell, because she mostly just looked knackered.

'I was hoping we'd have found somewhere by now. We're renting at the moment, and our contract's up at the end of February, although really we'd have liked to be in by Christmas, before...' She gestured at her bump, huge under her winter coat.

'Well, at least you won't be giving birth in a stable and laying your baby in a manger,' I joked. 'Come on, let me show you the property. There are three good-size bedrooms, so plenty of room for a growing family, and...'

I launched into my sales patter as I unlocked the door, describing the flat's proximity to good schools, newly refurbished bathroom and south-facing aspect.

'It's certainly convenient for my husband's work,' she said. 'He works horribly long hours – that's why he couldn't get away today. I do too – at least I will, when I'm back after my maternity leave. We've only recently moved to London, so we're just getting a feel for the place.'

As the viewing concluded, I found myself warming more

and more to this woman. She had none of the brashness of many of our usual clients – she was an ordinary, nice person wanting a home to live and raise a family in. By the time we said goodbye, with her promising to talk to her husband and let me know as soon as she could if they'd like a second viewing, the idea of my commission had all but vanished from my mind – I just wanted to do the best I could for her.

But when I climbed back into the car and checked my phone before heading home, I saw a message from Kimberley.

Sorry – Kildare Terrace is off the market. Brett got an offer accepted on it, from one of Tatiana Ivanova's contacts.

I felt a jolt of annoyance and disappointment, but that was all. There'd be other properties to show her, I thought – this was just a temporary setback.

It wasn't until later that I realised it was more than that – it was a declaration of war.

CHAPTER SEVEN

The buzz of the alarm yanked me out of a half-awake daydream the next morning. I'd snoozed it twice already, and now I was going to be late for work if I didn't get my arse in gear. Before the dream could wrap its seductive tendrils around me again, I forced myself out of bed with a jerk. The room was freezing, the windows running with condensation.

'Eff you, December,' I muttered.

Then I saw the Liberty advent calendar, balanced on my dressing table where I'd placed it the previous night, the gold-cased mini eyeshadow palette Clara had reluctantly handed over the previous day next to it, and my heart lifted. There'd be another delivery today and, hopefully, today I'd be home in time to receive it myself.

The thought galvanised me, making the day ahead feel suddenly less bleak.

I tapped on Clara's door, called out a cheerful 'Good morning' and waited to hear her muttered response before hurrying into the bathroom to shower and get ready for work.

Inevitably, Clara fell back asleep, I burned the breakfast toast, Portia was sulky and slow to start from the cold, and I only just squeaked into the office by half past eight. But throughout the day, my mind kept returning to the advent calendar with a pleasant glow of anticipation that not even the series of viewings I conducted of a 'bijou pied-à-terre' with barely room to swing a very small cat could dim. And I was able to spend several hours trawling through our database and send my applicant a shortlist of places that I reckoned might work for her, already imagining spending the commission I'd earn if she bought one of them.

My last viewing finished at two thirty, and I felt justified in heading straight home rather than returning to the office, arriving before Clara got back from school.

The flat was silent, peaceful and – for a change – relatively tidy. I heated up a can of soup and ate standing at the kitchen counter, before pacing the short distance from one end of my flat to the other, eagerly waiting for the delivery driver.

I didn't switch on the TV in case it drowned out the sound of a knock on the door. I didn't go to the supermarket and pick up something for our dinner in case I was out when the courier arrived. I didn't run myself a gas-bill-busting hot bath in case I had to answer the door in nothing but a towel and some soap suds – although, if I was honest, I could think of worse things than being checked out in a state of undress by those bright blue eyes.

I just paced – and waited. By four thirty, I'd almost given up, and then I heard the tread of boots on the walkway outside and sprang to attention.

I heard the thud of a bag being lowered to the floor, then the beep of a console, then – finally – the crash of the knocker, and I sprang to the door at lightning speed, flinging it open so quickly that the delivery driver recoiled in surprise before breaking into a rueful grin.

It was the same guy who'd come the other day, the smiley blue-eyed bloke with the turquoise baseball cap.

'Sorry,' I said, feeling my lips curve involuntarily into an answering smile. 'Did I startle you? Only I'm expecting...'

'A parcel,' he finished. 'Here you go, Mrs Connell.'

'It's Miss, actually.' As soon as the words were out, I felt myself blushing. *No need to ram your single status down the poor bloke's throat, Connell!* 'Thank you.'

I extended my hand and he passed me a flat brown cardboard envelope.

I looked at it for a second, confused. No beauty product I could think of would fit into this; it was barely thicker than the brown envelopes our council tax bills came in.

'Everything all right?' the guy asked, his smile fading.

I glanced at his face, noticing how perfectly all his features fit together – his strong jawline, straight nose and of course those amazing eyes. I wondered what colour his hair was, but it was hidden beneath his cap.

'Yes, I'm sure it's fine. It's just...' I turned the envelope over, but there, sure enough, were my name and address on the printed label.

'Were you expecting something else? I'll check if there's another parcel for you.'

He hitched his bag from his shoulder round to the front of his body and rummaged in it, his brow furrowing with concentration. While I waited, I tore open the envelope, the perforations in the cardboard parting when I pulled the tab.

Inside was a flat, translucent polythene bag, and inside that a slim piece of red plastic in the shape of a fish.

'There's nothing else here for you, sorry,' the delivery guy said.

'That's okay. Thanks for looking. I guess this is what I was expecting.'

He laughed. 'I mean, it is or it isn't.'

'It's kind of a surprise,' I tried to explain. 'My friends sent me the parcel you dropped off the other day, only it was empty, and they've said the stuff that was meant to be inside it would come over the next few days. Well, the next twenty-two, to be exact.'

'Like an advent calendar?'

'Yeah, like that. Only this is...'

'A fortune-telling fish.' He leaned closer, peering at the object in my hand – so close I could feel the warmth of his breath on my skin and an involuntary shiver run down my spine in response. 'It's like the ones you used to get in Christmas crackers. It should have instructions on it.'

I turned the plastic packet over, and there, sure enough, were a series of simple drawings of the fish's body in various contortions – tail to head, flipped over, twisting from side to side, and so on – each with a description next to it, which presumably indicated the user's state of mind.

'Why not open it and take a look?' the guy suggested.

I eased open the packet and slid the fragile object out into my palm. It was little more than a sliver of flexible red plastic film, thinner than the cellophane envelope that had contained it. Immediately, its head rose to meet its tail and it curled into an almost perfect circle.

'What does that mean, then?' I asked, looking down at the pack in my other hand, where the key was printed. 'Oh. Guess it thinks I'm passionate.'

'Oh, aye?' He grinned, and I felt my cheeks colour again.

'Go on then,' I said. 'You have a go.'

'I really ought to be... All right then.'

He pulled off his fingerless glove and held out his hand. Carefully, I tipped the fish from my palm into his. It lay there for a second, not moving at all, and then it flipped straight over onto its other side.

I looked down at the captioned pictures. 'False, something to hide,' I read.

We met each other's eyes, and now it seemed like it was his turn to redden. 'I'm honestly not.'

'Christmas cracker fish don't lie,' I countered, then I blushed again. 'Well, I guess it did about me, but...'

'Either the fish is telling the truth or not,' he said. 'Can't have it both ways.'

'But I'm not...'

'Then neither am I.' He was grinning now, his bright blue eyes crinkling at the corners, and I felt myself smiling back.

'It's just a stupid toy.' I held out my hand and he slipped the fish back into my palm, but I returned it to its plastic sleeve before it could respond to my touch. 'I'll show it to my daughter later. She'll have a laugh with it.'

He glanced at his watch. 'I'd better get my skates on. I just need...'

'A photo? Sure.' Reflexively, I smiled and turned my best side to the camera while he took it. 'Um... hope the rest of your round goes okay.'

'Only twelve more stops,' he said. 'I'll be done by six, six thirty.'

'That's good.'

We stood there for a second, awkwardly facing each other. It was freezing cold, I realised; behind me, the relative warmth of the flat beckoned.

'Guess I'll see you tomorrow then,' he said. 'For the next instalment. Hopefully you'll still be feeling passionate.'

'I'm not—' Then I realised he was teasing me, and burst out laughing. 'Trust me, I'll be just as passionate tomorrow as I am now. Thanks again.'

He smiled again, waved and departed, this time heading up the stairs instead of down, and I retreated into the warmth of the flat. I ought to have investigated the depths of the freezer for something to cook for dinner, but instead I found myself sitting on the sofa, the package containing the fish in my hand. Passionate? Was I? I knew it was just a silly gimmick, but the way the delivery driver had reacted had made me feel something I hadn't felt for ages.

Passion? Definitely too strong a word. But I'd felt a spark; a faint glimmer of a side of me I'd almost forgotten existed – a side that could, however tamely and tentatively, have an almost-flirtatious conversation with a handsome man.

A few minutes later, Clara came home, panting from her climb up the stairs.

'Did it come, Mum? What did they get you? Is it the eye serum?'

Wordlessly, I handed her the fortune-telling fish. She picked it up with her fingertips, inspected it from all angles, then placed it in her palm, where it gave a couple of listless flicks of its tail.

'Indifference.' Clara consulted the envelope with something that was more like contempt.

'It's quite fun really,' I protested.

'Seriously, Mum? Seriously? Do your friends actually even like you?'

'The delivery guy seemed to think it was cool.'

'He needs to get a life.'

And so do you. She didn't even need to say it.

'We studied these things in Science in, like, Year Six,' my daughter went on. 'It's just a gimmick. The plastic's coated with a polymer that reacts to the warmth and moisture on your hand. They cost about 60p for ten. Is this for real?'

'It said I was passionate.'

'God, Mum! That's so gross. And pointless. Why couldn't it have been another Anastasia Beverley Hills eye palette?'

'Clara, I couldn't expect my friends to give me the whole Liberty advent calendar. You know that. Those things cost a fortune. They just wanted to cheer me up. If Auntie— I mean, if Kate bought one, she'd be totally entitled to keep the loot inside for herself.'

'But then what would be the point in giving you the empty bloody box? That's lump-of-coal territory, right there.'

I could feel the brief amusement my encounter with the delivery driver had left me with fading rapidly in the face of Clara's scorn.

'Never mind,' I said. 'It doesn't matter. We've got tomorrow to look forward to.'

'Tomorrow's Friday and I'm at Dad's.'

'I'll show you what I get when you're back. I bought some oat milk and vegan cheese so we could make mac and cheese. Shall we—'

'Where's the packaging the fish came in?' Clara demanded.

'In the recycling.'

Clara rolled her eyes, stood up and rummaged briefly in the bin. *First time she's been near it in months*, I thought.

Then she returned, brandishing a scrap of paper, and flopped down on the sofa next to me.

'I knew it!' she said. 'The aunties— your friends would never diss you with a crappy present. Open it.'

Carefully, I opened out the page, which had been folded many times into a tiny square about three inches across.

Printed on it in Times New Roman were a few words: 'Await Mystic Martha's tarot reading at your home tomorrow, six post meridian.'

'Oh my God,' Clara gasped. 'That is so cool! Why do I have to be at Dad's?'

CHAPTER EIGHT

As he continued his round, Alex found the routine of parking up, retrieving a parcel from the van, knocking on a door and handing it over, photographing the recipient in their open doorway, and repeating the whole process over and over, a lot less tedious than it usually was.

Sure, there were elements of the job that he liked. The elderly lady on Tiverton Road, who lived alone with her West Highland terrier and was presumably lonely, because she always buttonholed Alex for a chat, and who turned out to have grown up in Glasgow too, not far from Alex's old home. The ginger cat that perched on the wall of a house whose occupants had a serious Shein habit going on, which always meowed at him for some fuss and then followed him the short distance back to his van. And, of course, the satisfaction of doing a job efficiently and politely.

But that aside, there was no doubt it wasn't exactly his dream career. The hours were long, the work was physically hard – not just carrying heavy parcels and climbing stairs, but sitting behind the wheel of the van for several hours each day. And, apart from the elderly lady, the ginger cat and the occa-

sional person who accosted him to ask for directions somewhere, it was pretty lonely work with little in the way of
collaboration or intellectual stimulation.

Now, though, Alex found he had something to divert him.
Every now and then, the image of the dark-haired woman
popped into his head, and he found himself shaking his head,
smiling, and repeating to himself, 'A fortune-telling fish!'

He tried to imagine a scenario in which he'd give such a gift
to someone. Not the fish itself – it was a novelty item, a joke
from a Christmas cracker. But the logic of it didn't stack up at
all. The fish itself would have cost pennies – far less than the
packaging and delivery charges. And someone – actually a
group of people; he was pretty sure the woman had said
'friends' – were planning to do something similar every day
until Christmas. 'Like an advent calendar.'

Why, though? What had inspired Rowan Connell's friends
to embark on this costly and inconvenient project, rather than
just, say, giving her an advent calendar?

Alex found it at once baffling, intriguing and touching.

And Rowan Connell herself – he recalled the way she'd
looked down at the polymer fish in her palm, her long eyelashes
casting shadows over her pale cheeks, her mouth curving
upwards in a smile as the fish moved, as entranced by the silly
little thing as if it had been something of real value.

Perhaps that was the clue, right there. Perhaps if someone
reacted in that way to a gift – however small and absurd – you'd
go to pretty much any lengths to please them.

Alex knew the next few weeks would get pretty brutal as
Christmas drew nearer. The ten-hour days would likely stretch
to fourteen or even longer, and it wasn't like his other commit-
ments were going to go away. He'd have limited time to spend
chatting to Mrs MacAllister and stroking the ginger cat, never
mind making the acquaintance of Rowan Connell.

Truth be told, Alex had more or less decided to jack in the

job before Christmas, so as to spend more time on other, more pressing aspects of his life. He owed Pegasus nothing, after all. The company would have let him go without hesitation if he needed it more than it needed him.

But now Alex found himself going back on that decision, and it wasn't because of the additional days working for minimum wage.

It was because he sensed that a story was unfolding, and he wanted to know how it was going to end.

CHAPTER NINE

The rain came down in sheets all day on Friday, so after much pleading by Clara over text message, I picked her up from school and drove her to Paul's. This was something I'd done regularly when she was too little to make her own way there by bus, then frequently once she could manage on her own, but I felt too protective if it was dark or she had anything heavy to carry.

But I hadn't done it since Hayley had been on the scene.

Call me pathetic but, as we approached the house, I felt a knot of nerves growing tighter and tighter in my stomach. I didn't want to see Paul. I really didn't want to see Hayley. And I definitely, definitely didn't want to see them together, all loved-up in their newly engaged state.

'You'll be okay to just jump out if I drop you at the gate, right?' I asked.

'Mmmm.' Clara didn't look up from her phone.

'We're nearly there.'

'Mmmm.'

I pulled Portia up outside the house. The wrought-iron

gates were open, and I could see lights on inside the house and a tall, illuminated Christmas tree in one bay window.

'Come on, jump out,' I urged. 'Have you got your keys, in case they're out?'

'Hold on, Mum. I'm just texting Jonny.'

Texting Jonny was something my daughter had been doing a lot lately, along with saying, 'He's just a guy, Mum. Stop asking me,' when I made what I thought were casual enquiries about him. So clearly there was no way she'd be hurried. Drumming my fingers on the steering wheel, I waited for her to finish.

But before she did, the front door swung open and Hayley stood there, her blonde hair shining under the porch light. She waved and made a 'come on in' gesture that couldn't have been clearer.

With agonising slowness, Clara put her phone in her coat pocket, then took it out and checked it again.

'Have a lovely time, sweetheart,' I said. 'I'll see you on Sunday, okay?'

Clara's eyes left the screen. 'She wants you to come in.'

'But I...'

'There's no need to be rude, Mum.'

I sometimes wondered if there was an acting career in my daughter's future; she could sound even more like me than I did myself sometimes.

'Oh, all right. So long as they don't mind me parking across their driveway.'

We got out, hurriedly pulled Clara's bag out of the boot, and ran together through the rain to the open door.

'You poor things!' Hayley greeted Clara with a hug and a kiss on both cheeks. 'You're soaked. It's absolutely pissing down. Do come in and have a coffee and a mince pie – I've been baking. I'm Hayley.'

'Lovely to meet you,' I lied.

She held out her warm, dry hand and I clasped it briefly in

my cold, wet one. The house smelled of Christmas: of pine and spices and marzipan. There were already a few wrapped presents under the tree, I noticed as I took a seat on the cream leather sofa where Paul and I had so often— But there was no way I was going to allow myself to remember that now.

Clara followed Hayley out in the direction of the kitchen, and I sat alone, consumed with awkwardness, not wanting to look around in case it might be construed as prying. Little seemed to have changed since the last time I'd been here; the room was cleaner, maybe; there were new cushions on the sofa and a new framed print over the fireplace of... Oh God. It was a nude of a woman who could only be Hayley. Not a full-frontal, page-three-style thing, but a tasteful black-and-white portrait taken from the back, Hayley's pale hair flowing loose over her toned shoulders.

I wondered whether Paul had been behind the camera, and my heart twisted.

'You okay, Ro? You look like you're miles away.'

I hadn't even heard my ex come into the room, but here he was, relaxed and smiling, his shaved head and dark-framed glasses as familiar as my own face in the mirror.

'Oh! Hi! Long time no... er... see.'

And the last time I had seen him, we'd ended up in my bedroom, shagging silently against the closed door, my back pressed against my winter coat and Paul's hands under my buttocks. It had been over in the time it had taken Clara to get the lift down to Paul's waiting car and send her father a text asking him if he'd died up there or what.

'It's been too long.' Paul sat next to me on the sofa, crossing one denim-clad leg over the other. He was wearing a new jumper, I noticed – bottle-green cashmere. 'You must tell me all your news.'

'Yes, I'd love to,' I said. 'But I really must be going pretty soon. I've got an appointment.'

'Mum's seeing a clairvoyant.' Clara came back into the room, carefully carrying a tray holding coffee and mince pies. The coffee was in a cafetière, the pastries on a doily, the china cups all matching. 'I'm so gutted I'm going to miss it. I'd love to have my future told.'

'Ro, you do know that's all bollocks, don't you?' Paul asked.

My face flamed. 'Of course I do. It's just a bit of fun. It was a gift, kind of.'

Paul looked at me, his eyes behind his glasses full of concern. 'Are you sure you're okay?'

'These charlatans prey on vulnerable people,' Hayley said. 'After my grandpa passed away, my nan spent hundreds on some woman who said she could reach him on the other side. All nonsense, of course.'

'I think it's pretty cool, actually,' Clara objected.

Paul ignored her. 'If anything happens – anything you're not comfortable with – you'll leave straight away, won't you?'

'She's coming to the flat,' Clara said.

Hayley gave a little gasp. 'Are you sure that's a good idea? To have some fraudster know where you actually, like, live?'

'Would you like me to come back with you?' Paul suggested. 'Just in case anything – you know.'

Worst. Idea. Ever. Judging by her face, Hayley thought the same.

'Look, it's very kind of you to worry,' I said. 'But I'm perfectly capable of looking after myself. I'm not taking it seriously, and I'm not handing over any money. If she tries to steal the silver – not that we've got any – I'll call the police. Okay?'

I sounded as sulky and churlish as Clara herself, I realised.

'Promise you'll record it, Mum? So I can listen afterwards?'

'Look,' Paul said, 'if your mother wants to expose herself to this nonsense, it's none of my business, I suppose. But I'm not having you—'

'I really have to go,' I said, standing up and struggling into my coat. 'Sorry I can't stay for coffee. The traffic's bound to be terrible.'

And I kissed Clara goodbye and left, vowing that if I never stepped back in that house again, it would be the best thing I'd ever done.

Still, in spite of my bluster, I found myself becoming increasingly nervous as I approached home. What if Hayley and Paul were right and I was putting myself at risk, allowing some random stranger I'd never even spoken to into my flat when I was there alone? What if the clairvoyant wasn't just a chancer trying to make a living out of desperate, credulous people but genuinely evil? What if she did have real psychic powers and hypnotised me into giving her my internet banking password or something?

Well, if she did, she'd enrich herself by all of seventy-five pounds, I told myself – the direct debit for the rent had come out the previous day and at this rate Clara's Christmas presents would be coming from the aisle of wonder at Lidl anyway.

Lost in thought, I reversed Portia into my parking place and climbed out. It was only as I was locking the car door that I realised the Pegasus van was parked in the next-door space and the delivery driver was leaning against it, watching me.

'Oh!' I started. 'Sorry, I didn't see you. I was miles away.'

'Barely more than a mile, surely,' he corrected. 'You only just missed me – I knocked on your door a couple of minutes ago, but you weren't back – obviously – so I put today's instalment through your letterbox. Hopefully it'll be an improvement on the fish.'

'Oh, but the fish wasn't the real present.' I felt compelled to fill him in on the details of the previous day's gift, not that there was any reason for him to be interested. 'There was a note in the envelope. I'm getting a psychic reading – tonight.'

'A what?' He stood upright suddenly, as if the panel of the

van was red hot. He was tall, I noticed – a good two inches taller than me, even though I was wearing my work shoes.

'I'm not going to give her any money or believe my late granny is trying to contact me from the other side. Promise,' I reassured him.

'What if she tells you you're about to meet a handsome stranger?' he said. 'Or you've already met one?'

'I could do with a bit more handsome in my life, I'm not going to lie.'

'Well,' he said, the sides of his mouth twitching upwards in a way that was undeniably attractive, 'let's hope your psychic delivers the goods.'

'If she doesn't, I know a reputable courier company that can help,' I joked, and then I realised what I'd said – implying that Pegasus was bringing me a handsome stranger, who could only be the one standing right in front of me.

'I mean – delivering stuff, that's what you do,' I backtracked frantically.

'Where you want it, when you want it, every time,' he quoted the Pegasus slogan, which was printed underneath the wing-shaped logo on the side of the van.

But it didn't sound like a courier company's piece of marketing, coming out of his mouth in that Scottish accent. It sounded like a deliciously filthy double entendre.

I genuinely can't remember how I got upstairs after that. I must have thanked him, said goodnight, watched as he climbed back into his van, maybe even waved. But it was like the wings of Pegasus himself had spirited me to my front door, where I found myself a couple of minutes later, fumbling with my keys, even more out of breath than the seven-storey climb justified.

It was just a joke, Rowan, I lectured myself. *Stop acting like a fourteen-year-old who's just had her first snog. He's probably got a girlfriend. There's no way he's interested in you, or flirting with you. Stop being ridiculous.*

But still, I couldn't stop myself from smiling as I tore open the parcel he'd left on my doormat, finding a gorgeous pastel-blue nail polish from a brand I'd never be able to afford to buy myself. I tucked it in my knicker drawer – that was one of Clara's presents sorted, at least.

The gift's arrival reassured me – my friends cared. They had my best interests at heart. They'd never arrange for some member of the criminal underworld to come round and read my fortune.

But still, when the door knocker tapped at five to six, I almost jumped out of my skin.

I slipped the security chain on and opened the door a crack. In the yellow light from overhead, I could see a woman standing. She was wearing a burgundy velvet coat and her head was covered with a scarf that cast her face into shadow. She smelled strongly of some musky scent, almost like incense. A tapestry bag was clutched to her chest.

'Rowan Connell? You wish to see your future?' Her voice was husky and heavily accented. In the shadow obscuring her face, I saw the brief flash of a smile.

Reluctantly, I unhooked the chain and opened the door. 'Mystic Martha?' I asked, just saying the words making me feel like the world's biggest plonker.

'The cards will reveal all.' She stepped into the hallway, the scarf slipping to reveal her vibrant red hair.

I burst out laughing. 'Naomi! Oh my God, it's you!'

'You don't think we'd pay some con artist to come round to your place and pretend to read your cards, do you?'

We hugged. I was still giggling, the tension draining out of me.

'Where did you get the fortune-teller get-up? And the perfume?'

'Perfume came in an advent calendar. Not your one – the Body Shop one. It's not a keeper but you're welcome to it if you want. Clothes are Patch's mum's, from her hippie days. Any chance of a glass of wine?'

'Of course. Come on through. So I'm not getting my fortune told after all?'

'You certainly are,' Naomi said firmly. 'I haven't been watching YouTube tutorials about it for the past week for nothing.'

Five minutes later, we were sitting on the floor on either side of the coffee table, our legs crossed in a manner that felt appropriately spiritual, and large glasses of cheap red wine by our hands, which didn't.

Naomi had produced a deck of cards from her bag and was shuffling them expertly. I remembered that she'd gone through a poker-playing phase a few years back.

'Now,' she intoned, a hint of the cod accent returning to her voice. 'First of all, you need to ask me – I mean Mystic Martha – I mean the cards, the question you wish this reading to answer.'

I thought for a bit. There were so many questions. Would I be single, lonely and skint forever? Were my dreams of Paul, Clara and me being a family together hopeless and even treacherous now that he and Hayley were engaged? Would my applicant complete the purchase of a multimillion-pound house and transport me to the life of luxury I dreamed of?

Was there even the tiniest chance of the hot delivery guy fancying me back?

'Where will I be in a year's time?' was the best I could come up with.

Naomi shook her head. 'That's no good. Too open-ended. This is an exact science, and you need to be specific if the cards are to reveal your deepest hopes and what the future holds.'

'I thought I was meant to be the client here,' I grumbled. 'Okay then. Since you're the expert here, you decide what we'll do.'

Naomi looked relieved. 'Why don't we go for a simple past,

present and future reading then? Three cards. I tried doing a Celtic cross when I was practising but it was well complicated.'

'Great. Past, present and future it is.'

So long as whichever card comes up for the past doesn't have a picture of me and Paul shagging on it.

Naomi looked at her slim, pale fingers shuffling the cards for a second, then looked up, met my eyes and smiled. It was dead strange – she was at once my mate, who I'd ugly-cried on and whose hair I'd held while she spewed from morning sickness, whose clothes I'd borrowed and whose babies' nappies I'd changed. But she was also a wise woman, a clairvoyant. A woman who had her shit together when I didn't.

And who had a pack of mind-reading, fortune-telling cards at her disposal, obviously.

'Right then, let's go,' she said, and I filled up our wine glasses.

She pushed the cards across the table and I cut them, chose one, cut again and repeated the process two more times. Naomi – or Mystic Martha, as I was trying to think of her – placed the cards in a row, her brow furrowed with concentration.

'First, we'll look at this one' – she tapped it – 'which represents the past. Okay?'

'Go ahead.'

She turned it over. On it was a picture of a guy in what looked kind of like medieval dress, standing on what was clearly meant to be a battlefield. He had two swords in one hand and one in the other, and two more lay on the ground at his feet.

'The five of swords,' Naomi explained, doing her concentrating face again. 'It's said to signify defeat, cowardliness or empty victory. Does that have meaning for you?'

I felt myself grow pale, then flush. I took another gulp of wine, remembering all the times Paul and I had had sex, how I'd known I was doing the easy, wrong thing, how my triumph that he still desired me had so quickly faded to self-disgust.

'Could it be something to do with Paul?' she asked. 'I mean, you mentioned a while ago that you two...'

'Yeah. We did. A handful of times.' *A handful of handfuls.* 'But now that's not going to happen any more, obviously.'

Naomi met my eyes. I had a feeling she knew that even if I was telling the truth, it wasn't the whole truth.

'It's probably a good thing that that's come up as the past, then,' she said. 'I think we're supposed to talk a bit about what you can learn from the card, but that's pretty blindingly obvious, isn't it?'

'Don't jump into bed with your ex when he snaps his fingers, even if he is the father of your child and you want to have a cordial relationship.'

'Quite. There's cordial and then there's – well, copulating.'

'Friendly, versus fucking.'

Naomi laughed. 'Best we don't dwell too much on that then. Now, how about the present?'

Again, she turned the card the right way up. The picture on the front was of a guy hanging by one foot from a tree – or possibly a cross, given he had what looked like a halo round his head.

'The hanged man,' Naomi said unnecessarily.

'Crikey. It's not looking great, is it?'

'On the contrary. The hanged man can indicate many positive things. Change, improvement, rebirth. But also boredom and a state of suspension.'

'Boredom is right,' I said. 'If I have to tell one more person about travertine tiles and integrated kitchen appliances I might chew my own tongue off.'

'And there we have it. You're bored in your job, in a state of suspension, and there's a need for change.'

'Too right there is. But how? As far as I can see, I'm stuck. I've got to pay the rent, and those Nike trainers Clara keeps pleading for aren't going to buy themselves.'

'I don't think the cards are suggesting you jack in your job and live on fresh air. But there must be other changes you can make – achievable ones.'

'I guess.' But at that moment, I couldn't for the life of me think what they might be. 'Why don't we see what it says about the future?'

If there was any justice in the world, I thought, my future card would be all sunlit uplands, with a daughter who loved me and a handsome man in my bed. Fat chance.

Naomi turned the card over to reveal a picture of a naked child holding a banner, riding a white horse. Behind her was a field of sunflowers and, in the background, a blazing sun rising – or perhaps setting, I thought pessimistically.

'The sun,' Naomi said, with a relieved sigh. 'This is a very positive card. It indicates accomplishment, success and joy.'

'And a boyfriend?'

'And love,' Naomi confirmed. 'Also, happy marriage.'

'For Paul and Hayley, I guess.' To my surprise, I found myself not entirely hating that idea.

'And maybe for you. I mean, if that's what you want.'

'Guess I'll have to meet the right person first. And right now that's looking about as likely as finding Zac Efron under my Christmas tree. But if the cards say so, it must be true, right?'

'Ro.' Naomi slid the three cards together and added them to the bottom of the pile. 'You know this is all a load of rubbish, right? Now how about we open another bottle?'

CHAPTER TEN

The following day, the smiley delivery guy knocked on my door just after two in the afternoon. I guess his round was shorter on Saturdays, or perhaps he'd got in an early start so he'd be able to spend the evening hanging out with his girlfriend, or down the pub with his mates, or getting in some self-care watching Only-Fans – whatever he did for fun. I had no idea.

In any event, I was in no state to make polite chit-chat about his weekend plans. Naomi and I had stayed up chatting until gone two, and one bottle of wine had turned into nearly three.

'You know what it's like,' she'd slurred, shortly after we'd raided the fridge to find that the only available food was a half-empty jar of slightly wizened olives and some cheddar that had gone cracked and dry in its beeswax wrapping. 'Night away from the kids. Patch in charge. And I've finally managed to stop breastfeeding them – after two and a half years, go me. Free at last!'

'Two and a half bloody years,' I said. 'You're nails, you are.'

'A fecking dairy cow, more like,' she said, and we'd spent the next hour exchanging child-rearing horror stories that frankly don't bear retelling.

I might even have offered to show her my episiotomy scar, which was probably what finally spurred her to order an Uber home. And after that, I'd collapsed straight into bed, still fully clothed and with my work make-up unremoved.

And that's where I still was when I heard the knock. I'd only moved to open the door to another delivery guy, the one who'd brought my emergency KFC bargain bucket.

'Oh! Hi!' I tried to sound bright when I opened the door to Mr Smiley Blue-Eyes, but he saw straight through me. At any rate, I bet he wished he had, as opposed to having to actually look at me.

'Rowan!' It was the first time he'd actually used my name. 'Christ. Are you okay?'

'Been better.' I pushed my hair off my face and tightened my dressing-gown cord. 'I had a friend over last night. At least, it turned out to be her. I was expecting a psychic.'

'You don't have the gift yourself, then?'

'Sorry?'

'I only meant, if you were psychic, you'd have known it was your friend and not the clairvoyant.'

'Oh. Of course you did. Duh. Sorry, I'm a bit slow.'

His smile turned into a grin. 'Maybe not your sparkling best this morning – afternoon, I mean.'

Strong work, Rowan, I thought. He had seen me a panting, sweaty mess after walking up the stairs, in a kind of moping daydream after seeing Paul, and now with a next-level hangover. It was amazing he even thought I had a sparkling best.

'Anyway, I've a package for you,' he went on, producing a small, square box from his bag.

'Thank you.' I took it from him, staying at arm's length so as not to subject him to the Malbec-and-chicken-nugget fumes I suspected were coming off me in waves, contrasting starkly with his own scent, which, at close quarters, I identified as something citrussy mixed with the smell of clean clothes. 'Great. Appreciate it.'

'What d'you reckon you've got there today? Another Christmas novelty item? Feel free to tell me to back off if I'm getting too invested.'

I hefted the weight of the cardboard box in my hand. 'Not this time. This feels like the good stuff.'

He's invested? I could feel a delighted smile spreading across my face.

'So what's in it?' He leaned forward eagerly, peering at the label.

'Want me to open it?'

'I mean... I wouldn't... I don't expect...'

'You do! Admit it. You're invested – you said so yourself.'

He grinned. 'You got me. Go on then.'

'I'll just...' I turned the box over, found the end of the tape that sealed it and started picking at a corner with my fingernail.

'Here, let me help.' He produced a Swiss army knife from his pocket, and I handed over the parcel and watched as he carefully slit the tape, then returned it to my waiting hand.

I lifted the flap and took out a small, green glass bottle. 'Bath oil. And it's geranium – my favourite.'

'Nice.' He raised his eyebrows appreciatively. 'Hot bath, water and paracetamol, and maybe more KFC, and you'll be right in no time.'

Shit. So I do stink of nuggets.

'It can only improve how I'm feeling right now,' I admitted.

'Then I'll leave you to it. Enjoy the rest of your day, Rowan.'

'Thanks. And thank you for the... you know...' I made a cutting gesture with my hand, unable for a second to think of the word 'knife'.

'Don't mention it.' He flashed a grin that made my chicken-filled stomach tumble a slow somersault, turned and strode off.

I retreated into the flat and turned on the hot tap in the

bathroom, figuring that I'd need a good old soak to get rid of the smell of wine and fried food – that, and something nutritious for dinner. Once I was feeling a bit more presentable, I'd head to the supermarket and buy vegetables, and maybe make a stir-fry.

While I waited for my bath to run, I eased the elaborate glass stopper out of the bottle of bath oil and breathed in the heady fragrance. There was only enough there for one bath. I thought of the nail varnish waiting in my drawer to be given to Clara and considered adding this to her Christmas stocking collection. But Clara hardly ever took baths – for that matter, I didn't either, at least not when she was around. A lecture from my daughter on how I was pillaging the planet by wasting precious water resources, not to mention the gas used to heat it, was enough to take the shine off even the most indulgent soak.

But Clara wasn't here.

So, after only the briefest hesitation, I tipped the contents of the bottle under the running water, watching it foam and fill the room with its luxurious scent. Then I stripped off my clothes and eased my body into the hot water, wishing I felt up to a glass of wine to complete the experience.

But there was no chance of that – just the thought of alcohol made my stomach churn.

I closed my eyes, breathing in the heady scent, and replayed my exchange with the delivery driver in my head. At the time, it had felt friendly – maybe even a tiny bit flirtatious. But now my hungover brain's analysis was harsher. I'd looked – and evidently smelled – awful. I'd forgotten the word for the thing you use to cut stuff. He probably thought I was mad.

And I was going to be seeing him a lot – almost every day, most likely – and somehow I was going to have to conceal the fact that I wouldn't mind him turning up in my stocking on the twenty-fifth, wearing a shiny red ribbon and nothing else.

For God's sake, Rowan, I told myself. *Get a grip.*

I fumbled on the floor for my phone and snapped a picture

of my toes emerging from the bubbles, thinking I'd send it to the Girlfriends' Club WhatsApp group, and thank them for the gift. But then I thought, *Why not thank them more publicly? They're doing this amazing thing for you, after all.*

So I typed a quick summary of what was happening, tagging my friends and adding a bunch of Christmassy hashtags and emojis, and posted the picture on my Instagram and Facebook pages. I hadn't posted in a while, but I still had loads of followers from back when I was doing wedding make-up. Gratified, I watched as a few people liked the post, and a few more commented saying things like #*friendgoals*.

And then a comment appeared on my Facebook post from Andy.

Very nice, Ro, but you might want to take that down before Mark Zuckerberg does.

What? It was only my feet. Hastily, I tapped on the image to take a closer look and felt mortification flood me as I realised what he meant. There, right next to my big toe, in the shiny chrome of the tap, was a perfect reflection of my naked breasts.

Once I'd frantically deleted the picture and returned to the privacy of WhatsApp to tell the Girlfriends' Club what I'd done, and thank them there, the bathwater was cooling. I eased myself out, dried and dressed.

Gloomily, I stared around my own flat, which apart from the string of tinsel and the few cards, looked just the same as it did every other month of the year.

Scrooge Connell, I thought. That was me all the way.

My friends wanted me to have a happy Christmas – a whole happy December. And I was doing very little to help their cause.

It wasn't good enough.

So, as well as stocking up on butternut squash, leeks and

onions in the supermarket (oh, and another tin of Quality Street), I bought a bag of oranges, a string of fairy lights, some more tinsel and a can of gold spray paint. I walked home through the park, in the cold twilight, feeling the promise of frost in the air, and gathered fallen twigs and pine cones, and harvested some holly from a hedge, carefully selecting the branches with the most red berries.

I had no idea what I was doing. I was hopeless at crafts of any kind, but within a couple of hours, with the help of YouTube tutorials, I'd fashioned a Christmas wreath on an old wire coat hanger. The pine cones and twigs glimmered with gold paint, the oranges smelled amazing after being dried in the oven, the holly berries shone like they'd been varnished. I'd found an ancient jar of cinnamon sticks in the kitchen and added those too.

It wasn't going to win any awards, that was for sure. I'd pricked my fingers on the holly leaves and cursed my stupid idea of creating an eco-friendly door decoration that would make my daughter happy more times than I could count.

But, hanging my creation over the door knocker, I felt a glow of pride and – could it be? – the beginnings of the Christmas spirit.

CHAPTER ELEVEN

Normally, I wouldn't have given work more than the merest passing thought over a weekend. But, that Sunday, I logged into the Walkersons Elite database and spent some time hunting for properties that might be suitable for my applicant. I'd taken her to see another one the previous Friday, which I knew was a bit of a stretch as it was right at the top of her budget and had only a balcony rather than the small garden she'd said was on her wish list. As I expected, she kindly but firmly said it wasn't suitable. But there were others that looked more promising, and I sent her over particulars of a few of them, assuring her that I'd be available for viewings all the following week.

The more time I'd spent with her, the more I found myself liking her. She had more money than I could dream of, of course, but she was still ordinary, friendly and unpretentious, and I found my thoughts turning not so much to the glorious, worry-relieving commission that I might receive, and more to finding a home where she and her husband could bring up their baby.

Because it was Sunday, I wasn't expecting a delivery from the smiley courier – he must get the occasional day off, I thought. But the idea gave me a stab of disappointment – not only would I have to wait until tomorrow for the next instalment of my advent calendar, but I'd miss seeing him. It was only when I realised that wouldn't happen until the next day that I allowed myself to admit how much I'd been looking forward to our encounter, however brief.

I even caught myself, at random points during the day, having imaginary conversations with him in my head, thinking how I could describe the Christmas display of toy Scottie dogs in tartan jackets I'd spotted in a shop window on Jermyn Street; inform him that the Tesco Christmas sandwich was clearly superior to the one at Pret and fifty pence cheaper; tell him about the viewing I'd done for Brett at a house in Mayfair where a specialist firm literally arrived while I was there and unloaded an entire truckload of Christmas trees, decorations and fake wrapped parcels without the owners having to lift a finger.

I'd imagined him listening, laughing, saying, 'That's nuts!' and telling me snippets about his day in return.

And now I wasn't going to see him, and all my daydreams were exposed as the adolescent silliness I should have known they were. It wasn't as if he'd have been going about his day having similar soppy thoughts about me, was it? I was being stupid, and I needed to get over myself.

Still, I found myself wandering through to the hallway, standing in front of the door and imagining myself opening it to his knock and seeing him there: his high-vis jacket, his warm smile, his blue eyes. The image was so clear I had to blink to remind myself that it wasn't real, and focus my mind back on what was: the jumble of post on the doormat – pizza delivery leaflets, estate agents' circulars, a flyer about a local baby signing group, the bill for our broadband and a bank statement, which I promised myself I'd open later.

And, at the bottom of the pile, a familiar brown cardboard

envelope. Alongside the usual printed label, there was a hand-written note scribbled in blue ink on the buff card.

Do not open this until tomorrow. Alex.

Tomorrow must mean today. And the previous day, after he'd handed over my bath oil, he must have waited and then slipped the envelope through the letterbox. Or perhaps he'd returned later on in his round to deliver it, and I hadn't even noticed.

My heart gave a little skip of excitement. I had a gift to open after all. And Mr Smiley Blue-Eyes had a name: Alex.

It felt strange to think of that. I mean, obviously he had a name – everyone does. But it made him seem more real, some-how, more like an actual person and less like an anonymous presence who would flit into my life each afternoon, make his delivery and then disappear again.

And who, after the twenty-fourth of the month, I'd rarely if ever see again, unless I developed an unsustainable online shop-ping habit.

I carried the bundle of post into the kitchen, binned the junk mail and tore open the envelope. A slip of printed, glossy paper slipped out onto the worktop.

It was embossed with a name – 'Studio Cleo' – and foiled with a figure – '£75'.

What was Studio Cleo when it was at home, I wondered. It could be a hair salon or a beauty therapy place. I could treat myself to a new look, have a massage or get my nails done. Or, more prosaically, have a wax for the first time in years. The way things were, the three wise men would need more than a star to find their way through that lot.

Excitement fizzing inside me, I tapped the name into Google on my phone and navigated to a slick website bearing the same swirly logo as the gift voucher. I scrolled down, and my finger froze on the screen.

There were a bunch of images of model-perfect women dressed in lingerie.

Proper lingerie, not like the cotton pants and practical T-shirt bras I wore every day. This was the real deal: matching lace sets in jewel colours, boned basques and floaty camisoles. The kind of thing women wore when they felt sexy, confident and desirable. The kind of thing they wore in bed with a man who fancied the pants off them – literally. The kind of thing I might have worn, back in the day, before the only man I shared my bed with was the Duke of Hastings when I watched *Bridgerton* on Netflix.

Then I looked at the address of the shop on the website and saw that it was just round the corner from work. And then I looked at the expiry date on the voucher and saw that it was Christmas Eve.

And then I really began to panic.

These women were my friends. What on earth had made them think I needed the kind of underwear that was clearly designed to impress some man, when I didn't have a man or any prospect of one?

(I was discounting Paul here, not just because of the obvious fact of his recent engagement, but also because the times we'd shagged in recent years had always been so furtive and hasty it hadn't mattered what we'd been wearing, and besides, we'd kept most of it on, removing only the bare minimum. And anyway, he'd been there when I pushed eight-pound Clara out of my lady parts, and the fanciest knickers in creation wouldn't have been able to erase that image.)

Did they think I was somehow magically going to discover my inner sex goddess between now and Christmas Eve?

Did they think that underneath my jeans, trackie bottoms and the suits I put on for work and sometimes wore for the Girlfriends' Club nights out, I was rocking underwear worthy of a Victoria's Secret model, and this would be par for the course for me?

Did they think I was somehow going to develop a booty I'd want to put on display in a pair of – I scrutinised the website – Brazilian tangas, between now and Christmas Eve? Did they not realise it would probably take from now *until* Christmas Eve to mow through the thicket my pubic hair had become?

Then I heard the thud of Clara's bag hitting the floor outside the flat and then her key in the lock, and I dashed back to the hallway and secreted the voucher in my bag as furtively as I'd concealed the sweet wrappers. I had no idea how she'd react if I told her about it – generous encouragement and incredulous scorn were equal possibilities, depending on her mood.

But I did know, with one hundred per cent certainty, that I wasn't going to disclose its existence to her.

All the same, the next day, in between answering yet another lengthy email from Tatiana about how the flat near Regent's Park I'd shown her wasn't quite right – almost, but not quite – and making my way to Knightsbridge to show one of Marty's potential buyers, a Saudi businessman, a four-bedroomed 'bachelor pad', complete with gym, wine cellar and parking for three supercars, I passed by Studio Cleo, just for a look.

If there was the slightest hint of bondage-style leather or latex, I promised myself, I wouldn't set foot in the place. The slightest hint of crotchless knickers and I'd be out of there. And if any of the staff looked like they belonged on the Pirelli calendar, I'd be putting that voucher on eBay, stat.

But I was pleasantly reassured. From the outside, the shop looked almost like an upscale hotel room, minus the bed of course. There were heavy velvet curtains across the window, almost obscuring the interior but allowing me to glimpse a few squashy sofas and racks of lingerie arranged discreetly around the walls. The top of a spiral staircase was just visible, presumably leading down to a fitting area, so I wouldn't be expected to parade around in my kecks with half of Regent Street enjoying the view. On one of the sofas, I noticed a fluffy ginger cat stretched out in a patch of winter sun.

The cat decided me. I hadn't had a cat since I was little, but I was willing to lay money on them having a low tolerance for nonsense. The first whiff of a bondage hood, I told myself, and that moggy would be decamping to live at the steak restaurant a few doors down.

I pushed open the glass door and entered the shop. A woman, middle-aged and sort of motherly-looking, with a tape measure draped around her neck, emerged from behind the counter, smiling warmly.

'Good afternoon,' she said. 'How can I help?'

'I've got a voucher. I thought I'd just have a look around, if that's okay?'

'Of course. Let me know if you'd like a fitting.'

I thanked her and glanced around again. Reassuringly, I could see some packs of cotton pants that, while far superior to my supermarket ones, didn't look actively intimidating. And there was a rack of the kind of simple, stretch lace bralettes Clara liked but was constantly poking her fingernails through. And the cat, when it saw me, yawned and stretched and rolled over onto its back in a welcoming fashion, arched like a large, furry banana.

'May I ask what size you're currently wearing?' the motherly woman asked.

'Uh... 34D.'

Back in the day, I thought bitterly, I'd worn an A cup when I'd bothered with a bra at all. Then I got pregnant, and my boobs went completely mental. I was downright alarmed at these two alien, beachball-like objects that appeared to have attached themselves to my chest; Paul had reacted like all his Christmases had come at once.

They'd never regained their old size or pertness. They weren't quite spaniel's ears, but it was close.

The woman was looking at me, her head on one side, an expression on her face like she was doing mental arithmetic.

'Maybe pick out a few things you like the look of in a 30F,' she said, 'and we'll see how you get on.'

My mind reeled – 30F? That was *Love Island* contestant territory, surely, not for mere mortals like me. And she hadn't even removed the tape measure from round her neck, nor had I taken off my coat. Did the woman have X-ray vision? Was she a witch?

Or were my boobs so freakishly huge that everyone could see them, all of the time?

Resisting the urge to leg it out into the street, I forced myself to stop thinking disparagingly about my own rack and focus on the racks of bras and pants, avoiding the small display of more in-your-face sexy items towards the back of the room. I selected one in black lace with a small butterfly on the front instead of a bow, which had unusual pewter-coloured hooks, a bright red satin number that I thought seemed suitably festive, and one in gold lace with threads of purple running through it, which looked like something the angel on top of the Christmas tree would wear. (Did angels even need lingerie, I wondered. Or did God just give them magic boobs that stayed perky through the power of faith?)

The woman escorted me downstairs and showed me into a large, curtained cubicle, pointing to a buzzer I could use if I needed any help.

Or if my norks get hoisted so high I poke my own eye out, I thought.

I hung up my coat, relieved to take it off as the shop was

warm, and quickly stripped off my jacket and shirt. I unhooked my bra and draped it over the chair where I'd placed the new ones. God, it really was a disgrace, I realised: a tatty thing that had once been nude but was now a kind of surgical-stocking greige, with bits of perished elastic sticking out of the straps and a permanent dent in one moulded cup because I couldn't be bothered to hand-wash anything.

I started with the safest option: the black lace bra. I slipped my arms into the straps and fumbled with the unfamiliar hooks behind my back, eventually getting them closed on the loosest setting.

But God, the thing was snug. I could feel pressure round my ribs and over my shoulders. Surely this couldn't be right?

I glanced in the mirror and almost reeled with surprise.

I looked taller, slimmer, more upright, like I imagined I'd look after a year of twice-weekly Pilates classes. My stomach looked flatter, my waist slimmer. And my boobs – well. They looked both smaller and perkier, like I'd had surgery. Experimentally, I put my top back on and gazed at my reflection with something like awe.

The woman *was* a witch. There was no other explanation.

Hastily, I tried on the other two bras. If anything, they were even better. The red was sexy without being over the top; the gold made me think that if angels didn't wear underwear, they were seriously missing out.

I peeled it off and placed it reverently on the chair with the others. Now, the only decision I had to make was which of the three to buy. But as I was gazing longingly at them, I heard the trill of my phone in my handbag. I'd sent my applicant details of another handful of properties that morning, in the hope that one of them would appeal and we could organise another viewing – perhaps it would be her.

And the name that flashed up on my screen was hers. But,

here in the downstairs fitting room, I could see I only had one bar of a 3G signal.

With frantic haste, I dragged on my top and coat, snatched my bag and dashed up to street level, exiting the shop (after sketching a 'back in a second' gesture at the motherly shop assistant) just as the call rang out.

'Damn,' I muttered. I'd give it a minute, see if she left a message and ring her back, then I'd return to Studio Cleo and emerge the proud owner of a gorgeous piece of new lingerie. Then I noticed the woman disappearing downstairs, presumably thinking I'd changed my mind and wouldn't come back – and, at the same time, I felt an unfamiliar looseness, a coolness around my chest, my nipples hardening uncomfortably under my coat.

Shit. I'd left my own bra downstairs in the fitting room. The embarrassing, tatty one with the frayed elastic.

There was no way I could go back there – ever.

CHAPTER TWELVE

'So I didn't actually buy anything,' I admitted. 'Not this time, anyway. But I will.'

I looked around at the faces of my friends. It wasn't the usual second Wednesday of the month meet-up, because it was December and everyone (well, everyone except me, it seemed) had work parties, family pantomimes and meet-ups with non-Girlfriends' Club friends. Clara was spending the night at her friend Lily's, and we were in Kate's flat, rather than the pub where we usually met.

'It'll be work Christmas party central,' Kate had said on WhatsApp.

'Men snogging their PAs and wall-to-wall Christmas jumpers,' Abbie had agreed.

'Our work party's tonight,' I'd confirmed. 'On a Monday – how grim is that? Thank God I'd already arranged to meet you lot, so I don't have to go.'

'Mass-produced turkey crowns and packet gravy,' Naomi had typed. 'God, I remember those days.'

She'd sounded a bit wistful, now I thought about it.

But anyway, Kate had offered to host and, as her flat was

really central, in a tall glass-and-steel tower overlooking the Thames, the lights of London spreading out below like they'd been switched on especially for Christmas (although of course they looked like that every night of the year), and also totally palatial, we'd all agreed.

Kate had said she'd lay on some snacks and predictably gone all out with turkey-and-cranberry vol-au-vents, home-made blinis with smoked salmon and *actual* caviar, honey-glazed chipolata sausages and French champagne that she said a grateful client had sent her. My offering of a bunch of flowers and a bottle of the best supermarket bubbly I could afford felt a bit inadequate by comparison.

We'd all dressed up for the occasion, too. Abbie was glowing in copper-coloured velvet, her hair freshly highlighted. Kate was wearing a floaty green silk maxi dress that showed off her tiny waist. Naomi was in black sequins, the stark colour contrasting with the brilliance of her hair.

I was wearing a strappy white dress I'd dug out from the back of my wardrobe and tried on without much hope of it fitting, but miraculously it did. I'd slapped some fake tan on my legs and painted my toenails and was praying that I wouldn't have to wait long for a bus home, because I'd get frostbite for sure.

'You look amazing, Ro,' Naomi said. 'That dress! Is it Ganni?'

'All Saints,' I admitted. 'It's so old it's back in fashion again. And I can't wear a bra with it, which is just as well, because I don't know if I'll be able to face my grotty old ones ever again after trying on those fabulous ones.'

'I'm terrible with vouchers,' Abbie said sympathetically. 'I'm always saving them and then they go out of date. It's such a waste, and I feel so guilty when I realise.'

'That's why I made sure it had a short expiry date,' Kate said. 'I know what you're like, Ro. And you, Abbie.'

'And me,' Naomi admitted. 'I've still got Mothercare vouchers from when I had the twins. I was so brain-dead from lack of sleep it was all I could do to tell them apart, which wasn't that hard given they're not even the same sex. Going shopping was pretty much beyond me.'

'It was such a lovely thing to give me,' I said. 'Honestly, I'm so grateful. But I kind of feel it's wasted on me, you know. It's not like I'm going to be whipping my kit off for some bloke and going "Tahdah!" any time soon. If ever.'

Kate looked at me sternly. 'Babe, it's not about some bloke. It's about you.'

'You sell yourself so short,' Abbie agreed. 'You're so lovely and stunning and special. You deserve to have nice things.'

'When my nana died,' Naomi remembered, 'we went round to her house to sort out her things. There was a whole drawer full of cashmere jumpers that she'd never worn, and the moths had got to them. And a beautiful tea set in the loft that she'd never ever used, proper bone china. That went to the charity shop – I'd never have been brave enough to use it with the twins about, and hopefully someone will buy it and love it. And the bath oil I used to give her for Christmas – bottles and bottles of it, all unopened in the cupboard under her bathroom sink. After that I promised myself I'd stop saving stuff up for best. It's there to be used.'

'Not kept for some mythical time in the future when it'll benefit from the male gaze.' Kate gave me a hard stare. 'Come on. You're worth more than that.'

'I know,' I said feebly. 'It's just it would be so nice to be fancied again. Just for a boost, you know. Maybe I should try online dating again.'

'Oh, Rowan.' Abbie glugged some champagne and filled up our glasses, then passed round a plate of canapés. Obviously, I took two. 'Listen to me. One, you are gorgeous and you don't need some man to tell you that. Two, you deserve to wear clothes that make you feel good, just because they make you feel good. And three... I've forgotten what three was.'

'And anyway, men,' Kate said. 'Trust me, if you take them at their own estimation, you'll never be good enough. I'm single too, and I know it sucks. You go on Tinder and there's some random dude whose profile says he's looking for a woman who "takes care of herself" – translation, is a size eight – and "has ambition" – translation, earns six figures – but is "nurturing" – translation, happy to wash his socks when she gets home from the office and babysit his kids while he watches the football.'

'I downloaded Tinder a few years ago,' I said. 'I've still got it on my phone, right on the last screen. I haven't looked at it in ages.'

'Can't say I blame you,' Kate said. 'Because these men, with their high standards – their ideas of the woman who'll finally be worthy of the privilege of shagging them – well. You take a look at their profiles, and what do you find? They're the wrong side of forty, unemployed and look like they've cut their own hair with the garden shears and haven't moved from the sofa in months. Years, even. Not since they had that photo taken on the back of some poor abused elephant in Thailand.'

'Not that there's anything wrong with being unemployed,' I said. For some reason, an image of smiling blue eyes and a thought popped into my head: *Or a delivery driver.*

'Nothing whatsoever,' Kate agreed. 'It can happen to anyone. It's just the sense of entitlement that gets to me. Like, because they're men, they get to take their pick of whatever woman they want, and then get narky AF when you say you're not interested.'

'It gets even worse when you're older,' Naomi said. 'My sister's in her forties and she says the only men who want to date her will never see sixty again.'

'Exactly!' said Kate. 'Because the ones her age are all looking for twenty-somethings without kids.'

'Guys, stop.' I drank the last of the fizz in my glass and put my head in my hands. 'If you're trying to persuade me to start dating, you're going about it the wrong way.'

'The point is,' Abbie said, 'you don't need a guy to boost your self-esteem.'

'Sometimes guys are the worst thing for your self-esteem,' agreed Kate. 'Especially ones online.'

'Are you saying I'm going to be single forever, then?' I asked.

'Not unless you want to be,' Kate said. 'I have to admit, I'm finding that prospect pretty appealing right now. But if you're not in a great place emotionally, online dating isn't for you. It's a bear pit.'

I noticed Abbie and Naomi exchange glances, and I knew what they were thinking. Their men might not be perfect, but at least they were there. At least – unless something awful happened – neither of them were going to have to create an online profile and put it out there to be assessed, weighed up against those of twenty-something blonde brain surgeons and discarded. Which right now seemed like the worst possible thing ever to me.

I said forlornly, 'If only Paul...' and then I stopped.

'If only Paul what?' Abbie asked gently.

'If only he wasn't getting married. If only things between him and me had worked out. It would be so much easier if we could be a proper family.'

'Oh, mate,' said Naomi. 'Come on. It's so much water under the bridge, isn't it? More than ten years since you two split up. You've both moved on, haven't you?'

'Paul clearly has,' I said bitterly.

'But not you?' Abbie asked gently.

'The thing is,' I said, 'when we first split, Clara was so young. All I wanted was for her to have a stable family. Me rushing around dating every guy who looked at me didn't feel like the right thing to do back then.'

'There's dating every guy who looks at you and then there's
—' Kate began, but I think Naomi might have kicked her under
the table with the pointy toe of her shoe, because she gave a
little gasp and shut up.

'And then my make-up business took off,' I went on, 'and I
was too busy building that up to really think about finding
another bloke. And anyway, if you had to pick the worst
possible career for meeting eligible single men, doing wedding
make-up would probably be it.'

'I dunno,' Naomi argued. 'I'm sure there are worse ones.
Astronaut on the International Space Station?'

'I bet there's loads of zero-gravity shagging going on up
there,' I said. 'Although how you'd do it in those spacesuit things
I'm not sure.'

'Lighthouse-keeper?' Kate said.

'Imagine if there was a shipwreck though. You'd have
dozens of horny sailors to choose from.'

'Being a cleaner in a convent?' suggested Abbie.

'Okay,' I admitted. 'That would be pretty bad. Although if
you were into nuns and they didn't take their vows too seriously... But where was I?'

'Not meeting single blokes because you were doing
wedding make-up,' Kate reminded me.

'Yeah. That.' I took a sausage and ate it without really
tasting it. 'So Clara was my top priority, and work was second.'

'And you were nowhere,' Naomi said.

'And Paul was just there,' I finished. 'And it felt like because
we were still being Mum and Dad to Clara, even though it had
ended between us, it kind of never really did.'

'But he was seeing other people,' Naomi pointed out. 'So
why was it one rule for him and a different one for you?'

'It wasn't a rule exactly, it just never happened.'

*And now I'm almost forty and I've got the self-confidence of
a used cotton-wool pad and it's never going to happen. I'm going*

to be alone forever. I thought about mentioning the handsome delivery driver, asking them if it would be totally weird to invite him in for a coffee, but then changed my mind. After all, what had passed between us apart from a few smiles and some very mild banter? Hell, I'd only just learned the man's name.

'But Paul,' Abbie began. 'I mean, we've all known him forever and he's a lovely guy.'

'And he's Clara's dad,' Naomi said, 'so there's clearly some fantastic genetic material there somewhere.'

Shame about mine.

'As well as yours,' Kate said. 'I mean, come on. You're stunning. And Clara's your total mini me. Gorgeous girl.'

'And she's so smart, and kind and funny.' Abbie kept on the 'let's big up Rowan' theme. 'You've done an incredible job.'

'Paul and I have done our best,' I said, sensing that I'd inadvertently wandered into some sort of love-bombing ambush.

'Shall I get the cake I brought?' Naomi said, confirming my suspicions. 'Well, it's a Yule log, but you know what I mean. Cake is cake.'

She stood up, staggered a bit on her heels, then made her way to the kitchen island, where she lifted the plastic cover off a stand holding an icing-sugar-dusted chocolate confection that had been raked with a fork to make its surface look like bark, and finished off with a sticky-out chocolate twig and a fondant icing robin.

'I bought it at a local craft market,' she confessed. 'I wish I could claim credit but I can't.'

'Anyway, so, Paul.' Abbie picked up the thread while Kate cut thick slices of cake and placed them carefully on the delicate porcelain plates she kept especially for occasions like this, adding antique silver forks to each plate. At least one of us didn't hold with keeping lovely things for best.

I dug in, tasting the rich chocolate frosting and the sponge that had clearly been soaked in some sort of delicious alcohol.

'I mean, he's nice and everything,' Abbie went on, sticking her fork into the Yule log. 'But seriously, Ro. You could do so much better.'

'Not that we think you're still hankering after him, or anything,' Naomi said.

'As if!' Kate added. 'Especially now he's getting married to Miss Insta Perfect.'

'It's exactly like what you were saying earlier, Kate,' Naomi said. 'Mid-grade men ending up with women who damn well ought to set their sights higher.'

'Okay, okay,' I said. 'I hear you. But enough about men. Come on, it's Christmas – well, almost Christmas. What are your best Christmas memories?'

At the rate the conversation was going – and the rate at which we were sinking the fizz – I might find myself blurting out the truth about exactly how ongoing my sexual relationship with Paul had been, and I wasn't ready for that – or for the loving telling-off that would inevitably result.

'This is going to sound pathetic.' Abbie levered the cork out of another bottle. 'But the last one. Matt and I had had such a rough couple of years. I really thought we weren't going to make it. But we have, and last year, having Christmas with just us and the cat was so amazing. Almost losing him has made me realise I actually really bloody love him. And Shrimp's realised how much she bloody loves roast duck.'

We all went, 'Awwww!' and, 'You guys!' and, 'Let's drink to that!'

'Can I have multiple ones?' I said. 'Like, when Clara was little, when she still believed in Father Christmas, it was so amazing getting everything ready on Christmas Eve. Putting out the glass of whisky for Santa and the carrot for Rudolph and dressing her in new pyjamas and thinking she'd never go to sleep so I could fill up her stocking. And the expression on her face the next morning, when she realised all the magic had happened overnight – it was just the most adorable thing.'

'Sometimes you wish they'd never grow up,' Naomi said wistfully. 'But Christmas without kids is pretty incredible too. About five years ago Patch and I saved up and went to Norway to see the Northern Lights – remember? God, it was incredible. There was snow everywhere, proper, deep snow, and we went husky sledding and drank all the vodka, and when we did see the lights they were so beautiful I legit cried.'

Kate said, 'I think my best was with you guys. Remember, when we rented that cottage in Cambridgeshire, with the hot tub in the garden?'

'Yes!' I agreed. 'They almost wouldn't let us book it because they thought we were a hen party.'

'We had to get Matt to ring them up and say he was going along to be the responsible adult,' Abbie recalled. 'As if! And we spent the entire time in that hot tub, because it was too cold to get out.'

'We had a karaoke session in there one night, remember?' Naomi said.

'We should do that now,' Kate said. 'Right now. Come on.'

Abbie, Naomi and I looked at each other blankly for a second, then I said, 'I think there may be a small flaw in your plan.'

'We're not in a cottage in Cambridgeshire,' Abbie pointed out.

'And there's no hot tub,' said Naomi.

'Doesn't matter.' Kate stood up. 'Follow me. Someone bring another bottle. Or two.'

Bewildered, we obeyed, trooping after her into her enormous en-suite bathroom. She turned the taps, and water gushed into the free-standing cast-iron tub, into which she squirted loads of Pomegranate Noir bath oil.

The water pressure must've been quite something, because it wasn't long before the tub was almost half full.

'I'm going in.' Abbie kicked off her shoes, pulled off her dress and stepped into the water in her bra and pants.

'Is there room for us all?' Naomi asked doubtfully.

'God knows,' said Kate. 'My arse needs its own postcode these days. But we'll give it a go.'

Soon, we were all in the tub, squeezed in next to each other, our legs hanging over the edge, glasses in our hands.

'Alexa,' I said, 'play Christmas music.'

And we spent the next hour in there, giggling like teenagers, murdering 'It's Beginning to Look a Lot Like Christmas' and 'Let It Snow' and 'All I Want for Christmas Is You' and all the rest, until the fizz was finished and the water was cooling.

And I realised it had been ages since I'd even given Paul a thought.

CHAPTER THIRTEEN

'Four pints of Kronenbourg, please, mate.'

Alex waited while the barman poured the drinks, then tapped his phone on the card reader and carried the glasses back to the table, balancing them precariously between his two hands.

'Cheers for that,' Carlo said. 'Where do I sign?'

Alex laughed and rolled his eyes. A lot of this long-overdue catch-up had so far been taken up with Carlo, always the group wag, taking the piss out of what he claimed was Alex's fall from grace, starting from his early gambit (right after 'What's up, you Weegie bastard?'), which had been, 'So how's the county lines gig treating you?' To which Alex had had to patiently explain that if he was running drugs, he'd expect to be paid a damn sight better than the minimum wage Pegasus offered.

'It's all done on biometrics,' Alex said. 'Your face is captured in the system now, and you'll get a weekly delivery of those cheese and onion Hula Hoops you made Fergus buy earlier.'

'Food of the gods,' Carlo protested. 'Don't knock them till you've tried them.'

'We don't need to try them,' Stevie said. 'We can smell them on your breath at twenty paces.'

'Seriously?' Carlo looked alarmed, cupped his palm over his mouth and exhaled noisily.

Although the evening had been billed as a boys' night, Alex knew that for Carlo, any pub was basically a stage on which his next seduction might take place. His attempts were mostly unsuccessful, owing to his reliance on pick-up lines gleaned from Reddit that were as cheesy as his favourite snack.

'Nah,' Fergus assured him. 'It's not your breath that puts women off.'

'It's you asking them whether it hurt when they fell from heaven,' Stevie finished, and they all laughed, confident that Carlo, with his ever-ready smile, olive skin and runner's physique, would have no difficulty finding a girlfriend eventually – or indeed a shag tonight, if he turned on the charm and dialled down the one-liners.

Then the conversation moved on to which team had the best chance of clinching the rugby league, whether non-fungible tokens would ever be anything other than a mug's game, and the best way to cook a tomahawk steak on the barbecue, if it would ever be warm enough to have one again.

Stevie assured the group that his wife and preschool-aged kids were doing okay. Fergus told them that his high-flying lawyer girlfriend hadn't yet come to her senses and dumped his arse, then updated them on the progress of the ongoing renovation of his house, using several choice phrases to describe the builders that Alex stored up to use next time he lugged a heavy parcel up six flights of stairs to discover the recipient wasn't in and none of their neighbours would accept the delivery.

Stevie described in great detail an amazing slow-roast brisket dish he'd recently cooked, and Alex asked him to email the recipe, even though he knew he'd never get the time to cook it.

Carlo had them in stitches about an ongoing feud with a work colleague who persistently thieved people's packed lunches from the office fridge ('I mean, come on. He knows I've gotta track my macros'), which had culminated in Carlo dousing his three-bean salad in so much chilli powder that the culprit would, as he put it, be shitting through the eye of a needle for days.

Before they could finish congratulating him on his devilish ingenuity, Alex noticed that his friend's attention had wandered. A tall blonde woman was standing at the bar, nursing a gin and tonic and glancing frequently and intently at her phone.

'Look over there,' Carlo said. 'Her Tinder date's stood her up – I'd lay money on it. We need another round anyway, so I'm going in. Hula Hoops, anyone?'

Alex, Stevie and Fergus shook their heads, but watched with rapt attention as Carlo ambled, faux-casually, to the bar, placed their drinks order and then turned to the blonde woman and spoke to her. They saw her smile, sip her drink, then laugh and shake her head.

With a slightly shamefaced grin, Carlo returned with their beers.

'Knocked you back?' Stevie said.

Carlo shook his head ruefully. 'Brutal. She's an ice queen.'

'What did you say to her?' Alex asked.

To his credit, Carlo looked embarrassed. 'That her eyes reminded me of IKEA, because I was totally lost in them.'

They all groaned.

'Oh my God,' Fergus said. 'Come on. That's bad, even by your standards.'

'Woeful,' Stevie agreed.

'So when I need advice on chatting up a woman,' Alex said, 'I know exactly who to ask. Not.'

Fergus picked up this like a dog with a bone. 'What? You're thinking of making a move on someone?'

'No more than usually,' Alex replied evasively.

'Come on then,' Carlo urged. 'Who is she? Share with the group.'

'Just someone I met through work.'

'What, another delivery driver? Your satnav led you to her?' Stevie quipped.

'Your eyes met across a crowded conveyor belt and you lost your heart?' suggested Fergus.

'No, you pair of idiots. She's someone I deliver stuff to.'

'And you've asked her out?' Fergus probed.

'Given her a special delivery?' Carlos said.

'No. Nothing like that. Not yet, anyway.' Much as Alex loved his mates, their banter felt somehow inappropriate when applied to Rowan. But he suspected that, if it was serious advice he was after, which he wasn't really – after all, there was nothing to advise on, given the fleeting nature of his contact with Rowan – he wasn't going to get it tonight.

'And speaking of the women in your life,' Fergus added, clasping a hand theatrically to his heart, 'how's Ailsa doing?'

Ailsa. Suddenly, Alex's phone, forgotten in the pocket of his leather jacket on the back of the tall bar stool, felt as if it was red hot. Reflexively, he reached for it and saw the message on the screen.

'Sorry, lads,' he said. 'I'm going to have to call it a night.'

CHAPTER FOURTEEN

Kimberley was alone in the office when I arrived the next day, slumped at her desk, a half-full glass of bright orange liquid next to her. She started upright when she heard the door open, her eyes wide and smudged with make-up. When she saw me, her face slackened with relief.

'Oh. Rowan. It's only you.'

'Are you okay? You look a bit...'

I didn't like to say it, but she looked a bit like Andy, all the times I'd seen him after a heavy night. And Andy's definition of a heavy night meant enough cocaine to fly all the way to the North Pole.

'God, Rowan, I feel terrible.' Kimberley pressed a white-manicured hand to her face. 'The party was great. But it got messy. We ended up in the flat in Corrigan Mansions – you know, the one with the view over Hyde Park? – because someone thought it would be a good idea to watch the sunrise.'

'Bloody hell, Kimberley. Sunrise was, what, half an hour ago?'

'I know. I went and showered and changed at the gym. These are yesterday's clothes. I must absolutely hum.'

Now that she mentioned it, I couldn't help noticing the odour of stale alcohol, cigarette smoke and yesterday's perfume emanating from her. Compared to hers, my own hangover faded into insignificance.

'Right. You finish your Berocca, then pop to the loo and fix your face. I'll run down the road to the greasy spoon and get you a bacon sandwich and make you a cup of tea, extra sugar. There's not much we can do about your clothes for now, but you can buy a new shirt from M&S at lunch.'

'I can't wear an M&S blouse!'

If I wore anything from M&S, unless it was off Vinted or in the sale, I thought I was doing pretty well for myself. But I didn't say that.

'Somewhere else then. Come on, up you get. Julz'll be here any minute.'

Kimberley stood up, swayed a bit, then brightened. 'He left early. I reckon he missed me being sick on the carpet.'

'That's good, at any rate.'

But Marty and Brett wouldn't have left early – poor Kimberley was in for a rough ride. Once again, I thanked my lucky stars that I'd had the cast-iron excuse of a pre-existing commitment with my friends so I'd been able to bow out of the work party. I hurried out, slinging my coat over my shoulders against the cold. The queue at the sandwich shop was long – clearly Kimberley wasn't the only one suffering after a work Christmas party.

'I'd like a double fried egg sandwich on white bread,' the girl in front of me ordered. 'A white tea, a KitKat and a packet of salt and vinegar crisps.'

'Anything else?' asked the man behind the counter.

'And an iced bun,' she added. 'And could you put it on two bills, please? The sandwich and the tea, and then the rest.'

Bless her, I thought, even in her broken state, she was too

proud to admit the whole lot was for her. But I knew, and I was willing to bet the sandwich shop guy knew too.

At last, carrying Kimberley's sandwich, I returned to the office. She'd repaired her make-up and was looking a bit less pale after a good go with the bronzer. Julz was at his desk now, too, scowling at his computer screen, a strong smell of sandalwood aftershave emanating from his corner, from which I deduced that although he'd left early, he'd also been hitting the negroni Bellinis enthusiastically.

I slipped Kimberley's sandwich discreetly on her desk.

'Drink, Julz?' I asked brightly.

'Black coffee, one sugar.' He didn't look up from his screen. 'I want you canvassing today, Rowena. There's loads of shit on that database. We need to clean it up, okay? Call every name and ask them if they're still looking for a property, and update their entry accordingly.'

'Right.' I handed him his coffee and Kimberley her tea, and took my own cappuccino to my desk. Canvassing was thankless work – by the time I left the office, I knew I'd have been shouted at, hung up on and sworn at – and reminded of the existence of the General Data Protection Regulations at least a dozen times.

Still, at least I'd be inside in the warm, I told myself. And at least I wouldn't be held up on a viewing, so I'd be able to make it home in time to catch Alex with my delivery, and maybe actually manage an intelligent conversation with him for once.

'Morning, morning.' Marty and Brett breezed through the door together, a full twenty minutes late. But Julz said nothing, only looked up from his screen again, stony-faced.

'Mate, I'm hanging so bad,' Marty said.

'Got a blowie off that girl from the Croydon office though,' Brett said. 'It's a Christmas miracle.'

'It's your irresistible charm, mate,' Marty said.

The two of them roared with laughter. Pointedly ignoring them, I called up the database on the customer relationship management app on my computer and slotted my headset over my ear. The printer whirred, and Kimberley stood up, gripped the edge of her desk for a second, then steadied herself and went over to collect her documents.

'Hey, Kimberley,' Brett said. 'How many Essex girls does it take to make chocolate chip cookies?'

Kimberley ignored him, squatting down to clear a paper jam.

'How many is that then?' Marty asked.

'Six. One to mix the batter and five to peel the Smarties.'

They hooted again, slapping the thighs of their Savile Row suits.

I glanced at Kimberley again. Her eyes were beginning to sparkle, but with unshed tears.

I gritted my teeth and dialled the first number on my list. It rang out to voicemail.

'Hi, this is Rowan Connell from Walkerson's Elite. I'm calling to ask whether you've found a property to purchase yet? We have had several new listings we'd really love to show you. Please could you give me a call back? Thanks, look forward to hearing from you, bye.'

'What does an Essex girl use for protection when she has sex?' Marty asked.

I could see Kimberley's shoulders starting to tremble. She was a tough, resilient woman, I knew – there's nothing like being told to get lost thirty times a day by strangers over the phone to cultivate a thick skin. But today she was vulnerable, and Brett and Marty knew it.

They were goading her like matadors in a bullring, and it was just as horrible to watch.

'A bus shelter.'

Before their shouts of laughter could even begin, Kimberley spoke.

'You know what, you two, that is fucking offensive. It's

sexual harassment and bullying, and it's not okay in the work-place, right? This is the twenty-first bleeding century. People go to court over that stuff. I deserve respect, and I expect to get it from you. And if I don't, I expect you to do something about it, Julz.'

She choked back a sob, grabbed a tissue from the box on her desk and wiped her eyes.

Finally, Julz turned away from his screen. Brett and Marty were still grinning, but their smiles looked ever so slightly anxious – their laughter had been forced but confident; now they were apprehensive, and it showed.

I darted a quick smile in Kimberley's direction.

'So you don't care for the way I run this business, Kimberley?' Julz drawled.

'I never said that. It's the way these two treat me I can't stand. It's not okay, Julz. You know it's not.'

'Very well. In that case, you can pack your things and leave.'

Kimberley flinched. 'I beg your pardon?'

'You heard me. HR will send on your P45.'

'But I...'

Julz turned back to his screen as if she hadn't spoken. Brett and Marty sat in their places, immobile. Both of them looked chastened, as if this served as a reminder that they could easily be dished out the same treatment.

I didn't need to be reminded.

Still, watching Kimberley fight back tears with a visible effort and gather her things, tucking the little white teddy clutching a heart that had lived on her desk into her bag, putting on her coat, doing a brief, panicky hunt for her phone that seemed to take hours, I couldn't just sit there and watch her leave in disgrace.

When she was ready, I stood up and moved to the door with her, hoping to have a quick chat outside. I didn't know what I was going to say – express solidarity, perhaps. Tell her how unfair it was. Ask if she was okay, even though she clearly wasn't. Wish her a merry Christmas, although it was impossible to see how she could have one after being sacked with it just around the corner.

But I never made it to the door.

'Rowena,' Julz said in a voice that commanded instant obedience. 'A moment.'

I froze. My heart was pounding in my chest like I'd sprinted halfway along Piccadilly. My mouth was as dry as a supermarket turkey sandwich, but my hands were clammy with sweat.

In that moment, if you'd offered me a thousand pounds to tell my boss my name was Rowan, I'd have told you to keep it and spend it on stocking fillers for your kids.

'Yes, Julz?' I managed to say, keeping my eyes trained on his face even as I saw the door swing shut behind Kimberley.

'You'll be taking over Kimberley's apps. We won't be able to get another negotiator onboarded before Christmas and we need to get those figures up. This office has slipped well below target.'

'But what about—' Marty said.

'Couldn't we split—' Brett began.

'Did either of you say something?' Julz turned his gaze on them, and I saw them both wilt like unwatered poinsettias.

'No, boss,' Marty said. 'Not a thing.'

'Not a dickie bird, guv'nor,' agreed Brett.

'Good,' Julz said. 'In that case, I'll thank you all to shut the fuck up and get on with your jobs.'

I turned back to my computer, my mouth dry with shock and relief. I didn't just have the one applicant now – I had lots. Those on Kimberley's list might not be the ones with the massive budgets – Brett and Marty would have seen to that –

but they were mine. They were a chance for me to earn some proper commission – a Christmas gift from the most unlikely of sources. A chalice I already suspected was poisoned, but wasn't able to turn down.

CHAPTER FIFTEEN

At lunchtime, Clara texted me to say she had a cold and wanted to come home early from school. I suggested she get some paracetamol from the nurse and tough it out, but she complained pathetically that she was 'legit dying', so I abandoned my tough love policy (not before reminding her that millions of girls around the world would kill for the opportunity of an education like hers) and relented.

When I arrived home, she was lying on the sofa eating Jelly Tots and watching CBeebies, a duvet pulled up under her chin so she looked like a baby kangaroo peering out of its pouch. She gratefully accepted the Lemsip I brought her, and I felt my heart swell with gratitude for the opportunities I still had to mother and coddle her.

'Feeling any better?' I asked, stroking her forehead to check if she had a temperature.

'God, Mum, I'm so bored,' she replied, so I assumed she was over the worst.

'Scrambled eggs on toast for tea?' I suggested brightly.

'I'm not that hungry.' Self-pity flooded her face again. 'I still feel awful.'

'Let's see how you are in the morning. I bought some industrial-strength decongestant from the pharmacy and some date-and-walnut bread from a bakery I passed in Notting Hill.'

And it cost more than five quid for a loaf, so it had better be good.

'Aw, thanks, Mum.' Clara heaved herself higher on the sofa cushions and started scrolling through the channels on the telly.

'Any deliveries?' I asked faux-casually, hoping that the courier hadn't been yet and that, if he had, Clara hadn't answered the door in the sports bra that appeared to be all she was wearing with her pyjama bottoms.

She shook her head. 'No sign of today's instalment. I hope he shows up. It's still raining out there, right?'

'Yes, coming down in sheets. The traffic was terrible. I'll just go and change.'

But before I could make it as far as my bedroom, I heard the welcome tap of the knocker.

Pushing damp strands of hair behind my ears and forcing my tired feet back into my work shoes, I hurried to the hallway and flung open the door, letting in a gust of damp air and a hint of some sort of cologne. Either today's parcel was a particularly strongly scented one, or Smiley Blue-Eyes (*Alex. His name's Alex*) had upped his grooming game for some reason.

I just wished I felt less drab by comparison. Perhaps next time I could open the door dressed in a lacy negligee. Only problem was, I didn't own such a garment. Still, I felt a lurch of nervousness when I saw him, which wasn't a bit unpleasant, and when I met his eyes, my heart beat faster in my chest.

'Afternoon, Rowan.'

'Afternoon, er, Alex.'

He grinned, if anything even more widely than usual. 'You got my note on Sunday.'

'I did. Thanks so much. It's... It's stupid, I know, but I really look forward to getting my parcel every day.'

'I bet you do. It's a cool idea. You've got good friends.'

'The best. I'm really lucky.'

He hesitated, then said, 'How about your boyfriend? Is he in on this?'

I grimaced. 'No boyfriend, unfortunately for me.'

'And unfortunately for the boyfriend. The one you don't have, I mean. I mean...'

He tailed off, and I waited expectantly for him to carry on, wondering if this just might be going in the direction I suddenly very much hoped it would.

'I just mean, if there was someone in your life, it wouldn't be just you that was the lucky one,' he said.

Our eyes held each other, and it genuinely felt as if he was looking deep inside of me, seeing things about me that I'd almost forgotten were there – things that would make my boyfriend a lucky person, if I had one. My heart was pounding so hard it felt like it was trying to escape from my chest, but when I opened my mouth to say something light and trivial – *Thank you, that's sweet* – no words would come out. Perhaps because those weren't the words I actually wanted to say.

'I'm sorry,' he said. 'Too much?'

His smile reassured me. 'It's not too much. It's a lovely thing to say.'

'Least I can do, say lovely things before I hand over your parcel.'

He rummaged in his bag, then pulled out a familiar brown cardboard sleeve and handed it over.

'Thank you.' I gauged the weight of the parcel and sniffed it but could smell nothing apart from the musky amber scent I'd noticed when I'd opened the door.

'It's a little one today,' he said. 'What do you reckon? Another of those fish things?'

'I'm sure they wouldn't duplicate a gift.'

For the first time, I realised how much planning must have

gone into the selection of my advent-calendar presents. Had they decided on all of them upfront, I wondered, or were they winging it, making it up as they went along?

'I need to get a hustle on,' Alex said. 'I'm running late because of the traffic and I've got... I've got to be somewhere.'

'Oh. Okay.' I wasn't sure why, but part of me had been hoping that he'd stay and watch while I opened the parcel, as he had a couple of times before. It had begun to feel almost as if his presence was part of the ritual – part of the magic. That, and I might get to feel his warm breath on my hand again, get a bit closer so I could identify whatever it was he smelled of. Maybe even allow my hand to brush against his and feel the zing of electricity that I hoped – that I knew – would be there. 'Hope you have a good rest of the day. Drive safely.'

'I guess I'll see you tomorrow.'

He smiled, and I felt an answering smile stretch across my face. 'I hope so. Thanks again.'

I backed slowly into the hallway again, watching as he shouldered his bag, pulled the baseball cap down over his face and hurried away along the walkway, waiting until he'd disappeared from view and I could hear his feet on the stairs. Even once he'd vanished from view, I could still see his face (those eyes, that smile!) and hear the warm timbre of his voice (that accent!).

'Mum?' Clara called. 'What's going on? You're taking forever out there.'

'I'm here. Come on – budge up and let me sit down.'

'I thought you'd died out there or something.'

'Well, I couldn't just grab the parcel from him and head back indoors, could I? It would be rude.'

'You always have before.' Clara looked at me from behind the curtain of her hair, her green eyes astute. 'When we used to have that other man doing the deliveries, the one with the BO, you couldn't get away from the door fast enough. And you still can't when it's the Amazon guy who likes to talk about the weather for ages.'

'Well, this is different. I'm going to see him every day until Christmas. Well, most of them. I guess he gets days off. We may as well develop a civil client–supplier relationship.'

'Hmmm.' Clara raised one eyebrow. It wasn't quite The Face, but it was close. 'Civil? Is that what they're calling it now?'

'That's enough backchat from you, young lady.'

I met my daughter's eyes properly, and we both giggled. It wouldn't be long, I realised, before I wouldn't be able to tell her off any more, not even jokingly. When she'd be a grown-up woman, able to make her own decisions and her own mistakes.

'Come on then. Are you going to open it or just sit there staring at it?'

'I might open it later, in bed, once you're asleep.'

'Mum!'

'All right then.'

I gripped the little cardboard tab, and the red plastic strip parted the perforations in the cardboard. The sleeve opened to reveal a small white cardboard box, about the size of a pack of cards but much lighter. I lifted it to my ear and shook it gently but heard only the faintest rustle.

'Want to guess what it is?' I asked.

'A sheet mask?' Clara hazarded. 'Stick-on nail art or false eyelashes?'

'Could be.'

I eased the lid off the box. Inside was a layer of tissue paper, which I lifted off. Beneath it were five small glass vials, the kind perfume samples come in. Each one held a different-coloured liquid, and a handwritten label.

Carefully, I lifted the first one out, holding its top and bottom between my thumb and middle finger. The room was dark, lit only by the flicker of the television, and I had to hold the vial close to my eyes to read the label. The script was a careful cursive that looked like it had been written with a fountain pen – Naomi, I guessed. She'd always had beautiful handwriting.

'Self-Esteem,' I read. 'Okay. That's nice.'

I placed the tiny bottle carefully back on its tissue-paper bed and lifted up the next one, Clara watching me sideways, her hair half covering her face again.

'Assertiveness.' I returned the bottle to its place and examined the next three, one after the other. 'Courage. Desirability. Risk-Taking.'

I laid the final bottle back, feeling oddly light-headed: at once seen and exposed but also with a sense of – something. Power? Not that. But the potential for power? Perhaps.

'Let me see.' Clara snatched the box from my hands then took out each bottle and scrutinised it, just as I had. 'Wow. That's like – what even are they? It's like something out of Harry Potter. Are they spells? Elixirs? Do you drink them or put them on like perfume or what?'

I retrieved the Self-Esteem bottle from the box in my daughter's hands and carefully eased out its tiny stopper, sniffing the contents.

'I think it's just a spirit base with some essential oil and colouring,' I said, remembering a long-ago visit I'd taken to a Paris perfumery, back when this sort of thing was my career. 'So I reckon you could do either. Without a fixative, the scent would fade pretty quickly. Might be better to drink them, if I'm honest.'

'Mum,' Clara pointed out, 'there's, like, a couple of millilitres in each one. That wouldn't even be enough to get Toby and Meredith drunk.'

'Not that any sane person would consider giving alcohol to Naomi's toddlers,' I said, giving her a side-eye to equal her own.

'Well, obviously not. God. But you know what I mean.'

She passed the box back to me, and I replaced the bottle in its place. We looked at each other for a bit, then Clara pulled a tissue from the box on her lap and blew her nose thunderously.

'I think they should be kept for emergencies,' I said. 'I'll put them in the bathroom cabinet. Any time either of us needs them, they'll be there.'

Maybe, I thought, the potions, or whatever they were, would give me the power to transform my life. Perhaps assertiveness was what I needed to prevent another property from being snatched from my applicant by one of Brett's cash buyers. Perhaps the risk I was meant to take was asking the handsome delivery driver to come in for a coffee; courage would enable me to do it, and desirability would make him say yes.

If that happened, I thought, I'd never diss the magic of Christmas ever again.

CHAPTER SIXTEEN

Alex hurried down the stairs, cursing the rain, the traffic and people who didn't put numbers in visible places on their houses. He was running more than an hour behind schedule, which meant he hadn't been able to stop to chat to the woman with the beautiful hazel eyes and the amazing smile (and the daughter who, strangely, never seemed to smile at all. Maybe that was the norm for teenage girls – he didn't have a clue. At thirty-four, it felt like his own teenage years had been lost in the mists of time), and see what her friends had sent her for her advent-calendar-that-wasn't-an-advent-calendar.

He'd become intrigued by her story. In between drops, he found himself wondering what had gone on in her life to make her mates think she needed cheering up, or whether they were just the type of people who did such random, generous things for one another. He hoped the latter – but feared the former. There was something about the woman – about Rowan – that made him think life had dealt her some shitty hands.

A couple of times when she'd opened the door, before the smile lit up her face, she'd looked harried and tired. And although her flat seemed warm and clean and homely, the lift had been out of order for almost two weeks now – he hoped she got her groceries delivered as well as her gifts, because shifting stuff up those stairs was no joke.

But any hopes he might have had of finding out more about her and her life would have to be put on ice for another day. His lateness also meant that he was going to have to change out of his courier uniform into his suit in his van, which was about as far as possible from ideal.

Fortunately, he'd had the foresight to bring the suit with him when he left home that morning, and to put his bicycle and helmet in the van when he left the depot, squeezing it into the small space left between the banks of cardboard boxes.

Keys in his hand, he hesitated outside the van, the wind biting like an axe blade into the space between his high-vis jacket and his baseball cap. Change here, or change at the depot?

Either way, he'd face gibes from his colleagues and probably a snarky comment from his foreman, who clearly thought Alex had ideas above his station. But if he changed here, he could put the high-vis back on over his suit, he realised. That would mean a reasonable chance they wouldn't notice, and a speedy getaway if they did.

He grabbed his suit off the passenger seat and opened the doors into the back of the van, empty now apart from his bicycle and his own messenger bag, black leather as opposed to the red canvas of his work bag.

He stepped in out of the biting wind, but the back of the van was freezing nonetheless. Quickly, he shrugged off his high-vis jacket and draped it over the handlebars of his bike, then peeled off his logoed sweatshirt, unlaced his heavy work boots and stepped out of his jeans, gooseflesh springing up all over his body.

He was in the best shape he'd been in ages, he thought with a hint of smugness. The cycle commute, followed by a day of lugging heavy parcels up stairs and along corridors, often with little time to eat anything in what was nominally his break, had shredded the last of the fat from his body and left new muscle in its place.

He was well on the way to a visible six-pack, which he hadn't achieved even when he was spending an hour a day in the gym.

'See,' he said aloud, through chattering teeth, 'total life goals, this job.'

It was just a shame there was nowhere for him to shower, and no time if there had been. Perhaps he could have asked the hazel-eyed woman in number 74 to use her bathroom, but that would have been creepy AF, especially if her daughter was home. Actually, maybe it would have been even creepier if she wasn't.

Just as well I didn't have that idea when I was up there, Alex told himself. It could have played out like the opening scene of a cheap porno, the delivery dude getting his kit off in her bathroom, she walks in by mistake and next thing you know…

He laughed aloud at the absurdity of the idea, buttoning his shirt and pulling on his suit trousers. They were too loose around the waist now, and his jacket was too tight across the shoulders, but he hadn't had a chance to get to the shops and knew from experience that if he'd done an online order, he wouldn't have got around to returning the stuff that didn't fit.

The irony of a courier driver not being able to take advantage of his own service wasn't lost on Alex.

He laced up his shoes, which were scuffed from cycling and which he hadn't had a chance to polish – or the polish to polish them, now he thought about it. Carefully, he knotted his tie, which was patterned with sprigs of holly. A cheerful nod to the festive season was the look he'd been aiming for when he'd grabbed it from his wardrobe that morning.

Now, he suspected that it just screamed 'desperate wanker'.

But it was too late to do anything about that now. He pulled on his jacket, which left him no warmer – chilled from the air in the back of the van, it felt like draping a wet towel over his shoulders. But the van's cab was heated – he'd warm up soon enough.

He glanced at his watch – four forty-five. If the traffic wasn't too bad, he'd make it on time. A pretty massive if.

Bracing himself for the onslaught of the wind, Alex stepped out of the van, hurried round to the driver's door and swung himself in. A quick check in the side mirror assured him that his tie was straight, he didn't have smears of dust on his face from delivery boxes and, even if he wasn't freshly shaved, he didn't look like a total reprobate. His hair was short enough that his cycling helmet wouldn't mess it up – the slick pompadour he'd affected a couple of years back was long gone. There was no room in his life for serums and waxes and fortnightly visits to the barber at this point.

Not the best, but he'd have to do. After a forty-minute cycle in the rain, all bets would be off in any case.

He started the engine and reversed the van out of the parking space, then swung through the gate leading out of the car park and onto the main road, easing into a gap in the stream of traffic. His stomach was growling – the chicken sandwich he'd wolfed down for lunch felt like a long time ago.

But it wasn't just hunger – he was kidding himself if he thought that. It was nerves as well. If he'd told the woman in number 74 where he was off to, and she'd given him that amazing smile and wished him luck, he'd have been feeling better for sure.

But she hadn't. Maybe she never would, unless Alex made sure she got the chance.

At the depot, Alex switched the van for his bicycle and headed out again into the steady stream of traffic, able now to slip past the streams of near-stationary cars, buses and lorries in the safety of the cycle lane. He tried to keep his mind on the road, but it was difficult – his thoughts kept veering to the panel of men in suits (it was almost always men) who he'd shortly be facing.

It was the fourth such interrogation he'd attended, and there would likely be a handful more before it was all over, all decided, one way or another. He knew his story, he was pretty confident he would be able to field whatever questions came his way, but still he could feel tension growing in his jaw, adrenaline heightening his reactions to the traffic.

It wouldn't do any harm, he told himself. A bit of stage fright was no bad thing – he needed his A game on, and if being shit scared made him give a better account of himself, he'd take it.

Two hours later, it was over, and Alex was on his way home. He cycled slowly across Tower Bridge, its lights arcing above him in the winter darkness, the wind buffeting him so hard he had to grip the handlebars to stay on course. Red buses glided past, the lights of the city spread out behind him, sparkling like gold coins tossed aside by someone with more money than sense.

Below him, the river was as dark as ink, its surface choppy from the wind and pitted by countless raindrops. The wet road ahead of him reflected the lights above so it, too, shone like precious metal – a path to riches. He smiled at his daftness, then brought his concentration back into sharp focus as a gust of wind almost sent him into the path of a double-decker bus.

To his right, he could see a Christmas market laid out along the south bank of the river, wooden chalets arrayed with sparkling lights, no doubt selling street food from around the world and probably artisan cheese: Alex's stomach rumbled at the thought. There was even a giant, illuminated reindeer presiding over it all, a robin perched on its back. Alex smiled at the kitsch over-the-topness of it all and resolved to pay a visit if he got a chance, even if he was mostly there for the cheese.

He reached the far side of the bridge and turned left, cycling past the old warehouses that were now luxury apartments, past concrete tower blocks and new high-rise towers, some clad in glossy panelling, some with their cladding stripped away.

Alex loved London. It didn't feel like home in the same way Glasgow had – not embedded in his DNA, virtually every brick familiar – but its unfamiliarity was in itself alluring. He loved the sense of potential with which the city seemed to swell, but also its anonymity. He was just a tiny cog in this vast machine, just one guy on his bicycle making his way home among countless others. Success or failure, love or loneliness, riches or poverty, arriving home in one piece or being mashed beneath a bus – it was all the same to London.

But that was no way to think. Alex was a man with responsibilities – London might not care if he never made it home, but there were others who did.

Returning his focus to the road, he kept pedalling, roughly following the course of the river as he navigated the familiar streets leading towards home, the brightly lit windows of bars and restaurants gradually giving way to fried-chicken shops, bookmakers and newsagents as he headed further east.

At last, he turned his bicycle off the main road into a quieter, tree-lined street, Victorian terraced houses stretching away on either side. Most of them were clearly numbered, Alex noticed with approval. His home certainly was: a brass '47' was affixed to the dark blue painted front door. He hadn't realised it when he moved in, but now the number felt significant – fortuitous, even: the reversal of the number he'd come to look forward to seeing every day, waiting for a moment before knocking, wondering whether today Rowan would be home, would swing open the door eagerly and smile at him.

He locked his bike away in the small storage shed in the front garden, rolling his shoulders to ease tension he hadn't been aware was there. He fished in his bag for his keys and unlocked the door.

'I'm home,' he called, then a second later added, 'You don't have to moan at me. I'm not that late.'

Then the door swung shut behind him and the street was silent and empty again, apart from a lone fox drifting through the shadows.

CHAPTER SEVENTEEN

I switched off the shower and hurried through to my bedroom. Showing up late for my first day after an effective promotion – although, I remembered, no increase in salary had been mentioned – wouldn't be a good look.

Still, I took more care than usual getting ready, applying bold red lipstick that I hoped would make me look like a badass, opening a new pack of tights in honour of the occasion and putting my hair up into a rather messy chignon, mostly because the rain was coming down like stair-rods.

Actually, I thought, peering unenthusiastically out of the window, it was more like going across than coming down. I could hear gusts of wind rattling the windows and whistling through the bare branches of the trees that lined the car park.

'Clara?' I called. 'If you want a lift to school, you need to get a move on.'

'I'm coming, I'm coming.' My daughter emerged bleary-eyed from her bedroom, knotting her school tie. 'What's the rush?'

'It's seven thirty, that's what the rush is. You've just got time for a piece of toast.'

'I'm not hungry. I'm still not feeling well. Can't I—'

'No. You're going to school. Have you got cash for a snack later?'

She nodded. Clearly I wasn't going to get any sparkling conversation out of her – like her mother, Clara was not a morning person.

But she surprised me, as we stood waiting hopefully for the lift, by saying, 'You look nice today, Mum.'

'I do? Thanks.'

'Will you show me how to do my hair like that?'

'Of course. Did you know, it used to be a thing that girls were only allowed to put their hair up when they were officially adults? Like, seventeen or something?'

'No way.'

'Yup. Hair up, long skirts, and you'd be married off as soon as your parents could find someone to take you.'

'God, that's so gross.'

The lift arrived and I stepped in, followed by Clara, relieved that – today at least – I wouldn't have to walk down the stairs in my high heels. I fumbled in my bag for my car keys, ready to sprint the short distance from shelter to Portia.

But once we were safely installed in the car, it refused to start. The engine turned over but wouldn't fire, and I knew from experience that attempting that too often would drain the battery, and then it would be game over.

'What's wrong with it?' Clara asked.

'Sweetheart, I have no idea,' I said wearily, remembering yet again the women's basic car maintenance course I kept meaning to enrol on but never had the spare cash for. Now I'd have to fork out for a mechanic, which made it the falsest of false economies.

'Suppose I'll have to get the bus to school. In the pissing rain. With the worst cold ever. God, I hate my life.'

'Well, yes, I'm afraid you will. Want to go upstairs and get your coat and an umbrella?'

'Mum! I'm fine. It's only rain.'

From burning martyr to resigned stoic in seconds, I noted, but I knew better than to point out her screeching U-turn.

'And I'll have to get the bus to the station and then a train and then the Tube,' I said.

What I'd do once I got to work, if I needed to get myself to any viewings, I'd have to wait and see. Walk? Jump on a Boris bike or a Lime scooter? Get an Uber I could ill afford?

In any event, turning up late and carless was preferable to not turning up at all.

I kissed Clara goodbye, wiped the red lipstick print from her cheek and climbed out of the relative warmth of Portia to brave the elements.

'God, what a vile day,' I muttered to myself. My coat was no match for the rain, and the gusty wind threatened to blow my umbrella inside out, or take me parachuting up over the rooftops like a grumpy second-rate Mary Poppins.

Grimly, I joined the scattering of commuters battling towards the bus stop. It was only a few minutes' walk, but by the time I reached it, my shoes were wet through and my coat sodden. And, inevitably, all the space beneath the shelter was occupied, people packed in like sardines, even around the edges where the rain drove in so hard it was barely a shelter at all.

Fighting to keep my umbrella angled into the wind, I took my phone out and checked when the bus was due. Predictably, I'd just missed one going in the right direction, and there wasn't another for ten minutes. Cars whooshed past, sending tsunamis of water over the pavement, wetting my shoes even more. My hand on my umbrella was white with cold, my sodden tights sticking to my legs.

I peered into the distance, praying that the app was wrong and the bus would magically appear. Instead, I saw a cyan

Transit van approaching. To my surprise, it stopped right in front of me, the passenger door swung open and a voice called, 'Rowan! Get in.'

It was Alex. Mr Smiley Blue-Eyes to the rescue, not on a white horse but in a turquoise Transit van.

I hesitated for a second. All my knowledge of what was safe and sensible told me that this was categorically not. Even in broad daylight – at least as broad as it got on an overcast winter morning – accepting lifts from strangers was crazy. Clara had known that since she was six. Absolutely anything could happen to me.

Apart from spending a few precious minutes alone with Alex, which felt like a prize worth taking just about any risk for.

And traffic was building up behind the stationary van. A car horn honked impatiently.

'Come on,' he urged.

And, without another thought, I wrestled my umbrella closed and scrambled damply up into the passenger seat. The wind almost snatched the door from my hands, but I wrenched it closed.

Alex grinned at me from under the peak of his baseball cap. 'Lovely weather for ducks.'

'I don't know about that.' I tried to catch my breath. 'Only if they like surfing.'

'On your way to work?'

'Yes, but Portia – my car – wouldn't start, so I was waiting for a bus to the station.'

'Portia?'

'It's her – its – name. Kind of a joke.'

'The green Fiesta?'

Shit, he's a stalker.

Then I realised that he'd have seen the car in my numbered bay when he parked his van. Still potentially a stalker, but more likely just observant.

'That's right. I've no clue what's wrong. I'll need to get it towed, I suppose. And then the mechanic will see me coming and charge me a fortune for something that actually takes five minutes to fix.'

He laughed. 'Always the way, isn't it? I sold my car a while back and cycle everywhere now. But I guess that's not always practical.'

He glanced at my high-heeled shoes and pencil skirt. He was right, of course – there was no way I could cycle anywhere in my work clothes without showing the whole of the West End my knickers.

But I wasn't going to say that to him, obviously.

'I'm an estate agent, you see. I have to get around town quite a bit during the day.'

'You're based in Central London?'

'Yes, in Mayfair.' Then I added hastily, 'But I don't expect you to drive me all the way there. It would take ages, and you'd end up being late for work.'

'I'd started my round already. Did my first drop just after seven – I just happened to be passing and saw you, and you looked like you could do with a lift.'

'It's really kind of you.' I felt the stilted awkwardness you always feel when driving with a stranger – like when you try to make conversation with a cab driver to be polite, and he either blanks you completely or starts giving you chapter and verse about his cryptocurrency investments, and you spend the rest of the journey quietly dying inside and wishing you'd never said anything.

Not that I had any reason to suspect that of Alex. I glanced sideways at him, taking advantage of his eyes being on the road to study his profile. He had a nice nose: straight and neither too big nor too small. Even when he was concentrating on driving, there was a slight smile on his lips. And the lashes framing his blue eyes were ridiculously long. His hands on the steering wheel were strong and almost elegant, and I could see the hard muscles of his thighs beneath his jeans.

Then he stopped at a traffic light, turned and caught me staring at him, and grinned.

'Don't worry,' he said. 'I'm not going to abduct you. I just thought if you're going into Mayfair, it would be easier if I dropped you at Brixton than Streatham.'

I'd been so busy staring at him, I hadn't realised we'd passed the station.

'Are you sure it's no trouble?' I asked.

'No trouble at all. I'll be working into the evening today anyway, with it being so busy in the run-up to Christmas.'

'Do you have anything nice planned for the day?' I asked politely. 'Christmas, I mean? Spending it with your family?'

I imagined Alex sitting by a roaring fire, maybe with a baby on his lap, a doting grandmother looking on as a smiling young woman – because how would he be with someone who didn't smile as easily and warmly as he did? – supervised a toddler trundling a toy train across the floor.

'I'm not sure, to be honest,' he said. 'I might be here, I might be up in Glasgow. Depends how things pan out. Anyway, being Scottish, Hogmanay's a bigger deal than Christmas. How about you?'

'I'm not sure either,' I admitted. 'Clara – that's my daughter – is spending it with her dad. So it'll probably just be me on my own.'

Me and my selection boxes, and probably an extra-large bottle of gin. Festive AF.

He looked at me again, sideways under the peak of his cap. His eyes were very blue, but he wasn't smiling.

'I reckon any special day on your own – whether it's Christmas or a birthday or whatever – is great if that's the way you want it to be. If you don't, not so great.'

'You're right.' I heaved a sigh that seemed to come out of

nowhere but was so deep it fogged up the windscreen in front of my face. 'Still, there's always next year, right?'

'There's always *this* year,' he said. 'Shame to have all that build-up with the advent calendar and then nothing on the actual day.'

'Ah, it's okay. It isn't that big a deal. It's only one day.'

We'd arrived now in the centre of Brixton. The Christmas lights were sparkling, and a massive tree stood in the central square. Outside the station, a Salvation Army band was playing, seemingly undaunted by the weather, their brass instruments bright in the gloom.

'Will you be okay from here?' Alex asked.

'Sure,' I said. 'Thanks so much for the lift. It made a big difference.'

'Want me to come and take a look at your car? I'm no expert, but if it's something basic, I could maybe help.'

'Really? Are you sure?'

'Sure. This evening, after I've finished my round?'

I wanted to demur, to tell him he didn't have to spend his time rummaging around in Portia's innards (although to be honest, if he'd offered to rummage around inside my pants, I wouldn't have said no), but the traffic was building up behind the van and I heard the angry blare of a horn. There was no time for me to linger, so I thanked him again and got out, not bothering to put up my brolly for the short dash through the rain, the music of the band following me down the escalator like a fanfare.

CHAPTER EIGHTEEN

Alex pulled up the van at Curlew Court, parking on a double yellow line so as to be close to the lift. It had bloody better be working today, he thought; he had fifteen parcels to deliver to the block, which would mean multiple trips and he'd prefer not to have to go up and down the stairs repeatedly, quadriceps or no quadriceps.

He'd been on the road since seven that morning. He'd had abuse hurled at him by a customer whose neighbour had signed for a delivery of a Louis Vuitton handbag but then denied all knowledge of it. He'd had his hand agonisingly swiped by the claws of the cat who lived at 34 Sycamore Road, whose greatest pleasure in life appeared to be waiting on the doormat for unsuspecting fingers to appear through the letterbox. He'd interrupted a dodgy-looking bloke with a crowbar hanging around the van and had to muster up his most threatening, 'Oi! What do you think you're doing?' before the guy, to Alex's relief, had fled.

Alex took his job seriously but not seriously enough to get beaten up by a member of the criminal underworld for it, that was for sure.

He rolled his shoulders, stiff from driving, or carrying boxes, or probably both. He was knackered and hungry and needed a piss, but he had a good three hours' graft ahead of him before he'd get home – and then another few hours at his laptop after that.

And at some point in between, he had a rescue mission to undertake on a car he had no idea how to fix.

What had possessed him, he wondered, to think that juggling the two parts of his life like this would be easy – fun, even, a new challenge, a learning experience?

He was learning, he had to admit that. Next time he put a card through the door of the house where that monster cat lived, he'd use the leather motorcycle gloves he'd brought along for the purpose.

Rowan Connell's little rust bucket of a car was parked in its usual space, but he knew that didn't mean she could be home. He'd knock at the door anyway – public transport might have got her back from town earlier than usual, or the daughter might be home, and she could sign for today's parcel, which was too large to fit through the letterbox. If the girl wasn't in, it would have to be left with a neighbour.

But, he decided, he'd do the deliveries to the other flats in the block first, just in case Rowan arrived home while he was there.

Before getting out of the van, he checked his phone – his personal one, not the basic Android model provided by Pegasus Express. There were several emails that he'd have to deal with in the evening. There was a WhatsApp from his mate Carlo about meeting up for drinks before Christmas. He scanned his Twitter feed, but there was nothing there to hold his interest.

But there was a missed call and a voice message from Ailsa. He pictured her, home on her own, looking out at the steadily falling rain and wishing she could go out for a walk. Flicking through the channels on the television, trying to concentrate on a book but not being able to stay comfortable for long enough to focus. Briefly getting up to pace the room, her long hair hanging down her back like Rapunzel's in the fairy tale – or like Rowan's when he'd seen her with it loose, not pinned up the way she wore it for work.

When he'd suggested to Ailsa that she watch something on Netflix, she'd sighed theatrically and said, 'I've *watched* Netflix.'

'Then you'll just have to watch it again,' Alex had told her callously.

He listened to her message but decided a response could wait – she was okay; she just wanted to moan. Not that he blamed her for that, but for now, he had a job of work to do.

Grimly, Alex got out of the warm cab into the rain, opened the back of the van and heaved out the first of the packages. It was large, heavy and unwieldy – some guys in his position would refuse to deliver it to the door, but not him. And not here. If number 34 had splashed out on a new TV for Christmas, he wasn't going to leave it down here to get wet – or nicked.

He headed for the lift – broken again. Rowan and her neighbours could do with a spot of assertiveness training, he reckoned – the management of this estate clearly needed a firm kick up the backside.

On the stairs, he passed a woman struggling with a baby in a buggy, a toddler and a child in school uniform who must have been about five, all of them drooping with tiredness after their long day, apart from the baby, who was screaming blue murder.

'Wait here,' he said, panting past them. 'I'll give you a hand when I'm done with this.'

After he'd delivered the TV safely to its new owner and helped the family to their flat, he returned to the van and made two more trips with smaller parcels.

He saved Rowan Connell's for last.

He was pretty sure that what he was about to do was a sackable offence, but he'd made his mind up – and Alex prided himself on acting on his decisions first and regretting them, if that turned out to be necessary, afterwards.

Or learning from them, as he preferred to see it.

He jumped back into the driver's seat, retrieved his personal phone from the jack where it was charging, and held the parcel carefully up to catch the light, since the sun had set a while back. Quickly, he photographed the label on the back of the box (the one on the front, Rowan's address, he already knew by heart), checked that the image was clear and legible, and swung back out of the van, locking it behind him.

He hurried up the stairs, knocked on the door and waited, but there was no answer. Instead, he handed the parcel over to Rowan's neighbour with a warm smile.

CHAPTER NINETEEN

By nine that evening, I'd pretty much given up hope. Clara had eaten dinner and retreated to her room. I'd had a shower (leaving her with strict instructions to listen for the door) and put on my pyjamas, and I was pretty much ready to go to bed.

Alex hadn't ever meant to come, I told myself. It was just one of those things people say to be nice. Or perhaps he had genuinely meant to come, but life had got in the way, and I was – understandably – way down his order of priorities. I was just some random woman, after all, one of hundreds he saw on his rounds every day. He probably smiled at all of them. He probably had quite the fan club.

Probably, if I searched on social media, I'd find #MrSmiley-BlueEyes trending like mad in my local area, hordes of lonely single women placing multiple online orders for things they had no intention of keeping, just to feel their ovaries flutter when that cyan van pulled up and those long, booted legs swung out.

Also, I'd definitely not changed into my nightwear on the basis that he was more, not less, likely to show up than if I'd blow-dried my hair and put on the slinky underwear I didn't actually possess.

And of course, I categorically was not overthinking this situation in any way, shape or form.

Which would explain why, when the door knocker sounded at ten past nine, I one hundred per cent did not jump out of my skin and spend thirty seconds running from the living room to my bedroom and back, wondering if I had time to change.

Okay, I did. And there was no time to change. If I attempted it, especially given the polite gentleness of the tap on the door, he'd have assumed I'd given up and gone to bed, and taken himself straight off again.

'Oh shit, I'm sorry, Rowan,' he said as soon as he saw me. 'It's too late. I feel bad. I would've been earlier, but my round took forever, and the traffic was terrible getting the van back to the depot.'

I'd never seen him without his Pegasus cap on before. His hair was dark brown, shiny as the conkers that had carpeted the paths of the park a few weeks back. I caught myself gazing at him in wonder, thinking that no one should have the right to be so effortlessly gorgeous. 'God, you don't have to apologise. You came. Don't tell me you cycled here?'

'Came on my sleigh,' he deadpanned.

For a second I gawped at him, then I laughed. 'Has Santa brought me jump leads?'

'Don't have any,' he said. 'Besides, we'd need another car to connect them to. I'm relying on the power of my manly intuition that enables me to diagnose mechanical problems at a glance. Oh, and Google. And a torch.'

Strong work, Rowan, I told myself. *You could have googled the problem yourself but you let a man come and help instead. Striking a blow for the sisterhood, right there.*

'I'm really grateful,' I said. 'You honestly didn't have to do this.'

'Well, since I'm here, why don't we get the show on the road?'

I shoved my feet into a pair of ancient Ugg boots that I wore to take the recycling out, snatched my keys off the shelf and stepped outside. My dressing gown – a shabby towelling affair that had once been pink but was now a depressing surgical-stocking beige – was no match for the cold.

'Are you sure you don't need a coat?' Alex asked.

'I'm fine.' I clenched my jaw to stop my teeth from chattering and hurried ahead of Alex to the mercifully operational lift.

We descended in silence and made our way across the car park to Portia, who to my eye looked somewhat forlorn, hunched in her slot between the covered hulk of a motorbike and my neighbour Sarita's newish Toyota.

'So what happened when you tried to start it?' Alex asked.

I shrugged. 'The engine kind of turned over, but nothing happened. And then I tried a couple more times and she – it – still wouldn't start. I didn't keep trying because I didn't want to drain the battery.'

'So jump leads would've been kind of redundant,' Alex said. 'Why don't you hop in and give it – her – a go?'

I nodded, glad of the chance to get out of the wind and the icy drizzle that had persisted all day. Not that the car was any warmer – the seat was so cold it felt almost damp under my bottom when I sat down.

'Open the bonnet,' Alex mouthed through the window, adding a hand gesture in case I couldn't hear or was too thick to understand.

For a second, the sight of his cold, cheerful face, lit by the strings of fairy lights the management committee had strung up between the arc lights a few days before, as if an expanse of tarmac could somehow be transformed into Santa's grotto through strategic festive illumination, stopped me in my tracks.

Did any man – any man whatsoever – have any right to look

so hot, especially in a high-vis jacket with his hair flattened by a cycling helmet and damp with rain? And more to the point, how could any normal individual respond with such cheerful composure to a near-stranger's trivial dilemma that had caused them to ride a bicycle across London in the rain late at night to attempt a rescue they were entirely unqualified to carry out?

It was almost a relief when he raised the car's hood, slotting the prop into place, and disappeared from my view.

'Come on then, Portia,' I said, as I always did when fitting the key in the ignition. 'Here we go.'

As I'd been taught when learning to drive years ago, I checked the handbrake, waggled the gearstick to make sure it was in neutral and depressed the clutch – a sequence that had passed into my muscle memory long ago.

And then I turned the key.

With a couple of splutters and a muted roar, Portia's engine obediently coughed to life. At the same time, I heard a series of human coughs from behind the open bonnet, and Alex's voice calling, 'Rev a bit more.'

I obeyed, then, conscious of the neighbours and the environment, killed the engine and stepped out, feeling like the biggest idiot in history.

'I don't know what to say,' I admitted. 'It seems fine.'

Alex nodded. 'In my expert opinion – well, according to Google – you most likely flooded the engine trying to start it earlier. Happens with older cars on cold days, apparently.'

'But I dragged you all the way out here on this awful night for nothing.' I was so mortified I'd even forgotten I was wearing pyjamas and Uggs. 'I could have done this tomorrow morning and it would have been okay. I can't believe it. It's almost like I—'

'Invented a problem with your car, hacked into the Pegasus routing system – which admittedly wouldn't be that hard; it's as leaky as your carburettor – to make sure I was in the right place at the right time, then used your evil feminine wiles to get me here so I'd see you in your jim-jams? Yeah, that's exactly how I think it played out.'

I stood there for a moment, the cold, wet air meeting my face like an almost welcome slap of reality, and then I started to laugh. Alex did too.

'I'm sorry,' I said. 'No matter how many times I say that, I won't feel like any less of a muppet. I'd offer to buy you a drink, but...'

'Going into a pub dressed like that would make you feel like a lot more of a muppet,' he said. 'And me too. Guy in work gear walks into a bar with oil on his fingers accompanied by a beautiful woman in a' – he leaned in closer and peered at the embroidery on the breast of my robe – 'Paddington Bear dressing gown. And the barman says...'

'It doesn't bear thinking about,' I admitted, shivering.

'You need to get into the warm,' Alex said. 'And I'm running late for a dinner appointment. Shall we never speak of this again?'

'Let's not,' I agreed. 'But thank you. Seriously. It was a massively kind thing you did tonight, and I'm so sorry to have wasted your time.'

'Rowan,' he said, 'you never waste my time.'

He flashed his smile at me, and I basked in the warmth of it and the glow of happiness his words gave me, knowing I'd replay them in my head over and over. *You never waste my time.* And the way my name sounded when he said it, like it was the most special name ever.

Then he shouldered his rucksack and turned, pulling on his cycling helmet before crouching to unlock the bicycle he'd apparently secured to the railings by the stairs earlier. I'd have loved to linger for a moment to admire the view of his pistoning thighs and tight glutes as he pedalled away, but I was too cold.

It was only once I was in bed, reliving the horrific cringiness of the experience – which Alex's calm competence had somehow made less cringy – that I remembered his parting words.

Dinner appointment. What dinner appointment, at almost ten at night? With who?

CHAPTER TWENTY

Over the past two days, I'd called about a third of Kimberley's –
well, it was mine now, I supposed – app database, with mixed
results that included a broken fingernail, a breakout of red spots
on my cheek from the headset and a persistent ringing in my
right ear – as well as four viewings, one of which I reckoned was
almost certain to lead to an offer. On Thursday, I showed Mrs
Choudhury, my original applicant, three more properties, one
of which she was dead keen to make an offer on. But when I
returned in excitement to the office, I learned from a smirking
Brett that it had been mysteriously withdrawn from the market.

Clara seemed to have recovered from her cold, but had
succumbed instead to a major fit of teenage grumps, which
seemed to have begun after a long call with her dad the night
before. That morning, in an attempt to lift her spirits, I'd
presented her with the hair treatment that had been
Monday's advent calendar gift, but she emerged after a long
shower and even longer with my hair straighteners in her
bedroom to announce that it was rubbish and had left her hair
looking like she'd washed it in chip fat. Although I could see
that she hadn't rinsed the treatment out properly, and my own

hair could seriously have done with it, I managed to say nothing.

That day, I at least managed to leave the office on time, and I was swinging Portia – purring and obliging now that she'd so comprehensively shown me up in front of Alex – into my parking space when the familiar Pegasus van pulled up in the visitor space next to me.

Alex swung out, then hurried to the back doors to load up his parcels, and I summoned the lift and waited for him.

'Afternoon,' he said cheerily, his blue eyes just visible between the peak of his cap and the large box he was carrying. 'Gorgeous day, isn't it?'

'Isn't it? There was frost everywhere this morning, but once the sun came out it was lovely.'

Together, we glanced towards the west, where the last of the sunset was glowing, surrounded by dark fragments of cloud that reminded me of the black lace skirt I'd had as a teenage goth, and worn until it fell to pieces.

'Isn't that beautiful?' I asked.

'Beautiful,' he echoed – but I couldn't help noticing that he was looking not at the spectacular sky but at me.

Hold on, is he saying he thinks I'm beautiful? I felt a glow inside that had way more warmth to it than the setting sun.

Alex noticed my smile and returned it, and we stepped into the lift together. In the confined space, I could feel the heat of his body. The harsh fluorescent light highlighted the angles of his cheekbones and jaw, and illuminated the tufts of dark brown hair that showed underneath his blue cap. I pressed the number seven and waited for him to ask me to do the same for which-ever floor he was headed to, but he didn't.

'You're not going up to the top?' I asked.

'No, I... I thought I'd drop your parcel first. Unless you'd rather I didn't?'

I realised that I'd been so distracted by the sunset, then by being in the lift with him, that it hadn't occurred to me to offer to take my parcel and save him a few seconds on his busy round.

'Of course. Thank you. I'm sorry, I should have offered to take it.'

'Don't worry, this lift journey's been the clear highlight of my day so far.'

'Sorry the rest of it's been so pants.'

'It's been great. Just this is better.'

The lift jerked to a stop, and Alex followed me the few steps to my front door and waited while I found my keys and twisted open the two locks. When I turned to face him again, he was holding my parcel: a flat box a little bigger than an A4 sheet of paper.

'Here you go.' He handed it over, then snapped a picture of me in the doorway as usual.

'Thank you.'

He hesitated, and I added, 'So should I open it?'

Alex glanced at his watch. 'Go on then.'

I stepped inside, dumped my bag and keys on the shelf, then turned back to him and pulled off one glove so I could grip the cardboard tab and tear open the box. Inside was a flat, rectangular object, clumsily wrapped in too much tissue paper so it was bunched at the corners, skewed pieces of Sellotape holding down the edges.

'Looks like a picture,' Alex said, leaning towards me.

'Yep.' I turned it over, but the thickness of the wrapping obscured whatever image might be inside the frame.

Most likely it was an adorable baby photo of Clara, or a picture of me, Naomi, Abbie and Kate on some long-ago night out, dressed up to the nines, toasting each other with cocktails, having the time of our lives.

'It's okay,' Alex said. 'You can wait until I've gone.'

I gasped out a surprised laugh. It felt almost as if he'd been reading my mind – knowing that as I scanned through the possibilities of what I might be about to see, what Alex would make of it had been at the top of my mind.

'It's fine,' I said. 'I'll open it. I wouldn't want to deprive you of the highlight of your afternoon.'

I tore open the tissue paper, turned the picture over in my hands and looked at it.

'Oh,' I gasped. 'Oh my God. How the hell did they get hold of this?'

In the frame was a clear, professionally shot and artfully retouched photograph of a woman in a low-cut, emerald-green evening dress, standing in front of a sparkling Christmas tree, a champagne flute in her hand. Her full lips were painted a glossy scarlet. Long dark hair tumbled down her back in natural waves, blown by a wind machine somewhere out of sight. Her eyes looked almost green too, her skin flawless, at once porcelain pale and glowing. Her teeth showed in what looked like a smile of pure excitement and joy.

'Crikey,' Alex said. 'Is that—?'

'Me.' The blush I'd felt begin was really going for it now; I could sense my cheeks flaming, and my hands felt too big, as if I might drop the picture and shatter its glass on my doorstep. 'I did a bit of modelling, ages ago, before I had Clara. This was on the cover of a fashion catalogue. It's probably the most expensive frock I've ever worn and so I was kind of...'

'Proud of it? I bet you were.' He leaned in closer – so close I could see the shadow of stubble on his jawline. I imagined how it might feel against my skin if he kissed me, and my blush deepened. 'You looked amazing.'

Looked. I noted the past tense.

'Yeah, well, those were the days, I guess.'

'You haven't actually changed,' he went on, quite unruffled, as if it was what he'd been going to say anyway. 'Just your hair's a bit shorter now. How old are you there? If you don't mind me asking.'

'Twenty-one, I think. God. Closer to Clara's age than mine now.'

'So is she planning on following her mum down any catwalks?'

'No! Jesus, no. I mean, it's her life and I'd support her in whatever dreams she wants to pursue, but... Still no.'

I thought of my beautiful daughter, perfect in every possible way. I thought how, just recently, she'd had one of those weird teenage growth spurts that had left her long and slender in the waist, but her legs hadn't yet caught up, and I remembered noticing that with a pang of sadness-tinged love, because that was the way Paul and his family were proportioned – but also relief, because as long as her shape stayed that way, no modelling agency would touch her with a bargepole.

'You didn't enjoy it?' Alex's question jerked me away from my thoughts of my daughter – and her father.

'Oh, at first I did. I mean, imagine. I was fifteen when I first signed to an agency. I got to go to London on my own, and later to Paris and Madrid and even New York. I thought I was living the dream.'

'Wow. That's a lot for a fifteen-year-old. Impressive stuff.'

'It was pretty amazing. Hard work, too, but cool all the same.'

'You must have some amazing stories.'

'What, like the time I was in a lift with a guy and I only realised afterwards when my mate told me that it was literally Bono? I mean, imagine. I hadn't even noticed.'

Alex laughed. 'I bet he was gutted by that.'

'Hey, at least I didn't shove in front of him, like, "Don't you know who I am?"'

'Yeah, that could have been awkward.'

We met each other's eyes, both half-laughing, and again I felt that... thing fizz between us, like an electric shock only nice.

'Good times,' I said, hoping my scarlet cheeks had faded a bit. 'I made some money and I had a ball. Until...'

'Until what?'

'Until I got too...'

You've got too fat. Like it was yesterday, I heard my agent's voice. The woman who'd supported and nurtured me; who I'd come to see as a kind of mother figure. There'd been nothing nurturing in her words then, only cold reality. *You need to lose a stone. Then we can try and get you some catalogue work. They'll take older, porkier girls.*

'Too big,' I finished. And then I saw a tear splat down on the glass covering the picture.

I hadn't even realised I was about to cry, and now I was. Proper ugly sobs that made me hold the frame up so the picture covered my face.

'Hey,' Alex said gently. 'Hey, Rowan. Are you okay? Do you need a glass of water?'

I nodded, the frame nodding with me. Alex put his hand around my elbow, not quite touching me, but so close I could feel the warmth coming off his skin, and guided me inside. Blindly, I stumbled to the sofa and sat down, and a few seconds later he was standing over me, a dripping glass of tap water in his hand.

'Thanks. Sorry to be such an idiot. It just... brought it all back, you know.'

Alex sort of hovered over me for a second, then he sat down next to me, not touching me but close enough to – and close enough for me to want him to.

'The disappointment?' he asked. 'Having to leave behind something you loved?'

'Yeah, that. But also...' I put the photo down on the coffee table, face down, then turned it the right way up again and pulled a tissue from the box we'd taken to keeping there since Clara had hit puberty and started crying at everything – and I mean everything, not just *Britain's Got Talent* and obvious things like that, but the news, *Antiques Roadshow* and even sometimes the weather forecast. 'Also, as a profession, it's kind of brutal. You're judged all the time. And trying to lose weight because I was told I needed to if I wanted to carry on working. It was... not fun.'

The cabbage soup diet. Oh my God. It had felt like I spent months on the damn thing. I could recite the regimen chapter and verse, even now: fruit on Monday, jacket potato on Tuesday, fruit on Wednesday, bananas on Thursday – and all the rest of the time, endless bowls of soup that stank out the kitchen and made me bloat so much I feared I might explode and fart so much I worried I might levitate.

But I definitely wasn't going to tell Alex that.

'It was horrible, not just being hungry all the time but feeling I was punishing myself and still not being good enough. Remember those Stairmaster things you used to get in the gym? I did three hours on one once. The soles of my feet literally went numb.'

I blew my nose and drank some water, and Alex cracked a smile.

'Not all glamour then?' he asked.

I shook my head. 'And some of the people... when I was younger and doing catwalk stuff, it wasn't so bad. We were all together and we looked out for one another. Even when we went to parties and there was booze and stuff, the other girls were always there and it felt okay, you know? But later on, some of the photographers and directors – ugh.'

'I hope...' Alex cleared his throat. 'Did anything bad happen?'

'Not really. I mean, not compared to some of the MeToo horror stories you hear. But being manhandled, treated like a piece of meat, groped a bit. It didn't help when I was feeling pretty shit about myself anyway.'

'So you decided to stop?'

I gulped more water. 'I met Paul, my ex. And he – he wasn't exactly the jealous type, but he didn't like it. Other men looking at me. In the flesh and in photos. So I decided to retrain, and I did a make-up artist course and liked it, and that was that.'

Alex looked down at the picture again, and my eyes followed his. I looked so happy, so radiant. No one, seeing it, could have guessed that I'd been so hungry I'd almost fainted, and the self-control it had taken not to neck glass after glass of the sparkling apple juice they'd used instead of actual champagne.

'Your friends don't know, right?' he asked. 'Or they wouldn't have sent you the photo?'

Of course, I realised, he was right. 'Nor gone to all the trouble of finding it and getting the catalogue masthead and cover lines Photoshopped off and having it framed and everything.'

'So you never told them?'

'No. I mean, I told them about having been a model and everything. But not really about why I stopped.'

I cast my mind back, trying to put myself in the shoes of twenty-three-year-old me, going for that first drink in the pub with Kate, Abbie, Naomi and Zara (who had still been part of the gang back then, before everything changed and her life zoomed out of our orbit), while our boyfriends played five-a-side football in the rain. We were meant to be supporting them, but it hadn't taken long to realise that – loved-up as we were – none of us could be arsed.

I remembered how impressed I'd been by them: by Abbie's cleverness, Kate's high-powered job, Naomi's sparkiness, Zara's glamour. I wanted them to like me, even admire me. I wanted to paint myself in the best possible light, and saying I'd effectively put myself out of a job because my arse had got too big wasn't going to hack it.

Alex nodded. 'That makes sense. Everything you've told me about them – they sound pretty amazing. Not like the kind of people who'd do something to make you cry.'

I looked down at the tissue in my hand. My tears had passed now, along with the shock of seeing the picture, and the emotions it had brought back felt almost distant, ready to be put back in the box of long-ago memories where they belonged.

'It was kind of a massive overreaction,' I said, managing a shaky laugh. 'Thanks for listening to me ramble on.'

'All part of the service.' He stood, and I felt his hand rest on my shoulder for a brief second, the spark of electricity I'd imagined earlier shooting through me for real.

'I'm sorry – you didn't even get yourself a glass of water,' I stammered. 'Would you like one? Or a cup of tea or something?'

'I'd love to, but I can't stay. I need to...'

'I've made you late,' I realised. 'You said you had loads of deliveries still to do, and I've been yammering on about my not-so-glamorous past.'

'Don't give it another thought, Rowan. I expect I'll see you tomorrow.'

'I hope so.' I stood too, and followed him to the door. 'Bye, Alex. And thanks again.'

We stood there for a second, and I felt every single cell in my body screaming out for him to touch me again. The brief moment when his hand had been in contact with my elbow had felt so potent, I was almost sure I'd imagined it. If he did it again, perhaps I'd know it had been real.

But he didn't. He flashed his amazing smile at me again, and I let myself bask for a second in the glow of his blue eyes, then opened the door.

I watched him stride off, the large parcel he'd left outside my door fortunately un-stolen and safely in his arms. Then, when he'd disappeared into the stairwell, I returned to the living room and looked at the picture for a bit before placing it on the mantelpiece above the gas fire.

When Clara got home from her school play rehearsal, she clocked it straight away.

'Jesus Christ, Mum, what the hell is that dress you're wearing? It looks like Nana's curtains.'

I laughed. 'It does a bit.'

Then she added kindly, 'But you look beautiful. Great hair.'

Later that evening, once my daughter was in bed, I inspected the picture again, and then I went to the bathroom and gazed in the mirror. My eyes were the same. My lips were the same, and I looked the same when I smiled. My hair was shorter now, and my cheeks had lost the sculpted hollows they'd had then. The hollows beneath my collarbones had gone too – and good riddance, given the days when nothing except cigarettes and salad passed my lips it had taken to achieve them.

But maybe, maybe, some of the glamour I'd had then had stuck around. And maybe seeing the picture would help Alex to see some of it in me now.

CHAPTER TWENTY-ONE

Clara's bad mood continued into the next day, and into the evening, when she retreated into her bedroom as soon as she got back from school. She didn't even emerge, as she usually did, when she heard Alex's knock on the door to see what that day's parcel contained. I emerged, however. I emerged like anything. I hadn't even realised until I heard the knock how excited I'd been for it, how much I'd been looking forward to the moment when I opened the door and saw his smile.

'Hey, Rowan,' he said, looking almost as delighted to see me as I was to see him.

'Hey, Alex.'

'Delivery for you.'

'Me? Seriously?'

'Yep. Look, it says right here on the label, Rowan Connell.'

Our eyes met and locked, and we both started to laugh, almost as if this silly pantomime was something we'd practised.

He handed over the box and, without asking whether he wanted to stay and see what was inside, I tore it open and tipped a pleasingly large glass bottle with an eyedropper top into my hand.

'What's that then?' he asked.

'It's a hyaluronic acid boosting serum.' I held it out for him to see. 'Full size too. It's a good 'un.'

'Wow. Hyalur-what? What do you do with it?'

'Put it on your face. It makes your moisturiser work better, so your skin appears plumped and glowing.'

'Blimey. And how much would that cost if you bought it on its own?'

'I'm not sure. Maybe seventy quid? That advent calendar's fantastic value.' I turned the bottle over in my hand again, gloatingly. Eternal youth was literally within my grasp.

'Does it work?'

'Um... I'm not sure, to be honest. I expect so.'

'How would you know? Would you, like, take a selfie every day for a month and see if it made a difference?'

'I expect some people do. Beauty bloggers and people like that. But no, I'd just slap it on and look in the mirror and be like, "Ooooh, I'm glowing!"'

He laughed. 'Surely that would just be because the stuff's wet?'

'Well, yes, but it... Look, stop doubting. It's Christmas. We're all meant to be thinking about virgin birth and a guy who flies round the whole world in one night pulled by reindeer.'

'When you put it like that, believing face cream makes you look nice doesn't seem like that much of a stretch.'

'Exactly. So when you see me tomorrow...'

'I'll have my shades on, so as not to be blinded by your radiance.'

'Good plan.'

He hesitated for a second, still smiling. I smiled back, and felt that... thing between us. That unmistakeable attraction. The awareness that I didn't just fancy the (taut, muscular) arse off the man, I actually liked him.

The thought made me feel like my heart or my stomach or

something had suddenly become too big to fit in my chest, making it difficult to catch my breath.

'I'll be off then,' he said. 'See you tomorrow, I guess.'

'See you tomorrow.'

'And, Rowan…'

'That's me.'

'You look pretty glowy right now, you know. Just thought I'd mention it.'

Before I could open my mouth to thank him, he'd turned and hurried off, his bag swinging from one broad shoulder.

I practically skipped back into the flat, rushing straight to the bathroom to look in the mirror to see whether what he'd said was true; to try and see for myself what he'd seen.

But I looked much the same as usual, apart from the cheesy grin I couldn't seem to wipe off my face. I had a bath, put a mask (sadly inferior to the one I'd donated to my daughter) on my hair, which emerged shiny and bouncy as promised, and smoothed the serum onto my face underneath my moisturiser.

I was definitely glowing. One hundred per cent.

But when I went into the kitchen to make a much-needed gin and tonic and there were no glasses to be found – not in the cupboard where they belonged, not in the sink, not on the draining board, not in the living room – I realised something was going to have to give.

There was respecting my daughter's privacy, and then there was drinking G&T out of a coffee mug.

So I knocked on her door, waited a second or two, and when there was no answer, pushed the door gently open.

Clara was lying on her bed, headphones in her ears, staring at her phone. I tried not to notice the chaos in the room: the clothes piled on the floor, bed and desk (a bad omen for homework), the drawers half-open, more clothes spilling out of them, the puddle of what looked like foundation on the windowsill.

And, in my initial scan of the room, at least six dirty glasses standing and lying on the surfaces, one half-full of sour milk, which I guessed accounted for the strong, yoghurty smell in the air.

'Evening, sweetie,' I said, as breezily as I could. 'I was just after a glass.'

Clara gestured, her eyes not leaving her phone. 'Crack on.'

Jesus. Okay, you're not going to talk to me.

'I thought we might splash out and have a takeaway tonight. Since it's Friday. What do you reckon?'

'Whatever.'

'Pizza? Curry? Burgers?'

Now she did turn her head to look at me.

'I don't care. Just leave me alone.'

'Okay.' *Bright and breezy, Rowan, bright and breezy.* 'I'll order and let you know when it's here.'

I collected the glasses, Clara watching me warily out of the corner of her eye lest I desecrate her sanctum by picking up a pair of knickers off the floor, and left. I washed up the glasses, fixed myself a strong drink and sat in front of the telly, scrolling without enthusiasm through the Deliveroo app on my phone.

Friday night takeaways had always been a treat for me and Clara, a chance to eat off our laps in front of a movie, occasionally chatting about our week or commenting on the film, or just sitting in companionable silence. When she was younger, she used to come and snuggle up next to me; more recently, she'd graciously allowed me to tickle her ankles.

I hoped that the promise of junk food and trashy entertainment would be enough to bring her out of her shell tonight.

Parenting teenagers was tough – I'd known it would be. And being a teenager was tougher. At least – so far anyway – Clara hadn't got into drugs or found an unsuitable boyfriend or been exchanging messages with creepy older men on Instagram. Not that I knew of anyway.

Mostly, we got along okay, I thought, broccoli face notwithstanding.

But now something appeared to be bothering my daughter that went beyond normal teenage angst. Something must have happened – maybe a bust-up with a friend, or with Jonny, whose name I couldn't recall hearing for the past couple of days.

Or maybe, I thought, the reality of Paul's upcoming marriage was starting to sink in. However much Clara liked and admired Hayley – and who could blame her, I thought rather sourly – it was a big adjustment, a seismic shift from her dad having a girlfriend to her having a stepmother.

I placed a random order for a couple of pizzas – ham and pineapple for me (I know, I know – say what you like, but it's the food of the gods), vegan deluxe for Clara, a portion of garlic doughballs and a tub of Ben & Jerry's Minter Wonderland, knowing my daughter had form for abandoning her no-dairy rule when dessert was involved.

And then I messaged Paul. Like I say, our relationship had always been good – too good, in ways I was trying my hardest to stop thinking about. But when it came to communication, we'd kept to the basics in recent years: what time I was dropping Clara off, when her after-school activities were changing, the dates of sports competitions and parents' evenings, that sort of thing.

We'd certainly never, ever mentioned us having sex, and I wasn't about to open that can of worms.

Hey, I wrote. *How are things? I'm a bit worried about C.*

I waited. Paul had been online a few minutes before; hopefully he wasn't now off taking Hayley somewhere fancy for dinner or making one of the elaborate cocktails he prided himself on, or tied up on their bed for hours of kinky sex.

The thought made me wince, so I forced it away.

But, as I watched, he began typing.

Worried how?

She's being kind of offish. More offish than usual. Has she said anything to you? Anything going on at school?

Not that I know of.

There was a pause. I imagined him frowning down at his phone, the way he did, like it held the answer to the mysteries of the universe or something.

Then he started to type again, and a message flashed up a few seconds later.

I think she might be upset about the bridesmaids' dresses.

What bridesmaids' dresses?

You know, the frocks the girls are going to wear to walk up the aisle with Hayley.

FFS, Paul, I know what a bridesmaid is.

Yeah, well... Hold on, I'll call you.

I put on my coat and slipped outside the front door. Plugged into her headphones as she was, I still didn't want to risk Clara overhearing me discussing her and her moods with her father.

As I pulled the door to, I felt my phone vibrate in my hand and saw my ex's name on the screen.

'Paul?'

'Hi, Ro. I thought it might be easier to explain on the phone.'

'Yeah, so. The bridesmaids' dresses. Go on.'

'Hayley took Clara shopping last weekend. Well, not actually shopping, she said, because she's not ready to buy anything yet. More just looking, she said. She's set up moodboards and all that sh— all that stuff.'

'Right.'

'Anyway, so she and Clara went to some swanky shop in Kensington and Clara tried on a dress, and when they got in she was made up about it. Really excited.'

'Lovely. I can't see what the problem is.'

'Then Clara went on the website and looked at the price of the dress and she freaked out.'

'Why? Is it expensive?'

Though even if it was, I couldn't see why that would upset Clara. Surely having a gorgeous, expensive dress from a posh shop would make her happy?

'Obviously.' Paul huffed a sigh that almost burst my eardrum. 'I tell you what, this wedding malarkey doesn't come cheap. That's why I had to tell Clara I'd cut her allowance.'

'You what?'

'She's so bloody materialistic,' Paul blustered. 'It's all about the stuff her friends have and she doesn't. Like her life's over because I can't buy her an iPhone 12.'

'Paul, for God's sake! What did you do that for?'

'I told you, Rowan, money's tight. With the wedding and everything.'

'Look.' I took a deep breath, trying to force myself to be calm. 'Try and see this from Clara's point of view. You're willing to spend however much on a dress for her to wear to your wedding, but the everyday money you give her to spend on herself suddenly isn't there any more. How do you think that makes her feel?'

'So you make up the shortfall, then.'

'You know I can't.'

I felt torn between annoyance, frustration and disappointment in myself. Because Clara stayed with Paul an almost-equal amount of time, he paid me very little to help support her. And although he knew how I struggled to make ends meet, he insisted that he 'didn't want to be a Disney dad' and spoil her with things he knew I couldn't stretch to. For the first time, I wondered if he was motivated not by a desire for fairness but by something else. But he'd always given her a reasonably generous amount of spending money – until now, apparently.

'Can't she get a job?'

'She's fourteen, Paul! God, we don't send children up chimneys or down mines any more, in case you hadn't noticed.'

'Rowan, I don't think you understand.'

I couldn't see Paul, but I knew from his tone he was drawing himself up to his full height. Five foot eight and a half – he was very insistent on that half inch – always had been, even though it still left him a full inch and a half shorter than me.

'I'm not a bottomless pit of money. I've the car to run. My mortgage is horrific. And this wedding...'

I took another deep breath, exhaling silently this time. *So what if you decided to buy a four-bedroom house when you were single? How is your BMW my problem – or Clara's? And as for your bloody wedding...*

Just a few days before, if you'd asked me how I felt about Paul and Hayley's forthcoming nuptials, I'd have said I wished them both every happiness. Now, suddenly, the word 'bloody' had appeared in my mind in front of the word 'wedding', as if it had always been there.

'I can't tell you how to spend your money,' I said carefully. 'But I do think you might want to rethink this decision, for the sake of your relationship with Clara.'

'Don't tell me how to parent my own child!'

'I wasn't. I was only trying to help.'

With a pang of guilt, I remembered the bath oil I'd used, which I could have given to Clara. I thought of the time I spent chatting to my friends on WhatsApp, when I could have been trying to draw out my daughter's innermost thoughts from wherever she hid them. I thought of my hardline stance on cleaning her bedroom and wondered whether I was teaching her about personal accountability or just being a lazy mare.

And I thought – literally for the first time ever – *What if I were to meet someone? What if I were to have a new relationship, like Paul had with Hayley? How would Clara react to that?*

'Well, don't.' Paul sounded as surly as if he was a teenager himself.

'Okay. Thanks for calling and explaining what's going on. Now I need to go – our dinner's ready.'

In fact, the Deliveroo driver was emerging from the stairwell, narky and panting after climbing seven floors, but I wasn't going to let on to Paul that I hadn't been slaving over a hot pan of nourishing lentils.

'Fine. Bye, Rowan,' he said.

'Good night.'

I thanked the driver and went inside with our food, wondering how to initiate a conversation with Clara about what I'd learned. But she was already emerging from her bedroom, some sixth sense having alerted her to the arrival of food.

'Pizza!' she said. 'God, Mum, that smells incredible.'

'And ice cream, too.' Her bad mood seemed to have evaporated, at least for the time being.

'I heard you talking to the delivery guy. Not the pizza one – Alex.' She took a slice of pizza from the box, scooping up strings of melted vegan cheese with her fingers.

'Yes, you probably did.'

'He's nice. I like him.'

I liked him, too. I felt a memory, or an echo, of the glow of pleasure I'd had earlier after talking to Alex, and I thought that – despite the fact that Clara was and always would be my number-one priority – there ought to be space in my life for my own happiness.

If – and it was an absolutely massive if, as big as the sleigh Father Christmas would need to carry gifts for all the children in the world – there was someone else in my life, I promised myself, I'd find a way to make it work.

CHAPTER TWENTY-TWO

I slept in the next day, doing that blissful thing of half-waking, realising I didn't have to go to work, turning over and slipping back into the weird dream I was having about having to cook Christmas dinner for Marty and Brett, and Alex turning up just as I was getting the turkey out of the oven. Luxuriating, I repeated the process a couple more times, not particularly caring about the strangeness of the dream, until, at about ten o'clock, I woke fully.

That was one positive of having a teenager, I reflected – on the weekends when Clara was with me, she slept even later than I did. Presumably she did when she was at Paul's too.

Paul. Abruptly, I remembered our conversation the previous night. It hadn't been a row – barely even a disagreement. But it was the first time I'd actively taken him to task over the way he behaved as a father to Clara.

And it had felt good – it had felt like the right thing to do. Obviously, he was and should be free to make his own mistakes as a parent, as I was. But when it came to my daughter's happiness, I was going to fight her corner.

I sat up, then got out of bed, walking softly across the

landing to the bathroom so as not to wake Clara. I cleaned my teeth and tied my hair back in a ponytail – that was the full extent of the grooming I planned to do for the morning. And then I noticed the plain white box that had come as my advent-calendar gift the Tuesday before, containing the little bottles of scented liquid – vodka, or whatever it was. I'd treated it as the jokey gimmick it was intended to be, slipped it into the bathroom cabinet and all but forgotten about it. But now I retrieved it, eased off the lids and read the labels on the bottles again.

Self-Esteem. Assertiveness. Courage. Desirability. Risk-Taking.

I'd conjured up a tiny bit of assertiveness with Paul, the night before. Perhaps next time I spoke to him, I'd prepare myself with a bit of the potion, just for an extra boost.

But for now...

I eased the stopper out of the Self-Esteem bottle and sniffed it. It smelled pleasant – like the grapefruit I sometimes used to eat for breakfast when I was trying to lose weight in my modelling days. Clearly, I remembered cutting the yellow sphere in half, inhaling its citrusy sharpness as I eased a knife around the segments to loosen them, thinking, *This won't be so bad. It might be quite nice, if it tastes as good as it smells.*

And then the overwhelming, mouth-puckering sourness of the first bite, the longing to dump spoonfuls of brown sugar over the thing to make it edible, and finally giving up after less than half.

As a diet food, they'd been bloody great – at least in that they'd put me off the idea of food entirely for several hours. But they did smell gorgeous.

Tentatively, I dabbed a little of the liquid behind each ear and onto my left wrist, pressing it against my right. I sniffed again – the smell was light and pleasant, and I suspected it would fade quickly.

But, for now, hopefully I'd given myself a good old dose of a quality I realised I'd been severely lacking.

I dressed in jeans and a jumper and made coffee, adding in a squirt of the gingerbread syrup I'd impulse-bought with the weekly shop (along with Prosecco-flavoured crisps, cheese footballs and yet another tub of Quality Street), and took a mug to Clara, who I could hear stirring behind her bedroom door.

She thanked me cheerfully enough, as far as I could tell given her head was mostly under the duvet, and when I suggested we wander down to the local high street later on to check out the Christmas lights and maybe have hot chocolate and cake somewhere, her muffled response sounded broadly positive.

Cheered, I returned to the living room and sat by the window, looking out at the clouds scudding across a clear winter sky. Then my phone pinged with a WhatsApp notification.

Kate: Morning! How is everyone? It's gorgeous out there. I'm in bed and don't plan to leave the house though. Bloody Christmas parties really take it out of you.

I imagined her in some glamorous bar, wearing a fabulous dress, sipping cocktails and dancing until the early hours, and felt a pang of envy. How long had it been since I'd had a night out like that? So long I could barely remember the last one.

Abbie: Matt and I are going ice skating. It's meant to be romantic and Christmassy but it'll be carnage. He's got two left feet and we'll be lucky if he only breaks one ankle.

Naomi: Thank God the sun's out – we can take the kids to the park and make them run around until they're exhausted. It's been cabin-fever central round here, and we're taking them to see Father Christmas later. The mood they're in they'd bite his beard off.

Kate: Ro, did you get a parcel on Wednesday?

I realised I hadn't. Distracted by all the drama with Portia and Alex's late-night rescue mission, I'd forgotten that day's advent-calendar gift appeared to have gone AWOL.

Rowan: No, I didn't actually. Hold on, let me see if there's a card.

I hurried to the door and checked the mail piled up on the table beside it, and, sure enough, underneath a white envelope that looked ominously like a bill and the menu for a new curry restaurant, was a card from the delivery company.

Left at number 73, Alex had written. And he'd added a smiley face. Involuntarily, I felt myself smiling back.

Rowan: It's with my neighbour.

It was with a sense of anticipation that I knocked on Sarita's door, and I was glad that her toddler was mid-meltdown, so she didn't keep me chatting as she usually did.

'Here you go.' She thrust a large, squashy parcel over to me. 'We're in the middle of World War Three here, apparently. I told Amina it was still almost two weeks until Christmas, and the news did not go down well.'

'Oh God, you poor thing. Worth ripping up the calendar and busting out the presents, just to keep the peace?'

'She's no fool,' Sarita said grimly. 'I'd have to do it every day between now and actual Christmas and there's only so much plastic tat in the world. Sorry I didn't get a chance to drop that round.'

'It's no problem. Hope things calm down a bit.'

'Me too.' She rolled her eyes, then added, 'You smell nice, Rowan.'

'Thanks. Early Christmas present. And this is another one.'

'Lucky you.'

We said goodbye and I skipped back to the flat, cradling the parcel in my arms.

Clara was up when I returned, sitting on the sofa wearing an oversized hoodie, the hem pulled down over her knees, her hands wrapped round her mug of coffee.

'What've you got there?' she asked. 'Doesn't look like a beauty product to me.'

'I don't think it is. Unless it's a bathrobe or something like that.'

But the parcel didn't feel like a bathrobe – it was softer, with more heft.

'Go on then,' Clara urged. 'Open it and let's take a look.'

The previous parcels had all arrived in cardboard boxes or sleeves, but this one was in a plastic mailing bag. With difficulty, I tore it open and slid out the contents. It was a garment, knitted in red acrylic fabric, with a strange, hard lump concealed within its folds.

Clara leaned over for a look. 'Maybe it's a Christmas jumper.'

'Maybe it is,' I agreed doubtfully.

What would I do with a Christmas jumper? Wear it to the supermarket, I supposed, trying to channel festive vibes with my daughter's lecture about the evils of garments that would only get one wear a year and end up in landfill ringing in my ears? It wasn't like I had loads of fun nights out at the pub lining up in my diary.

'Come on – let's take a look,' Clara urged. 'There's something inside it. Maybe that's the gift and this is just – I dunno, packaging.'

I shook out the jumper and Clara and I stared at it, open-mouthed.

It was bright scarlet. Around the neckline and sleeves was a sparkly green tinsel trim that I knew would itch intolerably from the moment you put it on until the moment – probably very shortly afterwards – you tore the thing off and hurled it away from you.

But that wasn't the worst of it. On the right side of the chest was a flesh-coloured plastic hemisphere, adorned with googly eyes and a sparkly red tinsel nose. Around its neck was more of the green tinsel trim.

'FML,' Clara said. 'It's Rudolph in boob form.'

'Boobdolph,' I said.

'A Titmas jumper,' Clara suggested, beginning to giggle.

I laughed too, torn between amusement and confusion. 'That is the most hideous thing I've ever, ever seen.'

'It's fricking awful,' Clara agreed. 'What were they thinking? Were they legit expecting you to wear this monstrosity?'

'It must be a joke,' I said faintly. 'But why...?'

All the other gifts had made sense, in their way. They'd either been luxurious treats, or something to amuse or challenge me; to make me reconsider the past or think ahead to the future. But this was just a random novelty item – and one so determinedly fugly I would never, ever wear it.

'Maybe it's a mistake,' Clara suggested. 'Maybe it got mixed up at the depot and you were meant to get something else.'

'Or Sarita ordered it and gave it to me by mistake.'

'God, imagine her in that.'

We both started to laugh again. But when I checked the label, it was my name and address on it, clear as anything.

'But what the hell am I meant to do with it? I can't exactly wear it to the office.'

'You can't bin it, Mum,' Clara argued. 'All that plastic, going straight to landfill.'

'Well, I'm not going to use it. You're the one who's always saying we're destroying the planet by accumulating too many redundant possessions.'

'I'm not sure a planet that has something that bad on it is worth saving,' Clara admitted, and we both started to giggle again.

'Maybe I'm meant to wear it. Maybe there's some kind of lesson in it. And it does seem ungrateful to...'

'If you ever, ever wear that, I'm disowning you. Fact. Have some self-respect.'

Her words chimed with something in my brain, and as I lifted the garment of doom up again, confirming that it really was as bad as I'd first thought, I caught a whiff of the grapefruit fragrance on my wrist.

Self-esteem.

Maybe the two things were somehow connected. Maybe someone with cast-iron self-belief would wear this jumper and not care how awful it was? Or maybe Clara was right, and by putting my own taste and feelings above a sense of politeness to my friends and a reluctance to get rid of an unwanted gift, I'd be giving my self-worth a much-needed boost?

But still, it was a gift. A gift from my closest friends. Getting rid of it felt ungrateful and cold and just weird.

'I guess I'll just leave it here for now.' I draped the jumper over the back of the sofa, knowing that every time I passed it I'd be confronted with Rudolph's reproachful red-nosed (or red-nippled) face.

That afternoon, like I'd planned, Clara and I walked through the last of the sunshine to the high street. There was a huge Christmas tree by the station, hung with lights. Every shop, however small, had gone all out to make its window display as festive as possible. Even the *Big Issue* seller was wearing a Santa hat.

We found a warm, brightly lit café and had hot chocolate

with marshmallows and squirty cream, and a massive slab of coffee-and-walnut cake for me, so rich it made my throat tingle, and a vegan carrot cake for her, which she said approvingly had loads of cinnamon in it. Although, as we ate, I couldn't help noticing that Clara seemed shifty and distracted, and that her bag was bulging as if there was something large concealed in it, even though her coat and scarf were draped over the back of her chair.

Then we wandered round the shops. Clara bought a mani-cure set for her friend Lily in Primark and a Tabac gift box for Paul in TK Maxx. I bought a couple of giant potatoes to have with beans and cheese for our supper.

Finally, we stopped outside the Cats Protection charity shop.

'Mum,' Clara said pleadingly. 'Can't we...?'

'We can't have a kitten,' I said, for the millionth time. 'I'd love one too, you know I would, but in a seventh-floor flat, it's just not...'

'It's not fair.'

'I know it's not. But it's— Look at that.'

Hanging in the window was a slinky, cranberry-red satin dress with shoestring straps, cut on the bias. It was a fashionable midi length, cut low at the front and back, and it looked like it was my size.

'What? The dress? It's nice.'

Clara had an expression of indifference on her face that I could have sworn was false.

'It's Ghost, I bet you. And in a charity shop! I wonder whether...?'

If it was under twenty pounds, I told myself, I'd go for it. It was a classic – it would last me years. I imagined Alex seeing me in it – his eyes (or, better still, his hands) travelling over my body.

Then I thought of the looming service-charge bill, and

remembered my panic at having no funds in reserve if Portia had needed to be repaired.

'Ah, better not,' I said. 'I don't have anywhere to wear something like that. I don't really need it.'

'Mum! Come on!' The indifference had melted away, and before I knew it my daughter had practically dragged me into the shop.

'Were you looking at the frock in the window?' the woman asked, smiling. 'It's designer, apparently. A label called Spirit, or something.'

'Ghost,' Clara said. 'My mum knew – she's got a really good eye. She used to be a model.'

I flushed with embarrassment and pleasure at my daughter's pride in me.

'It's barely been worn,' the woman said. 'Would you like to try it on?'

I held the dress up against my body, glancing in the mirror. I didn't need to try it on – I knew it would fit perfectly.

'I... Do you mind if I ask the price?'

'Twenty-five pounds. It's a size ten – looks about perfect for you.'

'But maybe you could give us a discount if we left a donation,' Clara said, rummaging in her bag. 'Like, for instance, this.'

Triumphantly, she produced the Rudolph Christmas jumper and handed it over.

The woman burst out laughing. 'Would you look at that? That'll get snapped up in minutes, this time of year. I'll call it a fiver for the dress, plus this.'

'Are you sure?' I asked.

'Quite sure. Funny, a lady dropped that dress off just yesterday and said she was pretty sure it would be gone soon. And here you are.'

'Well... thank you.' I dug in my purse and pulled out a five-pound note.

'Done,' the woman said, taking the money and slipping the dress into a paper bag.

'It's a Christmas miracle,' Clara said smugly as we left the shop.

And then my suspicions slotted into place.

'Sweetie, did the aunties... Kate and Naomi put you up to this? Did one of them leave the dress there?'

Clara grinned. 'Maybe.'

'Did they tell you I wouldn't want to get rid of the jumper and you'd have to prod me along a bit?'

'I can neither confirm nor deny that.'

I burst out laughing. 'Well, thanks. To you and them. And that self-esteem stuff, I guess. It took a while but, between you, you did the trick.'

Almost subconsciously, I sniffed my wrist, but the last echo of the grapefruit scent had faded away.

CHAPTER TWENTY-THREE

It was Sunday. Always a nothing sort of day. Even when I'd been working doing wedding make-up almost every Saturday throughout the summer, I'd struggled to find Sundays the relaxing me-time (or me-and-Clara time, when she still wanted that) they should have been. I used to spend the day going over my kit, cleaning brushes and making lists of what needed to be replenished, filling my social media with posts of radiant brides, catching up on queries and finalising bookings.

Now, I didn't even have that to do. Months ago, I'd finally chucked out the last of my bottles, tubes and palettes – as a professional, I couldn't bear to use manky, out-of-date products. All my brushes had been carefully cleaned and packed away, because there was nothing and no one for them to brush.

I stood in front of my dressing table, looking down at the small collection of make-up that was all I owned now, all I needed for my personal use. I knew what suited me for day-to-day and for rare nights out; I had no need for high-end stuff and no money to experiment with colours or looks that I'd only wear once.

From the next-door bedroom, I could hear Clara and her

friend Lily giggling. They'd been in there for a couple of hours; I'd given them lunch and then they'd retreated, Lily thanking me politely and Clara, taking her friend's lead, doing the same. The sound of their laughter made me happy – God only knew what they were up to in there, certainly not doing homework, which Clara had promised was part of the reason for Lily's visit. But they were happy, having fun listening to music or watching TikTok or talking about boys.

I ran my finger over the closed doors of the Liberty advent calendar, feeling the indents of the slots that opened the empty drawers. It was getting closer and closer to Christmas. If the calendar had been full, I'd have opened half of its doors. (Actually, who was I kidding? As my friends had known perfectly well, I'd have opened all of them the day it arrived.)

But that wasn't how they'd intended it to work. It had been meant as a different kind of present. There'd been lovely beauty products, of course, but they were there almost as extras, a way to pad out the true purpose of the gift.

Which was what, exactly? *We should do something lovely for Rowan.* It was lovely, and I was truly grateful. Having something to look forward to each day had buoyed me up immensely. But there was more to it than that. The tarot reading, the photo of me when I was a model, the little vials of scent with their affirmative names, even the ugly jumper – they were meant to do something else. To challenge me; to push me out of my comfort zone, in which I'd believed myself to be so uncomfortable I'd barely even realised it was one.

Because, let's face it, there are some things even an overnight enzymatic resurfacing mask can't fix.

It was just under two weeks until Christmas. Just under two weeks to try and capture some of that elusive festive magic that seemed to have scattered its sparkles over everyone but me.

I opened the drawers of the calendar, one by one, starting with the first and carrying on until I reached today's. Each little box, even though they were all empty, held something – a reminder of love and friendship, a promise of hope. When I pulled them out and sniffed them, I could just about discern the fragrance of the product that would have been there, along with the scent of expensive packaging, as evocative as Christmas wrapping paper.

I picked up the box holding the labelled vials and ran my finger across their smooth, curved surfaces, lifting out the one that said 'Courage'. When I eased out its stopper, the smell of roses met me.

Did I need to be braver? To grasp opportunities to change my life for the better, to actively pursue the things I knew I wanted: happiness, financial stability, love? Where would I even find those opportunities if I wanted them?

For the past two years – perhaps even longer – it had felt as if I was just marking time: waiting for my business to recover; realising it wouldn't; living for a while off dwindling savings before, in desperation, applying for the job at Walkerson's; muddling through there. Watching Clara grow up and away from me, snatching moments of illicit pleasure with Paul. Maybe it was time to be proactive, to get off my arse and make the magic happen.

Unbidden, the image of Alex's face came into my mind. The delivery guy, who I'd only met on a handful of occasions and not spent more than ten minutes at a time with. Why was I even thinking of him? He was just a guy, just someone I'd seen a few times, maybe even tentatively flirted with, someone whose smile made me smile.

When this was over – when the last gift was delivered on Christmas Eve, assuming I was even here to receive it – I'd hardly ever see him again – certainly not on a daily basis. Even before then, he might move on, get transferred to a different route or something. I didn't even know how that would work, but I knew that whenever we'd had deliveries in the past – from the Amazon guy, the DPD guy, the Yodel guy – my encounters with them had been so fleeting I had never even recognised their faces.

Alex was just another one of them, just another delivery guy. I was seeing him more frequently, that was all. And after Christmas, I'd barely see him at all, unless I decided to sign up for a Hello Fresh subscription or something.

That could be a plan, I thought. Healthy, easy-to-prepare food delivered to my door once a week by smiley, blue-eyed Alex. It could be life-changing.

But that was hardly courageous. I opened the vial again and sniffed, then dabbed some of the liquid on my wrist.

I needed a bigger, bolder, better idea.

Unfortunately, I didn't have one.

I sat down on my bed, picking up my phone from the pillow. I checked the Girlfriends' Club WhatsApp, but it seemed oddly quiet. I'd messaged earlier to ask how everyone was doing and whether they had any exciting plans for their Sundays, but apart from a vague response from Abbie saying that she might be popping to Bermondsey for coffee, there'd been nothing.

I could seek their advice – ask whether inviting Alex in for a cup of tea would be friendly – or weird. Whether asking for his number would mark me as a desperate, lonely stalker. Whether fantasising about him – there, I'd admitted it, even if only silently in my own head – was inappropriate.

But that would ultimately be futile, I suspected. I imagined the replies I'd get.

Kate: Is he on LinkedIn? I'm told sliding into people's DMs on there is a thing now. Actually, I'm not told. Pervy fuckers do it to me the whole time.

Abbie: That's so sweet and romantic! Just, you know, ask him out. What have you got to lose?

Rowan: Only my pride, and there's not a whole lot of that TBH.

Naomi: In that case, next time he knocks, open the door in your smalls with a rose between your teeth and go, like, 'Take me, I'm yours!'

I mean, I loved my mates, but sometimes their advice – even if I was only making it up – was less than helpful.

LinkedIn, though. Maybe Kate – if I'd asked her – would have had a point.

I googled Pegasus Express, and up popped a website with the familiar cyan-and-white branding. There was a load of waffle about how they made hundreds of thousands of deliveries a day, up and down the country, offering reliable, friendly service at competitive rates. There were links to arrange a delivery or a collection. There was an online chat bot.

And, hidden away right at the bottom of the page, there was a 'Contact us' link. I clicked it.

Pegasus customers could reach them through their UK-based call centre, which predictably was open from Monday to Saturday. They could send a letter to a PO box address in Leicester, which, given the carnage of pre-Christmas post, probably wouldn't get there until January. Or they could email hello@pegasusexpress.co.uk.

Fine. I'd do that then.

But what the hell was I going to say?

It was Christmas. That was a pretext of a sort. Starting a new email, I typed:

Hello

I've been receiving deliveries from one of your drivers, and I've been really happy with his punctuality, friendliness and commitment. As it's such a busy time of year, I'm particularly grateful that he's been willing to carry parcels up to my seventh-floor flat when the lift has been out of service.

With Christmas approaching, I wondered if it might be possible to send a gift to your office for him, to express my appreciation? Could you perhaps let me know his last name, so I can address it correctly?

Many thanks,

Rowan Connell

Like you couldn't give him a gift when he knocks on your door. Like they'll tell you his surname – duh, data protection. Like you don't come across as a right nutter.

Still, I pressed send.

On a bravery scale, I was hardly up there with Suffragette icon Millicent Fawcett – no one was about to erect a statue of me holding a banner saying courage called to courage everywhere. But it was something.

I opened my bedside-table drawer and looked at the half-empty Quality Street tin, thinking of rewarding myself with a chocolate or twelve. And then, emboldened, I thought of Clara and Lily hanging out in my daughter's room.

It was time for some power mothering, and time to tap into my inner Hayley.

I hurried through to the kitchen and found butter, sugar, flour and eggs. There were jars of spices in the cupboard: nutmeg, cloves and cinnamon. There were bottles of vanilla and almond extract left over from long-ago birthday cakes, and some icing sugar that I was pretty sure would have gone solid ages ago, but that was nothing some enthusiastic sieving wouldn't fix.

The Nigella biscuit recipe I'd made a million times when Clara was younger came back to me with no effort at all. At the back of a drawer, I found a selection of cookie cutters I'd all but forgotten I had. There was even, in a dust-covered shoebox on the top shelf of one of the cabinets, a rudimentary selection of sparkly sprinkles and some tubes of food colouring that were out of date but I reckoned wouldn't poison us.

Half an hour later, the smell of butter and sugar filled the flat, working its magic on the two teenagers. Clara's door opened, and she and Lily emerged, their faces glowing with highlighting gel, false eyelashes slightly askew on their lids, their nails painted in red, green and gold.

Lily smiled politely. Clara looked at me the way I imagined an urban fox would regard someone holding out a chicken bone.

'Mum. Have you been baking?'

I smiled cheerfully. 'Indeed I have.'

'Can we help?' Lily asked, taking a tentative step forward, her eyes on the baking tray I was easing out of the oven.

The biscuits were perfect: golden brown, fragrant and crispy round the edges.

'I was going to ice them when they'd cooled down,' I said casually. 'But we could do it together, if you like.'

'Cool!' Lily breathed.

'Yeah,' Clara agreed. 'Christmas has landed.'

Together, we mixed icing sugar and water to a stiff paste, divided the mixture into bowls, added colouring and got decorating, chatting and laughing together in the warm, scented kitchen while rain swished against the window. Clara piped green icing onto Christmas-tree-shaped biscuits and added gold and silver balls. Lily piped wonky white lines onto snowflake shapes. I went all out and chucked everything onto round biscuits, claiming they were baubles.

By the time we'd finished, the kitchen looked like a bunch of Santa's elves had had a drunken party in it, and we were more than satisfied with our handiwork. We flopped on the sofa, put a Christmas playlist on Spotify, and drank tea and ate most of the biscuits – although I was careful to keep the most garish of my bauble ones, wrapped in a paper napkin, to give to Alex next time I saw him.

CHAPTER TWENTY-FOUR

Alex thought of himself as a pretty confident guy. He had his ups and downs, just like everyone – moments of self-doubt and worry, and obviously those 'd'oh' facepalm moments. But normally, he was pretty much able to roll with the punches. You had to in his line of work – he'd learned that very early on.

So, normally, whatever challenges life sent his way – and there had been plenty – he faced calmly, head on, ready to take whatever tough decisions needed to be taken to offer the best chance of survival. Normally, finding himself in a situation where he really needed his A game, he'd be feeling eager, excited, perhaps even overconfident in his ability to field awkward questions, present himself well, give answers that were an appropriate balance between the unvarnished truth and what his questioner wanted to hear.

But today, he was worried he was out of his depth.

This was a new situation – one he was pretty much willing to bet no one had ever been daft enough to land themselves in. But he'd sought it out, engineered it, and now he was going to have to go in there and give the best possible account of himself

– and if he failed, if he was left feeling foolish, guilty even, then he'd just have to deal with that the way he'd dealt with other knock-backs in the past: by learning from the experience and, hopefully, moving on without making the same mistake again.

This didn't *feel* like a mistake. It felt bold, perhaps even reckless, but calculated risks were the name of the game for him, and he felt something of a familiar thrill knowing that he was about to take one.

He buttoned his shirt – a present from Ailsa, which he hoped might bring him luck. It was overdyed denim, dark blue, to match his eyes, she'd said. His jeans were black – he'd considered wearing a suit, but that had felt like total overkill, especially as it was a Sunday. He'd have worn his favourite leather jacket, charcoal-coloured now rather than black, because it had faded over the years since he'd bought it in celebration of a successful venture, but even he had to admit it wasn't equal to this frosty December day, the sun white and cold against a sparkling sapphire sky. So his grey herringbone wool coat would have to do.

He pulled on his trainers and tied the laces, fumbling slightly; his hands were literally shaking. *God, man, get a grip*, he chided himself. *This isn't life or death – you're just meeting some random women. You're even going to offer to help them out – do stuff so they don't have to. You're doing them a favour, if you think about it.*

But Alex didn't want to think about it. He wanted to get on with it, get the thing over with, leave feeling triumphant and hopeful or disappointed and foolish, whatever the outcome was going to be.

He couldn't get on with it just yet, though, otherwise he'd be early and that would strike entirely the wrong note. However he came across today, he didn't want to look desperate. That would be the kiss of death.

So, to kill time before getting the bus into town – he'd considered cycling but dismissed the idea for fear they might be the sort of women who cackled with contempt at middle-aged men in Lycra, if thirty-four even counted as middle-aged – he opened the back door and stepped out into the garden.

He was no horticulturist. The garden had been a non-negotiable when he bought the house, but it had remained in a state of what Alex liked to think of as benign neglect. The paving stones that covered most of its surface were cracked, and the luxuriant weeds that had sprouted there in the summer were mostly dead now – or more likely dormant, ready to spring forth with renewed vigour when the weather was warmer. A bay tree in a pot, which had been left by the previous owners, flourished despite Alex never having done anything to it – only Ailsa had pulled off a few of its leaves when she'd made a ragu. A sycamore tree, overhanging from the neighbouring garden, had scattered its wing-shaped seeds on the ground, so perhaps eventually the place would become a forest. Rewilding was a thing now, wasn't it?

But there was one part of his garden Alex did tend to. Hanging off the fence at the back was a bird feeder, little more than a plate suspended from chains. Every day – at least every day when he remembered – Alex would tip rainwater out of it and replenish the seeds he left out for the sparrows and finches – and for the squirrel.

At least, he assumed it was one squirrel – they all looked the same to him. It was there now, squatting on top of the feeder, its fluffy grey tail arched high over its back, its paws clutching a seed as it nibbled greedily.

'Got to keep you going through the winter,' Alex told it, approaching with the bag of bird food in his hand.

But when it saw him, the squirrel abandoned its lunch and shot off, running along the fence as lithely as the tightrope-walker Alex had seen in the circus when he was a kid.

'Fair enough,' he said. 'Discretion's the better part of valour, if you don't want to end up dead meat.'

He tipped seeds onto the plate, the squirrel watching him beadily from a safe distance.

'Chill out, mate, I'm all done now. You crack on.'

Shivering, he returned indoors. He pulled on his coat and tucked his phone, wallet and keys into the pocket.

Should he take some sort of ID? Business cards? No, that would be insane.

'Right, I'm off,' he called. 'Back in time for dinner, okay?'

There was no reply. *Sleeping or sulking,* he thought, *one of the two.*

He locked the door behind him and strode off in the direction of the bus stop.

As the bus inched painfully slowly through South East London, Alex felt his nerves building. He almost regretted choosing not to cycle, which would have kept his mind off the upcoming meeting, or taking the train, which would have been quicker. But he'd made his call – he'd hoped that the long, tedious journey would give him a chance to compose his thoughts and possibly do some deep prana tempo breathing – however you did that. He'd had a girlfriend once who was into that wafty stuff, but he'd been too distracted by the rise and fall of her breasts while she was doing it to ask.

How wrong he'd been – with each mile that passed, he felt his diaphragm rising higher and higher in his chest with tension, until he felt like he might puke.

He'd faced some tough crowds in his time. The guys he'd met the previous week had given him a proper grilling, digging into every aspect of his past until he'd almost expected them to enquire about the colour of his underwear (purple). This lot should hold no fear for him – but still, they did. He imagined their eyes on him, judging, assessing, finding him wanting. He imagined them jumping to the wrong conclusion entirely, and possibly calling the police on him.

Worst of all, he imagined them laughing at him.

By the time he reached his stop, Alex was in a right state. His imagination was in overdrive, so much so that it wouldn't have surprised him if the destination he'd been given was some sort of underworld dive. Not the kind of place he went to with his mates sometimes, which you accessed through a door disguised as that of a fridge, or where you had to give evidence to a private detective before they'd let you in.

No – far more alarming than that. His mind conjured up the sort of frou-frou place Ailsa liked, with pink everything and stands laden with over-frosted cupcakes. Or – another Ailsa special from his memory bank – somewhere that did wheatgrass smoothies and overnight oats, and when you asked if there was a ham sandwich on the menu they looked at you like it was literal violence. Or even nothing at all, just a bare street corner where he'd be set upon by gangsters put up to defend a woman's honour against Alex's not-noble-enough intentions.

But, in fact, it was a normal coffee shop. Normal for Bermondsey, anyway, with exposed-filament lighting, stripped wooden floors and a bit of taxidermy thrown in for good measure. And among the crowd of mixed-sex tables, couples with babies and solitary people spending their Sundays beavering away on their laptops, it was easy enough to spot his target.

There they were: three women at a table for four, the empty chair deliberately chosen to face away from the street. One slim and blonde, throwing back her head in laughter as she sipped her cappuccino. One red-haired woman, wearing the suburban-mum uniform of Breton top, jeans and Converse beloved of some of Ailsa's friends. One huddled in a faux-fur coat even though the room looked warm, her face mostly hidden by designer shades, like she was Anna Wintour or something.

Alex forced his nerves back down deep inside him where they belonged, strolled in as casually as he could, and introduced himself.

Then, seated at last with a double espresso by way of Dutch courage, he said, 'So. I wanted to talk about Rowan Connell.'

CHAPTER TWENTY-FIVE

On Monday, Alex delivered a lipstick in a gorgeous chunky gold case, and I handed him the Christmas biscuit in return. He waited by the door while I opened my parcel and breathed a gratifying whistle of appreciation when I wound it up to reveal a deep burgundy shade in a matte finish.

'Wow, look at that!' I said. 'It's gorgeous.'

He grinned. 'One for your daughter's Christmas stocking, then?'

'Uh... the colour's too old for her, really.'

'Is that right?'

'Yes,' I said firmly. Then I added, 'Besides, it's way too fabulous for me to part with, isn't it?'

'I wouldn't know. Lipstick's not really my thing. I'd have to see it on to judge.'

'You would? All right then.'

I don't know what possessed me – honestly, I don't. But before I could second-guess myself, I'd ducked into the hallway, where a mirror hung above the shelf on which we kept our keys and unopened post and that sort of clutter, and applied the lipstick. Normally, I'd have exfoliated my lips first with a soft flannel, used balm to moisturise them, and probably lined them so the shape was perfect and the colour wouldn't bleed.

Normally, though, there wouldn't have been a handsome man freezing his goolies off on my doorstep while I faffed around. So I went straight in: one sweep across my bottom lip, two more careful arches over the top, pressed my lips together, turned around and smiled.

'What do you reckon?'

'Swit swoo.' He raised his eyebrows so they almost vanished beneath the peak of his cap. 'Very nice. Are you going anywhere nice where you can wear it? Seeing anyone who's going to kiss it all off?'

I tutted. 'This is quality stuff. It ought to be one hundred per cent kiss-proof.'

Want to check? The words almost came out of my mouth, but I stopped them just in time. Instead, embarrassed by my almost-forwardness, I found myself burbling, 'I might be seeing my girlfriends the day after tomorrow – there was talk about meeting up – but no one's mentioned anything yet. I guess they're all too busy, with it being Christmas and everything.'

'That's a shame.'

'Yes, well... I can get dressed up to catch up on old episodes of *Bridgerton*.'

'Living your best life,' he said.

I forced a laugh. 'Trust me, that is my best life.'

Alex shook his head sympathetically, said something about how he was sure I'd get together with my mates soon and hurried off to finish his round, and I got on with my evening feeling oddly unsettled.

Had there been something in the way he'd looked at my mouth? Something that went beyond friendly banter? Had there?

Or was I just imagining it?

The next day, I promised myself, I'd do something to ramp

up the flirting – if it had been flirting. And if I could think what something might look like, beyond me grinning at him like a gormless chimpanzee, possibly with lipstick on my teeth.

But the next day, when Alex knocked on the door and handed over that day's gift (tickets to a Christmas fair, which I knew Clara would be delighted by), he seemed awkward and stilted. When I showed him the tickets, he said, 'Oh. That's really cool,' and then sort of hovered, as if there was something else he wanted to say but couldn't quite find the words.

'Do you need anything?' I asked. 'Hot drink? Toilet? Glass of water?'

He shook his head. 'I... uh... Rowan, I just wanted to let you know, my line manager passed on the email you sent to Pegasus.'

Oh no. I wasn't sure what I'd expected to happen after forcing myself to press send on my stilted happy-customer note, but it wasn't this. Although, now I thought about it, what else could I have expected? Obviously they weren't going to disclose the details of their employee – or self-employed contractor, as he probably was – to some random woman. I could have been an axe-murderer posing as an innocent single mother. I could have been a crazy, obsessed ex-girlfriend (and who could blame her?) stalking him. I could have been anyone.

As far as Alex was concerned, I basically was anyone. Or more likely, no one in particular.

His awkwardness had infected me, as if a virus had passed through the air between us.

'I thought...' I waffled, 'I thought it would be nice to say something, because... uh... you work really hard, and it's cold out, and there are lots of stairs, and the advent-calendar gifts have made a real difference to me, you know, and it kind of feels like you've been part of that. I'm really grateful.'

'I'm grateful too,' he said, his face serious as he met my eyes. 'I appreciate the thought, I really do. This job's tough in a lot of ways, you know. Past couple of days I've been working from seven in the morning until gone nine. Yesterday I didn't get a chance to eat.'

'That's awful!'

He gave a crooked half-grin. 'Cue the world's tiniest violin, right? I don't feel sorry for myself, honest. Some of the lads that do this have it much harder than me. But still, it's nice to be appreciated, and to see a friendly face. A few of the people I deliver to can be right... can be pretty unpleasant.'

At least he doesn't think I'm unpleasant. A weird stalker, maybe, but not unpleasant.

'I'm sorry to hear that. People are bastards, aren't they? At least a lot of them are, a lot of the time.'

He shrugged. 'Normally I'd call them out on it. Not that it makes a difference – it just feels better to stand up for yourself. But when it's your livelihood at stake, you can't.'

I thought of Brett and Marty at work, their sneering pleasure when the seller of a property one of Kimberley's former applicants had made an offer on had accepted a higher bid from one of Tatiana Ivanova's clients, and nodded sympathetically.

'I get that,' I said.

'Yeah, well, it's not forever, is it?'

Isn't it? What did he mean by that? Did he have another job lined up? Would I be getting a different, non-smiley, less blue-eyed delivery driver in the future? The prospect filled me with unexpected sadness.

But before I could frame the words to ask whether Alex was planning on jacking in his job at Pegasus, I heard an insistent bleeping from his phone, and he rummaged in his pocket for it, turning away as he did so.

I realised it was selfish as hell of me to have made him waste all the time he had, chatting on my doorstep, when he was working such brutal hours. He must have been desperate to get away, even if I was nicer to him than lots of other people.

Clearly, he was desperate to get away now.

But he turned, his phone halfway up to his ear already, and said, 'It's Winter, by the way.'

My face must have betrayed my confusion, because he grinned, pointed at his chest, and said, 'Alex Winter. And thanks again for the biscuit – it was delicious.'

And then, the next day, Alex didn't turn up at all. I'd shown my applicant and her husband – a tall, smiling Asian man – a flat that ticked all their boxes, and they'd agreed to put in an offer. So I returned home in triumph and on time, fairly confident that I wouldn't have missed Alex. But there was no sign of him over the next couple of hours, and no sign that he'd been by already.

When I asked Clara if she'd taken in a delivery, she rolled her eyes so hard I worried she might dislodge them, said, 'Like I wouldn't have told you, Mum,' and stomped off to her room.

I spent the rest of the afternoon on high alert, listening for the sound of footsteps outside the flat, the volume turned way down on the television so I wouldn't miss it. *He'd knock, Rowan – don't be daft*, I told myself, but myself wasn't listening.

At about five thirty, I thought I heard the familiar tread of boots, but it was just my neighbour's husband coming home from work, and he jumped about a foot in the air when I flung open the door. Twenty minutes later, there was a knock, but it was only some guy selling cleaning products, claiming to have been recently released from a young offenders' institute, but I'd heard they were scammers, so I thanked him and sent him on his way. At six, Paul came to collect Clara for her overnight stay, and she went happily off, no doubt relieved to be out of the way of her barmy mother.

Even though her presence wasn't exactly a ray of sunshine a lot of the time, with her gone I felt gloom settle heavily on me.

There'd been no gift that day, there'd been no Alex. And the Girlfriends' Club WhatsApp had been silent, with no one making plans for a meet-up.

I'd considered posting to arrange one myself, but I felt awkward about that – ungrateful, almost. They were doing so much for me, bringing me so much pleasure with their thoughtful and generous gifts. And it was a busy time of year – Naomi was probably relishing a quiet evening in, Kate probably had yet another client Christmas meal to attend, Abbie and Matt might be out for dinner together, their hands touching across a candlelit table.

I was alone, and I'd have to suck it up. It wasn't so bad, really. I had loads to be thankful for.

I showered and washed my hair so I wouldn't have to do it the next morning. I put a load of washing on. I looked dolefully in the fridge, but there was nothing I fancied eating.

And then I found myself standing at my dressing table, looking at the advent calendar. There'd never not been a gift before. Even on Sundays, when Alex didn't work, there'd been something for me to open, because he delivered the extra one on Saturday, with a stern note on the envelope saying, *Do not open this until tomorrow.*

But today there was nothing.

I slid open the drawers with yesterday's date on, and the day before's, but of course they were empty – they'd all been. Surely I couldn't dare to hope…

I slid out the box with today's date on the front. It was a smaller one; originally, it must have contained something not much bigger than one of the little vials of scented alcohol. But this one wasn't empty.

There was a piece of paper inside it, neatly folded so that it nested perfectly in the base of the box. My heart was literally hammering with excitement as I prised it out and unfolded it.

Be ready to leave at 19h30. You're going Out Out – dress to impress.

Oh my God.

I hadn't been so excited about going out since I'd been invited to my first party in Paris when I was a sixteen-year-old model – putting on a borrowed Hervé Léger dress in the tiny apartment I shared with my friends, drinking vodka and soda and smoking fags while we straightened our hair and trowelled on make-up that we hoped would make us look old enough to buy cocktails at Rex Club; dreaming about snogging a celebrity – or at least the hot photographer's assistant who'd caught my eye as I teetered down the catwalk. Or since my first date with Paul (which was lighter on the glamour, being all-you-can-eat night at Pizza Hut).

I leaped onto WhatsApp.

Naomi: Ro, are you there?

Kate: You don't have plans tonight, do you?

Abbie: Maybe we should tell her?

Rowan: YOU GUYS! I was so gutted there was no gift.

I added a crying-laughing emoji, even though Clara had told me no one used that any more.

Rowan: Where are we going? Where do I meet you? What do I WEAR?

Kate: It's a surprise, you daftie. That's the whole point. You'll be collected at the appointed time.

Abbie: You read the instructions. Dress to impress.

Naomi: See you later!

They signed off with a raft of emojis including clinking champagne glasses, high-heeled shoes and the dancing lady.

Dancing. Dress to impress. High-heeled shoes.

Shit. My A game was long gone, and I was going to have to find it, stat. Thank God my hair was sorted, at least. And thank you also, God – or rather the best friends any woman could ever hope to have – for my new lipstick.

I'd build my make-up around that, I decided. Skin as flawless and glowing as I could get it, minimal eye make-up and a strong lip, as we call it in the trade.

Despite being out of practice, I still had the old skills, and even working at top speed, I was able to get my face the way I wanted it within about twenty minutes. The rest of me was more of a problem.

What on God's green earth was I going to wear?

I pulled open my wardrobe doors. My work uniform of cheap suits and polyester blouses was a non-starter. The plain black yoga pants and three-quarter-sleeve cotton tops I'd worn to do wedding make-up were no good either. My off-duty look consisted of jeans, jumpers and Converse.

But now I had a dress! I'd almost forgotten it. The cranberry-red satin Ghost dress I had spotted in the charity shop, which had been planted there by one of my friends, surely with this exact occasion in mind. There it was, suspended slinkily from a padded satin hanger I'd got with some shortie pyjamas Paul had bought me back in the day.

I lifted it out, loving how its length pulled through my fingers, the way its colour changed in the light from almost scarlet to almost purple. I pulled it over my head, regretting the fact that I'd been too chicken to use the luxury underwear voucher. But no one was going to see my knickers tonight, I was fairly sure. I stood on my bed and scrutinised myself in the mirror from every angle, satisfied with what I saw, then zipped on a pair of old but still stylish gold ankle boots.

I was ready to go.

But go where?

I checked WhatsApp again, but there were no new messages. It was seven twenty-five. If they were sending an Uber for me, how would I know it was here? Was Patch, Naomi's husband, going to pick me up in their car?

I opened the front door and looked out, but the walkway was empty, the whole building apparently bunkered down against the frosty night. I could see no sign of life apart from Christmas lights twinkling in a few windows and a cat stalking through the car park seven floors below.

I'd freeze to death if I went out like this. I darted back inside and shoved myself into my everyday black wool coat, and dug out a sparkly vintage evening bag that just fitted my phone, keys and lipstick.

And then I waited.

It was almost twenty-five to eight when I heard footsteps outside my door, and my heart leaped. It couldn't be Alex. Could it? No, it was impossible. There was nothing for him to deliver today; my gift was the experience I was about to have – was already having. And there was no way my friends would have arranged for him to give to me a lift to... wherever I was going.

Still, when the knock on the door came, my palms were sweating and my mouth felt dry. I pulled the door open.

'Andy! Oh my God! How are you? It's been too long.'

'Been busy, haven't I?' He smiled his usual casual, radiant grin that looked like the sun coming out and opened his arms wide for a hug, pulling me against him and squeezing me, rocking me gently. Andy had always been a world champion hugger. He smelled amazing – of the androgynous violet-scented cologne that was his trademark – and he looked impossibly glamorous, as he always did, in his black silk shirt and long leather coat.

Honestly, if Andy hadn't been gay, I'd have fallen head over heels in love with him years ago.

Actually, if Andy hadn't been gay *and* in the throes of a massive cocaine-and-whatever-other-substances-he-could-get-his-hands-on habit.

'So you're my glass coach?' I asked.

'Coachman,' he corrected. 'I'll turn back into a mouse at midnight. But yes, I'm your designated driver. One of the perks of being sober. You look stunning, Ro. I love that lippie on you, and your pins are astonishing in that frock. Now let's get a move on or we'll be late.'

As we drove into London – Andy refused to disclose our exact destination – I begged him to tell me how this had been planned, for how long, and who was going to be there.

'God, Rowan, which part of the word "surprise" don't you understand?' he complained, but then he relented. 'Boring Paul's not on the guest list, in case you were wondering. But we've got a few of the old crowd together.'

'Not Zara?' I asked anxiously.

Zara, formerly the fifth girlfriend in the Girlfriends' Club before a major falling-out I'd never quite got to the bottom of, was in Paris, as far as I knew, working as a fashion journalist. She'd risen so far above our orbit she might well have forgotten we existed. I mean, Carine Roitfeld follows *her* on social media. And besides, Zara was Patch's ex, and if she turned up it would make things all kinds of awks for poor Naomi.

'Zara who?' Andy asked contemptuously, so I knew it would be all right.

'Dan's coming, though,' he went on, glancing over his shoulder as he changed lanes. His car was seriously swanky, I noticed – a new-ish Mercedes that would have put poor Portia to shame. 'Hopefully Kate will behave herself.'

Daniel – one of the old crowd who'd played football with our then-boyfriends back in the day – and Kate had always seemed to rub each other up the wrong way. I wasn't sure why.

'Kate always behaves herself.'

'Except when she's getting off with random strangers after too many negronis.'

'Andy, you know as well as I do that that's Kate's version of behaving herself.'

We broke into giggles.

'Stop being funny and let me concentrate,' Andy scolded. 'I almost missed our turning.'

He drove smoothly and skilfully, and I wondered when he'd got his licence, never mind bought this fancy car. The old Andy – he'd only been sober for about eighteen months – had never bothered to learn to drive and certainly wouldn't have had spare cash for a car.

'I'm working in sales now,' he said, without me needing to ask the question. 'Turns out I'm rather good at it.'

That didn't surprise me – Andy, with his easy charm and air of general fabulousness, which he'd always been able to summon even when he was at rock bottom, could sell ice to polar bears – which, given the shrinking of the polar floes Clara was always on about, might not be that hard after all. He'd make a much better estate agent than I was, I thought enviously.

As he drove, I caught him up on how Clara was doing and how work was going, glossing a bit over the unsatisfactory aspects of both. I told him about the advent-calendar gifts and how much I appreciated the surprise, and he told me he'd been in on the secret from the beginning.

'And the guy who delivers the parcels is kind of hot, which helps,' I admitted, feeling my cheeks colour, grateful for the darkness of the car.

'Oh, he is, is he?' Andy asked, glancing sideways at me. 'A delivery driver, though? Oughtn't you to set your sights a bit higher, Ro, if you want to be kept in the style to which you want to become accustomed?'

'I couldn't care less what he does for work. It's not like I'm exactly minted, am I? Anyway, all we do is chat on the doorstep. It's just a nice thing. I'm not about to ask him to marry me.'

'Well,' Andy said, 'you can tell me all about him while you drink a lovely cocktail, you lucky thing. Here we are.'

He pulled into an underground car park. I wasn't even sure where we were; we'd been too busy chatting. East London somewhere, maybe? I didn't know and I didn't particularly care – I was relishing being a passenger in all senses of the word, being out of control of my own destiny but in the hands of friends I trusted completely.

A few minutes later, we were stepping out of a glass-walled lift into a small, carpeted room. A Christmas tree, bedecked in red, copper, bronze and gold baubles and strung with twinkling lights, sparkled in one corner. A white-shirted waiter greeted us with a tray of champagne flutes, and orange juice for Andy. I could smell delicious food.

But before I had the chance to take it all in, I was surrounded by my friends, a glass of champagne pressed into one of my hands and a cocktail menu into the other.

'Isn't this place off the scale?' Kate asked, as bubbly with excitement as the Veuve Clicquot I was drinking. 'A client's a member here and he booked the private room for us.'

'He must've owed Kate a massive favour,' Naomi breathed. 'He put a load of cash behind the bar and paid for all the food and everything.'

'I didn't think that sort of thing was allowed any more,' Patch cut in. 'But she seems to get away with it.'

'It's because I'm so astonishingly good at my job,' Kate said. 'It's boring as fuck, but sometimes it's worth it.'

'You look totally amazing, Ro,' Abbie said. 'Look at your hair! Like Kate Middleton.'

'And that dress is seriously foxy,' said Abbie's husband Matt.

I blurted out the story of how Clara and I had found the dress in the charity shop, which of course my friends already knew, judging by the Cheshire-cat-that-got-the-brandy-cream expressions on their faces.

'You guys,' I said. 'I can't thank you enough. You're like fairy godmothers. And here I am in a designer dress I could never have even—'

'Stop putting yourself down, sweetheart,' said Daniel. 'You need to learn to be, like, "Oh, I picked it up in a sample sale."'

'Now have some food,' Andy instructed. 'And a cocktail, so I can live vicariously for you. What'll it be? Rum manhattan? Aviation?'

'What's an aviation?'

'Gin, lemon, crème de violette and maraschino.' Andy had always had an encyclopedic knowledge of all things related to mind-altering substances. 'You'll like it.'

'And if you don't, I'll drink it,' said Daniel.

But Andy was right – the purple drink was delicious, and so were the smoked salmon blinis, pigs in blankets, sausage rolls, melted Brie on toast with cranberry sauce, and endless other food that seemed to be pressed upon us as if we hadn't eaten in weeks.

We ate and drank and chatted and laughed, and I felt myself becoming light-headed, not just from the alcohol but from the feeling of being surrounded by people who loved me, who cared about me enough to have organised this amazing night just for me – just because I needed to be made to feel special.

Because I was special. Okay, maybe that was just the alcohol but, in that moment, I truly believed it. I might not have a man in my life; I might be single for ever and ever; Alex might never want to kiss me. But at least I had the most amazing friends in the world, who'd always have my back.

At around eleven, the last of the food had been eaten and the bar tab was running dry, and someone – probably Andy, whose capacity for enjoying himself seemed undimmed by sobriety – suggested we go on somewhere to dance.

'It'll be carnage,' Patch warned. 'Christmas party season is in full force, remember?'

'I saw someone being sick on the Tube at five o'clock this afternoon,' Kate agreed.

'Walking through the City was amazing,' Abbie said. 'Packed with drunk bankers in Christmas jumpers.'

'What are we waiting for then?' Daniel asked. 'Let's go and find Ro a drunk banker in a Christmas jumper.'

'Are you saying he'd have to be drunk to fancy me?' I teased.

'Nah. Just he'd fancy you more if he could see two of you.'

Giddy with laughter, we all piled out and made our way to a club that Kate said she'd be able to get us into, and, with her usual magic touch, she succeeded. We ordered more drinks and then we danced and danced, and I was tipsy enough not to notice that my shoes were beginning to hurt, and having too much fun to care how late it was or worry about work the next day.

I remember giving my number to a man in a Santa hat – whether he was a banker or not I never knew, because he never called. I remember being bought a glass of Prosecco by a handsome bloke in a tie with penguins on it, who told me I had the best legs he'd ever seen. I remember Kate snogging a bloke in a suit, who was one hundred per cent a banker (knowing Kate, she'd have checked his LinkedIn profile before getting off with him). I remember Andy telling me that he thought he'd met someone who might genuinely be The One, and making him promise to tell me all the details when I wasn't too pissed to remember them. I remember Daniel buying me a porn star martini and telling me he loved me, which I knew was meant in a friendship kind of way, and brought on by Christmas spirit as well as the actual spirits we'd been pouring down our necks all night.

I remember my cheeks hurting from smiling and laughing so much.

And I remember Andy saying, 'Come on, beautiful, it's chucking-out time.'

'What?' I twirled to face him, a glass in my hand, my hair sticking to my lipstick. 'It can't be much after midnight.'

'It's five in the morning, sweetie,' Andy said. 'Bit late for a school night.'

'Oh my God.' If I'd had less to drink, the news would have sobered me up; as it was, it just made me dissolve in helpless giggles.

'I'd better get home,' Kate said. Her eyes were a bit glassy, her make-up smudged, and she was swaying slightly on her high heels. The man in the suit was nowhere to be seen – and I was sure would never be seen again. Kate had form for copping off with people on nights out, just to make sure she hadn't lost her touch. 'Naomi and Patch left a while back – remember?'

Oh yes. I did recall them saying something about a babysitter, telling me they loved me and reeling off into the night. Daniel had departed shortly after – or, the way time was working on this magical night, possibly a couple of hours after.

'Thank God I'm working from home tomorrow,' Abbie said. 'I'll feel like crap, but at least I can stay on the sofa all day with the cat.'

'I took the day off,' Kate said smugly. 'Strong work, sober me.'

'Are you okay to see Ro home, mate?' Matt asked.

'Course,' Andy said. 'Come on, babe, it's long past pumpkin o'clock.'

We all said goodnight, got our coats and made our way out of the almost empty club. The cold morning air – still pitch-dark, of course – did little to dispel the warm glow I still felt.

'I don't want the night to end,' I slurred. 'Can't we go on somewhere else? Just for one more? Or get a kebab? I could go straight into the office. I'll be fine.'

Poor Andy had to almost carry me to his car, my legs going in all the wrong directions like a newborn foal's. A drunk newborn foal.

'Right,' he said, opening the passenger door for me. 'Jump in. You're in safe hands.'

'What am I going to do? How am I going to work tomorrow? I haven't been up all night since forever.'

'Relax. You're in the hands of an expert. *The* expert, in fact. I've thrown more all-nighters than you've had hot dinners. We'll get you home, you'll wash your face, I'll give you some parac-etamol with loads of water. Then a quick disco nap, shower, breakfast with lots of coffee, and you'll be good to go.'

'But there's no way I'll be in a fit state to drive.'

'True.' I could see Andy's mind working as he soberly navi-gated his own car through the London streets. 'I'll drop you off there. Tell them you've got a migraine and soldiered in anyway on public transport. They'll think you're a hero, even if you're a bit late.'

'Are you sure? You don't mind staying with me so I don't oversleep?'

'Not one bit.'

'But what about your work? Won't you be exhausted?'

'Rowan,' he said, 'trust me. There's nothing better to prepare you for functioning on the sniff of an oily rag than a fifteen-year class A habit. We've got this.'

We were almost home now. Expertly, Andy reversed the Mercedes into one of the visitor parking bays outside the main car park, just off the main road.

My mind already longingly on the prospect of a couple of hours' sleep, I leaned back against the leather seat and waited for him to come round and open the door for me.

'Out you get,' he ordered. 'No nodding off until we've got that slap cleaned off.'

He took my arm and helped me out, supporting me when I stumbled on my high heels, putting his arm around my shoulder and guiding me towards the entrance to the estate.

And just then, like something out of a dream – or a nightmare – I saw the familiar Pegasus van passing, crawling along in the already heavy traffic towards town.

And in the window, I saw Alex's face, watching us with an expression I couldn't even begin to read.

CHAPTER TWENTY-SIX

Jealousy wasn't an emotion Alex had any time for. People weren't possessions; they weren't to be squabbled over like you were feral pigeons going after the same scrap of mouldy bread on the street. He'd seen enough relationships destroyed by that kind of behaviour to know it wasn't for him.

Not that he had any kind of a relationship with Rowan Connell from 74 Curlew Court anyway.

She was just a customer. Just a nice, friendly woman who treated him like a person, not like some kind of bot that knocked at her door, handed over her stuff and then disappeared off again until next time.

But he'd be kidding himself if he pretended he hadn't been hoping for something. Something a bit more than just that customer–supplier dynamic. Even if it was just friendship.

Okay, now he *was* kidding himself. He didn't want to be her friend. He had enough friends and evidently so did she. He'd hoped that somehow, sometime in the ever-decreasing number of days left between now and Christmas, after which he'd no longer have the pretext of being her delivery guy under which to see her every day, he'd be able to move the relationship on.

Ask her out for a coffee. Get her number. Kiss her under the bloody mistletoe. Just something – something more than the, 'Hi Rowan,' 'Hi, Alex,' 'Cold, isn't it?' 'Freezing, but at least the sun's out,' 'What have your mates got for you today, then?' 'Oh look, it's a bath bomb,' 'That's nice,' 'Yes, isn't it? Thanks for bringing it,' level at which they were currently operating.

He thumped the steering wheel in frustration.

Maybe, if he'd shown a bit more initiative, she wouldn't have pulled that handsome man with the flash car on her night out.

Or maybe she hadn't pulled him on her night out. Maybe he was a regular boyfriend, or a regular friend with benefits or something like that – someone she hooked up with when her daughter was with her dad.

Maybe Alex had only ever been the delivery driver in her eyes, and if he'd suggested the coffee, asked for her number or – God forbid – found a sprig of mistletoe somewhere and tried to kiss her, he'd probably have got the mother of all knock-backs. Her letter to head office could have meant something – or nothing; more likely it was just a kind gesture from a grateful customer.

But being knocked back would've been preferable to being put in a position where he didn't feel able to at least try. And that was how he felt right now.

But maybe – the thought occurred to him as he pulled the van into the driveway of one of the big houses that lined a side street, a regular stop on his route – if the guy with the Merc was someone she'd pulled on a night out, she was open to that sort of thing. He wouldn't blame her if she was – hell, in her position, who wouldn't be? With the flat to herself and no responsibilities when Clara was staying with her dad, what more logical way to behave than to get some bloke off Tinder round or go out, get bladdered and come home for some nice, no-strings sex?

Nice, no-strings sex, Alex thought bitterly. *I remember that.*

He opened the driver's door and hurried to the back of the van, levering out two large parcels and carrying them to the front door of the house, which was decorated with an outsized green, red and gold Christmas wreath. In the window, he could see what looked like thousands of lights sparkling on a tree that must have been seven feet tall. Alex balanced the boxes awkwardly on one hip while he pressed the doorbell. A pretty, dark-haired young woman – the nanny, he assumed – answered, her finger to her lips.

Presumably they had a baby, and the baby was asleep. Smiling, Alex handed over the parcels, and the young woman smiled and whispered a 'Thank you' before closing the door softly behind her.

Every day, for the past three months, Alex had been given similar, fleeting glimpses into people's lives. The woman in one of the new luxury flats, who presumably worked from home and answered the door wearing full make-up, jewellery and a freshly ironed blouse over pyjama bottoms printed with images of Garfield the cat and pink, fluffy slippers. The old guy who lived alone with his two dogs, to whom Alex delivered a parcel every day (which from the sloshing within Alex guessed contained a bottle, and from the smell on the old man's breath he guessed was whisky), handing it over into trembling, nicotine-stained hands. The lady who ordered boxes and boxes of books, and opened the door with a parrot perched on her shoulder – she seemed quite nice, he reckoned.

So why, out of all the people he encountered, all with their passions and their weaknesses and their quirks, all living their lives in the build-up to what was meant to be the most magical day of the year, was it Rowan Connell who fascinated him so much? Why did the image of her hazel eyes, with that dark rim round the irises that looked like it had been drawn on with a felt-tip pen, the soft, white skin of her hands, the glossy fall of her hair, her husky laugh, seem so powerfully alluring?

It was her story, he realised. Her vulnerability. Whatever it was that made her friends care so much about her that they'd go to so much trouble and expense to try to – as she'd put it – 'cheer her up'.

Alex had wanted to be a part of that, to see her radiant smile light up her face because of something he himself had done, rather than just something he'd done on behalf of her mates.

The way she'd been smiling at the blonde bloke with the Merc, of whom Alex absolutely, categorically, wasn't jealous in the slightest.

Anyway, he'd taken the first step of his plan to do something for her, and he was going to go through with it, even though there was nothing in it for him. He'd made up his mind and he wasn't one to go back on decisions. But first, he had his round to finish. And then he had his appointed meeting with Ailsa.

Inevitably, though, Alex ran late. There was a street of houses where the numbers, instead of running logically upwards, odds on one side, evens on the other, appeared to have been allocated by some kind of lottery, and number 63, his destination, seemed not to exist at all. It took him over half an hour to find it, and when he did it wasn't number 63 at all but had been named Lilac Grove Cottage, despite the fact that it wasn't a cottage and there were no lilac trees in sight.

There was a delivery of a flat-packed dining table and eight chairs to the top floor of a block of flats, but the intended recipient wasn't in, and the neighbour refused to take delivery, saying, 'I wouldn't piss on that cow if she was on fire,' so Alex, cursing, was forced to schlep the whole lot back down to the van.

And there was Rowan's delivery, which Alex had deliberately left until later than usual in the hope he might be able to speak to her and get some clue about what was going on with Merc Man, but she wasn't in either, so he reluctantly left the parcel – too large to fit through her letterbox – with a neighbour and left.

At last, he made his final stop, returned the van to the depot – inching with painful slowness through streets clogged with traffic and slick with rain that had that semi-solid quality that was tantalisingly close to snow but would never actually become it. Not that Alex harboured any romantic ideas of a white Christmas – it never snowed in London in December, and if by some freak of nature it were to happen, it would only make his job more difficult.

At last, at almost nine, he reached his destination. Ailsa had been asleep, he realised when she greeted him, her eyes puffy and the imprint of the sofa cushion clearly visible on her pale cheek. Someone – Omar, probably – had put up a Christmas tree in the corner of the room, and its blue and silver lights were reflected in the gloss of Ailsa's dark hair.

She yawned hugely, kissed him and brought him a beer without him having to ask.

'What a woman!' Alex said, taking the glass and sinking gratefully into an armchair.

'I thought you weren't going to turn up,' she complained. 'You said seven.'

'You know me, the eternal optimist.'

'There's optimism, and then there's being two hours late.'

'You don't mind. You were having a nap.'

'All I flaming well do these days is nap. I can't even eat. I'm bloody miserable.'

'Well, you got yourself into this. You've only yourself to blame, really. And it'll all be over by Christmas.'

'It had better be. I don't know how much more of this I can take – seriously.'

'Hey.' Alex got up and moved over to the sofa, slipping his arm around her. 'Stop moaning. You're meant to be a strong woman.'

'I know. But it hurts.'

'It's going to hurt a hell of a lot more before you're done.'

'Yeah, thanks for that. I needed reminding.'

'Happy to help. Any time you start feeling cheerful, hit me up and I'll come over and remind you that everything hurts and it's only going to get worse, and you haven't had a decent sleep in weeks and you won't any time soon.'

Ailsa laughed, and then abruptly started to cry. The first time this had happened, Alex had freaked out, but he was used to it now. Anything set her off – the John Lewis Christmas advert on the telly, the sight of the poor trussed-up turkeys in the supermarket chiller cabinet, the idea of Rudolph being teased by the other reindeer.

'Aw, come on,' Alex said, but he tightened his grip around her shoulders. 'You know what they say. Don't upset yourself.'

'You're bloody upsetting me,' Ailsa sobbed.

'I'm not. I'm right here, comforting you.'

She cried a bit more, Alex patting her back as soothingly as he could. Funny, he thought, it had been ages since a woman last cried in his arms, and now two had in the space of a week. Like buses, he reflected. It didn't take long for Ailsa's fit of self-pity to subside; it was low-key crying, not like the storm of pent-up grief Rowan had unleashed.

'You're about as much comfort as a cactus,' she complained, when her tears had stopped and Alex had passed her a tissue – a clean but crumpled one from his pocket, because there was no box of them ready on the table like Rowan had had.

'That's because I'm not here to comfort you,' he said firmly. 'You've got a job to do.'

'Fine, let's get on with it then. Although why you can't buy someone a present without roping in all and sundry to help you, I'll never understand.'

'I just value your opinion.'

He reached over for his backpack and extracted a carrier

bag. It was stiff paper, creased where he'd folded it, but he knew the contents would be undamaged, because they were cocooned in layers of tissue paper. He extracted the first carefully wrapped bundle and placed it in Ailsa's lap.

'Brora cashmere,' she said. 'You're not messing about.'

She tore carefully through the sticky label that held the edges of the tissue together and pulled out a scarf. It was pale dove grey, with a sheen to it that made it look almost silver in the light of the log fire that burned in the hearth.

'What d'you reckon?'

'Nice. But let's see the others.'

The second scarf was a brilliant cherry red, the colour of Christmas. Ailsa held it up to her face, pressing her cheek into its softness.

'Better? Not so good?'

'Hard to say. I told you not to make me decide.'

'You're going to have to, so check out the other one.'

'You're such a slave-driver.'

Her hands slightly clumsy, because her fingers were swollen, as they had been for months, Ailsa unwrapped the third scarf. It was violet – a clear, brilliant purple like amethysts. She draped it round her neck, pulling her curtain of almost-black hair away from her neck so it fell down over the cashmere, mirroring its natural gloss.

'And?' Alex asked.

'This one. Definitely.'

'You sure?'

'One hundred per cent.'

'Then get up and give me a twirl.'

'God. Do I have to?'

'Yes.'

Alex helped her to her feet. She stood, her skin – alabaster pale like Rowan's – looking almost rosy in the firelight. Her eyes were more green than hazel, but he could see how Rowan's would look, their colour contrasting with the vibrant hue of the fabric.

The similarity ended there, of course. On Rowan, the scarf would fall in a clean, almost unbroken drape from her shoulders to her hips. On Ailsa, it ballooned out, supported by the shape Alex thought he'd got used to until it became even more extreme the next time he saw her.

'Okay?' Awkwardly, Ailsa performed a clumsy pirouette, then let herself sink back onto the sofa.

'Beautiful. That's the one then. I knew you'd be able to help.'

An hour or so later, Alex was back on his bicycle, heading through the sleety rain to work through the night. As he rode, he tried to conjure up an image of Rowan wearing the scarf, smiling, her elegant hand reaching up to caress the silky cashmere, but his mind obstinately refused to co-operate and it was only Ailsa's face he saw.

CHAPTER TWENTY-SEVEN

'I don't want to go to Winter Wonderland,' Clara said. 'I want to go bowling with Lily.'

She wasn't making her broccoli face now; she was making the face she used to make when she was about two and being asked to do something wholly unreasonable like open her mouth so I could clean her teeth or put the scissors down.

'But, Clara...' I began, and then my words trailed off helplessly.

The tickets to the Christmas funfair – which promised not only a Ferris wheel, rollercoasters and ice skating but also fresh cinnamon doughnuts, mulled apple juice and vegan frank-furters in buns – had sounded like Clara's idea of heaven. I knew my daughter and, for all her teenage cynicism, there was nothing she liked better than a bit of Christmas tat. There would be iced gingerbread and oompah bands and teeth-rotting candy canes, for God's sake. She'd love it.

Except, clearly, she'd love to go bowling with Lily more.

My gut instinct told me there was more to this than met the eye. Clara had been bowling before and hated it. 'God, it's the most pointless thing ever,' she'd said after a birthday party at All

Star Lanes. 'And why don't they make those ball things so that people with normal hands can actually, like, hold them?'

From which I'd gathered that Clara hadn't found her sporting niche in life. Which was fair enough – given she was my daughter, I reckoned it was highly probable she didn't *have* a sporting niche in life.

So this sudden change of tune must, I reckoned, be about something more than the desire to impress her friends by getting a strike. I remembered what it was like being fourteen: how the approval of my friends had mattered more than anything – with the possible exception of the approval of boys.

I wasn't going to ask her whether Jonny was going to be there, but I was pretty sure I knew the answer.

I caught Paul's eye. He'd been watching our exchange, which had begun as soon as Clara got out of his car, just as I was getting out of mine, with the same bemusement I'd felt, and I wondered whether he'd jumped to the same conclusion I had. He gave a gesture that was half eye-roll, half shrug with a bit of rueful grin thrown in, and made it clear he wasn't going to get involved in this disagreement.

'The Winter Wonderland thing was meant to be fun,' I said. 'If you think you'll have more fun doing something else, I'm certainly not going to force you to come with me.'

'Really? Are you sure?' The I'm-about-to-launch-World-War-Three expression had melted off my daughter's face as if it had never been there. 'You're so cool. I knew you'd understand. Lily's mum said she'd pick me up at six if you said yes. So I'd better get changed.'

She hoisted her bag higher on her shoulder and turned towards the lift.

Then she turned back, her face falling again. 'Mum? You're not disappointed?'

Well, I kind of was. It felt a bit like I was letting my friends down by missing out on this fun experience, which they'd presumably thought would be a great way for me to bond with Clara while reawakening the magic of Christmas. But at the same time, getting through a day of Brett and Marty's sniping with a weapons-grade hangover had almost broken me. Around lunchtime, I'd been ready to sneak off to the loo and have a quiet cry, but I'd remembered the tube of Berocca Kimberley had left in her desk drawer and helped myself to one, which basically saved my life.

So the prospect of a night in on my own nursing the last of my hangover had quite a lot of appeal. 'It's okay, sweetheart,' I said. 'I'll get over it.'

'Will you go on your own?' Clara asked.

If only I could go with Alex. The thought flashed unbidden into my mind, together with a picture of the two of us together, hand in hand under a frosty sky sparkling with stars. But as soon as it had appeared, it vanished again. There was no way, even if I'd had the chance to ask him, I'd have had the courage.

I shook my head. 'That sort of thing really isn't fun on your own.'

'I...' Clara hesitated. I could see her wrestling with her conscience. 'Mum, of course I'll go with you if you want to go.'

I almost laughed, touched by this rare example of selfless-ness. 'You'll do no such thing. You go bowling and have an amazing time. It really doesn't matter.'

Then Paul said, 'I'll go with you, Ro.'

'What?'

'That's such a great idea, Dad. You and Mum will have the best time.'

'But what about...' I began.

'Hayley's icing Christmas cakes all evening,' Paul said.

'She specifically said she'd like you out of her hair, didn't she, Dad?'

'I'm not much use when it comes to rolling marzipan, to be

fair,' Paul said. 'Come on, Ro. Let's do it. You know I love a mulled wine and a pretzel.'

It was true – I knew Paul would be delighted by the whole shebang, probably even more enthusiastic than Clara. And it was good for our daughter to see that we could be amicable, have fun together like adults in a friendly co-parenting relationship. Which, of course, we were.

Except, until very recently, we'd been that and then some.

'Okay,' I said. 'Let's do it.'

Paul followed Clara and me into the lift and sat in the living room with a coffee while we got changed, flicking on the TV as naturally as he had when it had been his living room too. Part of me felt a prickling resentment at his casual presence there. Part of me felt battered by nostalgia for the time when it had been the two of us and our baby daughter, a little family with the future ahead of us. And another, far more shameful part, was remembering the times, not so long ago at all, when we'd have waited there together, chatting casually, until Clara's friend's mum had picked her up and then ripped each other's clothes off and had sex without even making it as far as the bedroom.

Without even making it as far as undressing properly, if I was honest.

So I dressed hastily, throwing on jeans and a jumper, boots and a scarf, not bothering to repair my make-up or do more with my hair than pull it back into a ponytail and stick a pompommed beanie hat over it.

Clara, on the other hand, was taking her time. I waited impatiently, hovering in my room, not wanting to go and join Paul on the sofa, until at last she emerged, wearing denim shorts, a cut-off T-shirt, clompy black boots and a teddy-bear coat. She was dressed totally unsuitably for the December cold and she looked absolutely beautiful.

And it was my duty as her mother to comment on only one of those things.

'You look gorgeous, sweetie. Have fun.'

'You too.' She smiled, almost shyly, then kissed me, kissed Paul, tucked her phone and keys in her pocket, and hurried out, saying that her lift was waiting.

'She'll freeze to death in that get-up,' Paul said.

'She'll be indoors. No teenager's ever died of exposure in a London bowling alley, far as I know.'

'Always a first time. Shall we head off, or shall we—'

'Let's go. Our tickets are for six thirty.'

I wasn't sure what he'd been about to say, and I definitely didn't want to know.

We got the bus and then the Tube to Hyde Park, making our way through the crowds towards Winter Wonderland. All around us, it seemed to me, were couples. Couples holding hands; couples wrangling small children, couples snogging each other while they waited for the green man so they could cross the road.

I supposed anyone looking at Paul and me would think we were a couple, too. Parents enjoying a night out without their kids, maybe, or people who'd met on Bumble heading off for a first date, still too awkward to touch each other.

'So,' Paul said, once we'd reached the front of the queue and gained entrance passing under an archway covered with sparkling lights that felt like the portal to Christmas itself, 'what shall we do first? Hot chocolate? Ice bar? Go on a ride?'

'Mulled wine,' I decided. 'And something to eat. And then maybe the Ferris wheel?'

'Gotcha,' he said. 'I'll fight my way to the bar. Be right back.'

Paul had always been like that, I remembered – gentlemanly. If we went to a restaurant together, he'd always wait for me to sit down first. When it was our turn to a buy a round in the pub, it would always be him who went to the bar. He even opened car doors for me, and for Clara. Hell, if men still wore hats, you could guarantee that Paul would be whipping his off every time he so much as glimpsed a woman.

At first, I thought it was charming and respectful, then I'd got used to it and after a while I'd started to find it a bit too much. I was perfectly capable of wheeling my own suitcase through the airport, rather than having to wait for Paul to go off and find a trolley on which to stack both our cases lest I damage my fragile feminine shoulders – or his even more fragile masculine ego.

Still, I was glad it was him who was navigating the crowd at the bar – not to mention paying the extortionate going rate for a glass of mulled wine – and not me.

He returned a few minutes later, precariously balancing four cups of fragrant, steaming red liquid, and two smaller ones containing something clear.

'It's mayhem up there,' he reported. 'So I got us this round and the next plus a vodka chaser. Here, grab this before I drop it – it's hot.'

Carefully, I manoeuvred a mulled wine and a vodka out of his hands, and he put the spares down on the table next to us.

'Well, cheers,' I said. 'Happy Christmas. Thanks for coming along tonight.'

We tapped the rims of our glasses together and downed our vodka. The spirit blazed down my throat, cold at first, then warming, then threatening to awaken the last of my hangover and make me feel sick. But it didn't – I felt a pleasant glow begin to spread through me, aided by a gulp of warm, cinnamon-scented wine.

'It's nice being here with you,' Paul said. 'Weird, but nice.'

He smiled, the corners of his mouth and eyes crinkling in that familiar way, the end of his nose turning pink from the cold. I remembered the first time I'd noticed that his front teeth were ever so slightly crooked, the left just crossing over the right, and how that small flaw had made me love him more than

I'd ever dreamed I could love anyone. Paul – strong, masculine Paul – had an imperfection that made him somehow vulnerable, in need of protection.

Of course, none of the imperfections I'd observed after that had had anything like the same effect.

'It's been a while, hasn't it?' I asked casually, taking another gulp of wine.

Paul met my eyes and he winked. 'Sure has.'

Oh no. That wasn't what I'd meant – not at all. But if I denied it, I'd only be drawing attention to it.

Suddenly, it seemed very important that we finish our drinks and move the hell on.

'Thing about mulled wine,' I said, picking up my second glass and getting stuck in, 'is it's absolutely gorgeous when it's hot and absolutely minging cold. Don't you think?'

'Agreed.' Paul joined me, necking a good third of his in one go. 'Lots of things are better hot, I've found.'

Jesus. Is he flirting with me?

'Um... yes, totally. See also bread sauce and... um... hot-water bottles.'

Another couple of gulps. I was going strong – one more swallow and I'd be done.

'Soup,' Paul agreed. 'And feet. Nothing worse than cold feet in bed. Hayley—'

I was one hundred per cent not here for him slagging off his fiancée. Nor did I want to know anything at all about her feet. I'd been going to suggest we have a go on the ice rink, but a session had just started, and waiting for the next one would involve a period of hanging about that would inevitably lead to another drink and more of this – whatever this was.

'Look,' I said, 'there's hardly any queue for the Ferris wheel. Shall we have a go?'

'Good shout.'

Whatever Paul had been about to reveal about Hayley had

clearly been forgotten, at least for now. We put our empty cups in a recycling bin, I wound my scarf more tightly around my neck and we headed off to the funfair. The cold air smelled of toffee apples and frying doughnuts; I could hear brass instruments playing somewhere and, more distantly, the sound of a choir singing 'O Little Town of Bethlehem'. The lights of the rides arced through the sky above us, purple, red, green and gold, and more distant still was the clear arch of a crescent moon.

It could have been magical – would have been magical – if I'd been with someone I was in love with.

Just a few weeks ago, I would have found it magical being with Paul – all sorts of yearnings would have been released inside me, making my heart race and my knees tremble. But now I felt only sadness, that something that should have felt so special felt only tawdry; that a night I should have wished would never end couldn't be over soon enough.

Safety in numbers, I told myself as we waited to be let onto one of the glass-walled capsules of the wheel. In front of us was a couple with a small child – they'd do nicely. There's be no funny business from Paul with a five-year-old around. But as the capsule inched towards ground level and the people in it got out, the child seemed to have a change of heart.

'Mummy, I'm scared,' he said.

'Don't be scared, Rufus,' said his father. 'It's perfectly safe.'

'Come on, darling,' his mother cajoled. 'You've been looking forward to this for ages. We'll get to see the whole of London from up there – it'll be amazing.'

'I feel sick,' said Rufus.

'Maybe he shouldn't have had churros *and* a hot dog,' muttered his father.

'Well, it is Christmas,' his mum said defensively.

Then Rufus – clearly a child of action – proved his point by dropping onto all fours and unleashing a stream of technicolour vomit onto the grass.

'Oh, you poor possum!' His mother knelt down next to him, narrowly avoiding the sick. 'Pass me the wipes from my bag, will you?'

'I can't see them. You've got all kinds of crap in here but no—'

'In the side pocket. Where they always are. God, can't you ever—'

'I knew that hot dog smelled dodgy. You shouldn't let him have food that—'

'Come on, Ro.' Before I could object, Paul had steered me around the family and into the vacant capsule, which immediately began its inching ascent.

'Parenting, hey.' Paul reached over and patted my knee. 'It's a funny old business, isn't it?'

'That's for sure,' I agreed. 'Remember that time we took Clara to the seaside when she was two? It was meant to be the biggest treat ever and it all went horribly wrong.'

'We bought her fish and chips and she screamed like we were trying to poison her.'

'And then she dropped her ice cream on the sand and, oh my God, it was like the world had ended.'

'And you spunked about a tenner trying to get her a teddy out of one of those rigged games with the claw thing.'

'And when I eventually gave up...'

'Another epic tantrum.'

We laughed, my uneasiness dissolving somewhat.

'We're doing an okay job, I reckon.' Paul's voice was serious again. 'She's a good kid.'

'She's a teenager,' I said. 'It's not easy. It's like one of those filters on Instagram where the intensity of all the colours gets ramped right the way up so it hurts your eyes to look at it.'

'You mean the way she feels?'

I nodded. 'There's no shades of grey with her any more. She's either being absolutely adorable, or she goes all contemptuous and looks at me like—'

'Like she used to look at broccoli?'

'Exactly!'

We laughed again. Paul's hand was still on my leg, I noticed. There didn't seem to be a way to get him to move it that wouldn't seem somehow churlish and ungrateful.

Although why I should feel grateful just because he was being normal and nice, I couldn't be sure.

As the wheel continued to turn, our capsule rose higher and higher. Gradually, the whole fairground – the whole Winter Wonderland – stretched out below us. The glittering lights of the stalls, the spinning carousels, the sheet of silvery ice with skating figures circling over its surface like the wind-up toy my granny used to bring out at Christmas time, the smoky smell of grilling sausages rising through the cold air and the distant sounds of music coming up to meet us.

Then we rose higher, and I saw the expanse of blackness that was the lake, the Houses of Parliament in the distance, the loop of the London Eye, a much bigger Ferris wheel than this one, on the other side of the river, rendered small by distance.

Perhaps, I thought, the passage of time had made all the things that had gone wrong between Paul and me seem small and insignificant too.

'You know, Ro,' he said. 'Sometimes I kind of miss...'

'Miss what?'

'Us. All those times when we— you know.'

'Paul, what the hell are you even saying?'

'I'm saying I still want you, Rowan.'

And then, high up in the darkness with no witnesses except the rising moon, he kissed me.

CHAPTER TWENTY-EIGHT

Naomi: Oh my God! He what?

Kate: Jeez! The brass neck of the man!

Abbie: I can't believe it! What about – whatsername – his fiancée?

Rowan: That's what I said. When I'd managed to get him to stop sucking my face like a bloody Hoover. And when I'd got over the shock. What about poor bloody Hayley?

Kate: Quite right. What about her?

Rowan: He came up with a load of blather about how it had all moved so quickly, and now that they're talking about setting an actual date for the wedding, he's not sure about it any more.

Naomi: So cancel the wedding first, then snog your ex.

Abbie: Or better still, don't snog your ex! I mean, really. Who does he think he is?

I looked up from my phone. Julz was giving me the eye from behind his computer screen; presumably he'd seen me smiling, which I could never help when I was exchanging news with my friends – which, admittedly, I probably shouldn't have been doing at all during working hours.

But it was the first chance I'd had all day to share an update on the previous night with the Girlfriends' Club. Obviously, the first thing I'd said to Paul – like I said, once I'd managed to prise him off me; the man was like a bloody octopus – had been, 'What about Hayley?'

But, if I was completely honest with myself, that hadn't been my first thought. For a moment, Paul's kiss had transported me back to a time when it would have filled me with excitement, desire and even joy: the hope that maybe this was it, this was the moment when he would realise that he still loved me, that we were meant to be together, that we could be a proper family again.

This time, though, those thoughts simply hadn't been there. There had only been shock that this was happening, annoyance that he'd assumed I'd be fine with it – welcome it, even – and, strangely, revulsion.

It was as if, by the mere fact of being prepared to cheat on his fiancée with me, Paul had ceased to be fanciable.

Although – I tapped a few keys on my computer, hoping it would make me look busy – it hadn't been as sudden as that. The truth was, I'd stopped fancying Paul quite a while ago. I tried to recall the last time we'd had sex, at my flat, waiting for Clara to get back from her modern dance class so he could drive her over to his place. Like so many of the previous times, it had been furtive, rushed, awkward. It had ended with his climax and never even got close to mine.

I'd just let it happen to me, as if it was the closest thing I'd get to love.

And since then, something inside of me had changed. I wasn't sure how or why, but I didn't want to be a person things just happened to any more.

Especially not that thing.

I'd told him to stop, and he'd listened. I'd given him a bit of a lecture about inappropriate behaviour, and he'd looked shamefaced. I'd said that if he had doubts about Hayley, he needed to address them with her, not go around snogging other women like a randy sixteen-year-old, and he'd humbly agreed.

And by that stage, the wheel had come back down to earth – and it wasn't the only thing that had. We'd said goodbye and gone our separate ways, and the only communication we'd had since had been a one-word text message: *Sorry*.

I hadn't replied; I didn't know what to say. Part of me wanted to berate him for being so stupid and selfish and inappropriate. Part of me wanted to berate him for not changing his mind about me six months ago, when it would have made me ecstatically happy. Part of me wanted to reassure him that it was all okay, like I used to do when Clara was little and had apologised for squirting all my shower gel down the toilet or giving her Barbie doll a buzz cut.

And part of me, pathetically, wanted to say I was sorry too, although I couldn't think what I had done wrong.

The trill of my desk phone jerked me out of my reverie. I reached for it but, as usual, Brett got there first.

'Walkerson's Elite, Brett speaking,' he gabbled at top speed. 'Oh, hi, Tatiana. They have? That's great. Two point seven five mil? Awesome. That's a good offer. We'll let the seller know right away. You too. Speak soon.'

Gently, he lowered the receiver back into its cradle and turned to me, a smirk spreading over his face.

'Contact of Tatiana's has made an offer on the Gower Street apartment.'

'But I—' I began. But there was no point telling him that I'd submitted an offer on the same property on behalf of one of Kimberley's applicants just the day before, confident that it would be accepted. He knew. And it had been right at the top of their budget – there was no way they'd be able to stretch to another fifty grand to match the offer Brett had just received.

And this wasn't the first time this had happened. A few days before, another of my potential sales had fallen through after another 'contact of Tatiana's' with deep pockets had made a higher offer through Marty, meaning that he, not I, would get the commission.

I knew that the industry I worked in was brutal and competitive, but this was starting to feel personal. And I had no idea what I could do to stop it. I thought of the other offer I had pending, on behalf of my own applicant, and could only pray that that, at least, would be safe.

In silence, I gathered up my things and left the office.

For once, the traffic was on my side, and it was only just gone four thirty when I arrived home, easing Portia into her parking space and climbing out into the cold, damp, pitch-black evening. The wind bit into my neck above my coat collar, and I cursed myself for leaving my trusty black fleece scarf on the Tube the previous night – and Paul for discombobulating me so thoroughly I forgot I'd taken it off. I thought of the story I'd read Clara when she was in primary school, which my mum had read me, about the land of Narnia, ruled by the White Witch, where it was always winter but never Christmas.

In spite of there being only a week to go, in spite of the twinkling lights I could see in the windows above me, in spite of having overdosed on festive vibes the previous evening, in my heart, that was how it felt.

Without much hope, I pressed the button to call the lift. I

waited a few seconds then began to trudge wearily up the stairs. As I panted my way up from the fifth floor to the sixth, I heard hurrying feet above me and, seconds later, literally almost bumped into Alex coming down.

'Hello!' I was startled by how cheered I felt by seeing him. 'How's it going? I missed you yesterday.'

'I ran late,' he said shortly. 'Too many deliveries, not enough hours in the day. You were out when I knocked.'

I looked at him, startled by his tone. He wasn't smiling. His lips were set in a straight line, like a child's clumsy drawing of a face. Under the peak of his cap, I could see dark shadows beneath his eyes. He looked absolutely knackered.

'Yes, I was. I went to Winter Wonderland – remember, the tickets came a few days ago?'

For some reason, I didn't want to tell him I'd gone with Paul. And then I remembered – he'd seen me the previous day, with Andy. Was this the reason for his strange mood?

'That sounds like fun,' he said. 'Right, I'd better get on. Your parcel today fitted through the door, so it's there waiting for you.'

'Don't you want to see what it is?' I asked, in a tone that I meant to be light-hearted but just came out needy.

He half shook his head, looking past me down the stairs. Then he said, 'Oh, go on then.'

He turned, and I followed him the rest of the way up to the flat, making sure I took advantage of the view of his bum and strong thighs as he powered up the stairs.

He waited by the door while I unlocked it, bent over and retrieved the parcel: another of the flat rectangular boxes, about the size of a paperback book, which must have been designed specially to fit through letterboxes.

Alex watched as I pulled open the tab, standing so close I could feel the warmth of his breath on my hands, contrasting with the chilly evening air.

The box felt surprisingly heavy, and I soon saw why. Out into my hand, I slid a Christmas ornament. It was a glass star with veins of gold running through it and a slim gold ribbon threaded through its top.

'Christmas tree ornament,' Alex said.

'*The* Christmas tree ornament,' I corrected him. 'The star's the most important one of all, isn't it?'

A picture came into my mind of Paul holding two-year-old Clara up high so that she could fix the star to the top of the tree, the last Christmas we'd all spent together. I'd made that one, cutting it out of the cardboard back of a notebook and sticking gold paper onto it.

Now, Alex did smile. 'You're right. And that's a beauty.'

'Only problem is,' I said, 'we don't have a Christmas tree. We used to – just a cheap plastic one. But it got so shabby we had to throw it away. Half its branches had fallen off, and its stand was all wonky.'

'So get another one? This star deserves a decent tree, don't you reckon?'

I turned the star over in my hand, enjoying the feel of its cool, smooth surface. 'Yeah, I know. Only Clara's set her heart on a real one. I suggested just replacing the one we had and I got a massive lecture about microplastics in the oceans and the evils of a throwaway consumer culture. But I haven't got around to going and buying one, and even if I did, I can't see how we could possibly carry it up the stairs, and I don't know when the lift's going to be fixed.'

'You can order them online. Specify the type and height and everything. You can even get companies that'll collect the tree and keep it in a pot and you get the same one next year.'

'Really? That's cool. But it would cost...'

'Sixty or seventy quid. Yeah, I see the problem. Not a lot of money for some people, but—'

'It is for me.'

I looked back down at the star. Alex couldn't know, I realised, just how tight things were for me, money-wise. All the expensive gifts – and of course the ones that had cost nothing apart from my friends' time and effort – must have given him the impression that I was someone who, even if not exactly rolling in dosh herself, wasn't short of life's little luxuries. But then, surely, as a guy working a job that barely paid minimum wage, he'd get it?

'I get it,' he said.

'I can hang it in the window,' I said. 'It'll still look pretty and Christmassy. Clara will be happy.'

'Come on,' Alex said. 'I've got a better idea.'

'What? Come where?'

'Down to the van. There's a place about half a mile away that's got all the Christmas trees you could eat. We'll get you one there and I'll carry it upstairs for you. I've had plenty of practice.'

'But what about the rest of your round?'

'Half an hour won't make any difference one way or the other. Come on, before I change my mind.'

His amazing grin flashed out, properly this time. I felt myself smiling back, warmth filling me like I'd just necked a hot chocolate.

I slipped the star into my handbag, locked up and we hurried back downstairs. Alex opened the door and I climbed into the now-familiar interior of the Pegasus van. He drove, as he had the time before, carefully and economically, and it wasn't long before we were pulling into a parking space outside a garden centre, where fir and spruce trees were arranged in ranks by height, some festooned with lights, looking like a little Christmas army.

'Pick your poison,' Alex said.

Feeling as if I was in a dream, I got out of the van, the resin scent of the trees meeting me. It was like walking into a forest –

perhaps the forest in Narnia. Except now, although it was winter, Christmas was truly here.

The garden centre staff had lit a brazier, which they'd need if they were going to be working outdoors until late on this icy night, and I could see its flames licking upwards into the darkness and smell woodsmoke. Above the ranks of trees, multi-coloured fairy lights zigzagged, flickering against the sky as rhythmically as dancers. Somewhere, a radio was playing 'Jingle Bell Rock'.

Alex followed me as I walked through the avenue of trees, passing the tall six- and seven-foot ones, which would be far too large for the flat.

'You're sure?' Alex asked. 'What happened to go big or go home?'

'I wouldn't be able to fit into my home if I brought that monster in,' I pointed out, gesturing towards a Nordmann fir so large it would have filled my entire living room.

'You're saying you want to go for girth rather than length?'

I glanced at him and saw the determinedly deadpan expression on his face.

'Dimensions aren't everything, you know,' I said. 'It's about appropriateness for the available space.'

'Bet you say that to all the boys.'

'Only the ones who seem overly concerned with size.'

'Touché.' Alex laughed and I felt a fizz of happiness at my jokes landing with him.

At last, we came to the smaller trees, and I saw a four-foot one, perfectly shaped, not too wide and not too bushy.

'This one,' I said. 'It's perfect.'

'It's yours,' Alex said.

We had a brief tussle over who would pay for the tree and ended up compromising on half each, and by the time he carried the mesh-wrapped bundle to the van, any coldness there'd been in his manner earlier seemed to have thawed. He drove us back to the flat and, once again, I found myself panting up the stairs in his wake, losing sight of him, the tree and his back view by about the third floor.

By the time I made it to the top, he was standing by the front door, holding the tree upright by its top, his jacket slung over his shoulder. He was sweating slightly from the climb too, I was relieved to notice.

'Thank you,' I said, for about the millionth time. 'I'm so grateful, I really am.'

'Don't thank me,' he said. 'Let's get this bad boy up.'

I considered asking again whether he could spare the time off from his round, but I didn't – I was pretty sure he'd have left if he'd wanted to, and I realised that I quite badly wanted him to stay.

'Shall I make a cup of tea?' I suggested. 'And I'll see if I can dig out the box of decorations.'

'Tea would be great.' Alex was kneeling on the floor of my living room, adjusting the tree in its stand, leaning back to squint at it and check that it was upright. I paused for a moment, admiring the muscles in his back and arms.

Then I hurried off to the kitchen, returning a few minutes later with the box of decorations, two mugs of tea and a tub of Quality Street balanced on its top.

Together, we unwrapped my motley collection of baubles and tinsel from the squares of kitchen roll in which I'd stored them and arranged them on the branches, pausing occasionally for sips of tea and chocolates.

'There's something odd going on here,' Alex said, peeling the foil off a hazelnut noisette and hanging up a rather tatty cardboard robin that Clara had made in primary school.

'Odd how? What's wrong?' I almost dropped a gold pine cone when my hand accidentally brushed against his arm.

'All the good ones are left.' He gestured towards the choco-lates. 'That's not how it's meant to work. You eat all the green triangles first, then the purple ones, and then right at the end you resort to the dregs of toffee pennies.'

I felt my face colour. I'd almost forgotten the last time I'd lain alone in bed, trying to eat my feelings in the form of sweets, but forcing myself to leave the best ones till last.

'I... I prefer the toffees, actually,' I lied.

'Really?' He positioned a red felt Santa hat on a branch. 'You're sure? No one likes the toffees best.'

'I do,' I insisted, crossing my fingers behind my back the way Clara used to when she was telling a fib.

'In that case, you're my dream woman. Hell, you're everyone's dream woman.'

Our eyes met for a second, and I felt myself blushing so turned to the box of decorations, fishing out the last few and handing him a couple of scratched silver baubles.

'Shame it's not got me my dream man, then,' I said. 'I guess even an unlimited supply of those purple ones isn't enough to bring all the boys to the yard.'

'The boys don't know what they're missing.' He hung the baubles on the tree, drank the last of the tea and took a purple Quality Street – and I didn't even mind. 'How about... I mean, I don't want to sound like a stalker or anything. But I couldn't help seeing... the other morning...'

There was no hiding my blush this time – I was right there next to him, stretching up to put a gilt cardboard angel on one of the top branches.

'Oh my God, I was so drunk,' I said. 'So, so drunk. My mate Andy dropped me off and came in with me to make sure I could get some kip and be up in time for work. He's a recovering addict so he doesn't drink. But also, he's gay. Although I think he may have eaten a few of my chocolates while I was asleep, so you kind of have a point.'

Alex laughed. I'd never get tired of making him laugh, I thought – it was the kind you can't help joining in with.

'I like Andy already,' he said. 'He scoffed all the strawberry delights. No one with taste likes those either.'

Weird – I'd barely noticed their absence.

'I think we're about done here,' I said, surveying the tree. Even bedecked with my ramshackle collection of decorations, it looked great.

'Just one thing left,' Alex said.

'The star!' I'd almost forgotten it was there.

I took it out of my bag and held it up to the light, seeing it sparkle as it turned gently on its gold ribbon.

'You do the honours,' Alex suggested.

Carefully, I threaded the ribbon over the topmost branch. It dipped slightly under the weight of the glass then sprang upright again. Like a designer bag paired with a Primark outfit, it immediately lent an air of class to the whole tree.

We stepped back together and admired it for a moment. The shabbiness of the flat barely registered with me in that moment – the tree made everything magical.

'Thank you,' I breathed. 'Thank you so much.'

'My pleasure,' Alex said. 'Glad I could help.'

The formality of his words seemed to mute the closeness I'd felt to him – but I didn't want it dimmed. I stretched out my arms, inviting him in for a hug.

For a second, he hesitated, then he stepped into the circle of my arms and we embraced. Just for a moment, our bodies were pressed together, and I felt the heat of him against me, the strength of his back beneath my hands.

I could even smell him. He smelled amazing – the fragrance of clean clothes I'd noticed before and something else, a cedar scent that was almost like the Christmas tree itself.

Then we both heard the scrape of a key in the door, and we moved apart – not guiltily or urgently, just kind of naturally.

'Mum!' Clara called from the hallway. 'I completely forgot to tell you, Sarita next door gave me your parcel from yesterday when I was leaving for school this morning. It's been in my bag all— Oh my God.'

She took in the scene: Alex, me, the Christmas tree and the star. I waited, praying that there wouldn't be an outburst of – what? Horror? Disgust? Anger?

But she said, 'Did you bring the tree for Mum? You're ace.'

And she bestowed one of her special smiles on him, the ones that lit up her whole face.

'We did it together,' Alex and I said, our words colliding in mid-air. 'It was a team effort.'

'And the star came today,' I said, blushing like a loon again.

'It's awesome,' Clara said. 'But you're a day behind. Come on, open this.'

She chucked a parcel over to me. It was a larger, squashier one, a bit like the ill-fated Christmas jumper had been.

Alex said, 'I really need to make a move. I'm running way behind. Thanks for the tea, Rowan. See you later, Clara.'

'Thank you so much again,' I blurted, and Clara echoed, 'Yes, thank you, Alex.'

But he was already shrugging on his high-vis jacket, pulling the baseball cap back onto his head. Before we could say anything more, he'd disappeared with a brief wave, the front door crashing shut behind him.

'He's nice,' Clara said absently. 'Go on, open it.'

I wanted to sit and admire the tree, and remember the moments I'd spent close to him, how his body had felt, how he'd smelled. The warmth of his breath on my skin. The way his hands had looked on the steering wheel of the van.

But all that would have to wait until I was in bed alone, to be savoured – not mindlessly devoured like the chocolates I knew I wouldn't need that night.

I tore open the plastic package and let its contents slip into my hands.

Clara and I both gasped. It was a scarf – what we used to

call a pashmina, back in the day. I could feel from its almost slippery softness that it was a blend of cashmere and silk.

It reflected the light, not sparkling like the star on top of the tree but with a kind of rich gloss.

And it was the most perfect, gorgeous deep violet colour I'd ever seen.

CHAPTER TWENTY-NINE

When I walked into my living room on Sunday morning, the sight of the tree still took me by surprise. It wasn't like I'd forgotten it was there – of course I hadn't. But my mind was on other things – asking Clara to sort out the clothes on her bedroom floor so I could do a load of washing and she wouldn't bring shame on our house by having nothing to wear to Paul's parents' place at Christmas; the offer I had sent over on behalf of my applicant on Friday for the house on Wentworth Street; whether it was worth bothering to paint my toenails, given no one except me and my daughter would be seeing my feet.

So, when I was greeted by the scent of pine needles and the sight of the glimmering baubles and the glossy gold star, I stopped short, a smile spreading over my face. And the smile stayed there when I remembered the half hour I'd spent with Alex, decorating the tree. That, and the hug we'd shared. It had been a platonic, friendly hug, I told myself. There was no point getting worked up about it. He was just being kind.

All the same, my whole body thrilled remembering the feel of his arms around me, the clean man-smell of him, how strong and solid and – well, exciting – his body had felt pressed against mine.

I'm not going to lie, I was singing as I switched on the kettle. And for some reason, my brain picked 'Last Christmas' – my own personal Whamageddon, right there in my kitchen.

'God, Mum, stop making that racket,' Clara complained, shuffling in in her slippers, wearing a crop top and knickers. 'You know you can't sing. How am I meant to get any sleep? And it's freezing in here. Can't we turn the heating up?'

'It's half past ten,' I said. 'You were out like a light at eleven last night. And we can't turn the heating up because I got the gas bill yesterday and nearly had a heart attack. Put some clothes on if you're cold and stop parading about like a Victoria's Secret Angel. And have a cup of tea.'

Clara must have noticed my good mood, because she said, 'Hot chocolate? With marshmallows?'

'Oh, all right.' Now she mentioned it, I quite fancied one myself. 'And pancakes?'

'Pancakes? Yeah! I'm going to shower.'

A few seconds later I heard the sound of running water and smelled the honey and ginger shower gel that had been the previous day's advent-calendar gift. A different driver had delivered it, giving me mixed feelings of relief at not having to have an awkward encounter with Alex after our last delightful one, and disappointment that it wasn't him. When I'd asked the other driver where he was, he'd shrugged and said he was covering the route.

And there hadn't been a gift for today. It wasn't like I minded – I'd received so many amazing surprises. But there were only five days left until Christmas, and I was conscious that this magical, fun adventure would soon come to an end, and the prospect made me want to cry if I thought about it too much.

So I focused on frothing milk and beating batter, and

arranged maple syrup, cinnamon sugar, lemon wedges and Nutella on the counter, and by the time I was frying the first pancake, easing its lacy edges off the pan with a spatula, my mouth beginning to water at the smell of crisping batter, Clara had re-emerged, dressed in ripped mom jeans and a fluffy jumper.

'What are you up to today?' I asked.

'Going to meet Lily at Westfield.'

'Shopping? Movie?'

Did she even have money for either? I could spare twenty quid, I reckoned.

She picked up her hot chocolate, the sleeves of her jumper shielding her hands against the heat of the mug and blew on it. 'Just hanging out. I might try some stuff on.'

Ah, hanging out at shopping malls – one of the joys of being a teenager.

'Okay. I'll give you some cash so you can get lunch.'

I flipped a pancake onto her plate and poured more batter into the pan. The next one was mine by rights, and I was planning on some serious maple syrup action.

'Thanks, Mum,' Clara said, then added graciously, 'I'll sort some washing before I go.'

And leave me to wash, dry and fold it, like your domestic drudge, I thought ruefully. But it was a concession of sorts, so I said nothing, instead rolling up a pancake and biting into it, feeling the sugary hit of the syrup burst onto my tongue.

Half an hour later, fuelled with pancakes, Clara left to get the bus. Even though she was normally skulking silently in her room, the flat felt empty without her, and I realised I felt lonely. In just four years or so, she'd be off to university, and then it would be like this all the time. The prospect hit me with such a chill of fear that I pushed it out of my mind and busied myself tidying, cleaning, washing up and sorting laundry.

By early afternoon, I'd cleaned everything there was to

clean, including having a shower myself, and there was nothing more to do. The remainder of the afternoon stretched ahead, featureless. If the shops hadn't been shutting in a couple of hours, I'd have been tempted to go and hang out in a mall myself, like an adolescent girl whiling away the time until her life properly began.

But my life had begun – it might even be half over, if I was unlucky. I had my job. I had my friends. I had my daughter. One day, I might even have grandchildren – cute chubby babies I could cuddle when they were being cute and give back when they screamed.

But would I ever have love? Would I ever have anyone who was just for me, once Clara was grown up and gone?

My phone buzzed, jerking me out of my melancholy thoughts. It could be Clara, stranded somehow and needing a lift. It could be Paul wanting to make arrangements for me to drop her off on Thursday.

But it was a text from an unfamiliar number.

Good afternoon, Rowan. This is your Sunday advent-calendar gift.

There was a pause and then my phone buzzed again.

Today you'll be going on an adventure. Dress warmly. Click the link below when you are ready to begin.

An adventure? Well, whatever it was, it would be better than sitting at home feeling sorry for myself. Quickly, I put on some make-up and brushed my hair, then wound the beautiful violet scarf around my neck, stuffed my feet into warm boots, added my trusty beanie hat and fingerless gloves, and pulled on my coat.

Then I tapped the link. It took me to an app, which I downloaded after hesitating for a second to worry that it might be some kind of malware that would erase all my data and steal my bank details. But my friends wouldn't do that – apart from anything else, they knew that the contents of my bank account would just about stretch to a Terry's Chocolate Orange.

A background of twinkling stars filled my screen, and a message appeared.

Follow the directions in the link below to your first stop. Tick the checkbox when you arrive.

Again, I clicked, and a map appeared. There was a pin dropped on a location about half a kilometre from the flat, and the app asked for permission to access my location settings, which I warily granted.

Intrigued, I pocketed my phone and keys and set off on foot, giving Portia a quick pat as I passed and telling her to enjoy her day off.

It was three o'clock and beginning to get dark; the sun was sinking in a pallid, watery sky, but at least there were no threatening clouds. It didn't matter that I hadn't brought an umbrella, but I was grateful for the warmth of my new scarf around my neck, and the thick soles of my boots protecting my feet from the icy ground. The temperature was forecast to drop below freezing that night, and poor Portia would have to have frost scraped off her windscreen in the morning.

I followed the map onto the main road that led to the station. Was I going to have to get a train somewhere? Or a bus? Red double-deckers were whooshing past at regular intervals, some heading towards town, others into the suburbs towards the south. But no – the map guided me onto the high street, and then instructed me to turn left into a narrower side road that led off between the Favourite Fried Chicken and Poundland.

And suddenly, I found myself in a miniature version of the

Winter Wonderland Christmas market. Only here, it was local craftspeople selling handmade crafts, rather than the mass-produced goods I'd seen there. A woman stood behind a stall of hand-printed linen tea towels, some featuring kitchen utensils, fruit and vegetables, others more obviously festive, printed with bells, snowmen and holly. A bearded man was selling sloe gin, apparently made from fruit hand-foraged on the common nearby. A charity stall was set out with decorations handmade by local children.

In my pocket, my phone buzzed. I glanced at the screen.

Fancy a gingerbread person? the app asked.

Sure enough, I was just passing a table laden with cakes, biscuits and mince pies, the biscuits glossy with red and green frosting, the mince pies dusted with sugar, crumbly at the edges. The smell made my mouth water, and I stopped to look.

'Can I tempt you with anything?' the girl behind the table asked. 'My mum and I baked all of these.'

'They look amazing,' I said. 'And they smell incredible. But I don't actually have a choice in the matter – my phone told me I'm to have one.'

Her face lit up. 'You're Rowan?'

'What? I... yes, I am.'

'I've been expecting you.' She reached under the table and handed me a cellophane bag. 'Here you go – it's on the house.'

Baffled but delighted, I took the bag and peered inside. It wasn't just a gingerbread man – or a gingerbread woman – but a gingerbread family. Well, a mother and child at least, their gingerbread hands joined together. They both had long, choco-late-brown hair and identical frosting smiles. The gingerbread girl was wearing a school uniform and her mother had a purple scarf wound round her neck.

'Oh my God!' I squeaked. 'It's me! Me and my daughter! Thank you so much.'

'Merry Christmas.' The girl smiled, and I tucked the biscuit in my pocket to share with Clara later. Then I ticked the box on the app, checked the next destination on the map and walked on, my steps feeling strangely light in my comfy boots.

I was directed to the end of the side street and into a small park with a children's play area and a fenced-off rose garden. It was almost dark now; there was just a faint crimson glow on the horizon where the sun had set. Ahead of me, I could see the spire of a church jutting up against the dark sky and – faintly – I could hear organ music drifting out into the darkness.

Surely I wasn't going to be asked to go to church? I didn't have a spiritual bone in my body, and although we'd had Clara christened when she was a month or so old, that was more to keep Paul's parents happy than out of any religious conviction on our part. But the next pin on the map was definitely pointing to the church – St Catherine's, it was called.

Dubiously, I walked closer. The music was louder now, and I could see light glowing through the stained-glass windows. There was clearly a service already in progress – barging in would surely not be acceptable.

I hovered near the entrance, admiring the church itself. It was a huge, sand-coloured building complete with ornate pillars, pointy windows and all the other hallmarks of what I vaguely remembered from a school history class was Victorian neo-gothic architecture. It was certainly impressive, beautiful even, in the December night with the three-quarter moon hovering above its steeple.

As I watched, the doors opened, spilling a rectangular chunk of light onto the paving stones outside. The music swelled, and I could distinguish voices singing above the rich strain of the organ. It was a Christmas song, of course, the one about the three kings bringing gifts from their distant home. Now, people began leaving the church. But they weren't hanging around in groups and chatting – they moved with a purpose, still singing.

Most of the children and some of the adults were carrying candles stuck into oranges – I could smell the hot wax and the tang of the fruit. They were followed by choristers in red-and-white surplices, and the vicar in ornate gold vestments.

> *O star of wonder, star of night,*
> *Star with royal beauty bright.*
> *Westward leading, still proceeding,*
> *Guide us to thy perfect light.*

The music soared into the night, and I felt myself beaming, reminded of the beautiful star on my own Christmas tree.

The last strains of the organ faded away, and there was a rustle of paper as hymn-sheet pages were turned. A few people cleared their throats. They organised themselves into a group and headed away from the church, the choir leading the way.

In the darkness, the singing started again.

> *Silent night, holy night.*
> *All is calm, all is bright.*

Like I said, I don't have a spiritual bone in my body. But still, I was captivated, charmed by this Christmas tradition that seemed to belong in the past, yet was somehow timeless. I stood still for what felt like a long time, the cold seeping through my coat, until the carol singers had departed, the last glimmer of candlelight vanished, the clear voices faded away.

And then, my breath suddenly loud in the silence, I checked my phone ready for the next stage on my adventure.

The map on the app had quite a long blue line on it now, showing the direction I needed to go. It would be about a kilo-metre, I guessed – ten minutes' walk or so. I thrust my hands into my coat pockets and set off, pausing every now and then to check I was still on track. The route took me through residential streets, most with Christmas trees blinking in their windows, some with lights arrayed over the plants in the front gardens too.

It struck me that the route wasn't as direct as it could have been – at one point, I was instructed to walk three sides of a square before continuing in the direction I'd been going before. But I didn't give it much thought; I just kept moving through the cold, still air, enjoying the quiet roads and the endless Christmas trees.

When I was about halfway, I realised I'd begun counting them, and by the time I reached the next pin on the map, I was at 217. And the final house on the road was a doozy. The entire front garden had been turned into a Christmas extravaganza, with Santa and his reindeer perched on the roof of the house, a group of plastic red- and green-clad elves on the small patch of lawn, a giant inflatable snowman surrounded by polar-bear cubs and twinkling lights everywhere.

I must bring Clara here, I thought, snapping a photograph of the scene for the Girlfriends' Club WhatsApp group.

And then I thought, *Hold on. Did they plan this?* Because it seemed to me that whoever had, they had a pretty encyclopedic knowledge of the area of London where I lived. My friends never came here. Abbie lived in North London, Kate right in the centre on the river, and Naomi in the east, so when we met up, it was always somewhere central.

Whoever devised this knows my local area even better than I do, I thought.

I ticked the box on the app and waited for the next screen to flash up. The next leg of my journey was shorter, off the residential roads and onto a more main thoroughfare, leading me to an unfamiliar high street.

Unfamiliar because, surrounded as it was by large, grand houses, all the shops and restaurants here were decidedly upmarket, and there was no reason for me to have come here before. I passed an organic butcher, its shutters down but a sign in the window advertising free-range bronze turkeys. There was a cosy French bistro with paper tablecloths and couples eating steak by candlelight. There were boutiques selling designer children's clothing and fine jewellery and one that appeared to sell nothing but hats.

And finally, where the pin had led me, a cocktail bar.

On this Sunday evening, it was quiet, only a few tables occupied. The vibe was industrial chic, with stripped floor-boards, bare filament bulbs and exposed brick walls. I entered slowly, looking around to see if I recognised anyone, unsure whether this was the final stop on my journey.

But there were no familiar faces, so I took a seat at the bar.

'Good evening.' The barman greeted me with a smile, perfect white teeth showing above his beard. 'What can I get you?'

He slid a brown-paper menu across to me, then hesitated and said, 'Hold on. Is your name Rowan, by any chance?'

I nodded, speechless with surprise.

'One of the specials, then,' he said. 'With our compliments.'

He grinned again and turned to the array of sparkling bottles behind the bar, pouring and mixing and muddling and shaking. Then he presented me with a coupe glass containing amber liquid topped with egg-white foam, a cherry on a metal skewer balanced on its rim.

'Christmas sour,' he said.

Managing to find my voice, I thanked him and said it looked delicious.

'It's made with the brandy the bakery down the road uses to soak the fruit for their cakes,' he confided. 'And Amaretto, and – well, a few secret ingredients. Enjoy.'

I took a sip, relishing the warming alcohol and flavours of Christmas.

As I put my glass down, my phone vibrated in my pocket and I glanced at it.

Something to warm you for the last leg, it said. *Cheers.*

'Cheers.' My lips formed my reply silently, and I finished the cocktail, savouring every sip.

Leaving a tip for the barman, I got up to leave, checking my phone again as I pulled on my coat, spinning out the final few seconds of being inside in the warm. The map changed again, a new route revealing itself. It was taking me onwards, through more unfamiliar streets, but ending at a destination I knew quite well – or used to.

When Clara was about five, she went through a phase of being obsessed with dinosaurs, like many children. We took endless trips to the library to borrow books about them. She stomped round the flat on all fours, roaring and snapping her teeth. And we had to go, time and time again, to see the dinosaurs at Crystal Palace. Heavy on character and light on accuracy, the giant sculptures stood in an area of garden landscaped to look as its creator must have imagined a prehistoric landscape. Clara had loved it, playing with other children, admiring the vast figures, talking about it for ages afterwards and asking when I'd take her again.

Until one day, I'd offered and she'd said, 'Maybe next weekend, Mummy.'

That was the end of that obsession, and we hadn't been back since.

But now, I realised, I was just a few minutes' walk away from the park. I checked the map, but I could have found it easily myself, my footsteps following those of many Saturday bus journeys, my mind wondering what on earth dinosaurs had to do with Christmas.

But my question was soon answered: the park had a festive surprise in store. The map guided me through spectacular displays of lights: enchanted forests, fields of butterflies, a winged horse, swans surrounded by water lilies, an underwater world with tropical fish, a phoenix rising from the ashes.

I was as enchanted as my daughter had been by the dinosaurs, feeling like a little girl as each successive display made me stop, gasp and admire. I felt like a child coming downstairs on Christmas Day, looking at the bulging stocking hanging from the mantelpiece and squealing, 'He's been!'

I could have stayed there for hours, but the map was summoning me onwards, and I knew I was nearing my final destination.

And there, beneath the illuminated Crystal Palace itself, seated on a blanket with a bottle of champagne in an ice bucket next to him, was Alex.

CHAPTER THIRTY

I mean, over the past two hours as I'd explored the streets within a couple of miles of home, the idea that this had been something to do with Alex had stolen into my mind. I'd allowed myself to imagine – even to hope – that he'd had something to do with planning this adventure for me to go on. How, I couldn't imagine. The app, the free gingerbread people made to look like Clara and me, the barman who'd known my name – it was all so elaborate and probably expensive. How much did it even cost to get an app like that made? How long would it have taken? I had no idea.

But still, the hope had been there. My mind had formed an image of Alex driving those streets, day after day, noting where the best Christmas decorations were to be seen. I'd almost allowed myself to picture his grin when he saw the house with the over-the-top outdoor display, imagine him delivering a crate of small white candles to the church and noticing a sign telling the congregation when the carol service was due to take place.

But never had I allowed myself to expect that he might *actually* be here – the final stop on the adventure.

The ultimate treasure on the treasure hunt.

I walked towards him feeling like I was in a dream, my feet carrying me forward over the dew-drenched grass, my breath misting out into the chilly air. He stood up when he saw me approaching. He was wearing a dark-coloured down jacket and a beanie hat, similar to mine, pulled down over his ears. I'd hardly ever seen him without his high-vis jacket and turquoise cap, but if anything he looked less normal, not more. Not just another guy here to meet a woman to enjoy the illuminations on the last Sunday before Christmas but an almost magical, mythical figure.

I felt as if he, too, might be a trick of the light.

But he wasn't. His smile flashed out at me, easy and joyful. His arms wrapped round me in a warm, natural hug.

'Rowan! You made it. Are you freezing?'

Right then, I couldn't have told you whether I was roasting hot or on the point of developing frostbite. My body didn't feel like it belonged to me; my mind was still only beginning to process what was happening. The only thing that felt real was Alex's arms around me.

'I don't know.' I looked up at him and laughed. 'I think I'm in shock. How did you...?'

'I cleared it with your mates first,' he said. 'I hope you don't mind. Their details were on the dispatch notes, so I got in touch. I thought... I wanted to...'

His words trailed off, and I realised how much courage, as well as time and probably money, he must have invested in this.

'This is amazing,' I said. 'This whole thing. I can't even... I can't tell you how it's made me feel.'

'That's okay. So long as you're pleased. Would you like to sit down?'

My legs suddenly felt like cotton wool, and I realised I was going to have to. I sank down onto the blanket, and Alex passed me another to tuck over my legs, and a hot-water bottle.

'We're basically equipped for an arctic trek,' he said. 'Only thing I didn't have to bring was ice.'

He eased the cork out of the champagne bottle and filled two glasses. I took one with fumbling fingers. He was right – it was as cold as if it had come straight out of the freezer. I tucked the blanket more closely around my legs, over the hot-water bottle, and shifted closer to him.

'Uh… cheers.' I extended my glass and he clinked the rim of his against it. I took a sparkling, toasty-dry sip. 'And thank you. Am I allowed to ask what this is all about?'

'Oh, you know. It's just something we delivery drivers do sometimes, for our VIP customers.'

'Seriously?'

He laughed. 'Of course not. It's something I wanted to do for you. When I met your friends, Naomi said they were thinking of organising a treasure hunt for one of your gifts, and I said I might be able to help.'

'So the app and everything – how did you—'

'Mate of mine's a developer,' he said. 'There's some open-source software he used, and the rest was bespoke. That part was easy.'

'What about the rest?'

'Rowan.' He looked at me, his blue eyes steady. 'The only hard part was waiting here to see if you'd turn up, and then when you did, hoping that you wouldn't tell me to piss off, and that there was no way you were going to sit down and drink Bollinger with a deranged stalker.'

'Are you a deranged stalker?'

'Not last time I checked. Look, the thing is— Damn, this is awkward. I like you, Rowan. I wanted to see you – you know, properly. Like a date.'

'And what's wrong with "Fancy a pint sometime?"' I teased, light-heartedness covering the fact that every time I looked at him I felt my heart thump and my entire body tingle.

'Come on. When you like a woman and she's got a whole massive surprise-advent-calendar thing going down, complete with fortune tellers and being whisked off for nights out like bloody Cinderella, "Fancy a pint?" isn't going to cut it. You'd think I wasn't putting the effort in.'

It was my turn to laugh. 'I wouldn't have thought that. But I certainly think you've put the effort in now. This is... no one's done anything like this for me, ever.'

He looked a bit smug. 'Are you hungry?'

I realised I was. The pancakes had been a long time ago, and the gingerbread biscuit was still in my pocket, untouched and hopefully intact.

'You know what, I'm starving,' I said.

'Right. Hopefully this will work.'

He dug in his backpack and produced a few items, which he arranged on what looked like a slate tile. Then he struck a match, and a small flame leaped to life. From a plastic box, he scooped something into a small metal pan and set it over the flame.

'Cheese fondue,' he said. 'It should be ready in a few minutes. Please tell me you don't hate cheese?'

'I love cheese. Doesn't everyone? Even if it makes French people look cross in photographs.'

'What? Why?'

'Because they're all saying "fromage".'

It took him a second, but he got it, and we both giggled like idiots.

'Yeah, so I was like, "What if she's the only person in the world who doesn't like cheese? What if she's lactose intolerant?"' Alex went on.

'I'm not lactose intolerant.'

'Then I'll add that to the list of things I didn't know about you before, and now I do.'

'Add?' I said. 'What's on the list already?'

'You're brave. You've got a sense of adventure – if you didn't, you wouldn't have downloaded the app in the first place. You can read maps.'

'I'm an estate agent,' I reminded him. 'I'd be totally screwed if I couldn't read a map. And as for having a sense of adventure – well, I guess I do. I've never really thought of it that way.'

'How do you think of it?'

'Like, life's thrown me quite a few curveballs and I've just had to go with it. So I went with this. I trust my friends – I didn't think they'd get me kidnapped or anything.'

'But if you'd known it was me?'

'Then I'd have run for the hills, obviously.'

We both laughed.

'See, I knew I shouldn't have asked you out for a pint,' he said.

'Exactly. Hills, me – voom. But thanks to your elaborate deception...'

'Here we are.'

He filled up our glasses and peered at the fondue. The cheese was melting and beginning to sizzle round the edges, and a delicious smell was coming from the pot – cheese, obviously, and garlic, and some sort of alcohol. Alex unwrapped a couple of small forks and a baguette, which he sliced on the edge of the slate tile.

'You thought of everything,' I said admiringly. 'Fondue as well – seriously retro.'

'I took advice. And it's not retro, it's right on the cutting edge of culinary fashion. It's having a moment.'

'It is?'

'So I'm told.'

He turned down the flame beneath the pot and passed me a fork. I impaled a piece of bread, turned it in the cheese and lifted it out, a string of melty cheese following it. I twisted the fork and raised it to my mouth, hoping I wouldn't end up with cheese all over my face or – worse – my new scarf. Alex did the same, only more confidently, twirling his fork with elegant fingers.

'Oh my God, this is delicious,' I said.

'Secret recipe.'

'You're full of surprises.'

'I go skiing sometimes. The place where I stay does a legendary fondue, and I begged the chef for the recipe. This is it. I could tell you what's in it, but...'

'You'd have to kill me afterwards.'

'Correct.'

How does he afford to go skiing on a delivery driver's wage? I wondered fleetingly, but I was too hungry to care. I helped myself to more bread and dipped again. Alex produced a jar of sour pickles and I took one, and drank more champagne. I was barely conscious of the cold now; the hot-water bottle, the warm blanket, the gently simmering cheese and Alex's presence were filling me with a glow that made me impervious to the chilly night.

'So what about you?' I asked. 'You didn't know stuff about me until today. What do I need to know about you?'

He gave that flashing grin again – the smile I remembered seeing for the first time less than a month before. Already, it felt like I'd seen it a thousand times and wanted to see it over and over again.

'I worked that stuff out for myself,' he said. 'I reckon you should too.'

'I guess that's fair. So I've learned you make a mean fondue. You've got friends who work in tech. You like making complex plans. You managed to convince my friends – and they're a tough crowd – that you're legit and not a stalker.'

'All true. Especially about your friends being a tough crowd.'

'What did you do? I mean, did you email one of them or what? And when?'

It was too dark for me to be sure, but I could have sworn Alex was blushing.

'So I took a photo of one of the delivery dockets. It had the sender's mobile number on it, so I phoned. Turns out it was Kate.'

'And what did she say?'

'A whole lot of stuff about the GDPR – or whatever the new data protection stuff's called. I thought she was going to hang up on me, or report me and get me sacked. But then she said I should meet them all for a coffee, so I did.'

'My God. And they never told me a thing. When was this?'

'Week ago.'

'Were you nervous?'

'Terrified.' He laughed. 'But they were okay, once I'd explained why I wanted to get in on the present thing. I'm so pleased you're wearing the scarf.'

'Scarf?' Involuntarily, my hand moved to my neck and my fingertip brushed the soft violet fabric. 'I love it. Don't tell me you...'

'I chose it.' Alex ducked his head, grinning. 'Well, I had help. But I reckoned you'd like it.'

'I do. It's the best scarf in the world. And I left my old one on the Tube, so it came at the perfect time. Thank you. I've even managed not to drip cheese down it, which is pretty amazing.'

We'd finished the fondue and the bread, and were scraping the last bits of crunchy cheese off the bottom of the pot with our forks. Alex turned back to his bag and rummaged around a bit, then produced a Thermos, a couple of ceramic cups and a square, flat box.

'Mulled rum and chocolates,' he explained. 'I'm not sure if they'll work as a combo, but I figured it was worth a try.'

'That smells insanely good.' I watched as he poured out steaming, caramel-scented liquid and eased the lid off the chocolates. They were proper, posh ones, painted with a metallic sheen like expensive Christmas baubles.

'Oh no.' His face fell. 'I forgot. You like toffees.'

Shit. And I'd forgotten I hadn't been strictly honest about why I left the good Quality Street until last.

'It's okay. These will be lovely.' I took a chocolate and a sip of rum, feeling fresh warmth flood through me. 'They are lovely. But I need to ask – meeting the Girlfriend— I mean, Kate and Abbie and Naomi. Getting involved in the advent-calendar thing. Planning all this. Why?'

I heard his breath sigh inwards in the quietness of the night. Then he said, 'I like you, Rowan. I'm not going to lie – I fancy you. I think you're beautiful. I think you deserve things that make you happy. And I want to get to know you better.'

I sensed a new, different warmth spreading through me – one that was almost electric, not comforting and soothing like hot cheese and strong, warm alcohol, although it was just as intoxicating. And I felt a smile spreading over my face, totally involuntarily, as if the lights of a thousand Christmas trees had illuminated inside my head.

'I want to get to know you better, too,' I said.

'I can think of one really good way to do that,' Alex replied.

In the darkness, his eyes weren't the clear, deep blue I was used to seeing. They could have been any colour at all, with the lights reflecting off them. But his face was serious and kind – and, suddenly, very, very close to mine.

I leaned closer, putting my hand on his shoulder so I didn't topple over and face-plant in his lap, which would obviously have given a whole new meaning to getting to know a person better. He leaned in too, his arm finding my waist over the thickness of my coat.

And now our faces were close – so close everything was out

of focus except the brightness of his eyes. Then our lips met, cool at first and then warm, tentative and then exploring, friendly and then filled with desire.

I felt my hand move up to where his hair would have been, found his woolly hat instead, then caressed his neck, warm against my fingers. His hand was on my thigh, the pressure and heat of it just discernible through the layers of clothes and blankets.

The kiss lasted maybe a minute, maybe two. But seconds into it, I was sure that if he'd told me to get my kit off right there and shag him on the blanket in the icy December night, surrounded by other people, I'd have done so without a second thought.

But there was no shag. Just as we pulled away for breath, grinning at each other in wonder, I heard a phone ring. Not mine – an unfamiliar ringtone.

'Sorry, Rowan. God, I'm sorry. I need to—'

'It's okay.'

My breath coming in gasps, I sat back, watching as he pulled his phone out of his pocket. I could see the name on the screen: Ailsa.

'Hey.' Alex pressed the phone to his ear, half turning away from me. I could hear a woman's voice, urgent and strident, but not make out the words. 'Okay. Give me half an hour. And stop worrying, okay?'

He ended the call. 'I've got to go, Rowan,' Alex said. 'Sorry about this.'

Like water running out of a bathtub, all the warmth had left my body and I was conscious again of the freezing night and how far I was from home.

CHAPTER THIRTY-ONE

Normally, Alex was pretty good at keeping his head in a crisis – or, at least, faking it until he could make it. But now, he found himself dithering, even flapping. First, he couldn't make up his mind whether to get a bus or an Uber home – or, indeed, whether to go home at all. But he had to – he couldn't spend the night with Ailsa laden with a fondue burner that stank of methylated spirits, a cheese-encrusted pan and an empty bottle of champagne.

So, after pacing up and down trying to get a signal on his phone, he jumped into a cab and headed home. He dumped his bag on the floor, dithered again over whether to get changed or not, whether to take his bicycle or another taxi, and debated whether to let his neighbour know that he might not make it home before the following evening.

And before he could go anywhere, he had urgent responsibilities to see to. Work, at least, could be dealt with on his mobile in the hours of waiting he reckoned lay ahead – surely, however bad things got, he wouldn't be expected to stay with Ailsa throughout? There'd be stuff a man in his position wouldn't be allowed to witness.

'Yes, Balthazar, I know you're hungry,' he said, as plaintive cries followed him from the kitchen to his bedroom and back again. 'Just chill out for one second, okay? I'll be right there.'

His mind whirring and his hands unsteady, Alex tore open a pouch of salmon and tuna in jelly and squeezed the contents into a bowl, then hastily refilled the matching bowl with clean water. Everything else could wait.

At last, almost an hour after he'd said goodbye to Rowan beneath the glimmering lights of Crystal Palace, he found himself once more in the back of a car, tapping at his phone. God, the time he'd spent with her felt like days ago, not just sixty minutes. Already, the memory of her kisses was fading along with the pleasant light-headedness left by half a bottle of fizz.

He really shouldn't have been drinking, strictly speaking. He'd thought it would be okay – there was, in theory at least, still another week to go, and a good chance that Omar would have been able to step up and take charge of the situation he had, after all, been fifty per cent responsible for creating. But of course, on this night of all nights, it was happening, and he needed to get his shit together and pretend to be calm.

On my way, he texted. *Be about twenty-five minutes. Remember to breathe.*

Then he closed his eyes for a moment, focusing on his own breathing as the cab glided through the dark streets. It had begun to rain – a thick drizzle that had, at least, held off while he was outside with Rowan. If it had started to piss down while they were together, he'd have had no plan B – which wasn't like him at all; normally, he took all eventualities into account.

But tonight was different. He was utterly unprepared for what might happen between now and the morning.

His eyes still closed, he tried to summon up the memory of Rowan's face, so close to his. The way she'd smiled before they kissed, the knowledge of what was about to happen making her eyes shine. He remembered the clean smell of her hair and the way her scarf – the one Ailsa had chosen – had felt against his face. Her skin was winter pale – he wondered if she tanned in summer or whether that fair complexion stayed the same all year round, making her body look like a field of fresh snow.

But there was no point getting caught up in thoughts like that now – there was someone else he needed to think about. Two people, actually.

Alex was jerked out of his reverie by the taxi jolting to a stop. He thanked the driver, asked him to wait and hurried up the steep steps to the front door of the house. He could have had a key; the offer had been made, but he'd declined. So he tapped the knocker gently, as if there was an invalid in there or neighbours who were alert to any sound.

It felt like a long time before the door swung open. Ailsa was fully dressed, at least – if she'd been in a dressing gown and needed help getting her clothes on, Alex didn't know what he would have done.

'Hey. How's it going?' He stepped forward, wanting to touch her but suddenly almost afraid.

'Fucking awful. It hurts.'

'I know. Hang in there – it'll all be worth it in the end.'

'I don't need you to remind me of that, thanks all the same.'

'Come on. Tell me where your stuff is and I'll fetch it, and let's get you out of here.'

'There's a bag in the—' She broke off, pressing her hands to her back, leaning over so her forehead pressed against the wall, blocking Alex's way.

'Hey, come on. You've got this. Aren't you meant to be breathing or something?'

She didn't respond. Tentatively, Alex stroked her back. She was wearing a black long-sleeved T-shirt that had been through the wash so many times that the smiley face printed on the front of it had faded almost to invisibility. Every time Alex had seen her wearing it, it felt like Ailsa, too, had smiled with less and less conviction.

After what seemed like an eternity, she straightened up again, pushing her hair back from her face. She wasn't wearing any make-up and her skin was waxy in the overhead light.

'Bag's upstairs on the landing,' she said. 'Come on – let's get this over with.'

Alex sprinted up the stairs two at a time. He looked around for a second, bewildered by the sheer volume of stuff that cluttered the once-orderly space. Why hadn't she said? Why hadn't he guessed that all this lot would be arriving, at the last minute, the way they always did things, and Ailsa wouldn't be able to deal with it and Omar wouldn't be around?

But now wasn't the time to start messing around with power tools, even if he had any, which he didn't. He'd have to come back, hopefully tomorrow, and make a start on it. They'd have to sort out the details themselves later somehow.

Alex picked up the pewter leather overnight bag she'd packed, calling down the stairs, 'Sure you haven't forgotten anything?'

'Of course I have,' Ailsa replied. 'I haven't been able to think straight for months.'

'What do you need me to get?'

'If I knew, I'd have got it myself.'

Fair enough – Alex's bad for asking stupid questions. He slung the bag over his shoulder and started down the stairs again.

'Water? Snacks?' he asked.

'Got those.'

'Change of clothes?'

'Yup.'

'Toiletries?'

'Check.'

'Thingummy for the car?'

'Omar's got that.'

'Stuff for—'

'Look, stop with the Spanish fucking Inquisition and get moving. While I still can move. Unless you're planning to carry me.'

'I carried an armchair up to a third-floor flat the other day, but I definitely couldn't manage you. Sorry about that.'

'Right, then let's get in the— Oh, Jesus Christ.'

She did the head-against-the-wall thing again. Alex watched, helpless, wishing he could make it stop. But he couldn't – he could only be there, keeping his promise.

He walked slowly down the stairs, waiting for it to be over. There was going to be a lot of that in store for him that night, unless – or hopefully until – Omar showed up. And if he did, who knew what kind of state he'd be in. But at least he was used to this stuff, unlike Alex.

It took a few more minutes, but he got Ailsa down the steep steps to the pavement, which she'd struggled to navigate on her own for a few weeks now, and into the back of the waiting taxi. Alex fastened the seat belt for her. There was sweat on her face already.

'Is the lady all right?' the driver asked.

'I'm fine,' said Ailsa through gritted teeth.

'Just to the hospital now, please,' Alex said. 'My sister's in labour.'

CHAPTER THIRTY-TWO

The next day – the Monday before Christmas – I woke up with that feeling you get when you're having a really lovely dream, the kind you just want to escape straight back into, rather than getting up and cracking on with your day. I didn't open my eyes; I kept them closed, the duvet pulled right up to my chin, hoping that I could return to that magical moment under the winter sky when Alex had been about to kiss me and find out whether he would.

And then I remembered. It hadn't been a dream. It had really happened. I could safely wake up and remember the kiss as often as I wanted to.

Only then I'd also have to remember what had happened afterwards: how he'd walked me to the bus stop, solicitous and kind, but clearly distracted, and how I'd said I'd be perfectly okay and there was no need for him to wait until my bus arrived, and I watched him hurrying away into the night.

But I didn't want to remember that. I didn't want the feelings of doubt and confusion that threatened to overwhelm me when I recalled what he'd told me, how he'd explained that he was going to have to cut the evening short and leave.

I wanted to remember the good bits, to turn them over in my mind again and again, looking at them from every angle: the way I'd felt when I first saw him sitting there on the blanket waiting for me – my stomach lurching with surprise and amazement and anticipation like I was on a rollercoaster. The way he'd prepared everything for me so carefully, so thoughtfully, down to the hot-water bottle and the posh chocolates. The way he'd kissed me.

Oh my God, that kiss! I kept replaying it in my mind while I got up and dressed for work, and all the way to the office. The memory of it made my senses reel – and made me go sailing through a red light, earning an outraged hoot from the black cab driver I'd cut up.

'Focus, Rowan,' I told myself. 'If you total your car and wind up in intensive care, that's not going to do your happy-ever-after any good, is it?'

Thankfully, I managed to pull myself together and make it to the office in one piece, although admittedly still in a happy daydream. But my thoughts of Alex were banished – impossible as it would have seemed five minutes before – when I sat down at my computer and checked my email.

'Yesss!' I shouted, actually getting up from my chair and doing a fist pump.

'What are you getting so excited about?' Brett asked. 'Did someone leave a Rampant Rabbit on that seat or what?'

'Rampant Rabbits went out with vajazzles,' Marty said. 'Have you not got laid since 2005?'

Julz said, 'So, Rowena. What gives?'

'The Choudhurys have had an offer accepted.' I sank back down into my chair, suddenly feeling almost as weak-kneed as I had when I'd seen Alex at the end of my treasure hunt.

'Yeah? Where?' Marty's smirk melted off his face.

'Wentworth Street,' I said. 'It's perfect for them. Close to the hospital where the husband works, good schools nearby and a garden.'

'Well, aren't you the rising star?' Brett said. 'Champers on you on the twenty-third, before we knock off for Christmas.'

I couldn't prevent a massive, cheesy grin spreading over my face. I'd happily buy Brett and Marty – much as I loathed them – all the champagne they wanted. If this deal went through – and admittedly, it was a big if; there could be many slips between an offer being accepted and the money actually changing hands – my own financial situation would be improved significantly.

I did the sums in my head – the commission would be enough to pay my rent for six months. To pay for Clara's new school uniform many times over. Even to book a holiday for us in the summer.

And even better than all that, I'd be able to say I'd done it – I'd found the Choudhurys a home. Just in time, too, as the last time I'd spoken to my applicant, she'd said she was having regular Braxton Hicks contractions and was pretty sure the baby would be here soon. I was practically fizzing with pride.

But when I called her to deliver the good news, her phone went to voicemail, so I could only leave a message and imagine her delighted reaction when she listened to it.

After I'd ended the call, I hurried out to treat myself to a Christmas sandwich from Pret by way of a celebration. And on my way back to the office, I passed the lingerie shop. Since my first abortive visit there, I'd almost forgotten about the voucher, still languishing in my purse. But now I remembered.

And, I thought, perhaps the cheerful shop assistant would have forgotten all about my shabby old bra, left behind in the fitting room.

She hadn't. To my mortification, when she handed over the red bra, throwing in a pair of knickers for free because the sale was about to start, she slipped my old bra into the bag, carefully wrapped in tissue paper, saying that she'd saved it for me.

My elation carried me through the afternoon like a wave. The bright afternoon gave way to a spectacular sunset that lit up the Thames like a river of flame as I drove home over Vauxhall Bridge. The traffic was light. The festive lights on the high street sparkled cheerfully, reminding me that I might not be spending Christmas alone – and that even if I did, it might be for the last time.

And as I was reversing Portia into her parking space, I saw the Pegasus van pulling into the car park.

My heart leaped with excitement then set up a frantic drumming in my chest. I could feel my hands sweating and my cheeks flushing. I could have waited to compose myself, but I didn't – I sprang out of the car and hurried towards the van like a child going downstairs on Christmas morning.

Except the driver who got out of the van wasn't Alex. He was wearing the same fluorescent yellow jacket and the same turquoise peaked cap, but he was taller, lankier, with long locs hanging down his back.

'Afternoon, Miss.' He smiled at me broadly, showing perfect white teeth. It was a smile that would have charmed me, only it was the wrong one on the wrong man. 'You look excited. Expecting a parcel?'

'I... Yes, I am.' How could I ask him where Alex was without seeming rude, when he was being so friendly?

'What's the number, then?'

'Seventy-four.'

He stepped into the back of the van. I heard the hollow ring of his boots on the metal floor and the thump of parcels being moved around, then he emerged again, still grinning, and handed me a package.

'Special delivery, innit?'

'Thank you, that's really kind. Are you... are you filling in for our regular driver?'

If Alex had been kept up all night, perhaps he would have rung in sick, even if that meant sacrificing a day's wages. After all, he knew where to find me. He could knock on my door and see me any time he liked.

'Geezer's quit on us. Just like that, four days before Christmas. Can you believe it? So I'm covering part of his route as well as my own. It's going to be a long night, I can tell you.'

His cheerfulness undimmed by the prospect, he snapped a photo of me holding my parcel and stepped back in the van to load up his other packages.

All the joy seemed to have gone from the day. Alex had quit? Just like that? He wasn't going to be there to deliver the last four gifts from my advent calendar?

Numbly, I turned and started up the stairs, not even bothering to see if the lift was working. The rhythm of my feet seemed to be drumming out a message: *You might never see him again. You might never see him again.*

Although I was perspiring inside my coat by the time I reached the seventh floor, I felt cold inside. I unlocked the door and put the parcel on the hall table – I'd save it to open when Clara was home. It would be something to look forward to.

But I knew it would feel like a consolation prize.

I walked through to the living room and stood in front of the Christmas tree. Could it only be three days ago that I'd decorated it with Alex, made him tea, exchanged that first, magical hug that had opened the door to the magical kiss last night? I thought of the beautiful, expensive underwear wrapped in tissue paper in its bag – would I ever wear it? It had been bought with a voucher so couldn't be returned. Most likely, it would sit unworn in my drawer until eventually I donated it to a charity shop. Or maybe I'd become one of those women who wear sexy lingerie every day to work because it makes them feel empowered.

Somehow, I doubted that.

I reached out and stroked the cool glass of the star with my finger. What I'd felt with Alex had seemed so real. What he'd told me about why he had to leave had made sense: his twin sister, heavily pregnant with her first child, almost crippled by pelvic girdle pain and suffering, also, from the profound narkiness I could remember so well from the days before Clara was born. His sister, who needed him because she'd gone into labour and her husband, a surgeon, was operating and couldn't be with her.

It all made sense. It all had the ring of truth. I had no reason not to believe him.

But what if it wasn't true? What if I'd been taken in by his blue eyes and easy smile, and he'd been lying to me? I didn't even know his phone number. I only vaguely knew where he lived, because he'd said he needed to get back to South East London to feed his cat before making his way to Ailsa's home to get her to hospital in a taxi.

Hold on. Ailsa. Suddenly it was like a light had been switched on in my brain. At the time, I'd been so overwhelmed by our kiss and the abrupt ending to the evening that I hadn't made the connection, but now here it was. Ailsa, whose husband Omar was a surgeon, who was due to give birth any minute.

Mrs Choudhury was Alex's sister. The woman with the dark hair and the Scottish accent, who I'd been showing round properties for almost three weeks, racing to find a home for her before her baby was born. Now I thought about it, there were similarities between her and him – the warm smile, the blue eyes. But they were no more alike than any other brother and sister, so I simply hadn't made the connection – and why would

I? He was a delivery driver; she was the purchaser of a multimillion-pound property.

I imagined his amazed reaction when I told him – how we'd laugh together at the randomness of life and the chances it threw our way.

If I ever heard from him, that was.

Don't panic, Rowan, I told myself. *Don't despair. It's been less than twenty-four hours since you saw him. It's not like he hasn't been busy. He could have quit his job for any number of reasons. The other driver could have made a mistake, Alex could have just taken a day off after being up all night with Ailsa.*

Then I heard the crash of the door knocker and almost jumped out of my skin.

It's him! It's him! my heart sang.

It could be anyone, my head told me firmly.

Still, I glanced in the mirror in the hallway, smoothing my hair and checking my mascara hadn't smudged, before opening the door.

It wasn't Alex. Of course it wasn't.

It was Hayley.

I'm not going to lie, I almost didn't recognise her at first. I'd never seen her without full make-up before, her hair perfectly tonged, her outfit styled to the max. Now she was wearing a battered old anorak that I was pretty sure Paul had bought years ago when we went fell-walking together (not that any fells were walked; it pissed with rain non-stop and we stayed in bed all weekend. But I really didn't want to think about that right now), skinny jeans that anyone could have told her were so over they were practically back again, and trainers that looked like they'd been worn for actual training rather than kept box-fresh for maximum fashion points. Her face was shiny rather than glowy, and her hair was scraped back in a ponytail.

'Hayley!' I gawped at her for a second, baffled. She'd never been here on her own before, almost always with Paul and only a couple of times when she'd dropped Clara off.

Clara. She'd been spending the day hanging out at Lily's, she'd said, now school was done for the year; there'd been some mention of another trip to Westfield, which had clearly become my daughter's nirvana.

'Is it Clara?' I asked, cold fear trickling down my spine. 'Has something happened?'

Hayley shook her head. She looked, briefly, almost ashamed. 'Not so far as I know. We're not meant to be seeing her until Thursday.'

'Then what...'

'He's still in love with you,' she snapped. 'I thought you'd want to know.'

'What...? Who...? You mean Paul?' For a brief, intoxicating second, I'd thought she might have been referring to Alex. But that was impossible. She didn't even know he existed.

'No, Rudolf the Red-Nosed Fucking Reindeer. Of course Paul.'

'Hayley.' I took a deep breath. 'You'd better come in. I'll put the kettle on.'

She hesitated for a second, as if she could feel the moral high ground slipping away beneath her feet. Then she said, 'Okay,' and followed me into the flat.

I hurried to the kitchen and shoved teabags into two mugs, flicking on the kettle. It was more a gesture than anything else – the woman looked like she needed a strong drink, not PG Tips.

When I carried the tea back to the living room, she was standing there awkwardly next to the coffee table, her coat draped over her arm.

'Nice tree,' she said, turning and taking a mug from my hand. 'Thanks.'

I almost dropped the other one. Hayley was wearing a Christmas jumper. *The* Christmas jumper. The hideous one with the fake boob on it that had been my advent-calendar gift earlier in the month. Perhaps normally she could have styled it out – a bit of festive kookiness – but now it looked bizarre, obscene even, contrasted with her white, distressed face.

'Oh.' She looked down. 'This bloody thing. I found it in a charity shop. I was doing a video for my TikTok about ridiculous Christmas jumpers. I was in the middle of it when Paul came home and we had a row and he told me…'

I sat down on the sofa, hoping she'd do the same, which she did.

'What did he say?' I asked.

'He said he's not sure about getting married. I asked if it was because he still has feelings for you and he told me you – he said after you broke up you and him were still *intimate*.' She hissed the word out, like a scorned *Married at First Sight* contestant. 'Like, for years and years.'

Why did you tell her that, Paul, you utter copper-bottomed, ocean-going bell-end?

'Okay,' I said. 'I'm not going to lie, Hayley. We were. But not since you two met. At least, not since he told me about you. I'd never have done that. I shouldn't have done it anyway. But I was—'

'Lonely and desperate,' she said, her words dripping with scorn.

I flinched. 'Yes. I was.'

Hayley crumpled, like a Christmas cracker that had been pulled, its bang gone off, now only forlorn bits of crepe paper and a bit of loo-roll tube left to show for itself.

'I'm sorry,' she said. 'That was unkind. I'm just bloody hurt. And furious.'

'Of course you are. I would be, too.'

I was, too, when my wedding to Paul didn't happen.

'It's just… I thought he loved me.'

'I'm sure he does, really. Maybe it's just... I don't know. Pre-wedding nerves?'

I thought he loved me, too.

'We haven't even set a date for the wedding! How can he have pre-wedding nerves?'

'Hayley, I don't know. I'm no relationship expert. Look at me, I've been single for about a hundred years.'

She gave a watery smile. 'But...?'

'But you need to talk to him. Whatever happened between him and me is over. I don't feel that way about him any more.'

And I realised it was true. Not since the advent calendar – and Alex. And maybe even before that, but I'd let myself believe I felt like that, because it was all I had.

'Well, he'd better make his mind up, pronto,' Hayley said, with a return of her usual spirit.

'I don't know. Maybe putting the wedding off a bit, taking some time to think about things, getting to know each other better, would be—'

'It would certainly not,' she snapped. 'I want a baby. And I want to be married before I have one. And no one is going to come between me and my dream of a family. Especially not you.'

I felt stung by her words – and then furious.

'Hayley,' I said, 'I have no intention of coming between you and your dream of a family. I already have my own family: me and Clara. It might be small but it's perfect. But you need to remember that Clara is Paul's family too, and she always will be, no matter what.'

To Hayley's credit, she looked embarrassed.

'I... I didn't mean...' she stammered. 'I mean, of course Clara...'

Her confusion made me relent a bit. 'Clara's really fond of you, and I know she'll be really excited to be a big sister. And I can trust you and Paul not to ever let her feel second best or pushed out. Can't I?'

Almost meekly, Hayley said, 'Yes, Rowan. Of course you can.'

She left shortly after that. I stood in the doorway and watched her make her way to the lift, the absurd Christmas jumper covered again by her coat. And I thought that, perhaps, her outburst today could lead to something of an understanding between the two of us – that we might, eventually, even be able to become friends.

CHAPTER THIRTY-THREE

I woke up the next morning with a sense of what I'd like to be able to describe as steely determination but was more a vague feeling that Something Must Be Done.

I needed to talk to Paul. Like, properly talk. Read him the riot act, basically.

I needed to get hold of Ailsa or Omar and congratulate them, and try to get the wheels in motion on their house purchase before the seller lost patience and everyone knocked off for Christmas.

And I needed to get in touch with Alex. How, I didn't know. But I needed – and desperately wanted – to see him, to talk to him. And, if possible, snog the life out of him, obviously.

Rapidly and silently, so as not to wake Clara, who'd said she was planning a massive lie-in and then Lily might come over to watch Netflix, I showered and dressed ready for work. When I'd finished putting on my make-up – which I did with extra care, given that today was set to be a big day, all being well – I took the little box containing the vials of fragrance out of the cabinet. What was I going to need today? Self-Esteem, Courage, Assertiveness, Desirability or Risk-Taking?

Frankly, I thought, I could do with a massive dose of all five, and who cared if I smelled like I'd been Christmas shopping at the perfume hall in Harrods.

I opened the box, all set to douse myself liberally. But then I noticed a strange thing. There were only four vials in the box. One was missing. Risk-Taking had clearly taken matters into its own hands and gone AWOL.

Weird, I thought. I tried to remember when I'd last used it – had I splashed some on before my treasure-hunt adventure that had ended in meeting Alex? I couldn't remember – I'd been so filled with excitement and curiosity at the time, I could barely recall getting dressed, apart from putting on the purple scarf.

Back in my bedroom, I retrieved it from the hanger by the window where I'd left it to air and sniffed it. But I could detect nothing, only perhaps the faintest whiff of whatever scent Alex had been wearing. The musky memory of it, still clinging to the silken fabric, reminded me powerfully of that night and renewed my determination.

I was going to contact him, along with all the other things I needed to do. And I didn't need a magic potion to help me.

I hurried down the stairs, jumped into Portia – who to my surprise started first time, in spite of the icy morning – and set off for work.

It was when I arrived there that the whole day, with crushing inevitability, started to go to shit.

The first thing I saw when I entered the office was Marty's smirk. Like the Cheshire cat's, it seemed almost disembodied, too wide and unpleasantly gleeful to fit on his ferret-like face.

Immediately, I knew that his glee would mean bad news for me.

'Morning, morning, Rowena,' he said. 'Three days till Christmas. Got your fishnet stocking hung up yet?'

'Isn't it bad luck to hang up your stocking before Christmas Eve?' As casually as I could, I swung into my chair and switched on my computer. 'That's what I always told my daughter, anyway.'

Marty's leer widened, which I wouldn't have thought was possible.

'Here's one for you,' he said. 'What can society do to better support single mums?'

I raised an eyebrow in what I hoped was a glacial fashion. 'I'm sure you're about to tell me.'

'Build more strip clubs.' He guffawed, but without his wingman – Brett having already started his Christmas holiday, which he was spending with his parents in Spain – his joke fell flatter than he would have hoped.

'Hilarious,' I said, logging into my email.

Then he said, 'So, Rowena. Want to hear the good news or the bad news?'

Keeping my eyes on my emails, I responded with a shrug.

'Good news: your tits look great in that blouse. Not bad for an old bird. I would, if I had enough shandies down me.'

Urgh. Since Kimberley's departure, I'd kept my head down, hoping that the bullying banter they'd directed at her wouldn't now come my way. And it hadn't, until now. Evidently, having secured my first lucrative sale, I now had a massive target slapped on my head. Or, knowing Marty, on my arse.

If he so much as lays a finger on me, I'll lamp him, I promised myself.

But how to cope with the low-level harassment that had driven Kimberley to breaking point, I had no idea. My days of giving lecherous photographers the cold shoulder were far away in my past, and anyway, their advances had been driven by genuine desire – if only to take advantage of a vulnerable young girl – rather than Marty's compulsion to humiliate and gain the upper hand.

'Thank you,' I said. 'I'll bear that in mind.'

'Wanna hear the bad news?' Marty leaned back in his chair, popping two sticks of gum into his mouth.

'Not particularly, but clearly you can't wait to break it.'

'Nah, it's you that's going to have to deliver it.' Across the metre and a half or so that separated our desks, the smell of mint reached me, like a Christmas candy cane being chewed by a child – or a toothbrush being wielded by an overenthusiastic dental hygienist.

'Fine,' I said, trying to sound casual in spite of the sense of unease that was rapidly creeping between my shoulder blades. 'Hit me with it.'

'We're had another offer on Wentworth Street,' he said. 'For the asking price. Contact of Tatiana's.'

The sense of unease wasn't creeping any more – it was right there, a dagger in my back. Ailsa and Omar's offer had been a cheeky one; we'd discussed that – ten per cent below the asking price. But we'd banked on their ability to proceed quickly, with the lease on their rental property coming to an end. Although now, with a brand-new baby, who knew whether that would even be possible?

'Who's the buyer?' I asked, feeling like Santa in his grotto when he accidentally takes a mouthful of his own beard.

Marty shrugged, clearly delighted with the impact his revelation had had on me. 'Corporation in the Bahamas. The cash is all there, ready to go.'

'Can we not...?'

'Don't think we can. See how you like it up you, sunshine. I believe Spearmint Rhino are hiring. Now, I'm out of here. I've six viewings lined up in Belgrave Square.'

He stood up, hitching his braces up his shoulders, then putting on his too-waisted suit jacket, and over it his too-loud houndstooth overcoat. He glanced at his reflection in the window, smiled smugly at himself, then took the chewing gum out of his mouth and put the damp wad on my desk.

'Get rid of that, will you?' he said. 'Or you're welcome to it, if you can't afford your own. It's still minty fresh.'

And with that, he strutted out, heading for the parking garage where his BMW was waiting.

I picked up the gum with a tissue and dropped it in my wastepaper basket, my hand shaking. Now I knew what people meant when they talked about the rug being pulled out from under someone – I literally felt as if I was falling, my stomach rising into my throat as if I might be sick.

But I had no time to be sick. I needed to act, not stick my head down the toilet.

Paul and the talking-to I planned to give him would have to wait. I had more important matters to deal with: first, Marty's rival bid on the property I'd found for Ailsa, and second, getting hold of Alex.

Or maybe the other way around. Now, the two things were inextricably connected. I'd liked Ailsa from the moment I'd first met her, but her connection to Alex made it all the more personal. She wasn't just my applicant any more – she was his sister. She was a new mother.

And I wasn't going to stand by while the home she'd fallen in love with was snatched away from her.

A company in the Bahamas. I knew what that meant – I'd seen deals like it pass through the Walkerson's Elite system often enough. The company in the Bahamas would be owned by another company, possibly in Cyprus or Malta. And that in turn might be owned by another. The companies wouldn't manufacture anything, or even have an office – only an address, probably that of a law firm, or even just a PO box.

And whoever was actually behind the companies, whoever actually planned to buy the property (and most likely not even live there, or only for a few weeks of the year, when they were in London to shop in Knightsbridge or go to Royal Ascot or eat steak prepared by Salt Bae), would be unclear, opaque, hidden by layers of complex corporate structures and elaborate financial transactions.

They could be anyone at all.

I'd known it was happening, of course I had. But it hadn't affected me – those hadn't been my sales or my applicants. But now it was affecting Ailsa, and letting her down would feel like letting Alex down, too.

I needed help – and fast.

It had been a couple of days since I'd looked at the Girlfriends' Club WhatsApp, I realised. After my date – because it had been a date, hadn't it? – with Alex, I'd confided giddily in my friends about how it had gone, told them we'd kissed, and been about to quiz them for more details about him, what had happened when they'd met, what he'd said about me, and so on. I would most likely have carried on late into the night.

But then Lily's mum had dropped Clara off, and she'd wanted to debrief me about her shopping trip and the pizza restaurant she'd been taken to for dinner, and then it had been time for bed, and I hadn't wanted to disturb my friends late on a Sunday night. And then the following day – only yesterday, although it seemed like the distant past now – I'd been so swept away in the news of Ailsa's house purchase I hadn't thought to resume my interrogation. And then, of course, Hayley had shown up and dropped her bombshell, and I hadn't even got through processing that in my head, never mind telling my mates the news.

But, I realised, their input was exactly what I needed right now.

I'd missed a load of messages, it turned out.

Kate: Rowan, are you there? Come on, you only got about halfway through telling us what that snog was like.

Abbie: Only about 200 words and counting. Come on, I've been married nine years – I need to hear about other people's snogs.

Naomi: Not such an interesting topic, but WTF do I get Patch's mum for Christmas?

There was a load of chat about Molton Brown gift sets, chocolate subscriptions and Amazon vouchers.

And then they'd realised I hadn't been back to the group.

Naomi: Ro, are you okay? What's with the radio silence?

Kate: Have you heard from Alex?

Abbie: And did you get your advent-calendar gift yesterday? You haven't said.

Guilt flooded me as I realised I'd been so thrown off course by events, I hadn't even opened the parcel.

Rowan: Guys, I'm really sorry. Everything's gone haywire over here. Alex has quit his job and I don't know why or where he is. And the wheels have come off with Hayley and Paul. And work's a nightmare.

Abbie: Presumably Alex has just gone back to working on his start-up, though?

Rowan: His WHAT?

Naomi: He didn't tell you? WTF?

Kate: They were too busy sucking each other's faces off to exchange CVs – come on, guys.

Abbie: More likely, he wanted to know that Ro's feelings for him were the real deal, and she'd like him even if she thought he was just a delivery guy, not some shit-hot entrepreneur about to secure a massive funding round for his business.

Rowan: I don't even understand. You're messing with my head.

Kate: Are you at work?

Rowan: Yeah, and I need advice about that, fast.

Kate: I've just finished a meeting in Mayfair. Coffee?

Rowan: Life-saver! Five minutes?

Kate and I arranged where to meet and I left the office, putting the sign on the door we always used when everyone was out at viewings. Not that there'd be much in the way of passing trade to worry about, this close to Christmas. I pulled on my coat and hurried out into the street.

Although it was mid-morning, the day was dark, lowering clouds blotting out any memory of the weekend's sunshine. Sleety drizzle was falling and the pavements were slushy with grit. But that didn't seem to have deterred the shoppers and tourists who were crowding the shops and restaurants, laden with carrier bags, some even wearing Santa hats.

I entered Fortnum & Mason's through the ground-floor shopping area and regretted my decision almost immediately. If I'd walked round the block to the back entrance, I'd have got to the coffee shop way quicker; as it was, I had to fight my way through the crowds surrounding the racks of exotically flavoured tea and coffee, shortbread biscuits that were apparently the Queen's favourite, and chocolates so expensive I could feed Clara and me for two weeks for the price of a box.

Yesterday, with the thought of my lovely commission making me recklessly spendthrift, I might have splashed out. Today, there was no chance. The prospect – well, it was looking more like a certainty now – of that money slipping through my fingers was almost worse than if I'd never had it in the first place.

You'll manage, Rowan, I told myself. *You've managed all these years and you'll still manage.*

I inched through the crowds, barely hearing the Christmas music that played through concealed speakers, to the café. There was a queue of people waiting between red velvet ropes by the entrance, but Kate, with her usual uncanny ability, had already secured a table.

In her tailored woollen dress and high heels, her hair pinned up on top of her head, her squashy leather handbag on the seat next to her, she was a model of professionalism and competence – exactly what I needed. Just seeing her was as reassuring as the hug she gave me.

'I got you an eggnog latte,' she said. 'I was tempted by a sherry, to be honest, but it's a bit early.'

'Three days before Christmas, I reckon anything goes,' I said. 'But you're right. And I have to drive later.'

I sat down in a luxuriously padded chair and sipped my coffee, hoping that a hit of caffeine would provide the spark my brain so badly needed.

'So,' Kate said, 'where shall we start?'

Work, my head said. But my heart said, *Alex* – and it won easily.

'Alex,' I said. 'What the hell is going on with him? You said something about a start-up?'

'Yeah. It's an app for last-mile logistics – you know, getting stuff to the end customer, from a depot or supermarket or whatever. It sounds too dull for words, but the couple of articles I read on his LinkedIn page were actually quite fascinating. He's got loads of ideas about cutting carbon emissions and improving employment rights for drivers. He's a bright boy.'

'Wait – he's got a profile on LinkedIn?'

Kate looked at me like I was a recent arrival from the eighteenth century, sitting opposite her in a crinoline and powdered wig. 'You mean you never checked?'

'Kate, I'm not like you. I'm not a high-powered professional. I don't do LinkedIn. And I'm willing to bet your average delivery driver doesn't either. Why would I have checked?'

'Fair enough, I suppose. But after we met him for coffee, I thought it would be just as well to make sure he was legit, just in case. I mean, him saying he wanted to get to know you better and send you gifts and stuff – could be nice, could be dodgy AF. So step one was to make sure he was who he said he was. Actually, step one was to meet him. I reckoned between the three of us our creep-dar would be pretty much on point.'

'Why didn't you tell me?'

'Duh. Because he might have been a creep.'

'No, I mean about the whole start-up malarkey.'

'Because if you liked him, you liked him. Didn't matter if he was a delivery driver or a start-up gazillionaire. Not that he's a gazillionaire – just comfortable. He was a bit more gazillion-airey when he sold his last business, but then he invested loads in this one.'

'Wait, he... What?'

'You'll have to ask him. Our work here is done.'

'But I can't ask him, because he's quit his job and I don't have his number.'

'So go on LinkedIn.'

'But...'

Kate took pity on me. 'Of course I'll give you his number, Ro.'

She tapped a couple of times on her phone, which of course was on the table in front of her, because Kate was so high-powered, but upside down and on silent, because she wasn't rude. Seconds later, my own phone vibrated in my bag, and I took it out to check that the contact had arrived safely: *Alex Winter*.

'Thanks,' I said. Then I heard myself literally gulp. As far as Alex was concerned, my friends' work was done. It was over to me now, and I was as nervous as I imagined Clara would have been before seeing Jonny at the bowling alley.

'Anything else I can help you with?' Kate joked. 'Oh, hold on. What gives with the work thing?'

Work. Yes, there was that, still. Ailsa and Omar. And my commission on their house purchase, which had melted away before my eyes like the sleet on the pavement that would never turn into proper snow.

Incoherently, I blurted out the whole story to Kate, with loads of exposition and backtracking. She asked the right questions, which I answered as best I could. She told me what she thought I should do. I told her I'd never have the guts to do it.

She said, 'Ro, I really think you do.'

'Do I?'

'Of course.' She smiled. 'Risk-taking, remember?'

And then I remembered that the little bottle with that fragrance in it had been missing.

'I'll think about it,' I said. 'I'll try.'

'I believe in you,' Kate said. 'Now I'd better head off. I've got a lunch at twelve thirty.'

She paid for our coffees, hugged me and hurried off, her Prada bag slung over the shoulder of her cashmere coat.

I left more slowly, deliberately making my way through the crowded shop, taking a moment to soak up the pre-Christmas atmosphere, breathing in the smell of freshly baked cookies and expensive chocolates, hearing the excited babble of voices in many languages, enjoying the feel of the deep carpet under my feet, rather than cutting round on the street outside.

Before I got back to the office, I called the number Kate had given me for Alex.

But it rang out, going to a voicemail message that wasn't even his voice, and I didn't have it in me to leave a message.

CHAPTER THIRTY-FOUR

I didn't stay in the office for long: just long enough to make a phone call, leave a message, wait the surprisingly short time it took for my call to be returned and then put my coat on again. To my relief, Marty was still out at his viewings. If he'd known I was deserting my post for the second time in one day, I'd have copped a whole load of grief. But he didn't know.

Not yet, anyway.

I looked around the office: the familiar desks and chairs; the row of boards in the window, each bearing the particulars of a luxury property; the printer looming in the corner, silent and idle for once. I certainly wouldn't say I'd been happy here – often, I'd been pretty miserable. But for the past few months, it had provided a degree of stability and routine – things I'd realised I desperately needed.

But that was too bad. If I never came back, I'd never come back – there was nothing to be done about that. I'd made my decision, spurred on by Kate: I was going to take a risk and do the right thing, and if it came at the personal cost I suspected it would, I'd deal with that.

There were plenty of jobs out there, after all. When I'd met

Kimberley for coffee the previous week, she'd told me she was having to choose between three equally competitive offers. Although, of course, that was Kimberley, a shit-hot negotiator with years of experience, iron-hard self-belief and Louboutin shoes.

I had none of those things, and at the rate I was going, I never would.

With a sigh that seemed to come all the way from the soles of my feet, I picked up the framed photo of Clara from my desk and tucked it into my handbag. If I didn't ever come back, there was no way I was leaving that here for Brett and Marty to leer over, or mock, or chuck in the wastepaper basket.

There was no point driving to the City; the streets were clogged with pre-Christmas traffic – taxis and buses and private cars and delivery vans. Seeing those whizzing past in their various branded liveries gave me a pang of longing for Alex. I thought about calling him again, but now wasn't the time – I was about to get on the Tube, and after that I'd be tied up until I didn't know when, and if I did get to speak to him, I wanted to be able to do it properly, not in a distracted rush.

Half an hour later, I was pushing open the door of the Walkerson's head office, a building in the City I'd only visited once before, when I came for my initial interview, the one that had led to the second, successful interview with Julz at Walkerson's Elite. At the time, I'd been overjoyed to have been offered the job, amazed at my own success, convinced that they must have seen something special in me, and that great things – possibly involving riches I'd never dreamed of – lay in my future.

If only I'd known, back then, that business had been booming and they'd have hired practically anyone who had a driving licence and a nice smile. Well, I was about to find out if I'd be unhired just as quickly and easily.

Walking up to the reception desk – a swanky, marble-topped affair with a smiling blonde receptionist seated behind it and a silver-and-white Christmas tree glimmering beyond it – I felt just as nervous as I had the first time I ever walked on a fashion-show catwalk. I remembered realising, back then, that when people talk about your knees knocking with fear, it's not just a stupid thing they say, an exaggeration or a figure of speech. My legs had literally been trembling, the muscles jumping uncontrollably so I worried I might not be able to get one foot in front of the other and would celebrate my catwalk debut by stacking it like Naomi Campbell in her Vivienne Westwood platforms.

They were trembling like that now.

'I've an appointment with Oliver Bridges,' I said.

The receptionist looked at me, her face saying as clearly as if she'd spoken, 'You? Why?' But she just took my name and asked me to take a seat, which I did, wiping my clammy palms on my skirt.

A few minutes later, another smiling blonde woman came and escorted me into the lift, which whisked us up to the relatively giddy heights of the third floor. It could teach our lift at home a thing or two, I thought, and the idea somehow made me a bit less terrified.

Whatever happened, Clara and I had a roof over our heads, at least for the time being.

I followed the woman along a carpeted corridor with anonymous dove-grey-painted doors opening off it, realising as I walked that Walkerson's, despite being a London-wide firm that was rapidly expanding into the neighbouring counties, would certainly have no use for all this swanky office space. All the real business took place in the network of branches, of which the Mayfair one was the flagship. There must only be a handful of people based here, and the meeting rooms must only be booked for special occasions.

I guessed my visit was one of them.

Again, I felt a small increase in confidence. I was doing the right thing. I'd secured an appointment with the MD at short notice – almost no notice. This was a big deal.

The woman opened a door and waved me in. The room was small, furnished with a round, glossy wooden table set with bottles of still and sparkling water and two glasses. Through the gaps in the window blinds, I could glimpse vertical slices of the London skyline, office windows glimmering against the navy blue of the darkening sky. I took off my coat and settled myself into a comfortable, heather-coloured chair.

'Ollie will be with you very shortly.'

The door closed and I waited, resisting the urge to dig my phone out of my bag and check whether, somehow, I had a message or a missed call from Alex.

If I'd waited longer than a couple of minutes, I wouldn't have been able to resist. But it wasn't long before the door swung open again and Oliver himself strutted in.

He was shortish and plumpish, wearing a pinstriped suit a bit too big for him and a tie emblazoned with faces of red-nosed reindeers. His face looked freshly shaven, shiny and slightly flushed. He smelled strongly of expensive aftershave, and the hand he extended for me to shake was carefully manicured, soft as a child's.

My God, I thought. *He looks about twelve.*

He wasn't, of course. He was (according to his LinkedIn profile – thanks, Kate) about thirty-two, only a few years younger than me. And, of course, youth was no barrier to success, as he had proved, building Walkerson's up from a one-man band to the success story it undoubtedly was today.

Or would be, if my revelations didn't bring the whole show crashing ignominiously to the ground.

'Rowan?' he said. 'I'm Ollie. Lovely to meet you.'

'It's good to meet you, too.' To my surprise, I felt completely calm now that the meeting had commenced and there was no going back. 'Thank you for agreeing to see me.'

'Wasn't about to say no, was I?' His tone was jocular, but his face was serious as he sat down in the chair opposite mine. 'These are serious allegations you're making. Still or sparkling?'

It took me a second to work out that he was offering me a drink of water, which I realised I badly needed. 'Uh... still please.'

'Now,' he said, filling our glasses. 'Would you like to go into more detail about this... matter you wanted to discuss?'

I took a deep breath. 'It's been going on for a while. As long as I've been with the company, to be honest. At first I thought it was just the way things worked, but more recently I've been thinking something was wrong.'

'You're alleging that our anti-money-laundering checks haven't been as rigorous as they should be?'

'Yes, basically. There's a woman – a concierge, I suppose she is. Tatiana Ivanova. She views lots of the properties that come onto the books at our branch, and they're often sold to her clients. Who are, obviously, very wealthy.'

'You don't buy through Walkerson's Elite unless you're very wealthy, let's be honest,' Ollie said. 'Property in Prime Central London doesn't come cheap.'

'No, it doesn't.' I sipped my water. 'But I started noticing that many – even most – of our sales are going to companies based offshore, rather than to individuals. And I started wondering if maybe there was a reason for that. Like, the money that's going into the properties is... well, illegitimately obtained. And whether there's a reason for the buyers being anonymous. A lot of them are Russian, you know, and...'

'Potentially sanctioned individuals,' Ollie finished.

'Yes. Although of course you can't know, because the sale's in the name of a company that's owned by another company, and that's—'

'I get the picture.'

'And Tatiana works with lawyers who set everything up.'

'And are you suggesting' – Ollie took a deep breath that made his chest puff up like a pigeon's – 'that your colleagues and the branch manager are aware of this... this money laundering?'

'I don't see how they couldn't be, to be honest.'

'But if they were... uh, complicit in it...'

I waited silently, not moving my head at all any more.

'Then it really doesn't look great for Walkerson's as a wider firm,' Ollie concluded. 'Never mind the Walkerson's Elite brand.'

'No, it doesn't,' I agreed.

Ollie sprang out of his chair. 'Right. I'm going to have to get HR and legal onto this, pronto. Possibly engage an outside consultant who specialises in reputational risk. Why does it have to be bloody Christmas every time something like this blows up? Everyone's on fucking holiday already.'

'Including the manager of my branch,' I reminded him.

He gawped at me. 'Yes, I suppose so. Well, not on holiday any longer. Suspended pending a full investigation.'

'And what about...'

He paused, his hand already on the door handle, springing into action like the room was on fire.

'What about what?'

'What about me?' I asked, my voice sounding reedy and thin.

'You'll be on gardening leave too, naturally. I'll get someone from HR to look in now and go through the details with you.'

The door banged behind him and I sat there, frozen. I'd expected this – Kate had warned me it would inevitably happen. But still, the threat of losing my job loomed large over me. And what if it was me, the whistle-blower, who ended up getting thrown under a bus while Julz, Brett and Marty, the high achievers, kept their jobs? It was entirely possible. It was also not inconceivable that Ollie had known about this all along

– anti-money-laundering checks were, after all, meant to be carried out here at head office.

At least you'll know you did the right thing, I told myself. But it was cold comfort.

It was almost two hours before I finally left, HR's intervention having done little to reassure me of my long-term job prospects. Numb and exhausted, bewildered by all the talk of internal investigations, disciplinary procedures and legal representation, I let the lift carry me down and my feet carry me out into the cold afternoon.

The glass towers of the City loomed above me, as indifferent as icebergs. I wished I'd driven after all, so I could have slipped into the comfortable embrace of Portia and let her bear me safely home. But I was going to have to brave the Tube.

Before I descended into the station, I realised I hadn't thought to check my phone. Perhaps there'd be a message from Alex – something to relieve the awfulness of the day.

But none of the calls I'd received were from him. Four were from Clara, six from Paul.

Just when I thought things couldn't get any worse, it looked as if they had.

CHAPTER THIRTY-FIVE

At least I'm not meant to be at work, I told myself, finding a tiny crumb of comfort. If I was skiving off, I'd feel even guiltier than I was already.

But nothing could lighten my guilt about Clara. My daughter, who I'd failed more horribly than I could ever have imagined.

I thought back on all the times over the years I'd reassured myself I was doing my best, all the healthy meals I'd cooked, World Book Day outfits I'd cobbled together, parents' egg and spoon races I'd run – I'd genuinely thought I was doing an okay job.

Clearly I'd been kidding myself. Clearly I wasn't fit to look after a houseplant, never mind a teenage girl. I'd taken my eye off the ball, distracted by mooning over Alex as if I was fourteen myself, and by the giddy excitement of the advent calendar, as if I was about six. I was supposed to be a responsible adult, but clearly I'd blown it. Somewhere along the line, it had all gone terribly wrong, and when it had, I wasn't even there for her. Paul had got there before me.

But, I told myself, sitting on the Central Line willing the

train to go faster and faster, barely seeing the passengers around me with their loaded department-store bags bulging with Christmas shopping, self-reproach could wait. I had more than enough time to beat myself up over this – the whole rest of my life, in fact. Now, I needed to be strong, to put a brave face on things for my daughter's sake. To hide the volcano of fury and resentment I could feel bubbling up inside me at Paul and present a united front, same as I'd always done.

At last, the train inched its way into Shepherd's Bush station. They'd wait there for me for half an hour, Paul had promised, and if I wasn't there, he'd take Clara back to his place, even though it was a couple of days earlier than we'd arranged. It had been twenty-five minutes. I just had to find them in the vastness of Westfield shopping centre.

Of course, the mall was rammed. People were everywhere, wandering along with laden carrier bags, chatting and laughing. Christmas music blared relentlessly through the speakers.

Driving home for Christmas – that was what Clara and Paul would be doing, the day after tomorrow. It should have been a happy drive, but now it wouldn't be – it would be soured by blame and guilt and fear about our daughter's future.

I found them in Starbucks. Paul had an empty espresso cup in front of him; Clara a half-drunk gingerbread latte and an almost-untouched muffin. The normality of the scene was almost bizarre, until my daughter turned around when she heard me say her name and I saw her tearstained face.

Feeling as if I might almost be swept away by the wave of love, anger and fear that poured over me, I knelt down and took her in my arms. She returned my hug for the briefest second, nestling her face in my neck the way she used to do when she was small. She smelled strongly of a vaguely familiar violet scent, like she'd bathed in it. Risk-Taking, I remembered. Now I knew where that little bottle had gone – and why. Then she pushed me away.

'Mum, don't. It's embarrassing. People are looking.'

They weren't, but I let her go anyway and sat down at the table.

'Coffee, Ro?' Paul asked.

I didn't want anything, but I knew that he, tactfully, wanted to leave Clara and me alone for a moment.

'Just a water,' I said. 'Thanks.'

Then I turned again to my daughter. 'So. What happened?'

'Just what I told you.'

'Yes, but...' Her message had been garbled and incoherent, her breath coming in panicked gasps so she could hardly get the words out. 'Could you tell me again?'

'I took something. A bottle of perfume. From Space NK. And I got caught.'

Shoplifting. The pettiest of crimes – but not victimless, I knew that. *Why?* The word screamed through my mind, along with, *What did I do wrong?* The two of them had been playing tag in my mind all the way here; there was no reason why they'd stop now.

'And then what happened?' I asked.

'The store security guy took me into a back room.' Clara gulped, her face going from bone white to scarlet as she remembered. 'He said I could call you, but you didn't answer, so I called Dad and he came.'

I nodded. Paul had explained in his message that they'd decided not to involve the police – her crime (the word made me shudder, thinking of it in connection with my beautiful, innocent child) had been committed with a cack-handedness that indicated a total lack of premeditation (*Thank goodness neither they nor Paul knew about the Risk-Taking potion*, I thought); she'd taken only one product and it had been recovered; Clara was young and had never been apprehended doing anything of the kind before.

But a blistering telling-off had been administered, and Clara was still reeling from it.

Paul returned with my water and took his seat, pushing the chair back from the table slightly and scrolling through his phone, although it was impossible for him to avoid overhearing us.

'Can you tell me why?' I asked gently, although I suspected I already knew what her answer would be.

Clara looked truculent for a second, as if about to produce a monosyllabic teenage 'I dunno'.

But she didn't. She said, 'It was for your Christmas present, Mum.'

'You know I wouldn't want a present that you'd... got in that way, though.'

'I know that now,' she replied. 'But I was there, like, in Space NK and all the other shops and I just thought, it's so unfair. Just so unfair that we can't ever have nice stuff. We wear clothes from Primark and charity shops. I hardly get any pocket money. We haven't been on holiday for, like, years. You drive that embarrassing car.'

Poor Portia.

'Clara, I get it,' I said. 'But there are loads of people worse off than us. People having to use food banks. People who've lost their jobs. People who can't have new things ever.'

'Think of all the starving children in Ethiopia,' Clara said mockingly. 'Isn't that what you said Granny used to tell you when you wouldn't eat your dinner?'

At that moment, I felt a flash of sympathy for my own mother. This parenting shit was hard.

'Fair point,' I said. 'But the reality is, everyone wants things they can't have. You can't just go ahead and take them. You know that.'

I wanted Alex, and the chances of me getting him were

looking pretty slim. But I wasn't going to say that to my daughter of course.

Clara's face crumpled. 'I know. I'm sorry. It was stupid and I feel awful and... I'll never do anything like that again. Ever. I promise.'

I passed her a tissue from my bag. 'Come on, sweetie. Let's get you home.'

Paul switched off his phone and pushed back his chair. 'Shall I drive you both back?'

'I'd better go and pick up my car from town.' If I left Portia there overnight, the parking would cost a king's ransom. 'You take Clara home and wait there for me, okay?'

So we went our separate ways.

Before I descended into the car park, I tried calling Alex again, but again, his phone rang to voicemail. Again, I couldn't quite bring myself to leave a message. I drove home as quickly as I could and hurried up the stairs to find Paul slumped on the sofa watching a rerun of *Nigella's Christmas*, and Clara's bedroom door closed.

'Is she...?' I gestured towards the door.

'Conked out,' Paul said softly.

'What are we going to do?'

'Search me. I can't remember reading any advice on this one in *Toddler Taming*.'

Even *How to Survive Parenting a Teenager*, I reflected, didn't include a chapter on what to do if your child turned to a life of crime.

'We can't just let her off scot-free,' I said.

'God, Ro. I don't know. We could give her Christmas presents to charity or something.'

I thought of the carefully accumulated hoard in my bedroom: the nail polish, the clip-in hair extensions, the new wireless headphones I'd found in Lidl.

'That's harsh. Like, really harsh.'

'No Wi-Fi over Christmas?'

'Staying with your mum and dad? Come on. The poor kid needs to be able to chat to her friends.'

'Get her to volunteer at a homeless shelter or something?'

'Are you mad? She's fourteen.'

We talked around the issue for a few minutes but came no closer to a solution.

Eventually, Paul said, 'Looks like we've got nothing. Let's sleep on it and decide after Christmas. No point ruining that for everyone.'

I thought ahead to what the day held in store for me, in the flat alone, the Christmas lights flickering like a reproach, with my selection box for company and possibly a bottle of gin if I decided to push the boat out.

Then, all of a sudden, I found myself filled with indignation – anger, even.

'Paul, what the hell is going on with you and Hayley? She came round here and she said—'

'She came round here?'

'Yes. She told me that you two had had a row, and that you'd said you were getting cold feet about the wedding. And she told me...' I hesitated. Surely – *surely* – Hayley wouldn't have hidden her desire to get pregnant as soon as she could from Paul? But she hadn't said she was telling me in confidence, so I ploughed on. 'She told me she wants a baby. Are you trying?'

Paul ducked his head. 'Yeah. Well, she is at any rate. Told me she's stopped taking the pill and it's all systems go from here on. And if I don't like it, I can wear a condom or go without.'

I couldn't help feeling a spark of admiration for Hayley. She knew what she wanted, and she was laying her cards on the table in order to get it, while presenting Paul with alternatives I knew he'd find pretty unpalatable.

'Well, that's not exactly unreasonable, is it?' I said.

'I've got to admit, it kind of felt that way. So when she told me I – well, I flew off the handle a bit. I might have said she was trying to trap me into marriage.'

'Paul! What the hell? You already asked her to marry you. How could her getting pregnant – which, by the way, takes two people to achieve – be some kind of Machiavellian plot to make what was already going to happen happen?'

'I know. I did apologise, last night. But it just made me think – you've always been such an independent woman, Ro. Hayley's not like that. She needs me, in a way you never did. I know it was wrong, but I did say that it would be easier if she was a bit more like you.'

And Hayley, quite understandably given Paul's revelation about how recently we'd still been sleeping together, had flown off the handle and come round to have it out with me. It took me a second to digest that, and I realised it came as a massive relief. And me being independent? I'd never thought of myself that way – I'd always seen myself as muddling along, somehow keeping our heads above water. Perhaps it was true, though – perhaps people other than Paul saw me that way? Perhaps that was what the Self-Esteem potion had been for, to help me see it too?

I felt almost grateful to Paul for his words – but my anger was still there, increasing steadily until I could feel it was about to reach boiling point.

'Well, that's been very convenient for you, hasn't it?' I asked.

'I don't know what you mean.'

'Don't play dumb with me. You've barely paid a penny towards Clara, all these years. And I haven't asked, because I'm so "independent", and I wanted us to have a good relationship so we could be better parents to her.'

'I have her a night a week and every other weekend,' he protested.

'So you do – except when you don't. And I have her the rest

of the time. Seventy per cent of the time. Sure, you bung her some cash every so often, but every stitch of clothing that child owns, her school lunch money, every ballet class and swimming lesson, I've paid for. Every time I've asked you to contribute so she can go on a school trip you've ummed and ahhed and then said money's a bit tight right now. How bloody tight do you think it's been for me?'

'But you—'

'I've managed. I've managed because I've had no damn choice but to manage. What was the alternative? Starve?'

'But I—'

'And you know what? What Clara said today, about never having nice things. Of course what she did was wrong, and she knows it. But she's got a point. She hardly ever does have nice things, and she sees me not having nice things, and then she sees you and Hayley swanning around in your million-pound house and your BMW and your fancy clothes, and how do you think that makes her feel? She didn't used to be old enough to understand, but now she is.'

'So you're saying our daughter shoplifting a bottle of scent from Space frigging NK is actually all my fault?'

'Don't be ridiculous. Of course I'm not saying that. It's not your fault any more than it is mine. But what is my fault is letting this situation develop, where Clara feels her father doesn't support her. And if you and Hayley have a baby and the two of you bring it up together, Clara will see how different that is from her own childhood, and she'll draw her own conclusions. That's what I'm saying.'

'So what are you suggesting I—'

'And furthermore,' I went on, righteous indignation preventing me from letting him get a word in edgeways, 'what happened between you and me. All those times when we... when we had sex, after we split up. I shouldn't have allowed that to happen. It blurred the boundaries.'

Blurring of boundaries wasn't the only reason it would never happen again, but I wasn't going to tell Paul that. He opened his mouth to speak, but I still wasn't done.

'It let you take advantage of me in other ways, and I'm glad it'll never happen again. And as for what you did at the fair—'

He held up his hands, palms raised in apology or supplication. 'I'm sorry about that, Ro. It was wrong. Crass and stupid. But you know, the heat of the moment and the Christmas spirit, and you looked so beautiful, I—'

'I don't want your flattery, damn it.'

'So do you want from me, Rowan? I'll apologise again. I'll grovel, if that'll make you feel better.'

'I don't want anything. Not for me, anyway. But for Clara. Once all this has died down, I want you to pay her a decent allowance again. Not silly money, just enough that she can have some of the things she wants, normal teenage things. And I want you to put money aside for her so that once she's living away from home, she'll have a bit of a boost to get her own place, or buy a car or whatever.'

'I see. So I'm to be the one funding our daughter's future?'

'Do you seriously think I haven't been?' I stood up, looking down at him, and he almost quailed at the force of my anger. 'Every single month, even when I've had to live on beans on toast, I've put money into her savings account. There's quite a healthy sum in there now.'

I told him how much.

'And all I'm asking is that you match it. Fair?'

Reluctantly, Paul nodded. 'I didn't realise, Rowan. I genuinely thought you—'

'Were so feckless I wasn't making provisions for our daughter's future? Well – newsflash – I was. Thank you, Paul, I was sure you'd see reason. Now I'd better go and wake her and see if she wants anything to eat. Text me and let me know what time you're picking her up tomorrow, and we'll decide what to do about this other thing after Christmas.'

He left, and I collapsed bonelessly onto the sofa. I felt limp and exhausted, like I'd been in a fight – which I supposed I had. I could smell the sour perspiration of stress and exhaustion coming off my body.

Maybe, I thought, *that's what assertiveness smells like.*

CHAPTER THIRTY-SIX

Alex was being crushed. Slowly, relentlessly, beneath a weight he couldn't withstand, which pinned him down, impeding his ability to breathe.

When he was sixteen, he'd done work experience at an old-school accounting firm in Edinburgh, organised by a friend of his dad's. On his first day, one of the partners had casually handed him a thick Manila-bound folder and said, 'Take that down to the basement, will you, and file it in the archive cabinet under McPherson.'

Alex had obeyed, glad to have a task marginally more interesting than making tea and running out to the deli for sandwiches. He'd made his way downstairs, into a cavernous room walled entirely by giant filing cabinets, smelling of dust and ancient paper. He'd found the one labelled M, easy-peasy. But then he'd realised that it was in fact Ma–McB, this being Scotland. McD–McP was the next one along. He'd heaved open the topmost drawer, rifling through its contents from McPartland to McPhail to McPhee. McPherson would belong right at the back. He'd pulled the drawer out further, hearing the rusty creak of its runners.

And then the unthinkable had happened. The weight of the files inside had tipped the entire cabinet over. Alex had tried his best to fight it back, but within less than a second he realised it was a losing battle. Just in time, he'd sprung aside, and the entire cabinet had crashed down onto the bare concrete floor with a sound like a tank hitting a bunker, spilling files, papers, someone's carefully concealed pack of Benson & Hedges, a fossilised cheese sandwich and a family of spiders everywhere.

It would have been bad enough, except Alex had been so freaked out by the near-death experience that Mr Brody's kind PA had had to revive him with a cup of sweet tea, saying that the whole thing had been a health and safety nightmare in the making for years.

He'd seen out his work experience, but realised right then that any profession involving paperwork was not for him and done his degree in software engineering instead.

And still, almost twenty years later, Alex occasionally dreamed of a vast weight descending on him, slowly squeezing the life out of his body, his last sensory experience being the smell of mouldy cheddar.

He couldn't smell cheese now – nothing unfamiliar, in fact. But the sense of constriction was there, the weight pinning him down, the earth-shaking rumble directly next to his right ear.

Sleep banished, Alex opened his eyes.

'Jesus, Balthazar.' The coal-black, whiskery face was right there, inches from his own, amber eyes regarding him in a fashion Alex thought was unfairly judgemental. He could feel the cat's breath huffing against his top lip with every purr. 'You need to go on a diet. You weigh a ton. And what's this about breakfast? It must be, like, five a.m.'

Balthazar gave a stern meow that indicated his disagreement then immediately started to purr again, digging his claws determinedly through Alex's shirt and into the skin of his chest.

'Hold on. Let me just check my... Shit.'

He struggled upright beneath the weight of the cat, who jumped to the floor with a thud and a squawk that clearly meant, 'About time, too.'

'Where the hell is my phone?'

Of all the questions racing through his mind, Alex realised, it was a sign of the times that that was the one he'd articulated first.

Not 'Do I have a niece or a nephew?' or 'Did I nail that pitch?' or even 'How long was I asleep for and what the hell day is it?'

Mostly, he supposed, because his phone held the answers to those questions, and more.

Including 'Am I going to have the balls to ask Rowan Connell out on an actual, proper date?'

But locating his mobile would have to wait – he had even more pressing concerns. If he was going to mount an effective search for it, he'd need coffee. And Balthazar was twining round his legs, meowing piteously.

Alex went to the bathroom and cleaned his teeth. He was starving too – the cat would have eaten a lot more recently than he had, because when he'd got in, the first thing he'd done was tip two pouches of premium-quality food into Balthazar's bowl. The second had been to collapse into bed, where he'd fallen immediately into deep, exhausted sleep.

He had no idea how long he'd slept for or what time it was – his watch was the old-fashioned kind that needed winding, and according to it, it was three in the morning. Impossible, he realised, now he'd left the curtained darkness of his bedroom behind, as what passed for the sun on this midwinter day was already shining pallidly in an ice-blue sky.

Perhaps I've slept right through Christmas, Alex thought, then dismissed the idea as a fiction thrown up by his confused, disjointed brain.

Balthazar – almost six kilos of pure muscle, his coat glossy as a panther's – stalked ahead of Alex to the kitchen, his long tail held high. Every few paces he'd glance back over his shoulder to check that Alex hadn't changed his mind about providing breakfast, which he hadn't.

'Come on then,' he said. 'Let's see what's on the menu. Tuna and salmon? Turkey and goose? Let's go with turkey and goose – appropriately seasonal.'

He ripped open the pouch and emptied the contents into Balthazar's bowl, the cat keeping up a raucous chorus, his paws stretching as high up the kitchen cabinet as he could get. There were dusty paw prints on the worktop, Alex noticed – clearly, after a trip outside to inspect the squirrels, Balthazar had had a go at helping himself to food before opting to wake Alex.

Once the cat's face was firmly planted in his bowl, noisily chomping, Alex flicked on the coffee machine. It was seven o'clock in the morning, according to the clock on the microwave – and Christmas Eve. He'd been asleep for over twenty-four hours – unsurprising, given how insane the week had been so far – although he assumed he must have woken at some point to feed Balthazar, as there was no mangled squirrel corpse to be seen anywhere.

He pulled together his scattered memories of the three days since he'd arrived at the hospital with Ailsa. Explaining to the staff that he was her brother, not her husband or the father of the baby, only there for moral support and not – *categorically* not – to be present at the birth, no matter what. Ailsa adding that Omar would be there as soon as he was out of theatre, where he was carrying out a pulmonary thromboen-darterectomy.

Listening as Ailsa responded to the kindly midwife's sugges-tion that she might prefer to stay at home for a few hours, as she was only three centimetres dilated, by announcing that she intended to stay right here, close to where the good drugs were, because if it hurt this bloody much now, it was going to hurt a whole lot more before long.

Alex had applauded his sister's spirit, but if she had to stay, so did he – he'd promised her months before that if Omar wasn't able to be there, he would be, although he'd emphasised that he didn't intend to be anywhere near the business end of things, and Ailsa had said, 'My God. As if I'd ever let you see that.'

So he'd stayed. The two of them had done sudoku puzzles, read the back copies of *OK!* magazine that his sister had hoarded for the occasion, eaten jelly babies and watched *Come Dine with Me* – at least, when Ailsa wasn't moaning with the pain of a contraction and gripping Alex's hand so hard he feared she'd break a bone.

And at last, at almost eight in the morning, Omar had arrived, freshly showered but hollow-eyed and exhausted, having also been up all night. He'd kissed his wife and shaken Alex's hand, and Alex had been free to leave.

And then his phone had rung. The investor he'd been courting for weeks wanted a meeting, with a full presentation, first thing on Tuesday.

So Alex had raced home, showered, fed Balthazar and himself, then got to work on his laptop preparing a slide deck and putting together answers for every conceivable question they could ask, pulling an all-nighter to get it done. He'd been so engrossed in his work he couldn't recall checking his phone at all.

After only a couple of hours' sleep, he'd jumped on his bicycle while it was still dark and headed into town for the meeting, which had felt as if he was conducting it in a dream but had seemed to go well. After that there'd been a post-mortem with two of his freelance developers over lunch, which had then turned into a few beers in the pub.

And then he'd returned home, given the cat his dinner and fallen asleep – for the better part of a day.

But when had he last seen his phone?

He'd definitely had it when he and Ailsa had been in the hospital overnight; he'd composed several messages to Rowan and saved them as drafts but hadn't wanted to send them in the middle of the night. He'd read a text from Omar saying he was on his way. He'd rung the developers to check their availability for the meeting.

But after that? He had no recollection of seeing it.

The damn thing was officially missing in action, and it could be anywhere – in the hospital, in the office, in the pub or in literally any of the points between them. Also, he couldn't remember the last time he'd backed it up, but he was fairly sure it had been before he'd added Rowan and Kate's numbers to it.

There was nothing for it – he'd have to go round to Ailsa's, not only to ask about his mobile but because it was the simplest way to find out how everyone was. If they weren't there, he'd assume they were still at the hospital, hopefully just resting and getting some TLC.

As he stood under a jet of hot water in the shower, Alex found his mind clearing and, with it, worries descending. He shook his head to dispel them. This was the twenty-first century – women didn't die in childbirth any more.

Except when they did. And Ailsa had had a rough old time of this pregnancy, virtually housebound for the past couple of months except when she had dragged herself out to look round houses to buy, struggling to walk without crutches and in loads of pain from what she'd said was a common condition that would resolve once the baby was delivered. But what if it had affected her body's ability to... God! Do whatever women's bodies did. Dilate or whatever.

Alex realised, lathering his hair with shampoo, how little he knew about this childbearing malarkey. He'd had plenty of girl-friends in the past but none of them serious enough for the question of starting a family to arise beyond the vague idea that maybe, sometime in the future, he'd like to be a dad.

And his businesses had been his babies: the one before this, which he'd sold, and this one. The idea had come to him during the first lockdown when, finding himself with time on his hands and no need to bring in any money for the time being, he'd volunteered with an organisation that helped deliver essentials to people in Glasgow who were clinically vulnerable and unable to leave their homes.

The logistics of it had blown his mind. How, even with the tech at his disposal, it had been a massive headache to get stuff to the people who needed it. How complex the planning of a delivery route was, how even a minor glitch could throw everything off-kilter, and suddenly Mrs Miggins's frozen fishfingers weren't frozen any more.

And he'd got chatting to other drivers, the real ones, who did this stuff for a living. He'd learned how precarious their livelihoods were, how one customer refusing an order or one error on a delivery chit could throw out their entire day and leave them earning half what they expected and needed to keep afloat and feed their families.

There had to be a better way, he reckoned.

So, once the world started to return to normal and his services dropping off cornflakes and loo roll weren't required any longer, he'd begun formulating a business plan. An app, initially, which would streamline the last-mile logistics process from the driver's point of view. And then – Alex dreamed of this in his softer moments – a whole new company: one that would offer secure employment and a living wage for drivers.

At the same time, Omar had accepted a new job at a London hospital, which had meant he and Ailsa relocating. It made sense for Alex to do the same: London was where the venture-capital money was, after all. And it was where the vast majority of the nation's deliveries took place.

Always a believer in walking the talk, Alex had applied for a job at Pegasus, hoping to gain a greater understanding of what life was really like for the men (and the occasional woman) who made their living in this way. He'd planned on sticking it out for a couple of months, until December, then quitting and focusing solely on raising investment capital.

But then he'd delivered a parcel to a woman in a seventh-floor flat, whose smile had struck his heart in a way no one's had for the longest time, and he'd decided to stick it out for another couple of weeks.

And now here he was, with feelings for her that were quite startling in their intensity.

He towelled off, dressed quickly, assured Balthazar that this time he definitely, categorically wouldn't be home late and jumped on his bicycle, negotiating the familiar route to Ailsa and Omar's house in record time, only stopping en route to buy flowers and champagne, just in case.

The Christmas wreath, adorned with pine fronds and cinnamon sticks, which his sister had painstakingly made herself, saying that it was about the only thing she could do sitting down – what else was there, fucking crocheting? – still hung on the door where Alex had placed it. But below it, laminated and attached to the knocker with a piece of sparkly gold ribbon, was a note.

Delivery drivers – we have a new baby. Please knock quietly.

Alex wasn't a delivery driver any more, but he knocked quietly anyway.

Omar came to the door, dressed in a shabby grey tracksuit. He looked terrible – gaunt and almost green with exhaustion – but he embraced Alex warmly.

'Congratulations! You've got a niece.'

'Oh, man.' Alex pumped his hand, almost overcome by emotion.

'Come in. One of the neighbours dropped round a Christmas cake. We've got through almost half of it already.'

In the living room, the corner sofa had been expanded to its sleeper mode so it filled almost the entire space. Ailsa was lying down, her shoulders propped up against a pile of cushions, her dark hair scraped back from her shiny, flushed face, a tiny bundle clutched to her chest.

'Hey,' she said. 'Holly's sleeping, but she can't wait to meet her uncle.'

'Wow,' Alex said, sitting down and accepting the coffee Omar made, along with a slab of cake. 'So, how did it all... I mean, are you okay?'

'It smarted a bit, I'm not going to lie,' Ailsa said. 'And he got a fit of the vapours at the crucial moment.'

'You what?' Alex turned to his brother-in-law in surprise. 'But you're—'

'Cardiothoracic,' Omar said. 'Obstetrics is entirely different. Especially when it's your wife.'

'Anyway, he owes you an apology,' Ailsa said.

'What? Why?'

'Your phone,' Omar explained. 'I saw it just after you left, but things were too... so I put it in my shirt pocket for safe-keeping.'

'And then the midwife told me I was ready to push,' Ailsa said.

'And they told me to help her stand up and support her.'

'And so he bent over, and...'

'Your phone landed in the birthing pool,' Omar finished. 'Sorry about that.'

'We've put it in a bag of rice,' Ailsa said. 'But I think it's a goner, to be honest. There was blood in there and... well, all sorts.'

'It really doesn't matter,' Alex said. 'You're okay and Holly's here, and it's just a bit of tech. I can buy another.'

He leaned over, looking with wonder at his brand-new niece's tiny, scrunched-up face and perfect, shrimp-like fingers. Of course his phone didn't matter in comparison – but contacting Rowan did.

He was going to have to make another plan.

CHAPTER THIRTY-SEVEN

'Are you sure you've got everything?' I asked.

Clara nodded, her eyes on her phone.

'Chargers? Christmas presents? Period pants, just in case?'

'Yes. God, Mum, I'm going to Wales, not Outer Mongolia.'

I laughed. 'Fair enough. You'd have about as much joy buying period pants in Outer Mongolia as in Llandudno on Christmas Day, though.'

'Just as well I packed them, then.'

I eased Portia into a parking spot outside Paul's house, and we both got out. Opening the boot to get Clara's bags (and, to be fair, she'd packed as if she was off on a two-week trek across the steppes, not three days with her grandparents), I could see Hayley hovering in the doorway.

'Off you go, then. Have a lovely time. FaceTime me to say merry Christmas, okay?'

Clara nodded. Then she flung her arms around me and gave me a brief, fierce embrace.

'You'll be okay on your own, won't you, Mum? I left your present under the tree. Call me if you're lonely.'

To my surprise, I felt a massive lump forming in my throat.

In spite of everything, I'd managed to raise a girl who was kind, loving and thoughtful.

'I won't be lonely. Love you, sweetie. Merry Christmas.'

Hayley waved a 'come in' gesture, but I had no desire to eat mince pies and make polite chit-chat when I knew they needed to get on the road if they were to make it to their destination before dark, so I replied with a 'must dash' hand signal of my own, kissed Clara once more and climbed back in the car.

As soon as I'd shut the door, I felt a weight of loneliness descend. It was okay. It was only a few days. I had plans to catch up with the Girlfriends' Club for a boozy brunch on the twenty-seventh, and then Clara would be back that evening. I'd spent Christmas alone before and it had been fine.

But it wasn't what I had imagined. In my head, over the past week, I'd dreamed up too many scenarios that, somehow, involved Alex and me being together. Us sitting by a log fire in a luxury hotel. Us walking through the park beneath the bare trees, holding hands. Us lying in bed, our bodies intertwined under the duvet.

How we'd got into any of these, my imagination hadn't provided an explanation. But still, I'd played them over in my mind until they were tired and stale and no longer brought me any comfort or hope.

I thumped Portia's steering wheel in frustration. It was no good. However much I tried to imagine me and Alex having a life together, it wasn't working. I knew too little about him. The chance I had to ask questions on the evening when we'd had our picnic together had been thwarted first by my overwhelming desire to kiss him, and then by the message from Ailsa.

And since then, after trying to call him five times, I'd given up. If he wanted to get hold of me, he knew where to find me. But clearly he didn't want to.

So what have you lost? Nothing, said a sane – far too sane – voice in my head.

Nothing except a bunch of dreams of a future I thought I'd never have.

You thought you'd have it with Paul, and look where that got you.

Yes, I know, but I don't want it with Paul any more.

Just as well, because you're not going to get it.

I want it with Alex.

I want doesn't get.

The voice in my head sounded an awful lot like me telling five-year-old Clara off.

You can be perfectly happy on your own, the voice hectored. *Loads of women are. You've got your daughter, your career—*

Not any more, I don't.

Your friends.

Okay, they're great. But I want...

What?

I want to feel like I felt when Alex kissed me. I want to be in love, dammit. Is that so much to ask?

Probably. You'll just have to wait and see what Father Christmas brings you.

And with a final, cynical laugh from the voice in my head, I wearily swung Portia into her parking space outside the flat.

CHAPTER THIRTY-EIGHT

It was Christmas Eve, so Alex should have expected Covent Garden to be buzzing. But even so, the sheer volume of people wandering through the narrow streets laden with carrier bags, many with long rolls of gift wrap awkwardly rammed into them, took him by surprise.

After narrowly missing mowing down a woman cutting in front of him with her phone in one hand and a buggy in the other, he decided it would be prudent to abandon his bicycle and walk. He locked it in a stand with a load of others – hoping that the shiny, high-end ones on either side of it would prove more attractive to thieves – and made his way onward on foot.

The mist that had shrouded the world that morning had cleared, and the sun was shining determinedly in a clear sky, but it was still properly cold; even with gloves on, Alex's hands were stiff from gripping the handlebars.

Some Glaswegian you are, he chided himself. *You've gone all soft since you moved down south.*

And then he grinned to himself, realising that it wasn't just his tolerance for cold weather that had softened in recent weeks; his heart appeared to have been replaced with a marsh-mallow too.

Passing through the covered market beneath the giant swags of faux mistletoe, he couldn't help remembering kissing Rowan, and wondering when he'd get to repeat the experience. He could picture the look on her face as he'd leaned in – how she'd gone from, *Oh my God, is he going to kiss me?* to kissing him herself, in the space of a fraction of a second. He recalled the incredible softness of her skin against his cheek – clearly the fancy beauty products he'd been delivering to her had delivered on their hype. Or maybe she just naturally had skin like a rose petal. He could still feel the instant, potent swell of desire he'd experienced at her closeness, confirming that his feelings for her would translate from the world's most massive crush into genuine passion.

Soon, he told himself, she'd be standing in front of him in the doorway of her flat, her face lighting up with pleasure when she saw him. Or maybe she wouldn't – maybe the hours of silence and the impossibility of contacting him would have – understandably – pissed her off, and he'd have some fast talking to do. But that was okay – any talking to Rowan would be okay by him.

But first, he had an urgent errand to complete. He edged through the throng of people outside the Apple Store and pushed open the door.

Tech first, then love.

It took the best part of an hour to complete his purchase, retrieve his bike and navigate the crowds again, but soon Alex was back out on the open road, the icy wind cutting through his jacket and jeans as he whizzed over Waterloo Bridge, passing red double-decker buses, black cabs and lorries, and resisting the urge to cut up fellow cyclists in his haste.

No point killing yourself, or someone else, he told himself firmly. *You don't get the girl by landing yourself in Accident and*

Emergency. But impatience and eagerness were fuelling his legs, and he pedalled as if there was an Olympic medal at stake.

By the time he arrived, he wasn't a bit cold any more. His breath coming in gasps, he chained his bicycle up again and turned to the lift. Fortunately, it appeared to be working – he wasn't sure his quads could have taken the climb up the stairs after his breakneck ride across London.

Tucking his helmet under his arm, he smoothed his hair. *Gallant,* he told himself – *that's the vibe we're going for here. Gallant and poised. And hopefully sexy AF* – although, feeling sweat snaking down his back under his T-shirt, jumper and down jacket, he realised he couldn't guarantee that.

Alex suddenly realised he was nervous. He felt as jittery as he had facing the panel of venture capitalists whose decision could make or break his fledgling business; as anxious as he'd felt as a teenager turning up for his first day of that disastrous work-experience placement; as uncertain about what the immediate future held as he had been holding his sister's hand in the taxi on the way to the hospital.

Determinedly ignoring his churning stomach and pounding heart, Alex felt the lift jerk to a stop and stepped through the parting doors. He took a deep breath and walked, on legs that appeared to have been replaced by wet spaghetti, towards the door of number 74.

You daft fanny, he thought. *You've done this almost two dozen times before – how come now it's such a big deal?*

Because the other times I didn't know how I felt about her, his mind responded with implacable reasonableness. *The other times, I didn't know I was falling for her. Now I do.*

The realisation calmed him and brought a smile to his face. Now buoyant with excitement, Alex lifted his hand, raised the knocker and then let it fall gently, once and then again, and waited.

A long minute later, he was still waiting.

Rowan wasn't home, and nor was Clara. He imagined her in the car with her ex and daughter, on the way to Wales for a family Christmas after a surprise reconciliation. He imagined her drinking a cocktail in a flash bar with her handsome blonde friend, who she'd insisted was gay, but who knew? He imagined her stranded somewhere, her car broken down.

And then he realised how absurd he was being. It was Christmas Eve. The woman was out – that was all. And fortunately, Alex had come prepared for just this eventuality. He rummaged in his bag, found the white envelope, opened it, scrawled a few additional words on the page, refolded it and slipped it through the letterbox, as he'd done so many times before when no one had answered the door.

And then, with a final, reluctant backward glance, he returned to the lift, descended, unchained his bicycle and swung into the saddle.

CHAPTER THIRTY-NINE

Amazingly, the lift was working and it bore me up without complaint. I almost wished I'd had to climb the stairs, because now I'd be inside the flat, alone, for a few crucial minutes longer. I pulled the door open and stepped into the pine-scented silence.

As soon as I closed it behind me, the quiet descended on me like a smothering blanket, as I'd known it would. There was no buzz of music leaking through Clara's cheap headphones. There was no thump of her feet on the floor as she walked from the bedroom to the kitchen to get yet another glass of orange squash. There was no murmur of her voice as she chatted to a friend on the phone.

Even my own breathing sounded loud. There was noise from outside, of course – the hum of traffic on the main road; next door's toddler raising his voice in protest at something; the clock on the church tower striking twelve. But within these four walls, there was only me, only the clink of my keys as I put them down, the shuffle of my feet on the floor, the hum of the kettle as I mindlessly flicked it on, even though I didn't want a hot drink.

The afternoon stretched ahead of me, featureless. Of course

there were things I could do: I could blitz the flat from top to bottom, which I'd been promising myself I would for weeks. I could go to the shops and splash out on some Christmas food for me to enjoy on my own – cheese and cranberry parcels, chipo-lata sausages, the Brussels-sprout-flavoured crisps I'd seen, which I was pretty sure would be disgusting but wanted to try anyway. I could have a hot bath and plaster on some of the advent-calendar beauty products.

But I had no desire to do anything. Loneliness and sadness had me firmly in their grip, and I felt powerless to do even the things I knew would make me feel marginally better.

I kicked off my shoes and wandered through to the living room with a cup of tea, sinking onto the sofa and flicking on the TV. A cruise through the channels confirmed that there was nothing I wanted to watch – everything was either relentlessly Christmas themed or determinedly ignoring the time of year altogether, presumably aiming itself at people like me, who only wanted the day itself to be over so that they could return to normal depression without the expectation of jollity.

Then I heard footsteps on the walkway outside, and my heart leaped. It couldn't be him – it wouldn't. Whoever it was would surely pass by my flat. But the footsteps came to a stop and the door knocker tapped.

I sprang off the sofa, forgetting about the tea in my hand and sending a tidal wave of hot liquid down my jumper.

'Shit!' I put the cup down, hesitating for a second. Should I change into something clean? But what if Alex – *if* it was Alex – assumed I was out and went away again? There was no way I was risking that.

I hurried to the door and flung it open, and was met by the familiar wide smile, the familiar Pegasus baseball cap, the familiar high-vis jacket.

Not Alex. The new driver, the other one, the friendly guy

with the locs. I could barely see his face over the large card-board crate he was holding.

Disappointment hitting me like a punch in the gut, I forced myself to smile.

'Afternoon,' he said cheerily. 'What have we got here then? Says it's perishable goods. Tasty treats for Christmas?'

'Looks like it,' I agreed.

'Need a hand getting this inside? It's proper heavy.'

'Thanks, but I think I can manage.'

He passed the box over. He was right, it was heavy, but I barely noticed its weight.

'Give me a second,' I said. 'I'll just put this in the kitchen.'

A few moments later, I returned and tipped the guy a tenner. I could ill afford it, but if it made someone else's Christmas a little happier, that was okay with me.

'Many thanks,' he said. 'God bless you. Have a very merry Christmas.'

'And you.'

I turned away, feeling the smile drop off my face as if my muscles could no longer support it. Then I went to inspect the parcel. Just a few days ago, its arrival would have filled me with pleasure and excitement, but now my thoughts were only on getting whatever was in it into the fridge so it wouldn't spoil.

Taking a breadknife to the tape that sealed the box, I lifted the cardboard flaps aside and pulled out a layer of sheep's wool insulation, followed by a printed card bearing the logo of a fancy restaurant where I knew Kate often entertained clients. There was a menu on the reverse of it, but I barely glanced at it – I'd find out soon enough what the box contained.

There was a bottle of Veuve Clicquot champagne. There were lobster cocktails and Christmas crackers and venison wellingtons and cavolo nero with chestnuts and cream. There were goose-fat roast potatoes and maple-glazed carrots, and sage and onion stuffing. There were little pots of gravy, bread sauce and sloe-gin jelly. There were individual Christmas puddings and chocolate truffles and Stilton cheese and even a half-bottle of port.

It was a feast. A feast for two.

Wearily, I stacked it all in the near-empty fridge, putting the leaflet of cooking instructions on the kitchen counter. Looking at it all didn't make me feel hungry, just sad.

And, mostly, confused. My friends knew I'd be spending the next day alone. They knew I'd tried and failed to contact Alex and given up. They must, surely, know how this would make me feel – how it would serve as a reminder of the Christmas I'd have liked to have but wasn't going to get.

Perhaps it had been too late to cancel the order, and they hadn't wanted it to go to waste. Perhaps they had cancelled it, but the restaurant had made an error and delivered it anyway. It didn't matter either way. I'd ring the local homeless shelter and see if they could make use of it, and if not I'd drop it off with Sarita next door, and she and her husband could have a second Christmas on Boxing Day.

I returned to the sofa and my now cold tea, flicking off the television. There was nothing I wanted to watch – I'd already established that. And besides, I didn't want to risk drowning out the sound of another knock on the door, if by some miracle one were to come.

But there would be no knock on the door, my rational brain countered. There would definitely—

The door knocker tapped, and I leaped to my feet as if some prankster had stuck a pin through the sofa cushion from below. The rug skidded under my feet, I almost collided with the Christmas tree, and by the time I made it to the hallway, my heart was hammering and my palms were sweating.

Attractive, Rowan, I chided myself. *Alluring AF. Sweaty and covered in tea with two left feet – what a catch.*

But I didn't care. It was Alex – it had to be.

Composing my face into the calmest, most welcoming smile I could muster, I opened the door.

Standing there was a boy I'd never seen before. A young man, almost. He was tall and gangly. Judging by the way his wrists protruded from the too-short sleeves of his navy blue parka, he'd done a whole lot of growing very recently. Under the parka, I could see a suit jacket and tie, as if he was on his way to a church service with his family. His hair was braided into tidy cornrows.

He, too, was wearing a polite smile, but the eyes behind his round spectacles looked anxious. In his hands was a large square gold-wrapped parcel, tied with a red ribbon.

'Good afternoon,' he said, then paused to clear his throat. 'Are you Ms Connell?'

'That's right.'

He cleared his throat again. 'Clara's mum?'

Light dawned in my underpowered brain. This must be Jonny – could only be Jonny.

'Yes, that's me.' I felt a genuine smile come to my lips – his polite awkwardness was utterly endearing. 'My name's Rowan.'

'John Okoro.' He held out a hand for me to shake, clutching the parcel to his chest with the other.

'I'm afraid Clara's not in. She left for North Wales with her dad this morning.'

Jonny's face fell. I could have wept for him – if he'd only been a few hours earlier, he could have seen Clara.

'I was hoping she'd still be here... I bought her a Christmas gift,' he said, biting his lip.

'She'll be gutted to have missed you, I'm sure. But she can open it when she's back on the twenty-seventh. It's not perishable or anything, is it?'

He shook his head. 'It's just a hamper from Lush. Clara's been talking at school about all that beauty stuff she's into. I thought she'd like it.'

'She'll love it,' I confirmed.

Jonny's eyes grew anxious again behind his glasses. 'But it's, like, a surprise.'

'Of course! I won't tell her you told me what's in it. But I could WhatsApp her a photo of it if you like?'

He smiled, a wide, charming grin like the sun coming out. 'That would be amazing! Thank you, Ms Connell.'

'Rowan,' I corrected, returning his smile and taking the parcel from him. 'Thank you for bringing this. Clara will be thrilled.'

'It's my pleasure. And merry Christmas.'

'Merry Christmas,' I echoed.

Once he'd gone, I put the present under the tree and sent a picture of it to my daughter, anticipating her gleeful reply. And she was right to be gleeful, I reflected – the early signs were that Clara had significantly better taste in men than her mother.

And that, I realised, was the end of the excitement for my Christmas Eve.

Mindlessly, I found myself reaching for the new tin of Quality Street I'd had hidden in the kitchen, in case of emergencies. In a daze, I lay down on my bed, prised the lid off the tub and unwrapped a toffee penny. The first of many, because I intended to be here for some time.

CHAPTER FORTY

I woke up early the next morning, feeling absolutely dreadful. Like a hangover, only from too much sugar. My mouth tasted acidic and sour; my stomach was queasy; and my whole body felt leaden and exhausted.

I'd fallen asleep in my clothes, partially covered by the duvet, sweet wrappers scattered everywhere like the aftermath of a stag night, only held for one lonely, perma-single woman with chocolate issues. Even the sense of crawling dread and shame was there; the only thing missing was the dead body of a stripper I'd have to work out how to dispose of.

'Merry fucking Christmas, Rowan,' I said aloud, heaving myself upright.

And then I told myself to give my head a damn good wobble. I had no right to be miserable. I had a precious daughter who was healthy and mostly happy, when she wasn't turning to a life of crime. I had good friends who'd done all they could for a whole month to cheer me up. The sun was shining. Even if I never saw Alex again, I'd have that kiss to remember.

I'd get up, I told myself, and go out for a walk. The park

would be beautiful today, almost deserted apart from a few families test-driving their children's Christmas scooters, bicycles and inline skates. It would be cold, but bright and clear, sunlight dancing off the water of the lake where the swans glided. There might even be a robin in a tree, a symbol of Christmas. I could wear my purple scarf.

And when I got home, I could settle down on the sofa and watch all the cheesy Christmas films I wanted, without Clara sighing about how pathetic it was – *Love Actually*, *Home Alone*, *Little Women* – and cry my eyes out because of their cheesiness, not because I was actually sad.

I could eat all the damn Quality Street I wanted.

But before I could put my plan into action, I was drawn to the advent calendar. The gift that had started all this off. Slowly, I opened all its drawers, one by one, sliding them out of their close-fitting recesses, inspecting them and sliding them back again.

The first twenty-four were all empty, but the final one, the one with Christmas Day's date on it, wasn't.

Inside was a carefully folded piece of paper with handwriting on it. It looked expensive – the kind of paper you get in fancy stationery shops, cream-coloured and heavy, with a slight texture to it. The writing on it was a careful, tidy script that looked like it might have been written with a fountain pen.

Rowan,

Happy Christmas, darling girl. We started this to make you feel better – to remind you that you're special and beautiful and valuable. And you really, really are. Your kindness, thoughtfulness and humour have brought so much joy to us all over the years, and we hope this calendar has brought you joy, too.

We're honoured to be your friends, and we love you very much.

Naomi, Kate and Abbie

As I read, I felt tears starting to course gently down my face. I was so lucky, I realised. So blessed and fortunate to have these amazing friends in my life – women who'd be there for me no matter what; who'd put so much effort into this amazing journey they'd created for me, because they cared about me.

As long as I had them – and I was pretty sure it would be forever – I'd never truly be alone.

I pulled open the curtains and looked out at the clear, frosty morning. The sun was shining almost white in the clear, pale blue sky. Somewhere I could hear church bells ringing.

I imagined the vastness of London, street after street of houses, people waking up to this Christmas morning, happy or grieving, excited or frazzled, kissing or arguing. For all of them – and for my three best friends, for Clara and Paul in Wales, for Alex wherever he was – Christmas Day would unfold in different ways.

Suddenly, I didn't feel lonely any more. I felt strangely at peace. There would be other Christmases for me to celebrate in other ways. And today, although I was by myself, I didn't need to be sad. I could take care of myself, make the day special just for me.

I cleared away the sweet wrappers and put the empty Quality Street tin in the recycling. I showered and washed my hair and put on a bit of make-up. I dressed in the new underwear I'd bought and the slinky red dress I'd found in the charity shop where I'd left the hideous reindeer-boob jumper. I dabbed on some of the Desirability fragrance from its glass vial.

It smelled of orange blossom – a reminder that the longest night of winter was over and soon spring would come.

I walked through to the kitchen and switched on the kettle. Later, I might open the bottle of expensive champagne, but for now I'd make a coffee and drink it looking out of the window, enjoying the brightening sky and the new feeling of serenity that I'd found – or perhaps it had found me.

Then I noticed something.

There to the right of the doormat, as if it had been pushed aside as I'd opened the door and then half concealed by the other mail that had come through – a pizza delivery leaflet and a flyer about gutter clearing.

A plain white envelope with my name on it.

All my feelings of tranquillity vanished. My heart leaped into my throat, and my body went cold and then hot. How long had it been there? Since yesterday or even the day before?

I picked it up, almost gingerly, as if it might burn my fingers, and eased open the flap.

Inside was a piece of plain A4 paper, printed in standard Times New Roman.

Alex Winter would like to request the pleasure of your company on Christmas Day at 12 noon.

Below it was an address in South East London, a few miles from my home.

And below that, handwritten:

No need to RSVP. I'll be in.

Oh my God. *Oh my God!*

Feeling as if my legs had turned to water, I just about made it back to the sofa and flopped down, holding the page in trembling fingers and reading it over and over again.

He'd been in touch. He wanted to see me. Today. In just over an hour.

I wondered briefly whether I ought to be suspicious – perhaps this was some kind of cruel joke? Perhaps it was some way of Brett, Marty or Julz exacting revenge on me for telling the truth about their property sales? But none of them had a clue about Alex, or the advent calendar, or indeed any other aspect of my private life beyond the existence of my daughter.

Perhaps I ought to be suspicious of Alex himself. Perhaps he was trying to lure me to a strange address for some nefarious purpose? But I didn't believe that would be the case, and besides it was easily dealt with. I found the Girlfriends' Club WhatsApp group on my phone and quickly posted an update on the situation, after answering everyone's Christmas greetings and thanking them from the bottom of my heart for the letter.

Kate: Give us the address and send regular updates saying you're safe. If we don't hear, we'll send the peelers round.

Naomi: This is just the most amazing... Oh no, Toby's trying to murder Meredith with a satsuma. Gotta go.

Abbie: It's super-romantic! Honestly, he didn't seem like an axe murderer to me. Go for it, and check in with us when you're there, okay?

That was it then. Decision made. I couldn't even faff around spending ages getting ready, because I already was. I thought about taking the entire box of Christmas dinner out of the fridge along with me but decided that would be weird, so I just grabbed the champagne and put it in a carrier bag. Then I wound the violet scarf around my neck, put on my coat and boots, and picked up Portia's keys ready to go.

My heart drumming, I headed for the lift. Inevitably, it had gone on strike again. And then, as I turned to make my way down the stairs, I saw a familiar vehicle parked next to my car.

The turquoise Pegasus van. And then I heard the equally

familiar sound of footsteps on the stairs and, seconds later, Alex appeared, out of breath from the seven-storey climb, holding a bunch of red roses.

'Merry Christmas,' he said, holding them out to me. 'I wasn't sure if you'd have got my note, so I thought I'd drop by. Belt and braces. My old foreman lent me the keys to the van as a favour.'

His hair shone in the sunlight like it had been polished. His eyes were the same extraordinary blue I'd noticed what felt like a lifetime ago. He was wearing jeans and a battered leather jacket and he looked like a vision from a dream.

'I was just on my way,' I said. 'And... well, merry Christmas.'

'Even better,' he said. 'We'll go together.'

'I've got...' I began. 'I mean, yesterday's advent-calendar gift was a full-on Christmas dinner. Shall I bring it?'

Alex's smile flashed out, dazzling as the winter sun. 'Thank God for that. I thought perhaps they'd have cancelled it when I went all flaky on you. I lost my phone, you see.'

He lost his phone! The simplest possible explanation, and I'd been beside myself with angst.

While I unlocked the flat again and retrieved everything from the fridge, he explained what had happened.

'I came round yesterday to see you,' he said. 'But you were out. So I left the invitation, but then I got cold feet, worrying you were pissed off or hadn't seen it. So I...'

'You came round and surprised me.'

'I guess I did. Master of indecision.'

We laughed. I handed him the heavy box and he lifted it easily, and together we headed down the stairs to the waiting van.

'This is how it all started,' I said. 'So it's kind of nice that it's going to be part of Christmas. Don't you think?'

'How what all started?' He met my eyes, then swung into the driver's seat.

I felt myself flushing. *Us.* How we started. But I said, 'You know. The advent calendar.'

'And maybe something else as well,' he suggested.

Relief and happiness flooded me. 'Maybe.'

'I hope so, anyway.'

'Me too. Actually, I know so.'

There was almost no other traffic on the roads, and Alex drove confidently and easily, knowing the route without needing to use his satnav. We pointed out landmarks as we went: the church where I'd watched the carol singers, the house with the extraordinary display of decorations in the garden, Crystal Palace park where we'd had our picnic.

Incoherently, because it still felt like I'd only just figured it out myself, I told him that I'd been house-hunting for his sister and brother-in-law.

'Oh my God. So the estate agent she mentioned was you!'

'It was me. And they've had their baby?'

'A gorgeous girl called Holly.'

Already, it felt as if we had a shared history together, even though it only stretched back twenty-five days.

'It feels like a lot longer,' I said, thinking out loud.

'Knowing you? It feels like forever. Either that, or like I've been waiting forever. Which I guess I have.'

Perhaps I had too, I thought, a fizz of pleasurable excitement building inside me. Even though, just a few weeks ago, I'd still imagined a future with Paul, that seemed now like someone else's dream. And maybe it was – maybe it was possible to become almost a different person in such a short time.

Or the same person, but a changed, better version.

Alex pulled up the van outside a small row of Victorian houses, low brick walls fronting their gardens, their fronts painted in different pastel colours.

'Here we are,' he said, opening the door and stepping out.

I followed, feeling shy and tentative again. What if the

place was a hovel, full of the single-man detritus of dirty socks and empty pizza boxes, the way Paul's flat had been when we met? What if it turned out he was into hardcore S&M and there were manacles on the wall and whips everywhere? What if he had a ferocious dog that would leap on me and scare me or a weird dodgy housemate he hadn't told me about?

Carefully balancing the box against his chest, he unlocked the front door of a house with a cream-coloured wall and stepped in.

'Balthazar,' he called. 'Come and meet Rowan.'

Waaah! Dodgy housemate alert!

But the sound I heard coming from upstairs wasn't a human. Over Alex's shoulder, I watched as the biggest black cat I'd ever seen in my life came thundering down the stairs, its tail held aloft, emitting small squeaks of welcome.

'You're not allergic to cats, are you?' Alex asked as the beast twined itself round his ankles, threatening to push him over with the sheer force of its welcome.

'I'm not. I love cats. But this one's huge. Did he escape from a zoo or something?'

Hearing my voice, the cat abandoned Alex and approached me, giving me a hard stare through his amber eyes.

'Hello.' I squatted down to stroke him. His fur was as sleek and glossy as Tatiana Ivanova's coat, although it looked way better on the cat than it had on her. He butted his head against my hand, and I scratched his ears and almost immediately heard thunderous purring. 'Aren't you a beauty? Aren't you a black panther?'

Relieved of the crate of food, Alex reappeared. 'Come on in,' he said. 'Unless you'd rather spend the day in the doorway fussing the cat.'

I stood up. 'I can think of worse ways to spend the day. But also better ones.'

He met my eyes, and I realised he knew what I was thinking and felt my cheeks flush.

'Then we should get a bottle of champagne open,' he said.

'Deal.'

'I've got some smoked salmon as well,' he went on. 'I can't cook, but there's a great deli down the road so I bought some stuff in. We might have to share it though.'

Balthazar meowed, as if he'd heard the phrase 'smoked salmon' before and knew it was good news for him.

'Amazing,' I said. 'I love smoked salmon. There's something so Christmassy about it.'

'Stick around another month and you'll get haggis and neeps and tatties for Burns Night,' he promised.

I glowed. Never mind that I couldn't bear haggis and could never remember whether neeps were turnips or swedes – he thought we might still be together in a month's time.

A few minutes later, I was sitting next to Alex on a squashy grey sofa in a living room that – far from being a hovel – was considerably nicer than my own. It was only a cottage – 'bijou', I'd say, if I was describing it for a Walkerson's brochure. But the floors were stripped wooden boards, there were plaster ceiling roses round the light fittings, and a cityscape that I thought must be Glasgow hung above the mantelpiece. There was no Christmas tree, but a fire burned in the grate, a few clear, gold and silver glass baubles suspended from the mantelpiece above catching the light of the flames as they turned gently in the rising heat.

'I put up a Christmas tree, a couple of years back,' Alex had explained. 'Balthazar tried to climb it. Epic fail.'

I had a glass of champagne in my hand, and there was a plate of smoked salmon and lemon wedges, and another of buttered brown bread on the table in front of us. The cat was stretched out in front of the fire, toasting his belly.

It was the perfect domestic Christmas scene. But nonetheless, something didn't feel quite right. There was still an awkwardness between us, even though I could feel the air crackling with my desire to touch him almost as warmly as the flames licked at the burning logs.

'So,' Alex said. 'This is nice. And also, kind of weird.'

'It's really weird. It's almost happened too fast. Like, I woke up this morning, and I was going to spend Christmas on my own. And now, here I am.'

'With a man you barely know, and a cat you've just met.'

'That. And there's so much I want to know, but I'm not sure where exactly to begin.'

'I do know one thing, though,' he said.

'What's that?'

'I'd love to kiss you again.'

'It would certainly be a good start.'

I looked at him and smiled, shyly at first, then more widely as the warmth of his own grin filled me with the promise of happiness. He reached out his arms, and I put down my glass and slid along the sofa, easing into his embrace like I was meant to be there.

Like I'd always been meant to be there.

His lips met mine softly, gently. But there was nothing soft or gentle in my response. I kissed him back with an ardour that almost shocked me, my hand finding the back of his neck and pulling him closer, my tongue brushing his lips, my breath hungry for the smell of him, all clean and musky and just there.

And he responded in kind. I couldn't remember the last time I'd kissed anyone that way – not before the night of our picnic, at least. I felt like I was drunk already, even though I'd barely had half a glass of champagne. And as well as the scent of his body, I could smell the orange blossom coming off my own skin – desirability.

'Rowan,' he said, when we came up for a breath. 'Wow.'

'Wow,' I echoed. 'I... I don't know what...'

'I do,' he said.

And then he kissed me some more.

At some point, I must have unbuttoned his shirt, because I remember seeing the firelight gleaming against the bare skin of his shoulders and casting actual shadows over the ridges of his abs. Later, he slipped the satin dress off over my head, revealing the new underwear that was more beautiful than any I'd owned for years, and he said, 'Wow,' again. But I don't think it was the lingerie that did it – or not just that.

Feeling his hands on my body, gazing into his eyes and seeing his pupils wide with desire, I knew he wanted me. I knew he felt the same sizzling excitement when he looked at me and touched me as I did. I knew he thought I was as beautiful as I found him.

As I lay naked on the couch, Alex leaning above me on one elbow, he gazed at me like I was the best Christmas present he'd ever had, like he wanted to touch me all over with his eyes the same way he was with his skilful, questing fingers and lips.

And I did the same, discovering the contours of his hard, lean body, the swell of his erection that I couldn't wait to taste, the way his firm buttocks fitted perfectly into my hands – the way I knew he'd fit perfectly inside of me.

I knew I was about to have the best sex of my whole life.

And it was. From the first moment our lips met to the last, when he slid out of me, both of us gasping, our bodies glossy with perspiration in the firelight, it was bliss.

Afterwards, we realised neither of us had noticed Balthazar eating all the smoked salmon and licking all the butter off the bread, right there next to us.

'Well,' Alex said. 'I guess we got the beginning over with.'

'I don't think so. I want that beginning to happen over and over again.'

'Same. But maybe after some food. I don't know about you, but I'm starving.'

'God,' I realised. 'Me too.'

'But first, I've got something for you,' he said. 'Hold on.'

We untwined our bodies, and I watched with a smile on my face as his naked back view (Those glutes! The muscles in his back!) disappeared from view. A few seconds later he reappeared and I got to admire the front as well, only his chest was obscured by the glossy red cardboard box he was carrying.

'It's not from me,' he said. 'Your friends gave it to me for safekeeping.'

He sat down next to me and placed the box on my lap. I lifted the lid slowly, although I was pretty sure what I'd find inside – the smell gave it away. Not one smell, but many: the luxurious, heady blend of clashing scents that made me feel as if I'd stepped back into the Liberty beauty department.

Inside the box were all the products from the calendar, apart from those I'd already received. Eye cream and lip balm and acid toner. Perfume and bath elixir. Lipstick and volumising mascara. Stuff to give my hair body and stuff to make it shine. Stuff to put on my face and stuff to take it off with.

It was all there. I couldn't wait to have a proper look at it all with Clara and divvy it up between us.

I remembered how I'd felt walking into the beauty hall a month before: the promise those products had held. How I'd imagined them making me look younger, more beautiful, less tired. Glowing like I'd just had an orgasm or was falling in love.

I didn't need expensive products for that, now. I had the real thing. But the products were amazing all the same.

While I was looking through the box, sighing with pleasure at its contents, Alex had pulled on his clothes and topped up our champagne glasses. I dressed too, and we moved companionably to the kitchen to investigate the food.

Then I said, 'There's something I need to tell you.'

'What's that?' He slipped his arm around my shoulders,

which were bare in the skimpy red dress, and I leaned into his embrace.

'I wasn't completely honest with you about something.'

Alex looked at me, his face suddenly serious. 'Whatever you need to tell me, Rowan, it's okay.'

I said, 'I don't really like the toffees best. Come on – no one does. I just like saving the best for last.'

CHAPTER FORTY-ONE

SIX MONTHS LATER

'What time is it?' I mumbled, curling myself more closely into Alex's hard-muscled back. Since he'd stopped being a delivery driver and returned to being a full-time tech entrepreneur, he'd also returned to the gym, doing what sounded like terrifying things with kettlebells and pull-up bars three evenings a week, and there was no denying that I liked the results.

'Balthazar says it's breakfast time,' Alex replied. Over his shoulder, I could see the cat's black furry face on the pillow next to Alex's and hear the thunder of his purr.

'Balthazar always says it's breakfast time, especially when he's stomping on my head at four in the morning.'

'Well, you don't come here for sleep, do you?' Alex teased.

It was true. On the weekends when Clara was with Paul and sometimes on alternate Wednesdays, Portia and I made the journey across London to stay at Alex's place. And sleep was the last thing on our minds. Sure, we went out for meals together and drank cocktails in the garden together (Alex made a mean boulevardier), explored London together and hung out with his friends and mine.

But that was only once we'd satiated ourselves in his bed.

On the nights when he stayed over at mine, which I'd only suggested once he'd spent a few evenings with Clara, the two of them casually getting acquainted, sex had to be a bit more circumspect.

I mean, obviously my daughter knew exactly what I was getting up to, but I wasn't about to start swinging from the chandeliers in her presence, especially not since the heart-to-heart I'd had with her about staying safe if things were to get serious between her and Jonny, and ideally waiting until she was sixteen.

Now that I was making reasonable money at work, I'd been thinking of moving, buying a place for Clara and me that had a garden of its own but was still close to her school. But although things at Walkerson's had improved since Julz's departure (after a rapid but thorough investigation, Ollie had sacked him on Christmas Eve, by text, which I couldn't help thinking was a boss move) and Kimberley being brought back to manage the Mayfair branch, I wasn't about to rush into anything.

However, I did smile every time I remembered her first day in her new job, when she'd stalked into the office in her fearsomely high heels and fixed Brett and Marty with a stare that was one hundred per cent worthy of Christine from *Selling Sunset*.

'Morning, boys,' she'd said.

'Morning,' they muttered, not meeting her eyes.

'So, Brett,' Kimberley continued. 'How many men does it take to tile a bathroom?'

Brett developed a sudden interest in his tasselled loafers and said nothing.

'Marty?' she asked.

Evidently Marty's shoes were equally compelling.

'It depends,' Kimberley continued, her voice saccharine-sweet, 'on how thinly you slice them.'

And then, in tones of icy calmness, she'd told them that

head office had made the decision to dismiss them both on the grounds of gross misconduct, and their P45s would be sent to them in the post.

Tatiana Ivanova, a bit of strategic Instagram stalking had revealed, had moved to Dubai and was brokering property deals for wealthy Russian clients there.

But I wasn't going to dwell on work right now – and even if I'd wanted to, I couldn't. Alex had properly woken up now and turned over, my head was resting on his shoulder, and he'd begun gently caressing my arm. In the months we'd been together (I reckoned I'd always consider Christmas Day to be our anniversary, which was pretty cool as far as anniversaries went and meant there was no danger of either of us ever forgetting it), we'd had sex lots of times. I mean, like, lots and lots.

But still, every time he touched me, I felt the electric thrill I'd experienced the very first time.

I wondered if I'd ever stop feeling it. I hoped not – but I was quietly confident that if I did, it would be replaced by something even better.

I reached out my own hand and ran my fingers over his muscular chest. I couldn't get enough of those pecs, leading down to the ridged firmness of his abs, and below that the springing hardness of his cock.

Every time I touched him, I wanted to jump up and down with delight, crowing, 'He's mine! All mine!'

But I never had, obviously. That would have been immature and weird and creepy, as well as unfair on all the people who could never have Alex.

'What are you thinking, Ro?' he asked. 'You're smiling at something. You look as smug as Balthazar when he ate all the feta out of our salad the other day.'

'I'm thinking how lucky I am to have such a hot main squeeze.'

'Main squeeze? You mean you've got another squeeze?'

'Sure do. Balthazar knows at least half my heart belongs to him. And all my head, when he decides to lie on it.'

'Hmmm. My main squeeze is pretty foxy, too.'

'Foxy enough to kiss?'

'Foxy enough to never want to stop kissing.'

I turned my head and our lips found each other, meeting softly at first and then more urgently. The hand that had been lightly stroking my arm moved to my back, pressing the length of my body against his.

I felt his lips and tongue leave mine and begin to travel down my neck to my collarbone, then lower still to my breasts, and I closed my eyes, losing myself in the delicious pleasure of his touch. Right from the first time, my body had responded to him as if he'd always known what would give me pleasure, and practice had only made it more perfect.

My hands found the softness of his hair, and I stroked it as his mouth moved lower still, over the softness of my belly to the insides of my thighs. I could feel my whole body alive with anticipation of what was to come – the acute pleasure of his tongue on my clitoris, inside me, bringing me to orgasm almost instantly, and then again more slowly, until I pulled him away and rolled on top of him, unable to wait another second to feel him inside me, filling me, moving with me.

Afterwards, we lay together, our breath gradually slowing, our hands interlaced, smiling.

'Well,' I said. 'You'd better give that cat his breakfast.'

'And then we'd better get ready to go to that wedding.'

'Actually, I can't think of a better way to get ready to go to a wedding than what we just did.'

'All the same, you'd better get some clothes on, hadn't you? I'm not having your ex take one look at you and realise what he's missing out on.'

I laughed. 'That would be one way to put a damper on their big day. "If anyone knows any just impediment... blah-blah, speak now or forever hold your peace." And I run up the aisle starkers going, "Yes! He's a bit of a dick really!"'

I'd told Alex the backstory of Paul and me. I'd been worried about confessing it, but he'd taken it in his stride and said that the most important thing was that Paul and I were able to get along amicably as parents – and that I didn't plan to shag him again, obviously, which I'd told him, quite truthfully, that I wouldn't do if he was the last man on earth. And Alex had accepted that, because he trusted me.

Still giggling, we kissed and climbed out of bed, and Alex went to the kitchen to feed Balthazar and I headed for the shower. He joined me in there for a bit, and things would've got messy if I hadn't told him I needed to blow-dry my hair or I'd never be ready on time.

And so, an hour later, we left the house together, me in a floral maxi dress that I felt was appropriate for the groom's ex to wear and a pair of new Balenciaga heels I'd treated myself to with my commission from Ailsa and Omar's house purchase, and Alex in a kilt. (The first time I'd seen him in a suit, when he'd gone off for his final meeting with the venture capital firm that was backing Greenline, his delivery start-up, I'd come over all peculiar, like a swooning Victorian spinster. But I'm not going to lie, the kilt took things to another level.)

When we arrived at the church, my friends were already there, Kate and Daniel like bookends at opposite sides of the pew, Abbie and Matt holding hands and glowing with happiness, Andy looking like a movie star in a tuxedo, Naomi wearing an extravagantly feathered lilac hat. They waved us forward to the space they'd saved in the middle, and we squeezed in, hugging and kissing and softly chatting.

I looked at Paul, standing at the altar with Patch, his best man, by his side. He appeared hopelessly nervous, as any bridegroom would. But after the separate chats I'd had with him and Hayley, I was quietly confident that everything would work out okay. Paul was basically a guy who wanted a woman in his life – it just hadn't been me. And Hayley, with her unique blend of sweetness and bloody-mindedness, was sure to keep him in line.

I remembered speaking to Paul after they'd got back from Christmas with Clara's grandparents, sharing a bottle of Shiraz in a pub while Clara went wedding-dress shopping with her stepmother-to-be.

'I do still feel sad, sometimes, about how things worked out between you and me, Ro,' Paul had said. 'If we'd both just been a bit more... I don't know.'

'Compatible?' I said. 'Come on, Paul. We had the chance to make it work, and it didn't. We've both moved on, and a good thing too. And you know what? I don't regret any of it. We gave each other what we needed. We gave each other Clara.'

He'd looked solemn for a moment, then clinked his glass against mine and smiled, and I felt a glow of contentment knowing that whatever happened, whatever half-siblings were to come along, our daughter would always be the one he'd loved first – and the one I had.

The brilliant light that had been filtering through the stained-glass windows dimmed suddenly, and through the open church doors I caught the smell of rain – the sudden summer shower that had been threatening all morning deciding to descend and do its thing at the crucial moment.

'Poor Hayley,' Abbie murmured. 'I hope she's not going to get soaked.'

'Trust me,' I said, 'it would take more than a few drops of rain to put that girl off her stride.'

And sure enough, as the organ broke into Mendelssohn's 'Wedding March' and the church erupted in whispers of 'She's here!' before falling silent, I turned and saw a huge white umbrella filling the open door. Then it folded shut and the bride appeared.

Typical Hayley, I thought fondly. Everything about this day

was Insta perfect: the banks of pale pink roses and peonies massed at the altar; the four-tier cake I'd seen pictures of, decorated in the same flowers crafted from sugar paste; Paul's waistcoat and cravat in the same colour.

But Hayley herself was the most perfect of all, gliding up the aisle to greet the man she loved in an ice-white dress cut to skim over the barely visible bump of her four-month pregnancy, graceful as a swan, her blissful smile eclipsing the sun that had emerged as suddenly as it had vanished behind the clouds.

Actually, scratch that. More perfect still was my daughter. In her rose-coloured bridesmaid's dress, a smaller version of Hayley's bouquet in her hands, Clara looked serious but radiant. Her dark hair was pulled off her face by a circlet of rosebuds that matched the flush on her cheeks. Her eyes were wide and shining as she took in the crowd of people here to celebrate her father's joyful day. She shared a smile with the other bridesmaid, Hayley's best friend, and I saw a glimpse of the confident woman she was becoming.

I felt Alex's warm, strong hand enfold mine, and I squeezed it back.

And then he leaned over and whispered in my ear, for the first time, the words I knew we'd both been saying silently to ourselves for weeks.

'I love you, Rowan.'

'I love you, too.'

And although it was midsummer, at that moment I felt all the magic of Christmas in my heart.

A LETTER FROM SOPHIE

Dear reader,

I want to say a huge thank you for choosing to read *Santa, Please Bring Me a Boyfriend*. If you did enjoy it, and want to keep up to date with all my latest releases, just sign up at the following link. Your email address will never be shared and you can unsubscribe at any time.

www.bookouture.com/sophie-ranald

I'm writing this in early July, in the middle of a glorious London heatwave. The door to my garden is open, the cats have been sunning themselves outside most of the afternoon, and it will still be light at ten o'clock. Quite honestly, Christmas couldn't feel further away.

But by the time you read it, everything will be different. The nights will have drawn in, the last of the October bonfire smoke blown away, the first frosts nipped our noses and fingers. Perhaps you'll already have put up your Christmas tree; certainly your mind will already be full of festive plans and secrets.

Christmas in our house is a quiet one. Both my partner and I have families abroad, so we spend the day alone together, following the same time-honoured rituals: coffee in bed, a run around the near-empty neighbourhood streets counting how many Christmas trees we can spot, then lots of delicious food and drink, the former shared with our beloved cats.

Yours may be quite different. Perhaps you're in a bustling family home with multiple generations gathered together, gift wrap scattered on the floor waiting to be cleared away, toddlers and pets underfoot. Perhaps you're with friends, someone pulling the cork out of yet another bottle while you debate going for a walk, watching the monarch address the nation on television, or seeing if there's a pub open somewhere.

Or perhaps, as Rowan expected to be before Alex's surprise Yuletide arrival in her life, you're alone.

Whatever the case, I do hope this book has brought a sprinkling of Christmas magic to your day and a smile to your face, and I wish you and your loved ones a very merry Christmas.

And, for the record, I have never yet purchased the covetable Liberty beauty advent calendar. Perhaps this will be the year – I'll be sure to let you know on social media if that happens!

Thank you for downloading *Santa, Please Bring Me a Boyfriend*. I really appreciate the time it's taken you to read it, and would be very grateful if you could leave an online review.

With much love,

Sophie

facebook.com/SophieRanald
twitter.com/SophieRanald
instagram.com/sophieranald

ACKNOWLEDGEMENTS

Way back in late 2017 (how different a place the world was then!), I received an email from my wonderful agent, Alice Saunders at The Soho Agency, to tell me that an editor at Book-outure had expressed interest in seeing my next novel. As a self-published author, this was dream-come-true territory, and I set to work furiously finishing the first draft of the novel that would become *Sorry Not Sorry*.

It was the beginning of a truly wonderful journey with Christina Demosthenous, who has now worked with me on eight novels. Throughout that time, I've been overwhelmed by her talent, commercial acumen, humour and kindness. *Sorry Not Sorry* succeeded beyond my wildest dreams, and there are not enough words (especially at the end of a manuscript that contains close to a hundred thousand of them!) to express how grateful I am to her for believing in me, championing me, and making me a far, far better writer than I was back then.

Thank you, Christina, and thank you, Alice.

Huge thanks also to the rest of the team at Bookouture: Noelle Holten, Kim Nash, Peta Nightingale, Alex Holmes, Lauren Finger, Mandy Kullar, Sarah Hardy and Alex Crow, who work tirelessly behind the scenes on publicity, production and promotion; as well as my brilliant cover designer Lisa Horton, cracking copy-editor Rhian McKay and eagle-eyed proofreader Laura Kincaid.

I know that estate agents don't generally have the best rep, so perhaps my decision to place Rowan among their sharp-suited ranks could be seen as controversial. But, once I'd decided on my heroine's job, I needed to learn a bit more about how this competitive, sometimes brutal field works. So I put out a plea for help on a local Facebook group, and the moment found the man. Over a coffee at the very excellent Milk Café in Hither Green in South East London, Glenn Morrison regaled me with stories about his industry and career, providing a wealth of insight and detail as well as some scurrilous anecdotes. He could not have been more helpful, charming and self-aware, and proved to me that – as in any walk of life – there are many honest, decent people working in real estate. Thank you, Glenn. Any howling errors and inaccuracies are one hundred per cent my own.

And finally, to my wonderful friends, darling partner Hopi and precious cats – you're the best and I love you all.